FLOODGATES OPENING

His lips softened almost imperceptibly as his hands stroked downward to grip her waist. So gentle, Marianne thought. Far too gentle. It took away her will to fight him. All she could do was wait, wait until the enticing sweetness provoked by his kiss left her, so she might fight his embrace.

But the waiting never ended. Instead the sweetness swirled through her, holding her as helpless as any drug might. "My lord, please—" she whispered.

"Garett," he whispered back. "Think of me only as Garett of Falkham, who simply wishes to keep tasting you."

Falkham. The word rang warning bells within her. This was her enemy! How could she allow him to touch her like this? Worse yet, how could she derive so much pleasure from it? And as his lips moved to her shoulder, sending warmth like summer's heat throughout her body, she protested weakly, "One kiss, you said. Only one kiss."

He drew his head back and smiled, giving her a flash of even, white teeth. "Since when ~~~ men stop with one

"Royal Entertainment!"—Catherine Coulter

DECEIVED
by Mary Balogh

Beautiful Lady Elizabeth Ward had been young and innocent when she wed the man she loved, Christopher Atwell. She thought his love matched hers—until she found him in the arms of another, learned of his guilt in murder and worse, and saw him flee abroad. But now Christopher was back in England to claim the title he was heir to and claim innocence of all evil. He was back to claim Elizabeth as well. But how could Elizabeth forget the pain of betrayal? How could she trust her heart and happiness to this man who had so cruelly deceived her once and now was doubly dangerous the second time he pledged his love and cast his sensual spell?

Coming from Onyx

BY LOVE UNVEILED

by

Deborah Martin

A TOPAZ BOOK

TOPAZ
Published by the Penguin Group
Penguin Books USA Inc., 375 Hudson Street,
New York, New York 10014, U.S.A.
Penguin Books Ltd, 27 Wrights Lane,
London W8 5TZ, England
Penguin Books Australia Ltd, Ringwood,
Victoria, Australia
Penguin Books Canada Ltd, 10 Alcorn Avenue,
Toronto, Ontario, Canada M4V 3B2
Penguin Books (N.Z.) Ltd, 182–190 Wairau Road,
Auckland 10, New Zealand

Penguin Books Ltd, Registered Offices:
Harmondsworth, Middlesex, England

First published by Topaz, an imprint of New American Library,
a division of Penguin Books USA Inc.

First Printing, May, 1993
10 9 8 7 6 5 4 3 2 1

Topaz is a trademark of New American Library,
a division of Penguin Books USA Inc.

Printed in the United States of America

BOOKS ARE AVAILABLE AT QUANTITY DISCOUNTS WHEN USED TO PROMOTE PROD-
UCTS OR SERVICES. FOR INFORMATION PLEASE WRITE TO PREMIUM MARKETING
DIVISION, PENGUIN BOOKS USA INC., 375 HUDSON STREET, NEW YORK, NEW
YORK 10014.

If you purchased this book without a cover you should be aware that this book
is stolen property. It was reported as "unsold and destroyed" to the publisher
and neither the author nor the publisher has received any payment for this
"stripped book."

To Pam Ahearn, my diligent agent,
who believed in this book
through thick and thin.

And to Terry Olivier and Bob Mathison,
two wonderful bosses who understood
that my dream lay elsewhere and
who encouraged me to follow my dream.

Prologue

London, 1661

"Rest you then, rest, sad eyes,
Melt not in weeping
   While she lies sleeping
   Softly, now softly lies
Sleeping."
            —Anonymous,
               "Weep You No More,
               Sad Fountains"

One look in those clear, innocent eyes and guilt overtook Tamara like wind in a sudden storm. Such a despicable act she was about to commit—to drug her
own niece! Yet Tamara knew she had no choice. Sleep
would be a kinder fate than death.

"Drink your tea, Mina," she urged the young Lady
Marianne. " 'Tis one I made specially for you." *Once
I heard the news,* she added silently.

Marianne smiled, her lovely face lit with affection
for her aunt in the dim lamplight of the Gypsy wagon.
But that smile only increased Tamara's guilt. Eighteen-
year-old Marianne was her only niece, the sole child
of her late sister Dantela and Dantela's husband, Sir
Henry Winchilsea. Tamara had seen Marianne very
little over the years, but the Winchilseas' recent arrival
in London had brought her hope that she'd see more
of her niece.

To Tamara's delight, Marianne had come to visit her
aunt at the Gypsy camp early that morning. During
the visit, however, Tamara had been taken aside, away
from Marianne, to be told the sad news that destroyed
her pleasure.

Now she watched in silence as Marianne slowly

sipped the tea, her eyes closing as she savored the taste of chamomile.

"Mother always did like your tea," Marianne murmured, flashing her aunt a trembling smile that didn't quite hide the sadness she still felt.

Tamara sighed. She shared her niece's grief. Dantela had been dearer to her than anyone in the world. To have her taken away so quickly, snatched away by a fever neither Sir Henry nor his daughter could arrest, had been a blow from which Tamara knew she'd never recover. After two years, she still felt the sting of it, particularly when she looked at her sister's only child.

Anyone who saw her and Marianne together would find it strange that a girl with such delicate features could be related to a Gypsy. Marianne, with her coral-tinted cheeks and honey hair, didn't resemble Tamara at first glance.

But a closer look would reveal that Marianne's skin, a rich light bronze, was merely a shade lighter than her aunt's. And although Marianne's hazel eyes, which shifted from brown to green in the light, were far too light for a Gypsy's, her high cheekbones and lush mouth were like her aunt's, even more so like Tamara's much-mourned sister's.

The memory of her sister only firmed Tamara's resolve. "Drink it all, Mina," she said with a forced smile. "You know how healthful chamomile is."

Marianne tossed back her thick golden hair and eyed Tamara with amusement. "Is that your gentle way of saying I need a bit more color in my cheeks? You're just like Father, always worried I spend too much time alone preparing his medicines and studying." Still, she took her aunt's advice and gulped more of the steaming tea.

Tamara struggled to keep her bland smile in place, forcing her eyes away from the china cup. "Your father's a wise man. You should have been . . . should be at his side when he attends the king each day. How else will you ever find a suitable husband?"

Marianne arched one honeyed eyebrow. "A suitable husband? At Charles's court? Don't be absurd. The

Cavaliers preen before the king like so many peacocks, while the women try to catch His Majesty's eye, hoping to become his next great love." She frowned. "How many bastards has he fathered now? Ten? Twenty? All of whom will have titles and manors while people still starve in the streets of London. No, I'll find no 'suitable' husband at court, that's certain." Marianne lifted the cup again to her lips.

"Watch your tongue, poppet," Tamara cautioned. "In these turbulent days, 'tis folly to collect enemies."

Marianne looked contrite at the sight of her aunt's frown. "I'm sorry. Let's talk of more pleasant matters, shall we?"

Tamara nodded, then tensed as Marianne drained her cup. The time had come.

"Mina," Tamara said in a voice that trembled. She stared down at her hands. Then, angry at her cowardice, she forced her eyes back up to meet her niece's. "I'm afraid more pleasant conversation must wait. I've something important to tell you. Something that will displease you."

"Out with it, then," Marianne said blithely. "What dire prediction do you have for me now?"

Her teasing smile cut at Tamara's heart. "You'll never forgive me for what I've done."

Marianne laughed, a soft lilting laugh that only increased her aunt's unease. "What could you possibly have done to require my forgiveness?"

Tamara brushed away her niece's words with a wave of her hand, determined to plunge right into the truth. "You'll sleep soon, my sweet. I want you to be prepared for it when it comes upon you. And it will come soon. Among other things, the tea contains valerian root."

Marianne's face darkened as she heard the name of the sleeping herb.

"I had to do it," Tamara went on. "We must leave, and I can't have you fighting me."

"What in heaven's name do you mean? Why must we leave?" Marianne tried to rise from her seat. "What about Father?"

"I see I must tell you all of it," Tamara said, noting

that Marianne's limbs were already weakening as the drug took effect. "Your father's been arrested for treason. One of his remedies for the king was found to contain poison."

"It can't be!" Marianne protested, trying once again to rise from her chair, but failing. "I prepared those medicines myself!"

"I know," Tamara whispered. "And there's the rub. They're sure to know of your part in your father's work. They'll come for you next. When they do, I've made certain you'll be gone."

Marianne's eyes reflected her horror. "But I can't leave now! I must stop this madness! He's been falsely accused!"

"Of course he has. But they'll not listen to reason, I'm certain. The poison was there—the one who came to warn me assures me there was no mistake. Someone laid the trap for your father too well. Nothing you say will change their minds."

"Surely His Majesty doesn't believe Father capable of treason!" she protested. "His Majesty has always respected Father for his medical skill. He wouldn't have invited Father to serve as one of his physicians and join the Royal Society if he didn't trust him!"

Tamara sighed. "Mina, my sweet, listen to me. The king can trust no one in these dark times. Whoever chose your father for their treachery chose well. Your father had an unusual marriage. He's always refused to dabble in political matters. Those things make him suspect to men who consider politics their life."

Marianne stared in helpless anguish at her aunt. "But Father would never kill His Majesty! That would be against everything he believes in. He's innocent! I must . . . must tell them that . . ." Her voice began to lose its force despite her brave words.

"And what proof will you give them?" Tamara asked brokenly. "No, this is the only way. The men are already preparing to break camp. We leave when they're finished."

"Please," Marianne whispered, her eyelids drooping as the drug overtook her senses. "How could you?

How could you . . . you drug . . . me and take away . . . my will?''

Her head sank down onto her arms as her eyes slowly shut.

''Mina, Mina, how could I let them take your life?'' Tamara whispered, her hand stretching out to stroke one lock of her niece's dark golden hair away from her face.

Shaking her head sorrowfully, she stood and bent down to scoop her niece up in arms strengthened by years of hard work. Though already a grown woman of eighteen, Marianne was petite, a characteristic inherited from her mother. Tamara, on the other hand, was a hearty woman of peasant stock, so she didn't even stagger as she carried Marianne to the hidden cupboard at the back of the wagon. She opened the concealed doors and placed her niece on the pallet inside. Until they'd left London, Tamara wouldn't feel safe having Marianne where anyone could see her.

Then she closed the doors and made her way to the front of the sturdy wooden wagon. Her people must leave as soon as possible, she thought, before the king's men traced Lady Marianne to the Gypsy camp and before the drug wore off. As it was, the Gypsies couldn't move as quickly as she'd like, for they dared not attract attention to themselves as they headed toward the Channel and the relative freedom of France.

She sighed as she glanced back at the concealed cupboard. For now, Mina was safe. But how long could that last? Only until her strong-willed niece awakened from the drug and began harboring foolish notions about saving her father. Tamara would never be able to drug Mina again. This was her only chance to get her niece away. She threw her shoulders back, a look of determination stiffening the lines of her face.

No niece of hers would end up in the Tower of London. And if she had to lie, cheat, or steal to ensure Mina's safety, she would.

Chapter One

"Heat not a furnace for your foe so hot
That it do singe yourself."
—Shakespeare,
Henry VIII

Deep in thought, King Charles II passed into the sitting room of his spacious private chambers. He found it exceedingly refreshing to have a moment to himself without the demands and attentions of his court. The late afternoon sun created pools of dying light and darkening shadows across the lavishly furnished room. He surveyed the richness of his surroundings, a smile crossing his face. Even now he relished the trappings of royalty. He'd spent too many years without them not to enjoy them.

Then the smile froze on his face as a man melted out of the shadows to stand at the edge of the room.

"By God, Falkham, you startled me!" the king swore as he recognized his friend. "You have a nasty habit of appearing from out of nowhere when one least expects it."

"That habit has kept Your Majesty's enemies guessing these past few years, has it not?" Falkham replied with his typically aloof half smile and strode across the room to meet the king.

Charles tried to gaze sternly upon the young man standing before him, but he couldn't. Instead, he chuckled as he looked over Garett Lyon, the Earl of Falkham, whom he hadn't seen in nearly a year. On the surface, Falkham was little changed. The same mocking gray eyes met the king's assessing gaze, though they seemed more steely than before. The earl's thick nutmeg-brown hair still fell straight and uncurled to his shoulders. As usual, Falkham had no interest in wearing the elaborate, ringleted coifs sported by most of the Cavaliers.

Yet somehow Charles could tell that Falkham's air of bold confidence had increased in the past year, overlaid by a definite cynicism that shone in his eyes. Despite the hint of a smile that still touched Falkham's lips, his face was now a strangely harsh one, given that he was only twenty-three.

"I am truly glad to see you have returned," Charles stated. "I wish you could have joined us in our triumphant entry into the city last year, but it seems you made better use of yourself accomplishing the task I set for you. Lord Chancellor Clarendon tells me you were quite successful."

Falkham lifted one brow. "Aren't I always?"

"Only if it suits you," the king said with a shrug.

Falkham smiled fully this time. "I do only what suits my king. It's just that my king doesn't always know what suits him."

"Indeed," Charles replied dryly. "You'd best be careful, my friend. Your king may tolerate your witticisms, but others will not find them quite so amusing."

Falkham sobered. "I know that too well, Your Majesty."

"After the past ten years, you ought to. I tried to teach you often enough to curb your quick tongue." He frowned. "I'm afraid I wasn't the best companion for a young man who'd just lost his family. Between my bitterness and your hatred, we bred an unhealthy anger. Such anger can destroy a man, if he is not careful."

"Ah, but Your Majesty's bitterness was assuaged in the end. Your subjects have come to their senses at last." The teasing note in Falkham's voice was faint but unmistakable. He knew better than anyone that Charles's present hold over his subjects was tenuous at best.

Charles sighed. "That remains to be seen, doesn't it? A people so fickle bears watching. Yet I believe they're truly pleased to have me on the throne again. Unlike Cromwell, I don't feed them religion with their meat."

Falkham's loud laugh filled the room with its harsh, mirthless sound. "No, indeed not."

Charles debated whether to take offense at Falkham's oblique reference to Charles's "relaxed" way of living or to match it with another witticism. When he spoke, it was to do neither. "Now that you've completed your task in Portugal, I suppose you've come to claim your reward."

"If Your Majesty will recall, you did promise it to me." Falkham's whole body stiffened in expectation, though clearly he didn't seem certain he could trust even the king.

"I did promise it, although I almost wish I could withdraw the promise and thus keep you in my service." Charles threw the statement out almost as a challenge, for he did indeed wish Falkham had more of an inclination to remain at court and thus at the king's beck and call.

Falkham's grim smile showed he didn't appreciate the king's half-serious comment. "Those serve best who serve willingly, my liege," he said evenly.

Charles chuckled. "True. And I suspect that having you as an unwilling servant could be nearly as treacherous as having you for an enemy. At any rate, you have earned your freedom, that is certain, along with the funds I promised."

"And my estate, my lands?"

"That would have been yours regardless."

Falkham's face remained carefully expressionless. "Perhaps. But my uncle's said to be a very powerful man among Cromwell's old supporters. To cross him could mean risking the approbation of the very people Your Majesty wishes to placate."

Charles strode to the window overlooking his gardens and stared out at the Cavaliers and their ladies who wandered about the grounds. He chose his words carefully. "I shall have to take that chance. The promise I made to you must not be broken, for without your part this past year in arranging my marriage to the Infanta, I would be in dire straits indeed."

"I'm pleased I could be of service, Your Majesty."

"At any rate, you shall have your reward—and your revenge—with my blessing. I do not trust your uncle. Tearle paints himself a moderate, but I know a good deal more about his Roundhead companions than he realizes."

"Clarendon told me the Roundheads made an attempt on Your Majesty's life," Falkham remarked with the bland tones of a man accustomed to acquiring information without ever appearing to do so.

Charles frowned. "An attempt was indeed made by one of my attending physicians, whom I thought I could trust. But to my knowledge, he is not a Roundhead."

"So you don't know who was behind it."

"No, but we will find out. I have had my men state he was murdered while in his cell in the Tower, killed by his fellow conspirators. Clarendon hopes the rumor will confound the other assassins and provoke them into erring. Besides, we do not want his companions to kill him before we have a chance to question him. This gives us time to get the truth from him."

"Does Your Majesty believe him guilty?"

The king shrugged. "I do not know. 'Tis a very odd circumstance. Until he returned to London recently, he had not been much involved with affairs of state." Charles glanced away, an uneasy look on his face. "In fact, he'd been living a fairly secluded life in the country, near a town you know well—Lydgate."

Charles turned abruptly to witness Falkham's reaction to that news, but only a brief look of surprise crossed the earl's face before the impassive mask he normally wore dropped back into place.

"Why was this physician in Lydgate?" Falkham asked in a deceptively casual tone.

Charles didn't immediately answer. Instead he strode to a lavishly carved writing table that stood nearby.

Then he opened a drawer and removed something. His face grim, he returned to Falkham and placed the heavy object in the earl's hand.

"This should tell you. He wore it on a chain about his neck. The soldiers took it from him when he was arrested."

Falkham looked down at the unusual brass key and the chain dangling from it. His face became hard as marble as he hefted the key and then fingered its oddly molded end shaped like a falcon's head. His eyes seemed an unearthly shade of blue when at last he lifted his gaze to the king's face. "So he was the one who bought Falkham House from my uncle," Falkham stated.

Charles wasn't fooled by Falkham's seemingly calm response. He could smell Falkham's anger. "Yes, he was the one," Charles repeated quietly.

Every muscle in Falkham's face seemed to tense as the body of the gentleman became, almost in reflex, the body of the soldier. Charles could tell from the way Falkham's arms went rigid and his fingers clenched the key that he was struggling to control a fury he would normally have vented in battle.

Charles didn't blame Falkham for his anger. Charles himself had been stunned when he'd first learned eight years before that Tearle had sold the major cornerstone of the Falkham holdings. When Garett had heard of it as a lad of fifteen, it had merely served to calcify his hatred toward his uncle.

" 'Twas a mad world in those days, Garett," Charles said placatingly. "People passed around lands as if they were so many sacks of seed."

"But those lands were sold by their rightful owners, not by usurpers," Falkham bit out.

"Remember that except for your uncle, no one seemed to have known you lived."

"They know now . . . or they will tomorrow when I petition the House of Lords to have my lands returned to me."

Charles smiled. "And they will grant your petition. I will certainly give my approval."

Falkham fell silent for a moment, staring down at the key in his hand. Then he spoke in measured tones. "This physician—the one who bought my estate. Have you considered that he and my uncle might have conspired together to have you assassinated? They were bound by Falkham House. Perhaps this physician knew my fortunes were tied to you and thus so was his estate."

Charles turned to stare out the window once more, rubbing his chin absently. "Or perhaps Tearle and his Roundhead compatriots saw the advantages to be had in manipulating a man like the physician, who would appear to everyone else to be innocuous. I doubt, however, that the whole affair had anything to do with you and your return. The man probably was not even aware of your existence. And even if he knew—"

"If he knew, he shouldn't have bought the estate," Falkham finished.

Charles ignored the bitterness in his friend's tone. "You shouldn't blame him too much even then. During those days, everyone thought we were to be exiles forever. Even you and I believed it. So did your uncle."

"That's no excuse for Tearle's treachery."

"No. Still, I've never quite understood why you hate him so thoroughly that you'd risk all to have your vengeance."

Falkham looked away, a muscle working in his grimly set jaw. "I have my reasons."

Charles didn't doubt that. Sometimes he wondered what they were. But he respected Falkham's need to keep his thoughts private, so he didn't press him. "I doubt not that you will make your uncle regret his actions. You were too young to hurt Tearle then, but I almost pity him for what you will doubtless do now. I know you're justified in wanting your revenge. But remember—I want peace in my kingdom at all costs."

One look at Falkham's glowering countenance told Charles the nobleman was none too happy to be reminded of that. Charles plunged on. "You have the funds to restore your estate. You'll have your lands as well—"

"And what of this physician? Will you take Falkham House from him? The law says those lands sold during Your Majesty's absence remain with the buyers."

"He performed a treasonous act. I have confiscated his lands, of course. Gladly I return them to you. You see? You have everything you want. Do not seek to press my kindness by doing anything foolhardy against your uncle that might jeopardize us both."

"He deserves any retribution I see fit to give him," Falkham said with cold determination. "And I won't hesitate to mete out his fair portion, given the chance."

" 'Tis what I fear, my friend," the king replied. "This discord between kin—"

"He's kin to me only through marriage to my father's sister," Falkham protested. " 'Twas he who first severed the ties of kinship, not I."

"I know. But I speak now as your friend, not your king—I fear he will suffer less from your vengeance than you will."

Falkham's harsh laugh saddened the king. "Has Your Majesty now become like the Puritans, crying that vengeance is the Lord's? Will my soul be condemned forever if I make Pitney Tearle suffer for stealing away the inheritance of a defenseless boy?"

Charles ignored Falkham's thinly veiled insult. He'd known the young man long enough to understand the feelings that prompted his harsh retort. Charles forced a smile. "Nay, I think not. I believe the Almighty will understand." Then the smile faded. "Yet Tearle long ago planted the seed of bitterness within you, and now that it has sprung to life, I wonder if you will be able to stop its vines from choking your heart."

Falkham stared blindly away then, his eyes glittering with suppressed passion. "Your Majesty's fears are well founded. But after years of nurturing that seed, I can't root it out. When the time comes, I can cut the vines away. But before that happens, I'll see the seedling fully sprung and the vines grown firm to imprison Pitney Tearle."

With that solemn vow, he took his leave.

* * *

Marianne stared sadly around her at the once immaculate gardens of her cherished home. Falkham House. How well she could remember her first sight of it. For a child of ten accustomed to their cramped London home, Falkham House had seemed an incredibly magnificent palace. Built during the reign of Elizabeth and thus shaped like an E, the brick building had an imposing beauty with its myriad glass windows and graceful gables. Yet for all its solemn grandeur, it hadn't intimidated her even as a child. One look at the cheery red brick had assured her all would be well in this house.

Years of contented living had followed the move. The people of Lydgate, a town situated only a few miles away from Falkham House, had willingly accepted her Gypsy mother. Of course, they'd been told at the time—as had all her father's friends—that her mother was a poor Spanish nobleman's daughter. Would they have welcomed her so easily at first if they'd known her true heritage? Marianne wondered. Gypsies were hated creatures throughout England. The townspeople no doubt had thought it bad enough her mother was a foreigner.

Yet the squires of surrounding townships and the tradespeople of Lydgate had instantly warmed to her mother, whose sweet disposition and willingness to tend the sick had gained her their affection. Later, when the truth about her mother's race had slipped out, they'd jealously guarded her secret from the world. Her parents had been grateful, because their few friends among the nobility would never have accepted or understood.

Now a lump rose in Marianne's throat as she surveyed the neglected patches of sage and lady's mantle, oregano and dragon's blood. Even in their sad state, they were dear to her. She stooped to pluck a sprig of thyme growing wild and lifted it to her nose, inhaling the sweet scent. Her parents had so loved their herb gardens. Her father, in particular, had found strength in them after her mother died.

If only Father could be here now, Marianne thought, choking back a sob. This was where he'd always belonged. The Royal Society hadn't deserved to have him. He should never have gone to London. If only he hadn't taken her there. . . .

She fought the ready tears, knowing they brought no solace. *How could Father be dead?* she thought for the millionth time. It made no sense. He'd been killed for some inexplicable reason in a prison where he should have been safe. Why had someone wanted him dead? For that matter, why had someone felt the need to paint him the villain and cause his arrest?

"Come," a voice murmured at her ear, intruding upon her thoughts.

Marianne turned to face her aunt, who'd come up behind her. Tamara's stern expression forced a sigh from Marianne.

"Come now, Mina," Tamara insisted. "You agreed not to tempt fate by approaching Falkham House. If a stranger saw you here, he might ask questions. Everyone outside of Lydgate believes my tale. You drowned yourself when you heard of your father's arrest. Remember? Let's not give them reason to believe otherwise. Return to the wagon and leave this place."

Her aunt's warning fell on deaf ears. Seeing the house again forced to the surface the bitter feelings toward her aunt that she'd suppressed for three weeks. "You're right. I shouldn't be here at all," she said, not trying to hide her tone of accusation. "I never should have left London. Thus I would have been with Father when he needed me. Perhaps if I'd been at his side, those men wouldn't have murdered him."

Tamara's suddenly fierce expression reminded Marianne of her mother. "The soldiers wouldn't have let you share his cell, I assure you. Nor would they have hesitated to arrest you. Is that what you wished? To be tortured? To be forced to confess to a crime you didn't commit? Perhaps even to die beside your father?"

Marianne recognized the wisdom of her aunt's words, but still couldn't help resenting the way Tamara had chosen to protect her—by taking all choices from her. She turned her face away, conflicting emotions making her silent.

Tamara sighed, then spoke in measured tones. "I understand your feelings. But I couldn't let you act on them. Like all youth, you'd bravely risk your life to rail at the tempest. 'Tis a futile gesture."

Marianne drew herself up proudly. She loved her aunt, but it often galled her that Aunt Tamara, who was only twelve years her senior, insisted on treating her like a child. "It mightn't have been so futile," she said, a tinge of hurt in her tone. "Father was well respected. Even the king said his talent was amazing. I could have made them see reason."

A harsh laugh escaped Tamara's lips. "These are the days of saints and fools, Mina. You're neither. You have your wits about you. They wouldn't have listened to you."

"I would rather have discovered that for myself."

Tamara looked away, a flash of guilt crossing her face.

Instantly Marianne felt contrite. Wiping her face clean of reproach, she reached for her aunt's hand, then lifted it to her lips to kiss it. "I know, you did what you thought best."

It was true. She did know. Her aunt had taken the only possible action.

But at first Marianne hadn't been nearly so understanding. When she'd awakened to find the Gypsies a day's journey from London, she'd been furious. What was worse, nothing she'd said had changed her aunt's purpose.

Until Colchester. They'd been forced to stop for two days there and had heard the dreadful news of her father's death. After a few days of numbed withdrawal, Marianne had emerged from her sorrow to find a new purpose. Bent on vengeance, she'd determined to remain in England, knowing that if she didn't, she'd never have the chance to find her father's killers and restore his good name.

So she'd come to Lydgate. She'd known she could find refuge there. The townspeople wouldn't betray her, she'd felt certain. They might not prove eager to harbor her, she'd reasoned, but they wouldn't relinquish her to the soldiers, either. She'd have time to plan and consider her choices.

Tamara hadn't approved of Marianne's decision to part with the Gypsies and return to Lydgate. She'd argued until she was hoarse, but in the end she'd recognized that arguing was fruitless. Marianne was determined. The Gypsies had accompanied them to Lydgate, then continued on to France without them.

Tamara had grumbled the entire way, but once in Lydgate, she and Marianne had easily found a spot to settle. Marianne had quickly adjusted to spending her nights in the cramped confines of the wooden wagon and her days roaming the woods in search of firewood or going to town for provisions. It hadn't taken her long to realize how hard a life her aunt must have led, working at needlecraft to sell for money to gain food, using her wits to keep the wagon safe and warm, and keeping out of sight of the soldiers, who hated Gypsies.

Aware of how little money her aunt had to spare, Marianne began using her skills as a healer to help them earn their keep. She'd been proven right about the townspeople's refusal to turn her in. If anything, they'd been pleased to have her tend their sick and act as midwife to the women bearing children.

Still, Tamara hadn't given up hope that she could persuade her niece to leave. Even now as Marianne turned her face once more to her old home, Tamara again voiced her disapproval.

" 'Tis not too late to change your mind," Tamara whispered as she watched her niece's face. "We could meet the others in France in a few days."

Marianne shook her head. "I cannot. The cards are dealt, and I must play the hand out."

"I should have forced you to go with us to France," Tamara grumbled.

"You couldn't keep me drugged forever," Marianne said softly. The dark expression that crossed her aunt's face made her add, with a twinkle in her eye, "Besides, you didn't have to come, too. You could have gone on with the other Gypsies."

Tamara snorted. "Hah! As if I'd hurl my niece to the wolves! Don't think to be rid of me now, my poppet. I'll stay for a time. Someone must keep you from darting headlong into danger."

Marianne smiled and hugged her aunt, strangely comforted by the quiet determination that seemed to steel the woman's bones. "True. I daresay I'd be lost without you here."

"That you would be, I'll be sworn. And don't you forget it!" Tamara admonished sternly in her ear.

Marianne's soft chuckle set matters right between them. Then Tamara nodded her head in the direction of the isolated part of the forest where they lived in the wagon, and Marianne almost acquiesced and followed Tamara.

Suddenly a strange sight arrested her. Atop the hill that rose in front of Falkham House, a heavily laden cart appeared. Marianne watched the sturdy cart silently, expecting it to travel along the ridge and move off toward Lydgate. Instead, it began toiling down the narrow winding road leading to Falkham House.

"Look!" Marianne exclaimed. Another cart appeared over the hilltop and then another. "Who might they be?"

Her aunt's face registered alarm as she, too, saw the strangers coming over the hill. "Quick! We must leave!" She clutched Marianne's arm, but Marianne ignored her.

"No! Not yet. I want to know who comes here!"

Tamara pulled Marianne unceremoniously into a stand of apple trees standing at the garden's edge. " 'Tis the king's men, no doubt, and we're doomed," Tamara muttered in acute distress. "They've come to claim the house for the Crown."

Marianne glowered as yet another cart topped the hill. "How could His Majesty do that? Falkham House is mine!"

"You're forgetting everyone believes you dead. With no family to inherit, you've lost the house, I'm afraid. The king has surely confiscated and then sold it to another."

Marianne went cold. "That man must be the one who bought it," she whispered as a figure on horseback suddenly appeared silhouetted against the late afternoon sun. A wide-brimmed hat put his face in shadow, even if she could have made out his features from that distance.

What the distance didn't hide was his large build. Even though he was on horseback, she could tell he was taller than most men she knew. His gray cloak was thrown back, exposing wide shoulders. Oblivious to the two who watched him, he rode up and down the line, shouting commands to the men controlling the teams that pulled the carts. His thick, muscular legs, encased in black hose and gray leather boots, guided the massive stallion with expert ease down the rocky hilltop road.

"The gall of the man!" Marianne spat out, perturbed with herself for noticing his body at all. "How dare he move into my house as if he'd always owned it!"

One of the carts began circling the garden to move to the back of the house. In moments the cart would be behind them and their avenue of escape would be cut off.

"Now you've done it! We should have slipped away while we had the chance," her aunt hissed.

Suddenly the stranger urged his horse into a gallop and came up beside the cart. The driver halted the cart a few feet from the back of the garden.

"What happened to the kennels?" the stranger barked out, gesturing to the garden. Marianne gasped, and Tamara slid a hand over her mouth.

The kennels. Marianne distinctly remembered that the weather-beaten gray buildings meant to house hunting dogs had stood where the garden was now when her parents had bought Falkham House.

"They tore the kennels down, milord," the driver replied. Marianne recognized his voice as that of the man who'd once been a groom in her father's stables.

"Who tore them down? Tearle? That bastard—"

"No, milord. The ones who bought the 'ouse from 'im. You know. The Winchilseas. Sir Henry said 'e 'ad no use for kennels and wanted a garden instead." The driver's eyes traveled slowly over the garden. "'O' course, the garden were much lovelier before, truly it were."

Following the driver's gaze, the other man surveyed the weed-choked paths and tangled hedges, his hands holding the reins so loosely that his massive stallion pawed the ground in restlessness. "His garden has done none too well in his absence, has it?" he said uncaringly. "That's only fair, since he stole my estates and then had the temerity to alter them."

A surge of anger filled Marianne as she strained forward to hear more, but her aunt's sturdy arms held her back.

"Beggin' your pardon, milord," the driver said, "but did ye not know 'twas Lord—I mean *Sir* Pitney—who sold the 'ouse to Sir Henry? 'E's the one to blame, if it's blame ye're wantin' to put on somebody."

The stranger's body went frighteningly still. Marianne moved enough to catch a glimpse of his face. The unmistakable hatred in his expression sent trepidation through her.

"I know who sold my home and to whom he sold it," the man bit out. "That doesn't excuse Winchilsea for buying what he'd no right to own."

Marianne's breathing quickened at the stranger's callous statements. Who was he to talk of rights of ownership? Her father had bought the house fairly. So why did this arrogant man's words contain so much wrathful spite? And why did the driver refer to Pitney Tearle as "Sir Pitney" instead of "Lord Falkham"?

"Ye've a right to be angry, 'tis certain," the driver responded in a conciliatory manner, shrinking away from the furious glance of his master. "At least it all washed out properly in the end, eh, milord?"

"Only because I made it so," the man answered, his eyes glittering coldly. The taut smile that crossed his face merely enhanced its menacing lines. He swung his fierce gaze to the house, and the intensity in that gaze made Marianne shudder. He no longer seemed to notice the driver who sat awaiting his command.

When he spoke again, his words were more a vow to himself than an explanation to the driver. "I spent many a year and killed many a man for the chance to make Falkham House mine again. It shall never be anyone else's—never." Abruptly he swung his horse about and rode back in the direction he'd come.

Marianne's hands balled into fists, but her aunt held her tightly until the cart had passed behind them and disappeared around the back of the house.

"Come quickly," Tamara urged, keeping one eye on the stranger, who now rode back down the road and up the drive leading to the house's front door. But Marianne just kept staring at him. He seemed so cold, so controlled as he sat astride his horse in the drive. His words whirled through her mind, raising thoughts and doubts that wouldn't be quelled.

"Don't be hesitating now," Tamara commanded in a low whisper. "If we're caught here, there will be questions to answer that neither of us should want."

"This was his house," Marianne said, ignoring her aunt's warnings. As soon as she said it, she knew that Falkham House had been much more than "his house." Clearly, he considered it his ultimate possession.

From where they stood, they could see both him and the massive oak door of the manor. He seemed to regard the door intently.

"He must have owned it before Pitney Tearle," Marianne continued to speculate in a whisper. Her eyes narrowed as she remembered certain words of his in particular. "What do you think he meant about having killed many a man to regain it? Who is this—this bloodthirsty man? You don't think . . . you don't think he might have had a part in Father's arrest, do you?''

Tamara stared back fearfully at the stranger. She, too, seemed cowed by the dark man's impressive stature and ruthless demeanor. "I think not," Tamara clipped out. "He doesn't seem the sort to go the back way to achieve what he wants."

"But don't you find it odd that he said the house was his because he made it so?" Marianne persisted. "Could he have meant he took measures to make certain the owner was no longer in possession? And just consider . . . shortly after Father was arrested for something he didn't do, this complete stranger arrives to lay claim to Father's estate. Don't you find that a trifle suspicious?''

"I think you're being a bit hasty in your zeal to find your father's enemies." She gestured to where the man was dismounting from his horse. "He does look threatening. But that doesn't mean he's guilty of any crime.''

Marianne pursed her lips as she watched the man stand beside his horse and gaze at the house, the fine limbs of his body stiff with tenseness. Or anticipation? Marianne couldn't be certain.

Slowly he drew something from his pocket. She couldn't make out what it was. But when he stepped forward and fitted it into the lock of the oak door, the sun glinted off the metal.

She dug her fingers into her aunt's arm. Could it be? Her father had always worn the key to Falkham House on a chain about his neck. Surely this wasn't the same key!

Yet as the stranger paused at the door, his hand on the key, a sudden chill wrapped itself around her heart. Ignoring her aunt's insistent whispers and the danger to herself, she slipped through the garden toward the drive. Her heart beat so treacherously loud that she feared he'd hear her terror, but the stranger seemed too caught up in turning the key to notice her half crouching, half running through the overgrown rows and bushes.

She inched toward the front of the house, drawn by the incurable desire to know something—anything—that would tell her who this man was and how he was linked to her father. She had to know about the key. She had to!

As she crouched beside a hedge only a few feet from the door, he suddenly began chuckling to himself, his voice rising into a bone-chilling laugh. She sank lower to the ground, convinced he'd seen her.

But his laugh ended without his ever looking her way.

"It's mine now, Tearle, in spite of you and that physician," he stated fiercely to himself.

His hand fell away from the key as he reached to pull the door open, and she saw it. She only had a glimpse before the man withdrew it from the lock, but a glimpse was enough for her to make out the head of the falcon and the chain dangling from it.

The stranger was using her father's key.

Then the man entered the house with triumphant steps. As she watched him, a dark certainty gripped her heart. He could be no friend of hers, this man who wielded her father's key. No friend at all.

Chapter Two

"This made him long for home, as loath to stay
With murmurers and foes;
He sighed for Eden, and would often say,
'Ah! what bright days were those!' "

—Henry Vaughan,
"Corruption"

"I would advise you not to remove the mask at this moment," Mr. Andrew Tibbett told Marianne as she entered his apothecary shop, threw back the hood of her cloak, and began to take off the silk mask hiding her face.

"Listen to someone with sense," her aunt agreed behind her.

"But we're the only ones here," Marianne replied, "and it's far too warm today for the mask."

Her pleading look softened Mr. Tibbett's stern expression, but he shook his bald head in refusal of her request. "If the people of Lydgate are to shelter you properly, Lady Marianne, you must do your part and keep your face covered when strangers are about."

"I'll do my part, Mr. Tibbett, if you can remember to call me Mina," Marianne quipped. "I'm a poor Gypsy, remember?"

When his face fell as he realized his error, Marianne hastened to reassure him. "Don't worry. You're the first to forget. I've been surprised so many of the townspeople have acceded to my request. Of course, they have a stake in keeping me safe, for if I were found here, it would surely go badly for Lydgate. I should never have placed all of you in such danger."

Mr. Tibbett shook his head. "Nonsense. Our delight

was immense upon discovering you hadn't thrown
yourself into the Thames after all. Having you among
us again is to our benefit. The four months you were
in London were much too long for us to endure the
lack of your father's help in curing our ills. Fortunately, you have the skills of your poor dead parents,
God bless their souls, and we appreciate your using
your skills to aid us."

"Don't flatter the girl," Tamara grumbled behind
Marianne, but with a distinct note of pleasure in her
voice. Then she prodded Marianne with one insistent
finger. "The mask, Mina."

Marianne sighed, pulling up the hood and tying back
on the mask commonly worn by gentlewomen to protect their faces from the weather. She'd always scorned
such fripperies, but lately the mask had been a useful
tool for disguising her without drawing attention. Unfortunately, it also partially obscured her vision and
was occasionally uncomfortable.

"Now, then," Mr. Tibbett said. "What might I do
for your ladyship . . . er . . . for *you* today."

Marianne choked back a laugh at Mr. Tibbett's slip.
The poor man would never feel comfortable calling
her anything but Lady Marianne. The apothecary
might be a rather ponderous old Puritan much given
to platitudes and maxims, but she liked him just the
same. She and he had a special friendship that had
grown through the years as they'd learned from each
other about medicines and herbs.

At the moment, however, Marianne was most interested in his shameful tendency to pry into strangers'
affairs . . . and to gossip.

"We wish to know who bought Falkham House,"
Marianne said baldly, unable to keep the sudden tension out of her voice.

The apothecary swallowed, his florid face reddening
even more than usual. "I see you've heard the news."
He sighed in resignation. "I hope it hasn't been terribly upsetting for you."

Tamara spoke up. "No one told us anything. We
happened by just as the man was moving in." Tamara

glanced meaningfully at her niece. "Mina couldn't rest until she knew who'd stolen her home from her."

Marianne's hands suddenly felt clammy beneath her gloves. Now was the moment of truth. "I have the right to know who he is," she murmured in her own defense as she leaned forward and rested her trembling hands on the counter. "Please tell me."

Mr. Tibbett rubbed his nose nervously, then sighed. "The Earl of Falkham."

Tamara exclaimed, "Oh, poppet, a great noble no less! 'Tis disaster! We should leave here immediately, before you find yourself in more trouble!"

Marianne, however, ignored her aunt's outburst. What could Mr. Tibbett mean? The only Earl of Falkham she knew was Pitney Tearle. She shuddered. If Tearle had returned . . .

She thought back to when Pitney Tearle had sold Falkham House to her father for a song, having needed funds desperately at the time. Six years later, when his luck had turned, he'd suddenly been at their door, wanting to buy back the estate.

By then, she'd been old enough to form reliable judgments of people's characters, and she'd instantly decided she didn't like Tearle. Something about him had made her skin crawl. A faint scent of evil clung to him. She'd felt instinctively he was capable of any crime imaginable.

The man claimed to be a man for the people, wanting to serve his country alongside them. Yet she'd seen what a facade that claim was. She'd once helped her mother treat an old soldier, a destitute Roundhead supporter who'd been run down by Tearle's carriage after blocking its path to beg Tearle for help. The man's wounds had sickened Marianne. When her father had confronted Tearle about it, the earl had denied everything, saying the old man had lied. But Marianne hadn't believed Tearle's smooth talk.

Then later when her father had refused to sell Falkham House, Tearle had hinted to the superstitious villagers that Marianne and her mother were witches, spawn of the devil because of their healing abilities and Gypsy blood. Fortunately, Lydgate's people had ignored his pointed barbs. And her father had even more firmly refused to sell the house to Tearle. He'd thought little of the man, calling him a demagogue.

Now the specter of that demagogue seemed to have come back to haunt her.

"I don't understand," she told Mr. Tibbett. "If Pitney Tearle bought the estate, what was that other man doing there? Was the man his agent? He behaved as if he owned it."

Mr. Tibbett shook his head vehemently. "No, no, you don't understand me at all. We are not speaking of Pitney Tearle, but of his nephew, the real earl. It is he who has returned."

Before Marianne could even wonder at that, Tamara snorted and planted her hands firmly on her waist. "The real earl? Out with it, man! What is all of this about earls? Is Marianne in any danger of being discovered or not?"

"Not by the real Earl of Falkham, Garett Lyon," Mr. Tibbett emphasized. " 'Tis a very strange story, you see. All of us thought he'd been killed along with his parents during the war. Apparently even Sir Pitney thought so. Sir Pitney was merely a knight at the time, but since his wife was the only heir to the Falkham estate, he petitioned Parliament and won the right to the Falkham title.

"But from what I've heard," Mr. Tibbett added in a conspiratorial tone, "the real earl had actually resided all this time in France with the king. The real earl only recently returned. When he did, he reclaimed his lands." Mr. Tibbett bit his lip as he gazed at the two women, his eyes suddenly bright with distress. "And his lands included Falkham House. I have heard that he was incensed to learn the estate had been sold. Sir Tearle had no right to sell it, nor to claim the title for himself while the heir was alive."

"Had he not?" Marianne said dryly. "Then this— this heir shouldn't have hidden himself off in France somewhere if he'd planned to return later and demand his lands back."

The door opened and closed behind Marianne, but she was only dimly aware of it, so caught up was she in her indignation. Mr. Tibbett shot her a warning glance she ignored.

"Not that I sympathize with Sir Pitney," she continued, "but no one would have bought Falkham House from him if this heir had simply bothered to inform someone he hadn't died in the war. It seems terribly inconsiderate of the man, cavorting with royalty in France while everyone here thought him dead. It even makes me wonder—"

"Ah, here's that jar of rosemary you came for," Mr. Tibbett jumped in, his voice ringing loudly in the tiny shop as he took a jar from the shelf and thrust it toward her with jerky movements.

"Rosemary?" she asked in confusion, sliding it back at him. "What would I want with rosemary?" Mr. Tibbett looked positively apoplectic.

"I believe," rumbled a deep masculine voice behind her, "Mr. Tibbett is merely trying in his own subtle way to keep you from wounding my feelings even further."

Startled, Marianne swung around, knocking the jar of rosemary off in the process. It hit the stone floor and shattered, filling the air with the herb's pungent scent.

She tried not to gawk, but restrained herself only with difficulty. Before her stood the new owner of Falkham House, or, if Mr. Tibbett were to be believed, the old heir. Worse yet, she'd just been talking about him in the most insulting manner! A pox on her quick tongue!

Aware that Tamara had slid up next to her protectively, she stood there in uncertainty. Should she apologize or merely stay silent? Which would be less likely to keep his attention on her? Although he couldn't see her face behind her mask, she feared having him notice her unduly.

And well she should, not only because of what he might find out about her, but because of who he was. If he'd been with the king in France, then he was a

Royalist, and no Royalist would hesitate to hand her over to the Crown if he discovered who she was and what she and her father had been accused of.

He was an intimidating man regardless. Inside the shop, he seemed even taller than he'd looked from a distance, his head nearly touching the low ceiling. The harsh lines of his face bespoke a cynicism she'd seldom witnessed among the contented townspeople of Lydgate.

He certainly dressed like nobility, she thought as he studied her, too. She bent to pick up the shards of crockery, trying to gather her wits about her at the same time. At that level, her eyes instantly went to his jackboots of supple gray leather. As she straightened with the crockery in her hand, her eyes traveled up his form, taking in his hose of the best silk and his breeches of kerseymere. His gray woolen cape was pushed back over his shoulders, exposing his doublet and, underneath that, his practical yet fine holland shirt.

His expression turned to one of suspicion as she continued to be silent, not even offering an apology for her quick words. She knew his suspicion could only be heightened by the sight of her unusual garb. The late summer air wasn't yet chill enough for a cloak. Moreover, only ladies wore masks like hers, and then only when riding or for balls and such.

She stole a glance at her aunt, who seemed prepared to defend her niece if need be. At least Tamara's appearance wouldn't raise the earl's suspicions, Marianne thought, for although Tamara's dark skin proclaimed her a Gypsy, she didn't dress flamboyantly or otherwise make her social status known. She could easily pass for some poor gentlewoman's companion.

Yet Tamara's skin color and natural arrogance coupled with Marianne's cloak and mask were bound to make him wonder. Marianne cursed herself for having come to town. But how could she have known he'd come there as well? Why wasn't he at Falkham House, ordering his minions about?

Mr. Tibbett clearly wondered the same thing. "May

I help you, my lord?'' he asked, shooting a stern glance Marianne's way.

She took his cue and moved aside so the two men were face-to-face. She let out a barely audible sigh when Falkham left his intense perusal of her and turned his gaze to Mr. Tibbett.

"It's been a long time, hasn't it, Mr. Bones?'' Falkham said, the fierce mouth smoothing into a pleasant smile as he stared at the apothecary.

The smile more than the teasing nickname took Marianne off guard, for its genuine warmth seemed to belie the embittered lines of the face that wore it.

Mr. Tibbett seemed startled by the warm response. Then he reluctantly returned the smile, his eyes showing his surprise and pleasure. "Yes, my lord, indeed it has been. The days when you called me Mr. Bones are so long gone I wouldn't have thought you'd remember the nickname.'' His expression saddened. "In truth, I thought never to see you again in this life, nor to witness your return to your rightful place.''

"I'm thankful someone in England is pleased to see me,'' Falkham said, his glance turning mocking as it flickered briefly over Marianne. "Not everyone has been so eager to take my side. My uncle's Roundhead friends, some of whom are still in high places, would have seen me completely disinherited if they'd been able to accomplish it and had thought it would profit them.''

"Then God preserve us all,'' Mr. Tibbett said with a snort. At Falkham's raised eyebrow, he faltered. "Please accept my pardon, my lord. I—I only meant that your presence at Falkham House is preferable to Sir Pitney's.''

When Falkham remained silent, Mr. Tibbett continued more hesitantly. "Let me assure you that we here in Lydgate might have done much more to stop him if we'd only known of his treachery. He said you'd died with your parents. Then he took over your estates as if they belonged to him, as if he had the right! Imagine our disbelief when the blackguard went so far as to sell Falkham House—''

As soon as the words left Mr. Tibbett's mouth, he paled as he realized what impact his words might have on the other listeners in the room.

The stranger scarcely noticed Mr. Tibbett's abrupt silence. He smiled, and the wintry quality of that smile struck Marianne at once.

"It might have cost 'the blackguard' dearly if I'd returned to find the manor house sold and beyond my reach," he said, his hand moving unconsciously to the sword he wore so boldly at his side. "Parliament has been returning to their owners most of the estates seized by Cromwell, but not those sold to pay the family's fines and taxes."

Marianne grasped the ominous significance of that at once. The man standing before her wouldn't have been able to reclaim Falkham House if her father hadn't died. She went numb as her suspicions about this new earl solidified.

"Falkham House would have been lost to you," Mr. Tibbett said quietly, as if voicing her thoughts. "That would have been difficult for you if—if matters had been different."

Mr. Tibbett lapsed into an uncomfortable silence.

The earl had no qualms about being blunt on the subject, however. "Yes. Matters turned out well indeed."

As Marianne began to tremble with anger and fear, Mr. Tibbett hastened to smooth over the awkward moment. "In any case, I am certain I speak for everyone in Lydgate when I say we are terribly pleased you own the estate now rather than Sir Pitney. You'll be a good lord for Falkham House."

The stranger smiled grimly. Suddenly he turned to Marianne. "And what do you think, madam? Are your sympathies with me? Do you, too, think I'll be a good lord?" When she remained silent, aware of how dangerous it would be to engage in any conversation with this man, his eyes darkened. "Of course not. No doubt you preferred to have this Sir Henry in residence or even Sir Pitney, instead of the rightful owner."

Only with an effort did she keep her mouth shut,

though her eyes burned with unshed tears. Unconsciously, she clenched and unclenched her hands.

Mr. Tibbett spoke up in an attempt to change the course of the conversation. "We're sad to lose Sir Henry, of course, but we're equally glad to see you've returned. I know you would have felt the loss of Falkham House keenly if Sir Henry had lived and kept ownership of the estate."

"That wouldn't have happened," the earl said with assurance.

The tremulous words were out before Marianne could stop them. "Why not?"

He studied her masked visage. "I would have offered him so much money for the estate he would gladly have sold it to me."

That answer didn't appease Marianne. Didn't the earl know that his uncle had also attempted to buy back the estate and had been turned away by her father?

The stranger's triumphant smile chilled her. "Fortunately, that situation never even arose. The property is now free. Even though the Crown had seized it, His Majesty was more than happy to restore it and my other lands to me."

Mr. Tibbett seemed somewhat uneasy. "That won't please your uncle, I daresay. Sir Pitney was always a grasping tyrant with grand plans for himself and a tendency to use . . . ah . . . forceful means to achieve his goals."

"I don't fear my uncle," the stranger said tersely. "By now he must have realized he made the greatest mistake of his life when he strove to steal my inheritance. And if my regaining Falkham House didn't prove it, I won't hesitate to give him other proof. Either way, he'll learn his lesson, if I must teach it to him over and over."

The fringes of threat in his words sent a shudder through Marianne. Her every muscle tensed as his words whirled through her brain, raising a tempest of emotion. Clearly the man was obsessed with regaining his land, she thought. A man like that might do anything. A man like that might even be capable of causing the arrest of the innocent, if it would serve his purpose. Could it be her initial suspicions were well founded?

His status as one of those arrogant Royalists newly returned from France made it even more likely. Every aspect of his appearance shouted authority. Still, she had to admit he seemed different from the Royalists she'd known at court. His thick ash-brown hair fell uncurled to his shoulders, in defiance of fashion. And not a trace of lace adorned his shirt or doublet. Yet no air of the Puritan clung to him, either. He had a bearing more inherently assured and confident than any newly empowered Puritan she'd ever met.

It was that confidence, that bearing, which frightened her most of all. Such confidence could lead a man to commit all manner of crimes, could it not?

As if she could feel her niece's morbid thoughts, Tamara stepped forward. "We'll be leaving now, if you'll excuse us, sirs," she broke in, prodding Marianne toward the door.

Marianne briefly resisted her aunt's urging, burning to hear more of the conversation. But the warning look Tamara flashed her reminded her this was neither the time nor the place to find out what she wished to know, not if she were to keep from endangering both Tamara and Mr. Tibbett. With a sigh of resignation, she swept her cloak about her and walked ahead of Tamara.

The stranger's voice stopped them before they reached the door. "Please don't leave your business unfinished on my account," he said with a cloying civility she knew was directed at her. "I'd like to hear more about the pleasurable days I spent in France."

Inwardly Marianne groaned. He clearly itched to punish her for her words, and oh, how she'd like to spar with him, but she dared not. The last thing she needed was to draw attention to herself—to her mask in particular—and thus prompt more questions. She gritted her teeth instead, willing her aunt to extricate them from the situation with some semblance of dignity.

Tamara chose to ignore the challenge in his words. "We've finished our business, milord, but thank you for your consideration," she said, rising to the occasion with the smoothly ingratiating manner she'd often used with gentlemen who'd visited the Gypsy camp.

Both women turned to go, but apparently Tamara's words weren't enough for Falkham. He moved forward, placing his hand on the handle of the door as if to open it for them. But he paused.

"I see your companion has lost her tongue," he said to Tamara, although his gaze fastened on Marianne's masked face. "Such a pity, for I really wish to hear more of her spirited opinions. But if I may be so bold, I would at least like to know your names."

She knew he couldn't see her through the silk, yet she felt a blush creep up her cheeks under his intense perusal.

"After all," he continued more sardonically, "I've been away a long while and lost touch with those who once served my father. I may as well begin reacquainting myself with the people of Lydgate as soon as possible."

Marianne doubted he was truly interested in the "people of Lydgate." More likely, he merely wanted to know who'd insulted him, so he could take his revenge later. Unfortunately, he blocked their path, and they couldn't leave until he moved.

Her aunt hastened to remedy that, giving him a little curtsy. "I am Tamara, and this is my niece Mina. You must excuse her mask." She lowered her voice a bit. " 'Tis the smallpox, you see, milord. She was struck by it when young, and her face is quite disfigured."

Marianne choked back a gasp. Trust Aunt Tamara to find the most distasteful explanation possible for her mask, she thought wryly.

Falkham glanced from Tamara to Marianne, his face mirroring his skepticism. "I'm so sorry. I didn't mean to pry." But his eyes still searched the mask as if he weren't quite certain whether to believe Tamara.

Marianne knew instinctively he had indeed meant to pry. Somehow he struck her as the sort of man who trusted nothing and no one and thus must always be alert for treachery.

"We really must go," Tamara said in a slightly cajoling tone, her distress only evidenced in the way her hand tightened on Marianne's arm.

For a moment Marianne feared he wouldn't let them leave the shop. Then he opened the door with a mocking flourish. "By all means, don't let me hinder you. I'm certain we'll meet again."

When they were a few feet away, Tamara murmured under her breath to Marianne, "And I'm certain we won't—not if I can help it." As soon as they were out of earshot, she exploded. "You see? You should have listened to me! We were nearly discovered back there! We should leave Lydgate immediately."

"Nothing could make me leave now," Marianne replied in a voice steeled with determination. "Aunt Tamara, he could be the one who had Father arrested! He wanted Father's estate. Perhaps he decided the best way to get it was to rid himself permanently of Father!"

"You mean, plant the poison so your father would be blamed? But that would have risked the king's life as well."

"True, but we don't know what occurred with the poison. He mightn't have truly risked His Majesty's life, but merely made it look as if Father had done so! A man with his power could do all sorts of things to ensure someone's arrest."

Tamara shuddered. "Yes, I know. He truly might be dangerous. That's what frightens me. If he discovers who you are—"

Marianne laughed. "How can he? You conveniently gave me a reason to be wearing my mask all the time. That was quite brilliant of you, Aunt Tamara." Her eyes gained a teasing glint. "But did you have to make me sound so horribly ugly? First you tell everyone I threw myself in the Thames like some mad Ophelia when I heard of Father's death, and now you have me scarred for life. Truly, you'll have my reputation in shreds before the year is past."

"Better a reputation in shreds than your neck in a hangman's noose," Tamara warned.

Her aunt's words instantly sent shivers through Marianne's slender body, despite the warm day and the cloak. "Don't worry," she said with an earnestness born of determination. "I have no more wish to be hanged than you do to see me hanged."

"This earl may have something to say about that!"

Marianne's blood went cold remembering the earl's intense perusal of her and the way he spoke of taking vengeance on Pitney Tearle. He certainly was a man to be reckoned with.

"I'll simply have to avoid him," she replied.

Her aunt shook her head as she strode forward along the path. "This earl won't be easy to avoid, I fear. Be careful, poppet, you don't find yourself caught in his trap, for he would easily devour you."

"He's probably already forgotten about me."

But Marianne's heart continued to pound, like the heart of a bird hunted by the falcon, long after she and her aunt had passed out of sight of Lydgate.

Chapter Three

"Take heed lest passion sway
Thy judgement to do aught,
   which else free will
Would not admit."
—John Milton,
Paradise Lost

Weary to the bone, Marianne slipped out of the tiny cramped cottage where she'd just served as midwife to Mrs. Aiken. The poor woman had suffered tremendously, but at last had given birth to twin boys, sending her husband into raptures, for they'd previously had only daughters. Marianne was grateful now for the experience she'd gained from helping her mother serve as midwife.

With great reluctance, Marianne pulled up her hood and tied her mask in place. Moving about Lydgate in disguise had become very tedious. For three long weeks she'd suffered the mask and cloak, uncertain when she'd be able to discard them for good. She wished she could throw caution to the winds and do without them. But Aunt Tamara would scold her the minute she caught Marianne without them, so Marianne resisted the urge to tear them off.

She walked slowly through Lydgate, unafraid of being out in the streets late at night in the town she considered home. Although dark now and silent, it still seemed safe as a castle to her. Here among the stoic townspeople, she'd found a haven.

Then out of the darkness at the other end of the street emerged a thin man she'd never seen before. As he caught sight of her, he hastened his steps in her direction. Still feeling enveloped in a safe cocoon, she waited for him without fear. Strangers often sought her, needing help for their sick and having heard of her abilities. This man's urgent steps convinced her he was one of those.

"Be you the Gypsy healer they call Mina?" he asked as he approached, an anxiousness to his tone she couldn't ignore.

At her nod, he gave a great sigh of relief and clasped her arm, pulling her along behind him as he began to return the way he'd come.

"The men at the tavern told me to look for you here. Thank God I found you," he muttered as he took great strides, forcing her to run to keep up.

"Perhaps you could tell me where you're taking me?" she asked, a half smile on her face. The man was either so sure of her compliance or so flustered, he hadn't even bothered to introduce himself or to ask her to accompany him.

He stopped now, aware of his omission. "Sorry, madam. Didn't say, did I? I'm his lordship's valet, William Crashaw. His lordship lies wounded. The men at the tavern told me you could help him."

A cold chill gripped her heart. "His lordship?"

He nodded his head with impatience and pulled at her arm again, frowning when she stood planted. "The earl!" he said in exasperation. "Surely you know of him."

She stared at him numbly. She couldn't go to the aid of Falkham and risk his finding out who she was! Yet she couldn't ignore a wounded man. What was she to do?

Suddenly she thought of Mr. Tibbett. Yes, that was it. The apothecary could certainly care for the earl if the man weren't too badly hurt. "How serious is his lordship's wound?"

"Quite serious," the young man snapped in a voice that showed his growing anger at her hesitation. "And it worsens the longer we stand idle! Two men attacked him on the road. One of them stabbed him clear through the thigh. He'll die if someone doesn't stop the bleeding and bind his leg!''

She paled. "There's Mr. Tibbett—''

"A Puritan! I don't want one of his kind near my master,'' the man spat out. "Still, I'm desperate enough to consider it, but he's not there. The men at the tavern told me you could help my master.'' He eyed her coldly. "But if you're too squeamish to dress a wound—''

"I can dress a wound, fear not!'' The words were out of her mouth before she could take them back. Not that she would. If Mr. Tibbett were nowhere to be found, she'd no choice but to aid the earl. She couldn't let him die. "Depending on how bad the wound is, I may need you to return to the apothecary's shop once I see your master. Mr. Tibbett's servant can give you whatever remedies I might require.''

He nodded tersely, then stalked on in front of her.

She could also send William to Tamara's wagon, she thought to herself as she followed him. But she'd managed in the past few days to avoid the earl and his men, and she preferred they not know where she lived. No, Mr. Tibbett's servant was always there when his master was away. The servant could send her whatever she needed as long as this William could remember her instructions.

Her heart began to pound. She'd never dressed a serious wound, though she'd watched her father do it hundreds of times. And this wound of all wounds! How could she work on the earl, knowing he might have had her father arrested? How could she touch him when she was terrified of his discovering who she was?

She sighed. How could she not help him? She'd sworn to preserve life, as her father and mother had sworn. This man's life might not merit preserving, yet who was she to decide? A life was a life. She must do what she could to save his.

She hurried her steps to catch up with the anxious valet. As they reached the top of the hill and she caught sight of her old home, a lump formed in her throat. He was there in the home that had been wrested from her father! And she was expected to serve his need of the moment, when he might be the very one who'd sought to destroy her family!

For a moment she hesitated at the point where the road forked off toward Falkham House. Her mind swam with memories of coming home late at night with her mother after staying by a child's sickbed, of returning with her father from an evening's merriment at a friend's estate. This earl had possibly plotted her father's arrest. How could she help him? How could she?

William continued on a few paces before he realized she'd stopped. Then he turned to face her. Silhouetted against the moonlit sky, he seemed absurdly thin. But his voice didn't falter as he spoke. "Listen, madam. I'd send a man for Bodger, but he lives too far away. He couldn't be here soon enough, I fear. But if you can't help his lordship, I'll wait for the surgeon. I can't have you make a mistake that might cost my master his leg."

She stiffened at the mention of Bodger, a horrible surgeon who'd caused the loss of more lives than he'd saved. The thought of that despicable man working on anyone's leg appalled her. After all, she told herself, she wasn't certain the earl had been responsible for her father's arrest. If he died and wasn't guilty . . .

Her shoulders unconsciously lifted with determination. "I shan't cost him his leg, unless his leg is already too far gone to keep. However, I can assure you if you let Bodger cut on him, he'll be more fit for the grave than anything else. You can trust me to treat him."

Something in the calm assurance of her voice seemed to settle his mind.

"Come on, then," he murmured, turning back toward the house. "We're wasting precious time."

In moments they entered her old home. She walked beside the valet through the familiar rooms and climbed the stairs with a saddened heart, unable to stop remembering her past years there. The long hall on the second floor had been refurbished, but in their haste to pass through it, she had little chance to ob-

serve what had been done to it. Reminding herself of
the business at hand, she forced herself not to glance
longingly at the old memory-drenched alcoves.

Suddenly several booming curses rent the silence of
the house. She raced to the end of the hall ahead of
William to the master bedroom from which the sound
came.

The sight that greeted her when she entered the room
filled her with horror. One of the earl's servants, by
appearances an old soldier, stood poised beside the
earl with an empty cup in his hand. The earl himself
sat atop her parents' old bed with his legs stretched
out in front of him. A kettle was suspended over the
flames in the fireplace, and she could smell boiling
oil. The earl's face was twisted in pain as he soundly
cursed everyone within earshot.

For a moment, she forgot the crimes she attributed
to the man, forgot the hint of menace underlying his
voice the day they'd first met. All she could see was
the needless suffering of a man at the hands of a bumbling idiot who was using an outmoded and needlessly
painful method of cleansing the wound.

"If one more drop of that hits his skin," she threatened as she moved forward to the old man's side and
snatched the cup away from him, "I'll boil *you* in that
kettle!"

"But miss, we got to burn the poison away," the
man protested, automatically recoiling from the masked
figure all in black who threw the cup to the floor and
dared him to pick it up and fill it again.

"Burn the poison away indeed! Out, out, before you
murder him!" she instructed as she pushed futilely at
the stubborn old soldier, sickened by the smell of
scorched flesh that filled the room.

"Listen to the woman," Falkham stopped his cursing to grind out. "For God's sake, Will, get him out
of here!"

William quickly coaxed the old man to leave by
murmuring something in his ear. The soldier left,
grumbling as he went.

"I hope you haven't come to torture me more," the

earl growled from the bed. Only the sweat beading his brow revealed the extent of his pain, but one look at the angry red swollen area where the oil had burned the skin made her gasp. She couldn't have wished a worse torture on him if she'd done it herself. She ought to feel pleasure at his pain, yet she found only a desire to turn and run from the sight of his burn. Instantly she drew an ointment from her pouch and began to smooth it over the burn. He grimaced as she touched the sore spot.

"The sword wound hurts less than the old man's ministrations did," he grumbled through gritted teeth. "He took it upon himself to begin boiling my leg whole while I wasn't looking."

"He's a fool," she said in disgust, then began to survey the sword wound. Someone, probably the old soldier, had removed the earl's breeches to bare his leg. A sheet had been draped over his groin and left leg, leaving only his right thigh exposed. Her stomach grew queasy as she stared at the ugly laceration that gaped open close to where his leg joined his hip. "The wound is very serious," she said, trying not to let her voice shake. "But at least the sword went cleanly through. It doesn't seem to have severed the muscle, so it should heal well. Just be grateful the men didn't carry pistols."

"Actually one of them did," Falkham replied through clenched teeth. "But he was a poor shot, so I was able to wrest it from him. Unfortunately, he was a better swordsman than I expected."

William spoke behind her. "And you were a better one than he expected, eh, m'lord?"

Falkham's clear gray eyes clouded. "Yes, I suppose I was."

Marianne tried to ignore the ripple of horror that washed over her at that. Silently she moved to the basin of water someone had placed near the table and then wet the clean linen cloth that lay beside the basin. With slow, careful strokes, she began to wash the wound.

The earl's tight-lipped, harsh expression told her that

her every touch caused him pain, but she could do nothing about it. As gently as she could, she scrubbed away the dried blood and bits of fabric that clogged the wound.

"Do highwaymen often ride the roads hereabouts?" William asked her while watching her work.

"This is the first I've heard of," she responded tersely, concentrating on the task at hand.

"Those were no highwaymen," the earl bit out, a muscle working in his jaw.

William turned toward his master. "You think Tearle's behind it?"

"Certainly. He's none too happy I've regained the manor. Now he fears me as well. Perhaps he realizes how badly I wish to cut his throat. If it weren't for the king . . ."

He fell silent, his eyes fastening on her veiled face, for she'd stopped her movements at hearing his words about acquiring the manor.

Her heart began to pound as she hurriedly returned to cleansing the gore from the earl's skin, though less gently than before. Unnerved by the earl's continuing stare, she asked William, "Have you told the constable of the attack?"

"No need," William replied, peering over her shoulder. "His lordship left both men lying in the glade with their bellies open."

"That's enough, Will!" Falkham said sharply. She didn't miss the meaningful glance he gave his servant. "There's no need for the young woman to hear about such matters."

"I agree," she was quick to retort, her stomach churning at the image William's words had instantly brought to mind. "I abhor killing."

Falkham smiled at her tone of contempt. "You would have preferred they'd murdered me instead?"

She squelched her bloodthirsty urge to say yes, but only because she wasn't yet completely certain he deserved murdering. She fixed him with a somber gaze. "Of course not, but I'd rather not hear such deaths discussed so casually."

"Forgive me," he shot back, his eyebrow lifting. "I'm afraid Will and I have become far too accustomed to killing in the past few years. We saw many battles serving with the Duke of York."

She swallowed hard at that statement. Her eyes scanned his leg again, this time noting the many thin scars marring his skin, scars that could have been inflicted in battle. She knew the Duke of York's men had served the French and then the Spanish armies, winning honor and fame. This man had been one of those soldiers.

Small wonder he scarcely grimaced as she cleansed his wound. Small wonder he seemed deadened to the outrage of having been attacked near his own home. For a man as young as he appeared to be, he must have seen a great deal of death.

And how much of that death had he caused? She shuddered to think of the men he must have killed, even if some of them had been killed in battle.

By now she'd washed away enough of the blood to see what she had to work with. The wound looked better already. With some stitching and a healing poultice, he'd be moving about in a few days, she thought. Her eyes idly wandered up his hairy thigh.

Oh, no, she thought as with a sudden absurd horror she realized just how naked he was. Underneath her mask, a blush spread over her face. She'd worked beside her father when he'd toiled over many naked men, but this man differed considerably from them. He wasn't grizzled, dirty, and coarse like the soldiers she'd witnessed her father treat.

This man's voice was refined, his manner that of a gentleman. Yet even with his wound, he reminded her of a leashed lightning bolt, waiting to destroy anything that crossed him. He emanated strength, despite the slit in his leg. His thigh was pale from loss of blood, but it was powerful and solid nonetheless, sprinkled with curly dark brown hair. Her gaze moved helplessly farther up to where the sheet just missed covering a thicker patch of hair she knew surrounded his . . .

Her gaze dropped. Then she realized he watched her

intently, and her hand went instinctively to the mask that covered her face. She raised her eyes to his and nearly gasped aloud. His clear gray gaze seemed to see through the mask, clear through to her mind as if he could guess at her embarrassing thoughts.

"Well," he asked, his words tinged with sarcasm. "Can you save it?"

For a moment, she thought he referred to something other than his leg. Then she swore inwardly at herself for being such a dolt about his nakedness.

"Yes, of course, but I'll need your man to fetch some things from the apothecary's shop."

His quick, mocking grin instantly made her want to bite her tongue for reminding him of the circumstances under which they'd met.

"Just tell me what you wish fetched," William responded, oblivious to his master's odd smile as he started for the door.

"Tell the servant to give you a jar of wolfsbane ointment, and be quick about it," she said.

William nodded and opened the door.

"And William?" she added with a nervous glance at the earl. "Have the servant send a message to my aunt that I'll be late."

"If you tell me where you live I'll deliver the message myself."

"No!"

When both men gave her searching stares, she forced her voice to be more even. "I mean, there's no need for you to trouble yourself. Just send the servant. And don't . . . ah . . . mention whom I'm tending. My aunt would be alarmed if she knew. Simply tell the servant to say I'll return soon. Aunt Tamara's accustomed to my late hours, so she'll understand."

After William left, Marianne released a troubled sigh. Aunt Tamara would be furious when Marianne told her where she'd been. Since that day at Mr. Tibbett's, Aunt Tamara had stressed many times the importance of Marianne's remaining unnoticed by the new earl.

"Why will your aunt be alarmed to hear you're

tending me?'' Falkham asked, his gray eyes suddenly keen with interest.

Marianne's hand froze in midair as she was about to withdraw a heavy needle and some thick black thread from her leather pouch of herbs. She fought to keep her distress at his question from showing. Shakily, she pulled out the needle and thread, perspiration trickling down her breasts underneath her coarsely woven cloak. The room was close and hot, what with the fire still blazing, but the heat wasn't what made her perspire. Rather, it was the sudden realization that she was alone with this very dangerous man.

She chose her words carefully, hoping to keep the agitation out of her voice. ''Begging your pardon, my lord, but my aunt doesn't like nor trust noblemen.'' That was partly true, for Marianne's father had been the only nobleman Aunt Tamara could ever stomach.

Falkham surprised her by laughing. ''Why not? Are the nobility any less likable or trustworthy than Gypsies?''

''Some of them are despicable,'' Marianne retorted, angered by the slur he cast on the Gypsies.

''And so are some Gypsies. Perhaps your aunt has simply met the wrong noblemen.''

She bit back another retort, knowing it did no good to argue with him. After all, there was some truth to his words. Marianne's mother had once hinted that a nobleman had broken Aunt Tamara's heart, which was why she scorned the nobles so. But it was more than that. Aunt Tamara despised the few she'd met because she saw them as weak, spineless fops.

Marianne glanced at Falkham, whose stoic expression belied the pain he must be feeling. The earl was certainly unlike the noblemen her aunt had known. More was the pity. Since the man was far from being a fool, his presence at Falkham House made her situation all the more precarious. Her plan to stay out of harm's way was falling apart, she thought wryly.

At least he was wounded, so he couldn't come after her if she should need to flee suddenly. Yet she had the definite sense that if he wanted to follow her, he would do so, wound or no.

She'd just have to make certain he had no desire to do so. She looked at the needle she'd just threaded. After she finished sewing him up, he'd most likely never wish to be within a mile of her. She winced at the thought of the pain she was about to inflict on him.

Then she reminded herself of who he was. For the first time that evening, she glanced around the room he'd appropriated for himself, the room that had once belonged to her parents. Her dislike of him deepened as she witnessed the way he'd changed it. Her father's old well-loved chairs and writing table had been replaced with new walnut furniture lacking the warmth of the old. Her gaze fell on his bloodied sword, which lay on the rich carpet, staining it.

The earl was a ruthless killer, she told herself. He deserved whatever pain he suffered. Yet the blood darkening the sheets beneath his leg served as a reminder that he, too, was human; he, too, merited some mercy.

She'd best get the distasteful task over with, she told herself abruptly, lifting the needle.

"I'm going to sew the wound closed so it heals better," she told him as she approached the bed again. "It will hurt you, I'm afraid."

"It can't hurt more than it already does, but I certainly hope you're skilled with a needle," he stated acidly. "I don't want my leg to look like a patched doublet come the morrow."

His eyes followed her delicate fingers as she brought the needle to his leg.

"Don't you know? We Gypsies are famed for our needlework," she said lightly, trying to draw his attention away from her actions as she eased the needle through his flesh and pulled the thread through.

"You're no Gypsy," he muttered between clenched teeth.

His words threw her into such confusion she suddenly pricked him.

"Damn it, woman," he shouted, "I'm not a pin-cushion!"

"I'm sorry," she murmured as she forced herself to be calm. "What do you mean—I'm no Gypsy?"

"You speak too well for a Gypsy. Your aunt—she has an accent. But your voice is more refined."

She swallowed. This man was far too perceptive for her peace of mind. She must give him some explanation, but what? Then she remembered something her aunt had once said—the best lie was the one that came as close to the truth as possible.

"My father was a nobleman," she stated softly. "Only my mother was a Gypsy."

The earl's flint-hard eyes narrowed. "You're a no-bleman's bastard? That would explain your speech, but only if you'd been raised as a noblewoman. Are you saying your father claimed you?"

Thank goodness he'd leapt to the desired conclusion, and she hadn't been made to speak a complete lie. She forced her fingers to continue her stitching as a lump formed in her throat.

"Yes. I was raised in his house until his death," she whispered, her throat tightening. She wished the part about his death were no lie. "His family wouldn't accept me after that, so I went to my aunt. She has cared for me ever since."

A flicker of sympathy crossed his face, making her feel a slight twinge of guilt. She fought back the feeling. It was her life she had to protect, and her aunt's. Under the circumstances, surely a small lie could be forgiven her.

"You've had a hard life," he said quietly.

For a moment, his words confused her. Granted, she had no parents, but she had someone to care for her. Then she remembered he believed her to be dis-figured by smallpox. Suddenly she resented the pity her aunt's and her own deceptions had made him feel for her.

"My life hasn't been so terribly hard," she stated as she drew the needle through his skin yet again. "On the contrary, I've been very happy. For me, life is like an overgrown garden. You can spend all your time cursing the weeds, or you can work hard to pull them out. In either case, the flowers are what matter.''

His eyes became shuttered, cynicism turning the lines of his mouth rigid. "Some gardens are too overgrown to save.. 'Tis better perhaps to level those to the ground."

She dropped her eyes back to his leg, somewhat surprised at just how bitter his words sounded. "Perhaps. But then you must be sure to plant a new garden.''

He chuckled harshly. "You must have your flowers, I see. No matter what's done to your garden, you'll make it bear flowers.''

She smiled underneath the mask. "I suppose I sound a bit too cheery to a man who's just been wounded by highwaymen.''

"A bit. Or maybe a trifle naive.''

That stung her. "What would you know of hardship, my lord?" she bit out as she finished stitching the wound. "Have you ever suffered in childbirth or watched children starve? You've seen death in battle, 'tis true, but you no doubt gloried in the honor of it.'' She thought of the poor men and women her parents had treated and their awful, often needless suffering. "I've seen death come to those who didn't deserve it, who only died because they were born to the wrong families. Your kind never sees that suffering. No, your kind only causes it.''

He gazed at her intently, his eyes darkening at her outburst. "Your aunt isn't the only one who dislikes noblemen.''

She turned from him, confused by her reaction. Why had she suddenly responded with such venom? She didn't dislike the nobility. How could she? Her father was a baronet.

Yet she regarded the peerage differently than did others. Her mother had opened her eyes to the hardships the common people suffered, had taught her to treat them as she'd treat anyone else. That was why her father had been so reluctant to be a part of the court. Although his sympathies had always been with the Royalists, he'd been almost content under Cromwell. He'd even begun to think it might not be so terrible to have a government ruled by all the people, not just a few.

Now the court had returned—the idle noblemen led by a debauched king. She looked at the earl from beneath her mask. He might appear different, but at heart he was like all the other Cavaliers. He saw the world through jaundiced eyes, never once having experienced the despair and hopelessness of the poor. She continued to sew up his wound in silence, determined to keep her eyes steadily on her work until she was finished.

With angry motions, she began to rip a sheet into strips for bandages, still caught up in her feelings of resentment toward him and all those like him.

"Why do I get the feeling you wish it were me you were ripping into little bits?" he asked after a moment.

"Don't be absurd, my lord," she snapped. "I merely need something to bind your leg with."

He chuckled. "You've enough bandages there to bind both legs quite completely, if I'm not mistaken."

She stopped and looked down at the pile of linen she'd torn. "I suppose I have," she said ruefully, dropping her hands to her sides.

"If you really must use so many bandages, perhaps you should wound me in my other leg," he taunted. "You seem more than eager to do so."

How he could taunt her when his wound must hurt him terribly, she couldn't imagine. Perhaps it helped to distract him from the pain.

She tried to match his light tone. "Maybe I should. Then I could try your old servant's remedy on the other leg as well."

A dark scowl clouded his face. "Not unless you use those bandages to tie me to the bed. I shall tell him on pain of death that he's not to try his skill at doctoring anywhere within a hundred miles of my estates. My tenants will begin dying like flies if *he* starts treating them."

Slowly she lifted her eyes to his face, which now wore an expression of wry amusement. Just as she began to wonder why such a wicked man concerned himself with his tenants, William returned with the ointment.

"That aunt of yours was a mite troublesome," he grumbled.

Marianne took the salve from him with trembling fingers. "How did you find my aunt?"

"She was at the apothecary's, carping to that poor servant about her missing niece. I suppose she hoped to find you there."

Marianne released a pent-up breath. "I see," she murmured as she began to spread the salve liberally over the earl's sewn wound.

William grimaced. "She gave me a tongue lashing, she did. Said you weren't the townspeople's personal servant and you needed rest like everyone else. Then she scolded me for not telling her where you were. I told her you were safe. And still the woman lectured me. Said I was to remember you're an innocent and not to lay a finger on you."

Marianne bit her lip nervously when that last statement seemed to pique the earl's interest.

"My aunt is overly cautious. Pay her no mind," she murmured, taking a bandage and wrapping it carefully around the earl's hard, firm thigh.

" 'Tis hard to ignore a woman as sharp-tongued as your aunt," William responded, settling himself in a chair beside the earl's bed. "Then again, without the sharp tongue, she'd still be hard to ignore," he added enigmatically.

The earl seemed to understand what William hinted at. "Isn't the Gypsy woman a bit old for you?" Falkham quipped.

William's face grew stubborn. "She weren't that old, m'lord. And she weren't half bad to look at, either."

Falkham chuckled, his chuckle turning into a curse when Marianne tightened the bandage angrily on his leg.

"If you gentlemen are quite finished discussing my

aunt, I'd like to instruct William on how to care for the wound.''

The silence that fell on the room caused Marianne to look up. The earl's dark scowl was enough to send a timid soul running for shelter. Yet Marianne wasn't a timid soul. She met his gaze steadily.

''Won't you be returning to change the dressing?'' Falkham asked, his tone intimidating.

Despite the warm glow the fire cast on the inhabitants of the room, the earl's face seemed formidably dark. She ignored the whisper of fear it sent through her. ''I'm certain William can change your bandages quite well on his own.''

The earl caught her hand as she finished tying off the bandage. ''I'd rather you did it yourself,'' he murmured, his hold on her wrist tightening when she tried to pull it free.

''Please, my lord,'' she said, her heart beginning to beat rapidly in alarm, ''there's no need for it. I've others to tend.''

''Ah, but William is unfamiliar with doctoring and might worsen the wound,'' he said, suddenly taking a keen interest in the delicate hand he gripped.

The strength of his hold unnerved her. ''I—I'm certain he can follow whatever instructions I give him.''

''Perhaps . . .'' the earl replied absentmindedly, reaching out to snatch her other hand, which he studied for several moments. She could feel her pulse race under the firm pad of his thumb.

At last he dropped one hand, and his eyes jerked up to pin her with a suspicious gaze. ''Tell me, Mina, how did your hands escape being scarred by the pox?''

His question brought Marianne up short. ''I—I don't know,'' she stammered, uncertain what answer to give to lessen his suspicions.

''Isn't it odd your face was so badly scarred you wear a mask, yet your hands are as smooth-skinned and soft as a babe's? To my knowledge that's not typical of the pox.''

With his free hand he slowly slid the cuff of her sleeve up to bare her lower arm.

"You're the physician," he said, his eyes narrowing as he took in the healthy golden skin revealed beneath her coarse linen sleeve. "Tell me if the pox is generally so virulent in one spot of the body and so mild in another."

"It can happen," she said, her fear of him erased by a growing anger. How could he treat with such callousness a woman who claimed to be shy about her appearance?

"What do you think, William?" the earl asked as he easily resisted her attempts to yank her arm from his grip. "Have you ever known the pox to be so discriminating?"

She exploded, her role of timid, defaced young woman completely forgotten. "Release me at once, my lord!"

His lips curled in a mocking grin. "What if I should wish to explore this strange phenomenon further?"

She let out a gasp of outrage. "Then you'll merely confirm what I thought all along—that although you have all the trappings of a gentleman, you're as wicked as the rest of the king's courtiers!"

The smile left his face. "And what would a Gypsy know of the king's courtiers?"

She silently cursed her slip of the tongue, but retorted, "I've heard the stories, like everyone else. How the court sports itself with illicit pleasures. How noblemen such as you climb out of one loose woman's bed only to climb into another's. Are you so jaded with beauties you must now trouble a poor pockmarked maiden before she's scarcely finished tending your wounds?"

She wasn't certain which of her words did it, but something she said had the desired effect. Abruptly he dropped her hand, his mouth tightening into a thin line. "Ah, yes, my wounds," he said flatly. He glanced down at the neatly bound leg, his expression a mixture of anger at having his will thwarted and self-disgust for his behavior. "You tended my leg well. I had no right to embarrass you."

She reined in her temper, though it was difficult.

Begrudgingly he added, "I do thank you for your care."

Her urge to box his ears only slightly diminished. " 'Tis already forgotten," she said with a dismissive gesture, now eager to flee the room before he began questioning her again.

"Not by me. And I'm not going to let your skill go unrewarded, either. Will, fetch my pouch—"

"No, please don't!" she protested, afraid to be left alone again with the earl.

William paused in the doorway, awaiting his master's command.

Falkham's eyebrows lifted in question. "You must be paid for your services. I'm familiar enough with Gypsies to know they do nothing without expecting a reward."

She ignored the insult in his words. At the moment she was so anxious to get away without her identity being discovered she didn't care what he said. If she spent another minute alone with him, he might pursue again the question of her scars.

"I—I don't take money for my services," she insisted, hoping he'd simply let her leave.

But that hope proved groundless. He scowled. "Surely your aunt isn't so generous. I'll speak with her in a few days—"

"No!"

At her vehement protest, his gaze turned curious.

She wrung her hands as she realized she was handling this very badly. But she didn't want him to speak with her aunt. "I—I mean," she babbled, "she would say the same as I. The healing I do is for my own satisfaction, not for money. My aunt supports us with her needlework—we need nothing more. Please, my lord, don't concern yourself with us."

He stared at her with an intentness that curled tendrils of apprehension around her heart. Instinctively she knew she'd erred. She should have taken the gold and been done with it even if it had meant being left alone with him for a few minutes. But how could she have guessed he'd be so insistent?

Finally he gave her a curt nod, though she could tell by the gleam in his eye he found her reasons suspect. "As you wish."

A small sigh of relief escaped her lips. "Thank you. Now, my lord, I must go before my aunt becomes overly concerned."

"But you'll return to change the dressing?" he asked, more demandingly than she would have liked.

"If need be," she answered with reluctance.

It wasn't really a lie, she told herself later as she recalled the way he'd seemed to take her statement for a promise. If he needed her, she'd certainly return, but he wouldn't need her. He was strong and healthy, and the wound would heal well. Later, when William asked about her at Mr. Tibbett's, the apothecary could tell him how to change the dressing. And she'd not have to see this frightening earl ever again.

Unless, of course, the earl was determined to see her.

She forced herself not to worry about something that hadn't yet happened. If he sought her out, she'd find some way to discourage his curiosity.

She would, she told herself.

Only when she remembered the feel of his grip on her wrists did she doubt it.

Chapter Four

"Where guilt is, rage and courage doth abound."
—Ben Jonson,
Sejanus, His Fall

Marianne had sworn she wouldn't return to Falkham House. She'd never thought she'd need to. Yet here she was, only five days later, standing in the magnificent hall that stretched the entire length of Falkham House's second floor.

She couldn't help it, she told herself. Mr. Tibbett had said the earl was very ill. What else could she do? She had to determine why her stitching and poulticing had been ineffectual. Despite her suspicions of Falkham, the image of his strong, hard body wracked with fever troubled her. She knew she had no reason to feel guilt for his condition. Nonetheless, she did.

She glanced surreptitiously at her aunt, who was regarding everything with unveiled suspicion. Marianne couldn't blame her. The hall itself would raise anyone's suspicions about its new owner. The earl had transformed it into a gallery of rich, dark colors and disturbing, even violent images. Its paneled walls looked wholly different from when her father had owned the house. Although paintings and tapestries still adorned them, they didn't resemble the quiet scenes of shepherds and the sedate portraits of Winchilsea ancestors that her parents had preferred to hang.

Ancient medieval tapestries depicting battles now

lined the walls. The painted faces of fierce men and women, who all bore a marked resemblance to the earl himself, stared out at her. A painting of two half-naked, fleshy women reclining in the presence of two gentlemen made her blush to her toes. Yet something about its lush, dark colors and blatant sensuality drew her to stare at it in spite of herself.

Even the furniture seemed designed to intimidate the viewer. The expensive, carefully crafted chairs placed in the huge bay windows reminded her that Falkham's wealth probably far exceeded her father's. An ancient classical marble table caught her eye, the pedestal a circle of grinning satyrs who appeared to be holding up the tabletop. She turned away from their wicked eyes, only to be caught by a far more troubling sight.

Unusual weaponry hung along one section of the long hall. Crossed Spanish rapiers, wicked-looking sabers, and even a jeweled scimitar gave the hall a menacing air that hadn't existed before. What kind of man would hang such frightening accoutrements of battle on his walls? she wondered. Her answer followed swiftly—the kind of man who wanted to remind all who entered that he wasn't to be trifled with. The new owner of Falkham was a hardened soldier, accustomed to blood and horror and scarred from his many wounds.

So why hadn't he survived his sword wound better? she asked herself in bewilderment. She couldn't understand it. Surely he couldn't be as ill as Mr. Tibbett seemed to believe, for his wound had been no worse than those wounds he'd received in battle. Granted, she'd never treated such a wound before, but she'd cleaned it well and sewn it shut as she'd seen her father do. The wound shouldn't have festered, she told herself, nor should the earl now be unconscious with fever.

Aunt Tamara didn't believe he was, of course. After Mr. Tibbett had said he'd heard the news of the earl's poor condition from William Crashaw, Tamara had instantly insisted the story was all a trap to draw Marianne back to Falkham House.

"This is insanity," Tamara muttered now as they waited for the servant to notify William of their arrival. "I can't believe you came here again."

Marianne could scarcely believe it herself, but she didn't say so. "Mr. Tibbett fears the earl is near to death."

"Ah, but Mr. Tibbett was still against your coming. He didn't even see Falkham, so he couldn't vouch for his condition."

"I told you, William would never have let Mr. Tibbett near his master. He told me before that he doesn't trust Puritans."

Tamara snorted. "And you shouldn't trust noblemen. 'Twas foolish of you to go near the earl the first time. If not for your mask, who knows what might have happened?"

Marianne's eyes dropped guiltily to her hands. In memory she felt Falkham's firm, tapered fingers encircling her wrists. She hadn't told her aunt how close she'd come to discovery that night. Could William's claim that the earl lay ill really be just a trap, or was it genuine?

In either case, she was in a very dangerous position. If Falkham was truly ill, the townspeople might believe she'd purposely hampered his healing, whether that were true or not.

Marianne faced her aunt, and her petite form shook despite the heaviness of her wool cloak. "Have you thought of what will happen if the earl dies?" she whispered through her silk mask.

Tamara went very still, the lines of worry on her face deepening.

"If a nobleman of his standing dies after I've treated him, my fate is set," Marianne said grimly. "The townspeople dare not protect me then, and as soon as the soldiers discover 'Mina' and Lady Marianne are one and the same, I'll be arrested. Don't you see? I must help him, or I'll pay for it with my life."

Tamara's dark eyes glittered. "We could be far away by nightfall."

Tamara's proposition was tempting, but Marianne knew it wasn't the answer—not for her. "I won't abandon a man to a sure death," she said with a fierceness that seemed to fit the newly refurbished hall. "Besides, even if we escaped, this time they'd hunt me until they found me. They only left me alone before because of your trick."

Her aunt's expression grew tormented as she seemed to recognize the logic of her niece's words. Then she stiffened her shoulders. "At least I can protect you from that jackanapes William and his fearsome master while you do what you must."

"That's why you're here, isn't it?" Marianne quipped with a faint smile.

Marianne could almost envision Tamara wrestling one of the menacing swords from the walls to defend her niece's honor. The thought warmed her slightly, but it also made her wonder if she should have listened to Tamara and left well enough alone.

Something didn't seem quite right about the manor. Despite the quiet air of sorrow, even of death, in the long hall, the manor itself seemed very much alive. The sound of shoes tapping up and down the stairs mingled with the tuneless whistle of a footman in a distant room. Three servant girls passed noisily through the hall and eyed her and Tamara with barely disguised curiosity. Yet they didn't seem the least concerned about their master's condition.

Before she could worry any more, however, William entered one end of the hall. As he strode down its carpeted length, Marianne thought he looked much handsomer than she'd remembered. He lacked his master's intimidating build, but his lanky, wiry frame seemed imbued with a quiet determination she could respect.

"So you've come," he said in hushed tones as he approached them, his eyes not meeting hers.

His refusal to look at her instantly alarmed her. Was

she too late? she thought in a panic. "Is he—is he dead?"

Startled he looked squarely at her, then seized her hand. "Oh . . . oh, no, he's well . . . I mean, he's feverish. At the moment, he's resting some, but . . ."

His voice trailed off as he noticed Tamara, who stood behind Marianne.

"What are *you* doing here?" he asked Tamara, instantly wary, though his pale green eyes seemed to warm.

"I've come to help my niece, of course," Tamara staunchly replied as Marianne stood there bewildered by the tension that seemed to exist between her aunt and William. The two stared at each other as if she were no longer there. The gleam that leapt into William's eyes confused her until she remembered he'd met Tamara at the apothecary's shop the night the earl had been wounded.

William took Marianne's arm and pressed her forward, his eyes never leaving Tamara's face. "Please go on to my master's chambers. You know where they are," he said in a low voice, nodding Marianne in the direction behind him. As Tamara, too, moved forward, he stayed her with one hand. "You remain here."

Marianne turned back, her eyes narrowing with suspicion. "Why can't she accompany me?"

"Yes, why can't I?" Tamara put in, crossing her arms over her ample chest. "Where she goes, I go, sirrah. Let me pass if you want her near your master."

William looked from one to the other, his gaze full of concern, then cool calculation. He straightened, as if he'd made up his mind to do something. "You shan't see him," he told Tamara, stepping between her and Marianne. "I'll not have your evil eye making matters worse."

When Tamara harrumphed and started forward, he gripped her arms. " 'Tis bad enough your niece might have killed him. Together you could murder him for certain. No, I'll keep you here and make certain the girl doesn't harm him 'by accident.' "

"Why, you barbarous rogue, you shan't speak about my niece that way—" Tamara began, drawing herself up in fury.

But Marianne didn't share her aunt's indignation, for William's words worried her. She started forward, now even more determined to find out what had gone wrong with her treatment of the earl. She dare not chance William's calling the authorities. She'd just have to attend Falkham without the comforting nearness of her aunt.

William now steadfastly barred Tamara's way.

"Never mind, Aunt Tamara," Marianne called back as she headed toward the master's chambers. "Remain here. What can a sick man do to me anyway?"

With her aunt's protests ringing in her ears, Marianne hurried through the vaulted passageways of the manor, her steps quickening as she neared the earl's chambers.

She paused for a moment outside his door and patted her bag to assure herself she was prepared. What would she find behind that door? If he was near death, could she save him? She had to, for her life and her aunt's might depend on it.

Her heart pounding with dread, she pushed open the massive oak door and then slipped inside. She'd only just entered the warmly lit room when she froze in bewilderment. The bed was empty. She knew this was the master's chamber, so where was the earl? Had they carried him elsewhere? she wondered in increasing confusion. Meaning to question William further, she started to back out, then heard the door close behind her. She whirled around only to come face-to-face with the Earl of Falkham.

Dressed simply in an unbuttoned waistcoat, white holland shirt, and blue-black breeches, he leaned with casual ease against the door. His weight rested on his good leg, while his wounded leg was bent to take the pressure off of it. His loose-fitting breeches hid the bandage around his thigh so well, however, that no one except Marianne would ever have guessed he was hurt. Though his face was still a trifle pale, he didn't seem to be straining to hold himself up. Nor did a trace of fever flush his tanned skin.

In short, he was the very picture of health.

"So good of you to come," he murmured. His gray gaze locked on her mask, as if he could see what lay beneath. Then a slow smile crept over his finely chiseled face.

At that confident smile, a rush of emotions surged through her. Relief that she was no longer in danger of having killed an earl mingled with fear he might harm her, but another emotion dominated those two. Anger. A rage like fiery liquor filled her veins, even as she backed away from him, preparing to defend herself.

"So my aunt was right," she bit out. "Your 'summons' was a trick! How dare you! How dare you make me fear I'd brought you to the threshold of death when all the time you were well!"

His smile broadened. "Were you worried about me?" he asked with one eyebrow arched in skepticism.

"I was worried your man might have me hauled off to the gaol for killing his master. That's what worried me, you—you wretched scoundrel!" she spat out. "What possible reason could you have for spreading such a lie? Do you simply hate Gypsies? Was suffering a Gypsy's touch so distasteful to you?"

He came away from the door like a soldier given the call to battle, although she noticed he winced slightly when his weight came down on his wounded leg. "In truth, I'd thought to thank you," he said in a brittle tone.

"By ruining my reputation . . . by spreading malicious lies and rumors so the townspeople would avoid me? What manner of thanks is that?"

His eyes darkened until they were almost the color of iron. Determinedly he took a step toward her. "Will tried to find you, but no one would tell him where you lived. No one seemed willing even to acknowledge your existence. This was the only way I could think of to bring you here so I could express my gratitude. Tell

me this—has anyone in Lydgate really accused you?
Has anyone harmed you because of my little subterfuge?''

Her lips formed a reply, but she didn't at first speak
it. Had anyone harmed her? No. Her fears had been
fanned by her own worries and by her desperate situation, not by anyone's actual words. Of course, Mr.
Tibbett had worried she might accidentally have
harmed the earl, thus bringing the soldiers down upon
herself, but he'd certainly not accused her of any purposeful act. Still, she'd had ample justification for her
fears, and she resented the earl's casual disregard for
them.

''No one in Lydgate has accused me . . . yet,'' she
responded, ''but Gypsies are often held suspect in this
place, and your—your 'subterfuge' hasn't helped matters, I'm certain.''

He frowned at that. His face suddenly reminded her
of a painting she'd seen once of a vengeful devil scowling at the Creator. With a shudder, she gathered her
cloak more closely about her, belatedly realizing how
dangerous it was to be alone with him.

He seemed not to notice her action, but stepped
closer, still blocking her path to the door. ''I apologize for any inconvenience my trick may have caused.
But can you blame me for wanting to find the woman
who saved my leg, for wanting again to offer her some
means of recompense?'' When she remained silent at
that, merely tilting her head away from him, his eyes
warmed. ''If you wish, you may add my latest . . . ah
. . . thoughtless act to the debt I already owe you. It's
a debt I'm more than eager to pay.''

His words mollified her little. Her heart still beat
frantically from the terror she'd felt when she'd feared
being blamed for his fever. She wanted to speak a
million insults, to torment him as he'd let her be tormented, but she dared not. Now that her anger had
cooled somewhat, her sense of caution had returned.
This was no time to castigate an earl who had the
power to see her arrested. She must keep her wits
about her.

"You may consider the debt paid. Seeing that you are well and that my remedies eased your pain is enough reward for me," she replied, trying mightily to keep the sarcastic tone from her voice, but failing. "I'd best go now, before my aunt begins to worry about me."

Her carriage erect, she started to move around him toward the door, but he gripped her arm as she passed.

"You can't go yet, not without allowing me to repay my debt in full," he said earnestly.

Held momentarily captive, she strained against his arm, her heart pounding in fear. He stood so close she could see the spark of interest in his eyes. The intent attention he gave her mask sent alarm whirling through her body.

"Please . . . unhand me," she choked out.

Something in the quaver of her voice must have affected him, for he did as she asked. Yet he made no move to let her pass.

Words tumbled from her lips. "I never required your gratitude. What I did, I'd do for anyone." She paused, wishing with all her heart she'd listened to her aunt and had stayed away from Falkham House. "I've already refused your payment, so nothing else remains to be said."

"But I've something better to offer than mere coins. I've heard of a physician in London, a man named Milburn, who has a miraculous treatment for smallpox scars. He claims he can wipe them away completely, so the skin is as soft and smooth as a babe's. I'll send you to him. 'Tis the least I can do for the woman who saved my leg, possibly my life."

Her head swung up and she stared at him in shock. Those horrible scars she was supposed to have. Oh, Lord. She hadn't anticipated this possibility. Now she wasn't quite as certain about the brilliance of the idea of claiming she'd been scarred by smallpox.

Then her eyes narrowed. Why did the earl offer this? She, too, had heard of Milburn. Her father had denounced the man as a charlatan, but some had claimed to be helped by him. Milburn was most famous for treating the wealthy and always extracted large sums of money from his patients. Could Falkham really intend to spend such a huge amount of money sending a Gypsy to London for the treatment, particularly when Milburn's "treatment" might be nothing more than a fraud? It was amazing he'd even consider it.

Or would he? She peered at him through her mask, noting the way his eyes roved to her hands and then back to the silk covering her face. Could this offer of his simply be a trick to find out what lay beneath her disguise? How in heaven's name was she to refuse it without his becoming suspicious?

"I've no desire to go to this doctor," she replied after a moment of frantic thought. She lowered her face self-consciously from his unsettling scrutiny. "I've learned to live with my . . . er . . . unusual appearance. If this doctor failed to help me, I'd suffer far more than I've suffered till now."

She hoped her answer proved sufficient for him.

It didn't.

"You at first appeared to be a courageous woman," he said in a voice as carefully controlled as the expression on his face. "I didn't think you so cowardly as to fear the reward I offer for saving my life."

If only he knew, Marianne thought, wildly longing to flee his presence. She tried to discern from his face whether he was trying to see if she was lying about the reason for her mask or whether he was genuinely attempting to "save" her. To her consternation, his expression revealed nothing.

"I don't fear your reward, my lord," she finally answered with a proud tilt of her head. "I simply believe the physician's efforts would be futile. But thank you. I'm sure your intentions are honorable."

If he detected the note of suspicion in her voice, he didn't show it. "Think what possibilities my gift offers for you. It might enable you to find a husband who'd care for you far better than your aunt can."

Her head shot up at that, and it took all her will not to move away, not to show just how much she feared him. For he indeed looked fearsome in the light that streamed through the open curtains of his window, highlighting the broad, stern forehead and glinting off the thick chestnut brows drawn together in a deep frown. Even his lips seemed firm and purposeful, as if they only spoke words meant to be obeyed.

"I've already said I won't accept your gift, my lord," she said in a voice that wavered. She cursed herself for letting him so disturb her. "I'm pleased you've recovered fully, but I won't be forced to endure the probing of cruel strangers for naught when I can scarce endure the sight of my face myself. My scars are too deep, my face too hideous for any mere potion to heal."

She knew she exaggerated in her attempt to escape him, but didn't realize how she'd erred until he suddenly gripped her arm again and lifted his hand to the hood of her cloak.

"Let me see your 'hideous face' for myself before you refuse my help," he bit out, pushing back the hood and yanking the ties of her mask loose. "If what you say is true, you may leave this house without another word."

"No!" she protested in terror, but he was already lifting away the mask. . . .

Chapter Five

"No beauty she doth miss
When all her robes are on;
But beauty's self she is
When all her robes are gone."
—Anonymous,
Madrigal

Garett hadn't been certain what he'd find when he removed the Gypsy girl's mask. He'd half expected the scarred maiden she'd always professed to be.

But ever since the night she'd treated his wound, the touch of her hands had haunted him, hands with skin so golden and fine he'd been unable to believe her face could be any different.

Still, he hadn't understood what reasons a young healthy maiden might have for hiding her face. So when he'd yanked back the black hood, he'd been unsure what might lie beneath it.

He'd thought he was prepared for any sight. But the sight that now greeted his eyes stunned him. Two warm hazel eyes widened in fear in a face as arresting as it was unblemished. Not only had she no scars, but her skin was a light golden color—not the dark olive of a Gypsy, yet not the pale cream of a sheltered lady, either.

As his eyes roamed over the delicate-boned oval shape of her face, her rich, peach-tinged lips parted in shock. His eyes fastened automatically on the sweet mouth, so finely drawn. It was the mouth of a lady, not a Gypsy. He could well believe her father had been nobility. Yet he glimpsed in her face, in the stubborn set of her chin and the wild glint in her eyes, that she didn't always follow a lady's rules.

Hers was a face designed by nature to intrigue, entice . . . tempt. With him it succeeded.

As he continued to stare openly at her, drinking in the unexpected beauty before him, she seemed to recover her wits. She reached for the silk mask, but his fingers closed around her wrist.

"Don't," he commanded in a husky voice, his hands turning her slowly to face the sunlight that streamed through the multipaned window.

"You have no right . . ." she whispered as his free hand pushed the hood farther back until it lay draped about her shoulders. His action loosed her lustrous hair from its knot, allowing it to spill free.

He ignored the hint of alarm in her eyes and merely smiled as the sun lit her face and tipped her hair with antique gold. Drawn of its own accord, his hand moved to her face. Lightly he trailed his fingers over one smooth cheek, marveling at the softness of her skin. "It seems you have no need for the physician Milburn after all," he said with meaning.

She blushed then, the becoming flush infusing her cheeks with color. Her wide eyes darted to his. Then she backed away from the hand that caressed her and wrenched her wrist free of his other hand, her expression hardening.

"You never intended to bring me to him anyway, did you?" she responded tartly. "All of this—your offer, your lies—was done a-purpose to unmask me, wasn't it?"

He stared at her one moment longer, then shrugged. "Not entirely. But your tale of disfigurement rang false. How else was I to prove my suspicions? I assure you, if you'd been telling the truth and accepted my offer, I would have brought you to Milburn."

She tossed her head back, flashing him a skeptical glance. "Indeed. Well, sir, now that you've satisfied your curiosity, I wish to leave."

Her words angered him even while they challenged. Did she think he'd let her go that easily? She'd troubled his thoughts far too much during his recovery. Before he released her, he must know something of her.

She tried to push past him, but he halted her with ease.

"Satisfied my curiosity? Not at all. You've merely whetted my appetite. What other mysteries lie behind those beautiful eyes, I wonder? You might, for example, tell me why you wear a mask in the first place."

Her face turned abruptly to his, apprehension in her expression as she looked first down at the hand that restrained her and then up at his lifted eyebrows. Once again color suffused her face.

"I don't see that it concerns you, my lord."

Despite her bold words, he knew she feared him, for he could feel the trembling in her slender arm. She seemed poised to flee, like a cat waiting for the door to open so it could slip away unseen. He certainly didn't intend to let her slip by him this time. Not without some answers.

"Everything concerns me." Menace tinged his voice. "This is my domain. I don't like having two strange Gypsies roaming it, especially when one of them hides her face, and lies about the reasons for her disguise. It makes me wonder what mischief she is about."

His coldly spoken words seemed to disturb her.

"I intend no mischief," she averred, tilting her chin upward so that the light fell half across her face. "Isn't it enough that I saved your life? Must you know why I chose to keep my face hidden while I did so?"

He ignored the quick stab of remorse her words brought. He must know the reason for her disguise, if only to ensure she wasn't one of his uncle's minions come to spy on him. Of course, if she'd worked for his uncle, why would she have cared for his wounds so skillfully?

Yet there could be other, equally sinister reasons for her disguise, he told himself, reasons he must discover. Gypsies were capable of almost anything. After his years of dealing with lies and deceit, he knew better than to trust a Gypsy girl, no matter how lovely she was.

"Have you committed some crime?" he probed, his tone deliberately intimidating. "Are you hiding from soldiers or the guard?"

For a moment, some fear flickered in her eyes that made him wonder if he'd hit upon the truth. Then her chin stiffened.

"No, my lord," she said, contempt lacing her words. "I'm hiding from noblemen like you who like nothing better than to devour Gypsies like me."

Her deft answer surprised him. She wasn't easily cowed, that was certain. He chuckled. "What makes you think I'll devour you?"

His chuckle seemed to enrage her as much as did his question. "Aren't you holding me here against my will? Haven't you tricked me into returning to your manor when I didn't wish to do so? That's enough proof for me that you intend me harm. Because of men like you, Aunt Tamara thought it wise to keep my face and form hidden. It was, and still is, my only protection."

For a moment his gaze strayed over her face and then to her hair, which tumbled down her back like golden wheat spilling from a sheaf. "I understand why your aunt felt the need to protect you. But why do so by hiding your face? Wouldn't it be better to choose a protector?" As her eyes widened in shock, he smiled. "I see you understand my meaning. You're young and attractive. You could easily find someone other than a nagging aunt to shield you from the world."

She pinned him with a gaze as murderous as any he'd ever seen a woman give, making him wish he hadn't been quite so blunt. Why was she so outraged? She acted as if she were a well-born lady with a reputation to protect.

Her entire body stiffened in defiance, so that the cloak draped her form more closely, hinting at the womanly curves that lay underneath. "Only a—a thoroughly wretched man could offer such a solution!"

Wretched, he thought, trying to stop his mind from

wondering just what her cloak concealed. Wretched. That wasn't quite the word for what her nearness was making him feel.

Thinking how delightful it could be to have this sweet armful under his protection, he let his gaze travel over her cloaked form. "Gypsies have sought noble protection for years," he quipped.

She drew herself up in affronted dignity. "And that, my lord, is why so many bastards with Gypsy blood roam the countryside! Not to mention Gypsies with noble blood who've been thoroughly ruined because the hope of better things was dangled before their eyes, then snatched away at the last minute!"

He recognized she was throwing up a verbal barrier to keep herself from even considering the meaning behind his statement, and instantly moved to counterattack.

"Is that how you consider yourself?" he asked pointedly.

His question seemed to throw her off guard. "Wh-what do you mean?"

"Was the hope of better things dangled before your eyes, then snatched away? You said your father was a nobleman, and judging from your coloring, you must have spoken the truth. So are you one of those 'thoroughly ruined' Gypsies?"

She bit her lip in frustration, her dark golden brows drawing together in an uncertain frown. "Nay. 'Tis not myself I meant."

"So your father's 'protection' of your mother didn't ruin you," he persisted.

His comment seemed to startle her. Then she lowered her face from his and murmured, "I—I suppose not."

"But it has left you, as I pointed out before, with only an aunt and a flimsy disguise to protect you."

He felt her arm tense as she clenched her fist. "The two have been enough to deter most men," she replied uneasily, her stony face turned away from him.

He leaned forward until his lips brushed her ear. "Ah, but I stripped away your feeble defenses with little effort, didn't I?'' he whispered, inhaling her surprisingly clean scent as he did so.

She blushed despite her obvious attempts to ignore him. That blush absurdly pleased him, making him long to see if it covered the rest of her slim body.

He persisted in his taunting, determined to know more about this intriguing Gypsy. ''Perhaps I should have offered you my protection instead of my gold a few nights ago.''

Her head snapped around and her mouth opened to retort, but before she could express her obvious outrage, the door swung open and Tamara marched in.

''I knew it!'' she spat out as her eyes took in the sight of Mina and Garett standing intimately close to one another, Mina's mask dangling from her shoulder by one tie and her hood falling uselessly down her back. ''I knew it was all an unscrupulous trick!'' she accused Garett.

Behind her, William burst in rubbing his head, which now sported a large lump. Garett scowled at both Tamara and William, thoroughly displeased at having his interesting little conversation with Mina cut short.

William raised his hands helplessly. ''I didn't expect the wench to crown me with a vase, m'lord, truly I didn't!'' William protested as he tried to pull Tamara back out of the room.

The Gypsy woman ignored William's attempts to make her leave. ''Unhand her this instant!'' she demanded of Garett, whose fingers still gripped Mina's arm. ''How dare you touch my niece! And after what she did for you, you ungrateful lecher!''

Garett refused to move a muscle, his eyes traveling from the livid face of Mina's aunt to Mina's own defiant expression. ''I merely offered her a reward, woman,'' he replied with nonchalance. ''She hasn't had the good sense to take it. Yet.''

That seemed to give Tamara pause. She glanced at her niece's stony face, then back to the earl's mocking one. ''I can imagine what 'reward' you offered,'' she said, her eyes narrowing, ''and she would have lost all good sense if she'd taken it. She's not so foolish as to let a fine form and smooth words tempt her. Mina will take a reward, milord, but 'twill be in gold and naught else, for the other tarnishes far too quickly.''

Mina's face reddened at her aunt's bluntness. "I don't want his gold, either!" she protested to Tamara, wrenching her arm away from him. "I won't take it!"

Garett studied Mina. Why was she so adamant in her refusal to take his money? he wondered. Did she truly hate noblemen so much she despised their money, too? She simply wasn't what he expected a Gypsy girl to be.

Her aunt, however, was clearly quite willing to meet his expectations. "We'll take the gold!" she stated, with a glance at her niece that silenced her. "She's earned it well enough."

Indeed she had. He didn't begrudge her the gold. Garett chuckled. "Of course," he replied, unable to resist throwing a taunting glance Mina's way as he motioned to William to fetch the coins. Mina stared right back at him, her eyes blazing with impotent fury.

In moments, William returned with a bag. Garett removed a healthy portion of coins from it and thrust them into Tamara's hand. Tamara gave him a grim smile. When William muttered something about its being too much money, Tamara merely tossed her head back and fixed him with a glare that made him, too, lapse into silence.

Mina gestured to the coins Tamara was carefully slipping into a pouch hung around her waist. "Are you finally satisfied, my lord?" she asked sweetly, although her clenched hands showed that anger ruled within her. "You've done what you wished and recompensed me for my efforts to save your deceitful hide. Now leave me and my aunt alone. We have no use for your kind."

"Yes, you have your mask for protection, don't you?" Garett mocked.

"Just leave us alone!" Mina repeated before wheeling around and sweeping from the room. Tamara cast both men a contemptuous look, then followed her niece out, slamming the door behind her.

Garett watched them go with a mixture of triumph and suspicion. Mina's answers hadn't satisfied him. Far from it—they'd only made him wonder even more what she and her fierce aunt were doing in Lydgate. Why the mask? Her reasons for wearing it had been plausible, but he sensed she had other reasons she wasn't revealing.

Then there was the townspeople's mysterious silence whenever he asked about her. In a town like Lydgate, people never kept their opinions to themselves. Did they simply have no interest in the Gypsies? Or was there more to their silence?

"Two fine-looking wenches," William muttered as he stared at the closed door. "But their tongues are a mite too sharp for a man's enjoyment, eh, m'lord?"

"Indeed," Garett replied absently.

"That Tamara has a strong arm when she's wielding a vase," William continued with a grin, "but I'll wager she's soft as silk when a man's got her 'neath him."

Tamara didn't interest Garett in the least. But Mina . . . Mina had a soft mouth too tempting for words. He'd wager it was softer than silk.

"Shall we leave them alone like they requested?" William asked, throwing his master a sly glance.

A slow grin crossed Garett's face, all thoughts of his revenge against his uncle temporarily fleeing his mind as he remembered the way Mina's hair had shone in the sunlight. Mina might be wary, but he knew he could ferret out her secrets, given enough time. Right now the thought appealed to him immensely.

"Leave them alone?" he murmured aloud as he turned away from the door. "Not if I have something to say about it."

William then smiled, too. "And you do have something to say about it, don't you, m'lord?"

"Oh, yes," was the terse answer.

On a small, secluded estate not far from London, Bess Tearle watched warily as her husband paced from

one end of her bedchamber to the other. He wore his
now graying hair as had all the Roundheads, cut all
around in one line even with his chin. Yet she knew
better than anyone that only his hair was Roundhead.
From the tip of his expensive hat to his imported
French stockings, he was as driven by money and the
desire for titles as the Royalists he despised.

Until recently, he'd publicly disdained the Cavaliers'
intemperate habits, seeking the approval of Puritan and
Anglican alike, for they'd held the reins of power. But
privately, he'd indulged his desires whenever he'd gotten the chance. For the most part, he'd always been
able to obtain what he desired, for who would deny a
man of his position and wealth anything?

But someone had thwarted him lately, she thought,
for his too full lips were pursed in anger and his still
handsome face wore a permanent frown. This wasn't
a good time to ask him what she wanted to know, but
lately no time had been good. His sullen silences and
dark moods weren't unusual, but they told her something was wrong. It was time to find out what troubled
him. If she left him to brood, he would eventually
begin taking his anger out on her.

That led her back to her question. Somehow she
knew what his answer would be, knew his anger was
related to what she wanted to ask. Yet she hesitated to
ask it, wondering if it weren't better not to know.

Still, she gathered up her courage and asked. "Why
haven't we moved to Falkham House yet? You said
we'd move into it soon. You said it was ours now. But
we've been out here in the country for weeks, and
you've not made the first effort to have our belongings
moved or—"

She broke off as Pitney swung about, his light blue
eyes looking less colorless in his anger.

"Don't mention that place to me!" he snarled.

Temporarily cowed, she fell silent. But she couldn't
remain that way. She had to know. "What has happened?" she asked timidly. "Please, Pitney, tell me
what—"

He slammed his fist against the wall. "Damn it,

woman! You try my patience sorely!'' Then he looked at her, and a sneer formed on his face. ''All right, you might as well know the truth once and for all, so I can get some peace. You'd learn of it eventually, since my efforts to keep it from happening have all proven fruitless. Falkham House is lost.'' He watched to see how she reacted. ''I couldn't secure it as I'd expected. 'Tis someone else's now and has been for some weeks.''

That was the answer she'd feared he might give. Five months pregnant with her first child, she was devastated to learn they wouldn't be returning to Falkham House at last. She'd been looking forward to raising her child in her own beloved childhood home.

She swallowed, fighting the tears that welled in her eyes. ''Who has it?''

Pitney's pale blue eyes glowed with pure hatred. Though she knew the hatred wasn't aimed at her, she trembled. Pitney was a complete beast when someone had crossed him.

''Your nephew owns Falkham House now, madam. What's more he's taken the title and all the lands. I'm no longer an earl nor you a countess, thanks to your nephew.''

His words left her numb with confusion. Her nephew? But he had died in the war, along with her dear brother. That was the only reason the lands had passed to Pitney, because she was left to inherit.

''I don't understand,'' she murmured, her hands twisting the material of the fashionable gown she wore.

Pitney's face filled with rage as he strode to the bedside where she sat. His eyes took in her tears, but the tears only seemed to enrage him more.

''Your nephew escaped being killed when your precious brother Richard was murdered by the army. Somehow Garett made his way to Worcester and joined the king there. When Charles fled, Garett accompanied him. So you see, your nephew has been living in exile until just recently. Now he's returned, and he's taken Falkham House from us.''

Bess could hardly believe what her husband was telling her, yet she knew he had no reason to lie. Her brown eyes began to glow with joy as the meaning of what Pitney was saying sank in. "Garett lives," she whispered. "The dear boy lives. Thank you, God, for that."

Her husband sneered. "Yes, you would be happy about it. Don't you care that he's stolen back the estates that should have been mine? Doesn't it matter to you that he has both the title and the lands—even Falkham House?"

" 'Twas his all along," she replied, emboldened by the knowledge that her nephew was alive. She'd grown so accustomed to thinking herself left without any of her family that the very fact of his existence gave her courage. "He is the rightful owner, after all."

At that, Pitney became incensed. "You can say this, after all I did to get it back for you, for us? I thought you wanted Falkham House back at all costs."

She looked up at the face she'd grown to despise and said evenly, "I wanted it to belong to my family again. And now it does. It matters not to me if my nephew owns it, as long as it's owned by a Lyon."

"A Lyon!" he spat out. "Your damned family has caused me more grief than a hundred Royalists. Thanks to your whoreson nephew, I've lost it all, including Falkham House!"

She knew she shouldn't taunt him, but the words spilled from her mouth nonetheless. "You should never have sold it in the first place! If it hadn't been for your greed, it wouldn't have left the family at all."

He raised his hand to strike her, but when she merely stared back at him bravely, he lowered his hand with a muttered curse.

"A pox on him!" he hissed. "Now the man's even got you thinking to defy me. Well, you'd best thrust that idea from your mind, madam, for it won't serve you. He wants nothing to do with either of us, so if you're contemplating running to him for shelter, think again. He'd as soon kill you as look at you."

Her lower lip trembled, but she ignored the fear creeping through her. "Why should he hate me? He surely can't blame me for inheriting what he wasn't here to claim. We didn't even know he lived!''

At that, Pitney's head swiveled and he pinned her with a triumphant stare.

"We didn't know, did we?'' she asked uncertainly. He smirked, and she felt her heart sink. "Oh, dear God,'' she said helplessly, "*you* knew! You knew he lived, but you didn't tell me!''

She thought the horror of it would surely rip her asunder. Her own nephew abandoned willfully, and she'd known none of it.

Pitney took her pale face in his hand and tipped it up, rubbing his thumb over the still beautiful lips. "I didn't know at first,'' he said coolly. "But then letters came from France, from Garett. He asked me to protect his lands for him until he could return. His pride kept him from asking for money, but I knew he must have needed that, too.'' His eyes filled with hatred. "I had thought he'd died with them, with his parents. I had thought at last the world was mine. The title, the lands—I had it all. Then to find it all a trick—''

"Why didn't you tell me about the letters?'' she asked in a whisper.

"And have you whining around the house, trying to bring him back? Cromwell himself wanted me . . . *me* . . . for his minister. But that was because of my title—he needed nobility on his side to bring the other noblemen around to his cause. With that Royalist brat here I would have lost my chance, 'tis certain.''

"So you refused to bring him back,'' she said, understanding instantly how her grasping husband would have reacted to the news that his title was but ashes. "How did you explain that to him? How did you explain you didn't want him around to spoil your plans?''

Pitney stared at her in surprise. "Explain? You don't think I told him anything, do you? I ignored his letters, you fool. He sent five of them, each more desperate than the last, and I tore up every one of them.''

"No,'' she whispered.

"Yes,'' he replied, his eyes narrowing. "I'd thought for certain he'd starve in France with the other exiles,

if I just waited long enough. After a time had passed,
I didn't hear from him. I assumed he was dead. But
no, I should have known your beloved nephew would
insinuate himself into the right circles so he could return to England and take it all back. I never thought
the Royalists would return, never!''

She twisted her head away from her husband's hand
as a dull numbness beset her. Her nephew and Falkham House were lost to her now. Her husband had
seen to that. Garett must have suffered untold hardship
with his parents dead and no one to help him. She
thought of him as he'd been at the age of ten, shortly
before her marriage. He'd been a quick-witted boy,
with a confident air that resembled her dear brother's.
She'd always thought him a strong child, who hid his
strength beneath his quips.

What might his years of abandonment have done to
him? How had he survived? Despite what was more
commonly believed by those who'd listened to Cromwell's tales, she'd heard the exiles had barely kept food
on the table during those years. Pitney had once
boasted even the king was destitute. So what must
Garett have endured as a young exile with no money
and no parents?

She felt ill from the weight of it all. Garett was
certain to blame her as well as Pitney. How could he
not? Could he ever forgive her for his abandonment?

Then her face brightened. Though Garett had been
but a lad of thirteen the last time she'd seen him, he'd
known her husband well enough to know how ruthless
the man was. Surely he hadn't forgotten. He'd believe
her when she told him she hadn't known. He'd help
her escape her wretched marriage. At last she could
leave Pitney and not fear what he might do to her if
she did!

Pitney caught sight of her softened expression and
closed his hands in her dark hair, twisting her head
around so she was forced to stare up into his face.

''I know what you're thinking. You'd best forget going to your nephew, my dear deceitful wife, for I'd kill

both of you if you deserted me. You know I could do it.''

"I hate you!'' she bit out, ignoring the aching in her head from where he held her hair.

"Do you?'' he snapped, jerking her head back hard so she cried out. His free hand lifted to her collar and loosened the buttons at her neck. Then he slipped his hand inside and down until he had her breast firmly in his hand. Roughly he fondled it, while she fought down the bile that rose in her throat. "You may hate me all you wish,'' he said with a leer, "but you still belong to me, my noble little wife. So if you're considering running away to that nephew of yours, remember I hold your life in my hands.'' He squeezed her breast hard, but she refused to give him the satisfaction of crying out again.

"I don't care what happens to me anymore,'' she spat at him, her eyes blazing. "And you don't have the courage to kill Garett or you'd have done so by now.''

Pitney merely chuckled, his hand groping lower into her loosened shirt until it rested on the slight curve of her belly. "Would you risk your child's life, then, too?'' he asked.

A sob caught in Bess's throat. Surely he didn't mean it. Not her babe. In spite of being childless the first fourteen years of marriage, she'd somehow managed to conceive. She'd wanted a child for so long, someone she could love and lavish affection upon after fourteen long years of enduring Pitney's contempt.

"You wouldn't harm your own child,'' she whispered as she felt the babe leap in her belly under Pitney's hand.

His eyes hardened. "If he were mine he'd be safe. But I'm not certain he's mine,'' he replied with coldness as his hand slipped up again to tweak her breast painfully.

"He's yours,'' she asserted, hoping her face didn't reveal that she lied. She wished she could taunt him with the truth—that he'd never been able to get her

with child, that one of the handsome merchants he
dealt with had easily impregnated her.

Yet she dared not. He'd hurt her and her child. Then
he'd ruin her merchant lover, the man who'd shown
her the only kindness she'd seen in a long while. Her
lover didn't know about the child, and she had not told
him, for she'd known what Pitney would do if she ever
fled to the merchant. She would not risk it. She must
make Pitney believe the child was his, no matter what
happened.

"The babe concerns me not," he whispered cruelly
in her ear. "I can destroy the mother without destroying the child. Don't try my patience, madam. Go to
Garett, and I'll see you and your nephew dead, and
leave the babe without a mother."

Her hands shook where they lay on the silken counterpane. Once again he had her trapped. She didn't
know how she could bear it, staying with him any
longer. Yet bear it she must, for the sake of her child.
She couldn't die and leave her child to be raised by
Pitney.

At her silence, his pale eyes sharpened with desire.
"Do you promise to be obedient, then, wife?" he
asked, his hand still groping inside her clothing.

She lifted eyes clouded with sorrow to his jeering
face and with all the quiet dignity she could muster,
she nodded her head.

He gave her a pleased smile, then released her hair.
But she wasn't free yet, for his hand went to his petticoat breeches. He loosened them, then let them fall
to the floor. She could see him thickening underneath
his long shirt, and she shuddered.

He slid his other hand up to her shoulder. With cruel
insistence, he pressed her down, forcing her off the
bed and onto her knees on the floor in front of him.

"Let's see just how obedient you shall be, wife,"
he muttered, his fingers closing around her head and
forcing it forward toward his jutting member.

"Please, Pitney," she whispered as loathing filled
her. How had she ever been such a fool as to marry
him, thinking him daring and strong? She should have

listened to her brother when he'd said Pitney wasn't to be trusted. But she'd been blinded by Pitney's mature age, smooth words, and good looks.

She thought now of what he was asking her to do and hesitated, as she'd hesitated so many times before.

"Remember the babe," he said with menace, pulling her head toward his groin. "You'd best prove your obedience to me if you wish to live to raise the brat."

Her heart and mind detested him, but it mattered not, for he was stronger than she. So with tears streaming down her face, she proved she was obedient.

Chapter Six

"To the glass your lips incline;
And I shall see by that one kiss
The water turned to wine."
—Robert Herrick,
"To the Water Nymphs
Drinking at the Fountain"

Dawn's light washed the Falkham House gardens with sudden fire, making every dew-drenched leaf and twig twinkle magically. Yet Marianne tarried only a moment to note the beauty of the morning. Then she drew her heavy cloak more tightly about her and pressed on between the small shrubs and weed-choked paths, her breath forming misty clouds in the cool fall air.

At last she stopped beside an overgrown stretch of rows. She cast a furtive glance about her, but no one stirred in this secluded part of the estate near where the apple trees stood. This had been her mother's special herb garden. Her eyes carefully searched the tangled mess. She knew she'd find what she sought if she looked long enough, for the plants couldn't have died. As silently as possible, she crept over the rows until she came upon the scarlet berries and deep purple flowers signifying black nightshade.

Thank heavens they'd survived the months of neglect. Nightshade was a common enough plant, easy to find in fields and ditches, but this was no common nightshade. Her father had gone to a great deal of trouble to bring the specially grown variety back from France years before. The French had learned to cultivate its special properties, so this nightshade was the most useful of all the varieties. And the most deadly.

Still, nothing else was as efficacious for halting spasms and healing heart troubles. Unfortunately, heart troubles seemed a common complaint among the elderly of Lydgate.

She withdrew the small spade hidden inside her cloak. Then she knelt and carefully dug up two or three of the plants, intending to carry them away and replant them in a less dangerous place for her. Unconcerned about the damp dirt smearing her hands, she packed the nightshade's roots carefully with soil, then wrapped them in wet cloths she'd brought for that purpose. With infinite care, she slid the wrapped plants into her pouch.

Once again, she glanced back at the silent manor looming behind her. No one stirred yet, but a quick stab of anger went through her as she surveyed the unseeing glass windows that caught and gaily reflected the first rays of dawn. She should be inside and not skulking about in the damp cold! How unfair that she, a lady, had to sneak about her own gardens, pretending to be other than what she was! She would make the earl pay for that injustice if it was the last act of her life!

She turned back to the garden and paused. Now that she had the nightshade, she ought to leave. Yet where else could she find so many of the herbs she needed for the garden she wanted to cultivate? Mr. Tibbett used powders and dried herbs brought from London. He'd always claimed he wasn't a gardener. Sometimes he had what she needed, and sometimes he didn't. If she was to continue as a healer, she had to have the necessary fresh herbs. And one of the townspeople had given her a little patch of land for her garden.

But it would take months for seeds to take root. She was here now, and no one in the manor seemed to be stirring, or if they were, they were paying no mind to this remote part of the estate. Why not take what she needed while no one was about to bother her?

Once her mind was made up, she crept through the garden like a ghost, stepping here and there to dig up plants she knew she'd need. Lady's mantle and woundwort, lad's love and mugwort—all were delicately worked loose from the ground, some dirt left clinging to them, and their roots wrapped carefully in more wet cloth, to be added to the pouch along with the night-shade. Fortunately, she'd brought plenty of cloths and bags. She knew some of the plants wouldn't survive the transplanting, but enough would live to make the beginnings of a respectable garden.

As she worked, she tried not to think of the earl who slept so close by. In the past week, she'd tried to forget the day he'd found her out, tried to push out of her mind the insulting proposition he'd put to her. But forgetting him had been difficult, what with Aunt Tamara giving her daily warnings about the foolishness of having anything to do with a man such as he.

Marianne certainly wanted nothing to do with him. Yet he seemed determined to have a great deal to do with her. She shivered as she remembered the way he'd looked at her in his room, as if he could see beneath her clothes. Worst of all, however, his touch hadn't repelled her. She'd been alarmed, even terrified of him, but never repulsed.

'Tis only because you've had so few dealings with men, she told herself, yet that wasn't entirely true, and she knew it. Because of her father's status as a mere baronet and his unusual marriage to a woman most people thought was a Spaniard, the Winchilseas had lived in seclusion from the rest of the nobility. Not that they hadn't attended the occasional ball or private dinner, but a baronet with a "Spanish" wife was not the toast of the town. Except for a few close friends, the Winchilseas had socialized little with people of their class.

Her father instead had made his friends among the intellects, the eccentrics whose mutual interest in medicine had made them unconcerned with his private situation. Marianne had grown up surrounded by men so engrossed in the fever of learning they took little time to notice her. Even as she grew older, she'd been treated more as a young sister by her father's friends than a possible conquest, as she might have been among the nobility.

Dantela Winchilsea had worried about her daughter's prospects as her daughter grew older, but Marianne hadn't been the least concerned she might find herself husbandless. She'd always wanted to follow in her parents' footsteps, and she didn't need a husband to do that.

Then when her mother had died, there'd been little time for going to dinners and balls. She'd had her hands full taking care of her father's household. Once in a while one of her father's younger friends had noticed her; one had even stolen a kiss. But she'd taken none of them seriously.

Now after years of being regarded as a mind without a body, she didn't know quite how to deal with a man who seemed to see her as a body without a mind. No, that wasn't quite it, either, for he hadn't disparaged her for her wit.

But he'd stared at her with such . . . such hunger. Yes, that was it—like a starved man admitted to a feast for the first time in months. Coping with that look was difficult. So was resisting it.

That's enough thinking about the earl, she told herself sternly. No sense in letting him ruin yet another day for her. Besides, she had things to do, and if she didn't finish with these herbs and get away, someone might find her. Then she'd be in a world of trouble.

"Stand up very slowly if you wish to live another day," a deep voice said behind her, breaking her concentration.

So much for getting away before I'm found, she thought dismally, her hands going very still. Then she recognized the rumbling timbre of that voice and wished she could melt into the very earth. It was as if she'd conjured him up by her very thoughts. Suddenly something sharp prodded her ribs, making her stiffen. For heaven's sake, she thought, the man was actually holding a sword to her back!

"Stand!" he commanded, and she did as he bade, silently cursing her all-encompassing black cloak that made her look like any thief in the night.

" 'Tis only I, the Gypsy," she whispered, her voice

scarcely audible in her terror that he might kill her before she could speak. "I mean no harm, my lord."

As suddenly as it had come, the sword point left her ribs. She gave a great shuddering sigh of relief, but the silence behind her did nothing to lessen the terror-filled pounding of her heart.

"Turn around," he said tersely, and she obeyed so quickly she nearly tripped over her cloak. Her eyes widened as she saw his finely hewn face, grim and implacable in the early morning light. Underneath the gray cloak draped casually about his shoulders, his clothes were in disarray, as if he'd dressed in a great hurry. Nonetheless, he held his sword in readiness, looking for all the world like an avenging angel, albeit a decidedly untidy one.

His keen gaze fastened on her mask, which she'd worn in case a stranger came upon her. Then it traveled to her cloak stained with rich dirt, grass, and the morning dew. With one hand she held her pouches of herbs hidden from view under her cloak, but they made a noticeable bulge and his gaze next fastened on that.

"Remove your mask and cloak," he said, his expression unchanging.

"I will not!" she protested. "You know who I am!"

He lifted the sword threateningly. "Remove them!"

She considered refusing again, but she was truly uncertain whether he'd harm her or not. And he had every reason to be suspicious of her, for she'd been trespassing in his gardens. Releasing her pouches so they slid to the ground, she did as he asked, her fingers shaking as she fumbled with the ties of first her mask and then her cloak.

As soon as the cloak hit the ground, she became aware of several things at once. First, the air was far more chill than she'd realized. Second, her hands were smeared with dirt. And finally, the earl had lowered his sword and was looking at her in a way that boded trouble.

His gaze paused for only a moment to take in her cheeks pinkened by the cold and her hair that had been hastily tied back with ribbon earlier that morning.

Then his eyes moved over her body, lingering over her long, slender neck and the thin cream muslin of her chemise that bunched over the tops of her breasts. A slow smile lit his lips as his eyes moved downward past the boned bodice of her simple chocolate-brown gown, to her naturally small waist, and then to her shapely hips. She wore few petticoats these days—she had no place to keep them in her aunt's wagon—so despite her clothing, her form appeared much as nature had intended it.

"Enchanting," he murmured at last as his eyes lifted back to her face, "but I felt certain you would be." Without taking his eyes off of her, he sheathed his sword.

It took a few seconds for her to realize he'd only made her remove her cloak so he could satisfy his lustful urge to gawk at her body. But as soon as the realization hit her, she snatched up her cloak indignantly.

"You—you, sir, are a lecher!" she cried, fumbling to fit her cloak back around her shoulders. She struggled to retie it, but at last, too nervous to make the knot, she abandoned the ties and the cloak slid from her shoulders again.

He chuckled mirthlessly. "And what are you, my little Gypsy? A spy? A thief?" He gestured to the pouches that lay exposed at her feet. "What are you doing, skulking about in the wee hours of the morning, alarming my cook so she rouses me out of a deep sleep to confront the intruder?"

She reddened under his scrutiny, which now had turned decidedly suspicious.

"I—I merely wanted to b-borrow some of the plants from your garden, my lord," she replied. She knelt down and pulled one of the more innocuous plants from her bags. "You see? I want to start a garden of my own and . . . well . . . I thought you wouldn't mind if I took a few of the ones difficult to cultivate. After all, you have plenty, and you certainly don't use them. In the spring, I could bring you some from my own garden, once these have taken root and . . . and multiplied."

Skepticism in every line of his face, he stepped nearer, then knelt so close to her she started. He searched through the pouches, but when he found nothing but plants, he stood again. He held out his hand to help her rise, but she ignored it, rising on her own.

"So the testy Gypsy who won't take my money isn't quite so independent as she would lead everyone to believe, is she?" he said with a calculated air of superiority. "Would it have been too much for you to humble yourself and ask for the plants? Think you I would have begrudged you a few paltry herbs?"

She tossed her head back, her hazel eyes warming to a green that matched the garden's lush greenery. "I really don't know what you might begrudge me, my lord."

He said nothing to that, but he scanned the garden as if searching for signs that she'd been doing something other than taking plants. Then his eyes narrowed.

"My gardens are rather extensive," he said in a tone laced with distrust. "How did you know where to find what you needed? You couldn't have been here more than half an hour, yet you've clearly put aside a goodly supply of plants."

His question caught her off guard. She sought to hide her confusion as her mind searched for an answer that might pacify him. Then she hit upon it.

"I've been here before," she said hesitantly, then hastening on as she saw the shuttered look that crossed his face. "The former owners allowed me to take what I wished." With that half-truth, her next words came more readily. "That's why I didn't think anything about coming here now. I'm accustomed to gathering what I need when I need it."

Before she knew it, he'd stepped forward and taken her chin in his hand, forcing her head up so her eyes were level with his.

"Is that why you came at this hour, when you thought no one would see you? I'd say that's the habit of a thief, not a guest."

Her eyes brimmed with hot tears that threatened to spill over at any moment. "I'm no thief," she whispered. Then when she noted the half smile playing around his lips, she grew irate. "The Winchilseas never called me such, nor will you! You don't care about the garden, so what care have you if I take a few plants? For all the attention you pay them, they could be just weeds!"

His mouth thinned into a hard, implacable line. Releasing her and then stooping down, he pulled one of the plants loose from the bags. Her pulse quickened as she watched him hold out the nightshade.

"Just weeds?" he clipped. "I wouldn't call belladonna a mere weed, would you?"

She willed herself to remain calm. If he recognized the plant, even knew the Italian name for it, he must know what the nightshade's properties were. He was certain to consider her use of the plant in the worst light possible.

"I use belladonna for poultices," she said in an even voice.

"And here I thought it was to make those entrancing eyes of yours look more mysterious," he replied with heavy sarcasm.

That, too, was one of the properties of the plant—Italian ladies used it to dilate their pupils and give their eyes an unnaturally enticing, sensuous appeal.

"I've no desire to look mysterious."

He laughed, and the grimly bitter sound of it raised Marianne's alarm even further. "You've no desire to look mysterious—so you lurk about in a cloak and mask, sneak into my garden, steal my plants, particularly the poisonous ones—"

"I wish to poison no one, my lord," she cried in desperation. "I merely want the nightshade to use for medicines! And the other plants are nothing but herbs—you can see that for yourself. Why must you make such a commotion over a few plants?"

It was so unfair! These were her gardens, her plants, yet she had to explain to him why she wanted them, what she wanted to use them for! Curse him for being so suspicious about what was really nothing!

His jaw was set with an unyielding firmness. With one booted foot, he turned over a bag of plants that lay before him. "The plants don't concern me, not even the belladonna, for you can find any number of poisons in the woods. But I won't tolerate your lurking about this garden without my knowledge. I have enemies—" He stopped, breaking off as if angered with himself he'd said so much.

She strove hard to ignore the cold wisps of fear curling around her insides at that statement. Most men had enemies, to be sure, but what crimes had this man committed to make him feel threatened in his own house? Of course, there was Sir Pitney, but surely Sir Pitney wouldn't venture this close to Falkham House. He couldn't be that stupid. No, Falkham's suspicions just proved he was a man prone to making enemies, prone to stirring up trouble.

Falkham glanced at the manor before turning his piercing gaze back to her. "You knew the Winchilseas?" he asked abruptly.

At first his casual question seemed to come from nowhere, yet she had no doubt he had a reason for asking it. She sensed he was waiting for her answer with a great measure of curiosity. And more suspicion. She'd best tread very carefully in answering.

She dropped her eyes before his inquisitive gaze. "I knew the Winchilseas well, although I've only lived here a short time." She felt pleased with herself. So far she'd told him mostly the truth, though she'd cast it in an unrecognizable light.

"I know very little of the ones who lived here before," he surprised her by saying. "Tell me about them."

"Wh-what do you wish to know?"

"This Sir Winchilsea. What manner of man was he?"

Her desire to paint her father truthfully warred with her common sense, which told her she should say as little as possible. The former won out.

"He was a wonderful man, kind and gentle," she said, unable to hide the soft pleasure she took in speaking of her father. "He cared about everyone here, rich and poor alike. I learned a great deal about doctoring from him."

A shadow passed over Falkham's face, his jaw stiffening. "You seem to have known him better than I might have thought, considering you're a Gypsy. What's more, you seem to have cared for him. Perhaps you've had more experience with protectors than I first realized."

Her eyes widened in shock as she realized what he meant. "For shame!" she said, shaking a finger at him. "How dare you imply that Sir Winchilsea and I . . . that we . . ."

"Yes?"

"Only a reprobate such as you would think such a thing! Why, the man was old, and he loved his wife! What would he have wanted with . . . with the likes of me?" She cast him a look of such Puritanical disdain his face lost some of its rigidity.

Her petulant glare seemed to affect him. His mood abruptly changed. "What indeed would he have wanted with you?" he asked almost unwillingly as his slate eyes raked over her body, gleaming with a familiar light. "I can easily answer that for you, sweetling. A man would have to be either blind or a fool not to consider your form an enticement to all manner of pleasures."

The raw desire underlying his words put Marianne on her guard. Silently she cursed herself for once again stepping so near the lion's mouth. With her body poised to flee if he should pounce, she backed around the hedge behind her until she'd put it between them.

"Please, my lord," she said as he stalked her at a leisurely pace. "I think I'd best leave now. My aunt will worry."

"Let her worry," he replied without a break in his step. "You weren't too concerned about her when you came sneaking about here in the first place, were you?" He took a few more steps forward, strategically placing himself between her and her plants, though the hedge still lay between them. "Besides, you wouldn't want to leave without taking what you came for."

Her eyes darted to the pouches that lay strewn haphazardly on the ground, the plants half in, half out of them. "I—I don't need them after all," she lied.

"Nonsense. You wanted them badly enough to steal them. What can I do with them now? They'll die unless someone replants them, and I assure you, I'm no gardener. By all means, take them with you."

He knelt and scooped them up, his hands surprisingly gentle as he placed them back in their bags. Then he lay them on the hedge that separated him from her. But before she could snatch them up, he vaulted the hedge with ease, landing between her and the plants.

"You do still want them, don't you?" he asked, laying one hand casually on the pouches that now rested on the hedge behind him.

"Ye-es," she answered, backing away from him until she came up against an apple tree, one of the stand that marked the edge of the gardens. She groaned as she realized he had her trapped.

But he didn't take advantage of her position to move forward, not at first. "Then you'll have them, but for a price."

He smiled triumphantly, instantly making her wary. She didn't think she wanted to know what his price might be.

But he told her anyway.

"One kiss. That's all. Then you may take the plants and do as you wish with them."

One kiss? As if she would so much as touch the lips of this . . . this killer! Fury overrode caution as she planted her hands on her hips and railed at him. "That's all you wish, is it? One kiss? Trust a nobleman to ask for the unthinkable. How dare you even ask such a thing?"

"Such indignation from a Gypsy! You'd think you were a princess. Remember, you trespassed in my gardens. One kiss is a small price to pay for my ignoring your criminal behavior."

She knew he spoke the truth, but she was beyond all reason in her outrage over what he wanted. "Since when do noblemen stop with one kiss, my lord? I'm not so innocent as to let you talk me into such foolishness. My aunt has warned me often enough about men like you, and I plan to take her warnings to heart."

His face darkened with a dangerous quickness that made her aware of how frighteningly alone she was with him. The servants might be about in the manor, but she and Falkham were far enough away that he might harm her without anyone's taking much notice.

She glanced around, hoping for some weapon to come to hand, but none lay nearby—not so much as a tree limb.

"I should remind you, madam," he said harshly, moving closer to her than she'd have liked, "if I wished, I could turn you over to the constable and have you thrust in the gaol."

Her eyes blazed. "You would do that, wouldn't you? And all for a few herbs. I should have expected as much from a . . . a varlet like you. Well, then, send me to the constable. I daresay he'd rather have me free to help his wife with her sickly newborns than locked up at the whim of a mad nobleman!"

She knew she dared much with her words, but the thought of willingly kissing him terrified her. Still, she hoped he didn't call her bluff. Although the constable had supported the townspeople's harboring of her, if the earl brought her to him, the constable would be forced to act. No, at the moment she must avoid being brought to the constable.

But she needn't have feared that. His face mirrored his surprise at her audacity. Yet a glint of something like admiration shone in his eyes as well. "Very well, then, I see I can't have you clapped in chains or the town will cry out as one against me," he said, his words heavy with sarcasm. "But I still won't let you take the herbs—not without the small payment I request. I don't understand why a Gypsy should risk the anger of a lord of the realm for such a paltry reason.

Few Gypsies would hesitate to pay what I ask for their freedom.''

The devil take him! Must he always remind her she acted more like an affronted lady than a wheedling Gypsy girl? What would a Gypsy girl of her age do? Probably use his passion to eke out some small reward for herself, Marianne thought wryly. She should give him his kiss and be done with it. Then her head snapped up as she thought of something more. Why not play the part completely?

"One kiss, my lord? I think 'tis too high a price to pay for mere plants. Now, if you were to offer me more of an enticement . . ."

His eyes narrowed. He closed the distance between them, his hands pressing on either side of her, trapping her against the trunk of the tree.

"So now the Gypsy princess shows her true colors, does she?" he hissed.

Instantly she regretted her foolish attempt to best him. She stared back at him, defying him to touch her even while she quaked inside. His eyes were the color of winter sleet as they dropped to her lips, then darted back to meet her stare.

"You're right," he murmured. "One taste of your sweetness would be worth more than mere herbs, but I'm afraid the bargaining is done. No Gypsy maid shall defy me. You'll satisfy my whim, sweetling, whether you give the kiss freely or I'm forced to take it."

Now truly frightened, both by his nearness and by the desire she glimpsed in his expression, she pressed her hands against his chest. "Please, my lord, I didn't mean to defy you. I-I'll give you what you wish . . . if you'll give me but a moment to . . . to prepare myself."

His eyes took in the very real fright in her face. He drew back, but he didn't move far enough away for her comfort. She grew flustered under the intensity of his gaze, which disturbed her more than anything. Frantically, she sought for something she could say to change his intent.

"Come to me, Mina, for I will have my taste," he

murmured in a voice so consciously seductive it washed over her like sun-warmed water, holding forth a rich promise just as enticing. She fought the urge to do as that mellow, deep voice commanded.

Shaking off the lethargic feeling, she reached up to pluck one of the apples hanging plentifully from the tree and thrust it at him. "If you're hungry, my lord, perhaps this will serve your needs better," she said in a feeble attempt to put him off.

"An apple may have been Adam's undoing, my little Eve," he said with dark foreboding. "But a man doesn't fall for the same trick twice."

With that, he took the apple from her and tossed it aside. Then he pulled her resisting body up against him, making her all too aware of the hardness of every part of him.

"I'm not—" she began to protest, but his lips came down on hers, cutting off what she'd intended to say.

His mouth was hard, as firm as the flesh of the apple he'd just thrown aside, and as his lips pressed demandingly against hers, all thought fled from her mind. Her hands pushed against his chest and her body stiffened against the mastery of his, but those were unconscious actions born of surprise and fear. Nor did they bring her any respite from his strength. His arms held her anchored against him, as if she'd float away if he released her.

Then his lips softened almost imperceptibly as his hands stroked downward to grip her waist. So gentle, she thought. Far too gentle. It took away her will to fight him.

His lips played over hers until her mouth grew pliant and soft of its own accord, and her body began to tingle with an odd anticipation. His chin, scratchy and rough with the morning's whiskers, brushed harshly against her silky skin, but all she could do was wait, wait until the enticing sweetness provoked by his kiss left her, so she might fight his embrace.

Yet the waiting never ended. Instead, the sweetness swirled delightfully through her, holding her as helpless as any drug might. Unconsciously she curved into him, her mouth clinging to his like sugar to a pastry.

Only when her body rested limply against him did he lift his head from hers, his eyes a whirling tempest of emotion. "Ah, Mina," he murmured, his breath soft on her face, "one taste of you is like a taste of wine to a drunken man. 'Tis never enough."

Then he kissed her cheek, his lips trailing down over it to nibble at the skin beneath her ear. She gasped. "My lord, please—" she whispered.

"Garett," he whispered back, nuzzling her neck. "My name is Garett, sweetling. Think of me only as Garett of Falkham, who simply wishes to keep tasting you."

Falkham. The word rang warning bells inside her muddled head. This was her enemy! she reminded herself, fighting the lethargy that was fast overcoming her will. What madness was this? How could she allow him to touch her with such intimacy? Worse yet, how could she derive so much pleasure from it?

Even as his lips moved to her shoulder, sending warmth like summer's heat throughout her body, she protested weakly. "One kiss you said. Only one kiss."

He drew his head back and smiled, giving her a flash of even white teeth. " 'Since when do men stop with one kiss?' " he murmured, echoing her earlier words.

His statement conjured up all the images her aunt had drawn for her of Gypsy women seduced and abandoned by lesser nobles than the earl. And she was a lady—educated to know better than to let a man seduce her. Like a bracing blast of air, those thoughts cleared her head and brought her out of the haze he'd led her into.

Her heart pounding with the desire to escape him, she balled up her fists and struck his chest, surprising him as he was about to lower his head to hers again.

"Would you take an unwilling maiden, then?" she demanded, her sudden anger and fear lending force to her words.

His eyes went cold, the passion dying as quickly as it had been born. " 'Twas no unwilling maiden who trembled in my arms a second ago," he taunted, though his arms slackened about her waist.

He told the truth about that. Her body still throbbed with the intensity of the feelings he'd roused in her, but she swore she'd never let him know it. She told him in measured tones, "You asked a price of me, my lord, and I paid it. You said the kiss had to be given willingly. It was. Do you now intend to use the very conditions you placed upon it to demand yet another price?"

Her matter-of-fact tone forced a scowl to his face. He stepped back from her, his gaze scrutinizing her body, taking in her rapid breathing and the flush that gave her cheeks their glow. Under his scrutiny, she blushed with embarrassment, fervently aware her scornful words hadn't fooled him. Then he lifted steely eyes to her face.

"You talk like a fishwife discussing her wares," he scoffed. "Deny it if you will, but that kiss was more than any payment. An honest woman would admit it."

"And an honorable man would let me leave now and torment me no more with whims and prices," she retorted, wanting only to flee before she revealed how his perceptiveness disturbed her.

For a moment his eyes traveled downward, assessing her body. Then they slid upward over every inch of her simple gown, and wherever his gaze alighted, she felt her blush spread to cover the area. His gaze fastened at last on her lips, which she knew were swollen and red from his kiss.

As he watched, she deliberately lifted her hand to her mouth and wiped her lips, as if to eradicate the feel of his mouth on hers.

He grew rigid with anger. Stiffly he turned away from her and snatched up the bags of plants that lay on the hedge behind him. Then he turned back to her, thrusting the bags in front of him.

"Here. Take them and get off my land," he snapped.

Hesitantly she reached for them, but as her hands closed around them, his fingers closed around her wrists.

"Run back to your aunt, to your poultices and patients," he ground out. "But next time I find you lurking about where you shouldn't be, I won't take a mere kiss for payment. Nay, my scornful Gypsy—next time the stakes will be far higher for your freedom. Remember that when you make your plans."

With that he released her. Then he gave her a mocking bow, whirled on his heels, and stalked from the gardens, leaving her to stand there vainly attempting to still the frenzied beating of her heart.

Chapter Seven

"The jury, passing on the prisoner's life,
May in the sworn twelve have a thief or two
Guiltier than him they try."
—Shakespeare,
Measure for Measure

Two days had passed and still Garett couldn't banish
Mina's image from his mind. As he rode his stallion
Cerberus briskly down the road bordering his fields,
he cursed himself for once again letting his mind wander
to the stubborn little Gypsy.

He knew why she captured his thoughts. When she'd
shed her cloak, she hadn't revealed her secrets. Her
secrecy obsessed him. One moment he believed she
had nothing despicable to hide, and in the next he
toyed with the suspicion that she worked for his uncle.

Even if she was his uncle's lackey, could she do him
any harm? he thought. She was clearly unskilled in
real treachery, and Garett had seen enough truly
wicked manipulation to know how to counter any hindrances
she might throw his way. Yet if Tearle had sent
her, she could prove more than a mere nuisance, particularly
when she distracted him so.

Distractions were the last thing he needed now, not
if he was to accomplish his aim. That aim absorbed
him more and more these days. Returning to Falkham
had started anew the pain he'd felt when he'd learned
of his parents' deaths.

When he'd first been told of their deaths, he'd accepted
the explanation that it was one of the tragedies

of the war. But as time had passed, he'd come to a few realizations.

Only Garett's uncle had known his parents were fleeing to Worcester in disguise to join the king. Only Tearle had known how to find them on their journey. And now Garett felt certain only Tearle had betrayed them to the Roundheads. He couldn't prove it, but in his heart he believed it.

Through the years his suspicions had engendered within him a burning desire for vengeance. Now he could scarcely believe that after long years of planning, he was finally to achieve his revenge.

His vengeance had begun with his appearance before the House of Lords and the regaining of his lands. Although none of the circumstances of his exile had been revealed, his sudden return had spawned rumors. Those rumors were even now growing to assurances, and it wouldn't be long before society would draw the right conclusions about Tearle without ever having heard one word of the facts. As suspicion of his duplicity spread, Pitney would soon find it difficult to show his face among the gentry or nobility.

Then Garett could begin tightening the noose. Already he was carefully laying the groundwork. And soon, very soon—

The sound of men shouting pierced the afternoon quiet, bringing him out of his thoughts. Jerking Cerberus about in the direction of the noise, he saw tendrils of smoke curling upward from his fields. *Damn it all*, he thought, *someone's set fire to my fields!* Instantly he spurred the stallion forward. Then he heard a horrible scream and dug his knees more urgently into his stallion's sides.

In moments he came upon three men in the midst of a scorched patch of ground from which smoke still rose. He didn't recognize the man who lay very still on the ground, blood rapidly drenching his shirt and doublet. But he knew the two who were thoroughly engrossed in shouting at each other. The taller of the two still gripped a bloody sword. And both men worked for him.

Rapidly he dismounted. "Stop this madness!" he shouted as he came between them.

Immediately, the tall man jerked about to face the newcomer, his face twisted with rage and his sword suddenly at the ready. Then his gaze steadied on his master, whose expression of fierce anger would have frozen the blood of Mars himself.

The man blanched instantly and dropped his sword. "M-milord, I didn't realize—"

Garett's dark glowering look made him lapse into silence. "Tell me what happened," Garett demanded, keeping a wary eye on both men.

The tall man, a villager hired to aid in the harvest, recovered his composure and hastened to relate the tale. "This villain here"—he gestured to the man lying prone—"tried to set fire to the fields. And he would have succeeded, too, if I'd not gutted him before he could do his dirty work."

The shorter of the two men, the tenant of the fields in question, shook an angry fist at the tall one. "You only 'gutted' him after I showed up to knock the torch from his hand and out of harm's way. He weren't armed. If not for yer foolishness, I'd have taken him prisoner. His lordship could've questioned him. 'Twould have been better to know who sent the bastard to burn us out than to have a nameless dead man to bury."

Garett once again surveyed the scene. The torch had rolled into a patch of green grass and had clearly burned only a few moments before sputtering out. Garett studied the prone figure of the man who'd attempted to set fire to his fields. If he carried a weapon, it was hidden.

Garett said nothing, but merely leveled a steady questioning gaze on the tall villager. The villager glanced from the tenant farmer to Garett as if studying how best to defend his actions.

"Perhaps I acted hastily," the tall man muttered at last. "But how was I to know the man wasn't armed? I did what any soldier would do."

That comment gave Garett pause. "Your name's Ashton, is it not?"

The tall man nodded.

"And have you been a soldier?"

Ashton bit his lip uncertainly, his gaze shifting to the ground.

"When you came in search of work, you said you were a farmer," Garett prodded. Then his voice took on a steely quality. "Answer my question. Have you ever served as a soldier?"

"I merely meant, milord, that I sought to defend myself, just as any soldier would."

"So you haven't been a soldier."

"Nay."

Garett's gaze flew to the bloodied sword in Ashton's hand and then to the wounded man on the ground.

"You're dismissed," Garett said coldly. "I don't require your services anymore."

The tenant farmer grimly nodded his approval while Ashton stared at Garett in confusion.

"B-but milord, why?"

Garett's eyes met Ashton's and under the earl's steady, piercing gaze, Ashton's face grew flushed.

"I don't countenance liars," Garett remarked. "Mere farmers don't carry swords, and what need have you to hide that you once served as a soldier?"

For a brief moment Ashton's expression changed, as if someone had ripped a mask from his face. His eyes took on the quality of a wild man who'd been cornered.

"Milord, I—I wasn't certain if I should tell you I was once a soldier. Soldiers don't always make good farmers. But if you'll keep me on, you might find it an asset to have a soldier on your side."

Garett smiled, though his eyes remained cold and gray as winter. "I might find that indeed. But lying soldiers I have no use for."

Ashton's face paled, but he didn't seem to want to acknowledge the insult. "Your lordship would find me loyal—"

"Loyal to whom?" Garett asked grimly. "That's

the key question here. No, I believe it would be best for us both if you left my employ, before your 'loyalty' jeopardizes me and mine and forces me to act.''

The hint of warning in that statement made Ashton's face flush once again, but he merely gave Garett the slightest of nods, acknowledging Garett's dismissal. Then he whirled around and strode off toward Lydgate, his back stiff but shaking with suppressed anger.

The tenant farmer stared after Ashton with contempt. "Mark my words, m'lord. That one's a villain, a true villain despite his deft talk. You won't regret the losing of him.''

Garett's expression was somber. "The true villain was the man who sent him, and that man will pay as soon as I can prove his treachery.''

Suddenly the two men heard a low groan coming from the man lying on the ground. Garett moved swiftly to his side. The man's eyes fluttered open briefly.

" 'Tis of no use,'' he murmured, "no use . . . no use at all.''

Garett knelt down and lifted the man's head. "What is of no use?'' he demanded, but the man's eyes had already closed again, and he'd lapsed back into unconsciousness.

"Mayhap this one will live yet,'' the tenant farmer remarked. "If you can wring a confession from him, you may trap his master.''

Garett nodded as he surveyed the man's body, this time with a keener eye. It was impossible to tell how bad the man's wounds were beneath all the blood he'd shed. But if the man could be saved, he might be more than willing to reveal what he knew in exchange for leniency in his punishment.

"I know just the one to keep him alive,'' he murmured aloud. Abruptly he stood. "Make him as comfortable as you can. I'll fetch the Gypsy healer.''

The tenant farmer nodded his head. "If it's Mina you mean, she's a good choice. Aye, Mina will bring him back if anyone could. She can't bear to see anyone suffer, villain or no.''

As Garett mounted his horse, he thought on the farmer's words. Mina was indeed softhearted. She might not think well of his desire to keep a knave alive only to hear the man's confession. It would be best not to tell her what he planned, or she might not do as he wished.

He rode in a frenzy back to Falkham House and beyond it into the forest. He knew Mina had thought to keep her abode secret from him, but that day in the garden, he'd followed her at a distance. Now he made his way to the clearing with grim purpose. She'd need convincing to go anywhere with him, but her soft heart would win out in the end. He could count on that.

When he reached the clearing, at first he could see no one. The fire in front of the Gypsy wagon had a few glowing embers, but the pot dangling from a curved iron stake above it was empty. He dismounted, intending to look around. Then he heard voices raised in heated argument coming from behind the wagon. Rounding the wagon, he found Will and Tamara facing each other like a bear and a dog in a bearbaiting, except they exchanged words instead of bites and blows.

"For a Gypsy wench, you have mighty high ideas!" Will shouted.

"And for a gentleman's servant, you, sirrah, have the manners of a thief!" rang out the feminine reply. "Don't you have duties elsewhere? I don't want you here."

Garett noted that Tamara's lips were reddened and her hair mussed. "Apparently Will found it more interesting attending to you than attending to his duties," he remarked dryly, startling the two combatants so that both jumped. When he had their complete attention, he went on. "Normally I wouldn't interrupt such edifying conversation, but I have need of both of you."

Tamara's instant defensive stance didn't hide the quick flush that crossed her face. "Have you come to join your lackey in attacking me, milord?" she asked, casting a derisive glance Will's way.

"Attacking! Why, you're a fine one to talk—" Will muttered.

"I don't attack defenseless women," Garett answered impatiently, getting a glare from Will for his pains. He plunged on. "At the moment I have greater concerns. Where's Mina?"

Tamara's eyes narrowed. "Why?"

"I've need of her services," he retorted impatiently.

Tamara didn't seem to like his answer, for she planted her hands on her hips and scowled at him. "I'm sure you do, milord," she said with silky sweetness, "but she won't lend them to you."

Garett stepped forward a few paces and gripped Tamara's shoulders, throwing her off guard. "Listen, woman. A man lies dying not two miles from here. Your niece might save him. I don't have time to waste in overcoming your objections, so either you tell me where she is or I'll take you off to the constable."

At that Tamara's eyes widened, though he could feel her shoulders grow rigid under his hands. She sniffed and lifted her face to him defiantly. "Well, then, be about it, milord, for I shan't tell you a blessed—"

"I'm here!" a voice rang out from the woods. Then Mina stepped into the clearing. "There's no need to threaten her, my lord. I'll do as you wish."

Garett turned his face toward the voice, arrested by the sight that greeted him. A few days and he'd already forgotten just how much she affected him.

She wasn't an astounding beauty like the bejeweled, painted ladies of the court whom he was accustomed to seeing in Charles's presence. Yet something about her calm assurance, her look of good health and radiant youth struck him half dumb every time. Now she stood with twigs and dry leaves clinging to her skirts, her dark golden hair down and wind-tossed. Cradled in her arms were two bundles of dry branches, which she held as gently and reverently as two babes. If there was a goddess of autumn, she would be it, for she looked as if she'd just emerged from the very essence of the brilliantly hued trees themselves.

No, he thought as he continued to stare, his mind wandering to more lascivious things. She looked as if the god of autumn, whomever he might be, had just tumbled her there in the crisp leaves. Garett could easily imagine her lying prone in the woods, her hair the only mysterious beacon of light in the dark shadows of the forest. That wayward thought sent a surge of desire through him so powerful he nearly shuddered with the force of it.

Even her quick frown couldn't squelch that burst of wanting.

"What do you want with us?" she demanded, her gaze flitting briefly to his grip on her aunt's shoulders.

For a moment he was tempted to blurt out what he really needed from her. Then he forced himself to return to the serious matters at hand. "There's been an accident. I require your services as a healer," he replied, releasing his grip on Tamara.

The Gypsy fell back a step into Will's waiting arms. Tamara shrugged Will off, but he stood beside her nonetheless, intently watching the interplay between his master and Mina, even while he kept one hand lightly on Tamara's shoulder.

"It seems to me, milord," Tamara said before her niece could reply, "that you attract 'accidents.' I'm not so certain my niece should be in your company. You seem to bring bad luck."

Garett glanced at Mina, but she stared him down, her expression much the same as her aunt's mutinous one.

"At present I'm inclined to agree with you," he said. "I could certainly use any luck you're willing to offer." His eyes didn't move from Mina's face, though he directed his words to Tamara. "If you want to accompany us, you may, but only if you intend to be of some service. If not, you and your luck may stay here with Will. Either way, Mina is coming with me."

Tamara stepped forward, but Will's gentle hand became an iron grip on her shoulder. She shot him a look of venom. He simply smiled and shrugged.

Mina moved closer and threw down the branches.

Her expression showed she was clearly not at all pleased by the familiar way Will held her aunt. "If you'll call your dogs off," she retorted to Garett, gesturing to where Will had snaked one arm around Tamara's waist, "then I'll consider your request."

Garett gave Will a curt nod, and Will released Tamara, grinning as he did so.

"Come, then," Garett directed Mina once he saw Tamara was free. He turned back to his horse and took a few paces, but when Mina didn't follow, he halted. Slowly he pivoted to fix her with a stare designed to make it clear to her where her duties lay.

But she wasn't so easily intimidated. "Is this a command or a request, my lord?" Mina asked, tossing back her hair in an unconscious gesture of rebellion.

He gazed at her until she flushed, but her eyes didn't waver from his. "Which one will make you come freely?" he asked, a trifle impatiently.

Mina's face softened as she searched his face for some sign he really cared what answer she gave. Her eyes locked with his, a strangely endearing fierceness in their depths. "A request," she said with a haughty tilt to her chin. She clearly didn't intend to move a step until they settled that point.

"Madam, would you come with me now while the man still breathes?" he replied tersely, tired of coaxing her.

She hesitated at his statement that was neither quite a request nor a command.

"Please," he added, even more tersely.

That last word seemed to satisfy her. "As you wish," she responded, giving him a regal little nod. "I'll fetch my medicines." Then she pivoted and walked gracefully to the wagon, leaving him to wonder at her sudden complete acquiescence.

As Mina left them, Tamara mumbled something under her breath, but she said nothing to stop her niece. The moment Mina was inside the wagon, however, Tamara strode up to Garett with eyes flashing. "If you seek to seduce her this way, milord, you toy with the wrong maiden. She won't hop into your bed out of sympathy for your troubles.''

Angry that Tamara had so easily read his interest in her niece, he retorted with attempted nonchalance, ''Don't be absurd, woman. What need have I to seduce a Gypsy?''

Tamara's eyes narrowed. ''Mayhap I've used the wrong word. Mayhap you mean *take*, not *seduce*.''

That wasn't at all what he'd meant. His brows drew together in a dark frown that she ignored. Will stepped forward as he recognized the dangerous glint in his master's eye, but Tamara continued on, oblivious of the two men's reactions. ''You know, milord, the Gypsy's reputation for being a soothsayer is unmatched. Shall I tell you your future?''

As his frown deepened, she went on. ''If you should force your will on my niece, I know I can do little about it. But be forewarned. You won't find it easy to cast her aside after one night, as you've no doubt done with others. That girl is pure sweetness throughout— her innocence is like a balm to those bitter at heart such as you. If you're not careful, you'll find yourself needing the balm more and more often till you'll die without it. And when you come to that pass, be sure you have her heart well in hand or 'tis you will suffer for it, not she.''

Garett strove for control of his mixed surprise and anger at her boldness. ''Don't worry, Gypsy,'' he bit out. ''Your niece is a comely maiden, I'll warrant you, but I've never forced a maiden. Nor do I intend to begin doing so now.''

She scrutinized him, and when he didn't turn away from her stare, she relaxed. ''Then we'll deal well together, milord, for I know she'll never go willingly to your bed.''

He wondered about the certainty in Tamara's voice. Apparently she didn't know about her niece's foray into his gardens . . . and his arms. If Tamara had known her niece had already willingly given him one kiss, she'd not be so certain Mina would deny him other liberties.

Tamara clearly thought she knew her niece well, but in this one thing she was wrong. Mina might have her pride and her strange, noble-bred pruderies, but she'd been wild, sweet passion in his embrace. And she'd be so again. He'd make certain of that.

Chapter Eight

"I'll give thee fairies to attend on thee;
And they shall fetch thee jewels from the deep,
And sing while thou on pressed flowers dost sleep."
—Shakespeare,
A Midsummer Night's Dream

The half-moon's silvery light trickled through the trees as Marianne and the earl rode toward the Gypsy wagon. Numb from exhaustion, Marianne shifted slightly in Garett's uncomfortable saddle, too tired to worry that half her body rested against his. Her every muscle ached, and she longed for the relief of her pallet, hard though it was.

Never had she worked so hard to save one patient. But then, never had she seen so terrible a wound. Earlier that afternoon when she and the earl had arrived at the scorched clearing where the man had lain, she'd nearly despaired. He'd had the worst kind of wound, one in the stomach. She'd feared he would die, even though the number of scars on his body marked him as an old soldier accustomed to wounds.

The man had been blessedly unconscious, but his tenacious heart had clung to life. Only that thread of a pulse had kept her from giving him up for dead. Then she'd had little time to wonder about the scorched ground or to question why someone had plunged a sword into the laborer's belly. Instead, she'd gone right to work.

Under her direction, Garett and a tenant farmer had moved the man carefully into a carriage William had fetched from the manor. Then Marianne had sat with the wounded man throughout the slow, tortuous route over the rutted road to Falkham House. Another hour had been spent moving him into a chamber—her old bedroom, ironically enough. Then she'd had to work quickly, calling for water to be boiled, herbs to be mixed and steeped, and linen bandages to be prepared.

Bathing the man had taken most of her will, for his wounds sickened her. Yet she couldn't give up when he fought so hard to stay alive. Determined that his fight wouldn't come to naught, she'd stayed beside him constantly, bathing his wounds, forcing broth and medicinal concoctions between his feverish lips, and trying to stanch the bleeding as best she could.

When at last Garett had taken her from the chamber, ordering her to go back to the wagon for some much-needed sleep, she'd argued with him, although she'd done all she could, for the present. In the end, of course, he'd prevailed.

Now she was glad he'd insisted. Her body felt as if someone had beaten it with a sack of potatoes. Her eyes were scratchy with a desire for sleep, and her lids slid down almost of their own volition, lulled by the rocking gait of the horse.

Garett settled her more closely against him. She ought to hold her body stiffly apart from his, she told herself, but his warmth felt so good she couldn't bear to move away. Even when his arm tightened about her waist and he rested his chin against her head, she couldn't summon up the energy to resist.

"If I didn't do so earlier, I must thank you for what you've done for me this day," he murmured in a husky voice.

" 'Twas not done for you, but for that poor, wretched man. I'm not even certain he'll live, but I did all I could for him."

"Indeed, you nearly killed yourself tending to his wounds. 'Twas probably more than he deserved."

Briefly Marianne pondered the earl's words and the strange bitterness that crept into his voice as he said them. "Everyone deserves to live, my lord, even the poorest beggar. He may not have great estates and fine friends in London, but he enjoys the starling's song and the smells of autumn just as you do. And to hear and smell those things again, he deserves to live.''

Garett sighed. ''You've misunderstood me, Mina. I don't begrudge any man, poor or rich, the chance to live. As a soldier, I've taken it away from too many not to realize life is precious. Besides, I've seen villains among the rich and saints among the poor. So I agree that a man's worth shouldn't be measured by the coin, or lack of coin, in his purse. I merely meant that one can never know the true state of another man's soul, nor the true extent of his capacity for villainy.''

She heard his words in silence, confused by his voicing of the same sentiments her father had sometimes voiced. What was she to think of this strange earl? Today he'd worked beside her to save a man's life. The man was no one of consequence that an earl should strive so hard to save his life.

Too, Garett's concern for her puzzled her. He'd been so solicitous that he'd many times demanded she take a short rest. His manner had often been close to gentle in dealing with her.

What kind of man was he? Ever since she'd met him, she'd kept her eyes and ears open, hoping to find proof of what his role in her father's arrest had been. When she'd met his servants in Lydgate, she'd questioned them—discreetly, of course. Unfortunately, they'd known little, since most had been newly hired. His men, whom she'd occasionally treated for minor injuries, were loyal to him to a fault. They always praised him for his just manner and prowess in battle.

Garett himself wasn't terribly communicative about his past. The only thing he'd freely admitted was that he'd killed men in his lifetime. Yet all soldiers had. She needed more proof of his true character than that. Was he the kind of man who would betray an innocent man simply to steal his property? Heaven take her, but she wanted to know very badly. After all, if he'd not had her father arrested, her attraction to him wouldn't bother her so much.

And she certainly was attracted to him, much as she hated to admit it. Even now, in her exhaustion, her body thrummed with an awareness of his. His sinewy arm rested directly beneath her breasts so that it brushed those sensitive mounds every time the horse moved. The earl's stallion walked at such a slow gait they seemed to slide through the night on a dream, the moonlight changing everyday trees and bushes into fairy creatures guarding their way.

As if to take advantage of the mystical evening, Garett's hand, which had rested on her waist, began to rub caressingly up and down along her ribs. She stiffened, but his hand only grew bolder, slipping up her side until his thumb rested underneath her breast. Although the back of his thumb barely pressed the bottom of her breast, it felt like a burning brand searing into her. She shifted to put some distance between them, but his arm, which encircled her waist, only settled her more tightly against his body.

Then he lowered his head to nuzzle her bare neck below her coil of hair.

"M-my lord . . . what . . . are you doing?" The words left her lips, but she hardly knew she'd said them, for his mouth now pressed tiny kisses on the skin behind her ear, making every inch of her body tingle.

She shouldn't encourage him, but his kisses felt like balm on the tired tendons and taut skin of her neck. Under his ministrations, she tilted her head back until it rested on his shoulder.

He took that as an invitation and tugged on the reins. Then the horse stopped its movements, whinnied softly, and lowered its head to graze. Before she could even think how alarming all of that was, Garett had shifted her until she lay back in his arms. Then his mouth was on hers.

At the first touch of his kiss, she froze. But his tongue slid along the crevice of her lips, begging entry, and the jolt of heat that caress sent through her made her gasp. His mouth devoured hers, his kiss exerting a force too powerful for her inflamed senses to reckon with.

Somehow he'd done it again, she thought dimly. He'd swept her inhibitions away with his infernally dark kisses. She fought to regain her power over her own body . . . until his tongue darted into her mouth, heralding the surge of pleasure that then stole through her.

His lips claimed every part of her face. They felt warm, so very warm against the skin that lay exposed to the chill night air. Like Galatea, the beautiful statue whom Pygmalion's devotion had brought to life from the cold, hard stone, she awakened under his kiss. His caresses made her blood roar in her ears.

"What a creature of passion you are," he drew back to murmur wonderingly, as if he'd read her thoughts. Gently he planted a kiss against her tightly wound coil of hair. "I long to see what secrets this sweet form of yours holds for me."

"N-no secrets . . ." she murmured as he nibbled at her earlobe, sending a strange new heat radiating upward from her belly. "Please . . . please . . ." She broke off, not certain what she wished to say.

"I'd bid you return with me this instant to Falkham House if I didn't know how tired you are. Tonight it would be sheer cruelty on my part to take you to bed." He slid his hand over her cinched waist, resting it just beneath her breasts and making her shiver from the fire that inflamed her flesh. "Then again . . ." he muttered, lowering his lips to hers.

Take you to bed. The words echoed in her mind, striking the alarm. She thrust her fists against him, determined to show him she would not be going anywhere with him this night.

When he tore his lips from hers, his eyes questioning her, she whispered in a voice fraught with fear, "Please, my lord. . . ."

For a moment he tensed, his hands gripping her waist. His gaze played over her anxious face. Then he groaned and lifted his fingers to brush her swollen lips. "I know. As tired as you are, I have no right to press you. I suppose we'd best end this dallying, before I find myself doing what I'd regret on the morrow.''

Reluctantly, he settled her body back as it had been before he'd started kissing her, although his arm seemed to hold her more intimately than before. Then he took up the reins and set the horse in movement again.

As they rode on, her body flamed with shame. How thoroughly mortifying! He'd only stopped out of concern for her weary state. Otherwise, he'd have taken her behavior for an invitation, and rightly so. Oh, how could she have come to this pass? She fought to clear her befuddled brain. Her tiredness had so weakened her will that she'd allowed him flagrant liberties. Clearly he thought her the perfect wanton, eager to go to his bed after a few kisses.

She scolded herself as they neared the clearing where the Gypsy wagon lay. This was what came of dreaming of the night and the fairies it hid. It made a woman forget the central baseness of all men. She'd do best to remember this was no fairyland and Garett was no fairy prince. He very likely was a murderer, and she mustn't forget it.

By now they'd reached the Gypsy wagon. Garett easily dismounted, then caught her at the waist and lowered her to the ground. She tried to slip around him, but his hands lingered on her waist, holding her trapped between him and the horse.

''What? No kiss for the night, my Gypsy princess?'' Garett whispered. ''Are you angry that I put a temporary end to our pleasures?''

Righteous indignation made her grit her teeth as she lifted eyes flashing with fury to his face. ''Nay. I'm angry that in my weariness I didn't make my true emotions known to you.''

She could scarcely see his face in the dim shadows of the forest, but she could see that her words had annoyed him.

''Oh? So I merely imagined you were soft and willing in my arms. Was it a trick of the moonlight, perhaps? Or is it the trick of a Gypsy who's peeved she didn't get her way?''

"Peeved! Peeved! I'm not peeved. I'm infuriated! You play your nobleman's games with me, and somehow you force my will out of my very head! 'Tis maddening! You make me forget the very thing I should remember—that . . . that . . .''

She trailed off, suddenly aware that in her rage at herself and him she'd said too much.

The moonlight glinted off his eyes eerily, giving him the appearance of an avenging gray-eyed angel as his gaze bore into hers. His hands closed on her upper arms, and she could feel the tension in his fingers as he said, "Yes? What do I make you forget, Mina?"

She dropped her gaze from his. *That you're a villain,* she thought to herself, but merely said, "That we're too different.''

Her answer seemed to startle him. "Too different for what?''

"For anything!'' When that response brought her nothing but silence, she stumbled on. "You regard me as some sort of amusement, someone you can toy with while in the country. I want naught of that.''

Only after his fingers relaxed on her arms did she realize how hard he'd been gripping her. "And if I should tell you that isn't what I want?''

She raised her face in surprise. "If you told me such, my lord, I'd call you a liar, for you wouldn't mean it.''

He shrugged. "Perhaps. But then I've never wanted a woman as much as I want you. Now. This instant. So much that tomorrow I'll wonder how I ever managed to tear myself away.''

His words set her emotions into turmoil again. "But I don't want you!'' she said in despair.

He lifted his hand to caress her cheek. He stroked the full curve, then trailed one finger downward to tip up her chin. His lips brushed hers so lightly she found herself feeling disappointed and wanting more. Unconsciously, she swayed against him, so that he caught her about the waist and pressed a quick, hard kiss on her mouth that she returned despite herself.

His voice held a hint of triumph when he spoke again. "You don't fool me, Mina. You may not want to desire me, but your desire is there nonetheless, like a lantern-encased flame I can see and dimly feel, but not yet touch." He smiled then, the smile only giving greater credence to the determination already in his eyes. "I'm a patient man. I can wait for you to break the glass, to join my fire with yours. Just don't make me wait too long or the blaze may consume us both."

Abruptly he released her. Her heart pounded from the power of his words and the force of his nearness. He'd taken the weariness right out of her, and replaced it with confused yearning. How could she answer him, when he thought he'd proved all her protestations to be lies?

Perhaps he had. She didn't know. All she knew was she must escape him before his presence drove all thought from her head. Quickly she slipped from between him and the horse, hurrying to the wagon as if her life depended on it.

"Good night, little coward," he called after her, his soft chuckle mocking her.

She ignored it, hastening into the wagon without an answer. Then she stood for several long moments just inside the door, holding her breath in case he decided to stay and tempt her more. But at last she heard the tramping of his horse across the forest floor, and she released a great sigh.

"Did he harm you?" came a question out of the darkness, startling her.

"Nay, Aunt Tamara," she managed to choke out, "nay, he didn't harm me."

A long silence ensued before she spoke again. "But he kissed you, didn't he?"

Marianne blushed, thankful her aunt couldn't see in the dark. Or could she? "Why think you so?"

"I heard his horse approach some time ago. The two of you must have been doing something all this time. It wasn't talking, for I could hear when you were talking."

Marianne groped her way to her pallet in the hidden

cupboard at the back of the wagon. "I'm tired, Aunt Tamara," she murmured as she began to undress. "I'd really like to retire now."

"He's a handsome one, poppet, I'll grant you that. But don't let his manly looks sway you. Remember, you're not a lady anymore, but a poor Gypsy girl. This man isn't honorable like your father was. His heart's filled with bitterness, with hate and revenge. If once he captures your affection, he's sure to turn your heart of sweet water into water of bitterest wormwood."

With the taste of the earl's kiss still fresh on her lips, that warning unsettled Marianne. "Don't you think it might happen the other way?" she couldn't help but snap. Then she hastened to add, "Not that I would ever fall prey to such a man's snares. Still, if I did, might I not turn the bitter water into the sweet?"

Her aunt's cynical snort cut through her. "Nay, poppet. I think 'tis not possible. It takes a strong love to turn wormwood water into wine. I don't think this nobleman has that in him."

Marianne didn't answer as she slid onto her pallet and underneath the coverlet. But some small persistent voice within her still whispered that wine wasn't made overnight, and Gypsies couldn't always see the future.

The next day Marianne found it difficult to concentrate only on her patient. She hadn't wished to return to Falkham House, to be confronted with Garett's presence so soon after their last encounter, but her conscience wouldn't allow her to abandon the wounded man who now lay ensconced in her old bedchamber.

To her immense relief, the earl made only a brief appearance in the sickroom early in the morning. Once he determined the patient was still unconscious, he left the doctoring to her, telling her he'd return later in the day.

Sometime around midmorning, Marianne was bathing the wounded man when his eyes briefly fluttered open, and he murmured a few words.

She leaned over him in excitement. "What is it? Would you like something? Water, perhaps?"

His eyes closed again, but a small measure of relief pulsed through her. At least he was partly conscious. She finished bathing him and tried to make him more comfortable. Then she left him resting to search for the earl.

As she descended the stairs, the sound of loud, belligerent voices wafted up to her from the entranceway.

"I told you before. His lordship won't see you and m'lady. You must leave," said a voice that was unmistakably William's. His tone was exceedingly rude, even for him, and Marianne descended farther down the stairs, curious to see who could make William behave so abominably.

"I don't care if he wishes to see us or no," came the harsh reply. "I would see him. We shall not leave until I do, so you'd best tell his lordship we await his pleasure."

With that the man pushed his way into the hall adjoining the stairwell. Marianne crept silently down the stairs, stopping short a few steps from the bottom at the point where she could just see into the hall.

First she saw a lady dressed richly in a satin morning gown with fur-trimmed overskirts. The woman herself, though at least ten years older then Marianne, had a lush, ageless beauty. But her face wore a deeply sad expression as she twisted a silk kerchief she held clutched in her hand. Marianne instantly pitied her.

Her pity only deepened when the woman's husband came forward and snatched the kerchief from her hand, muttering something under his breath that made the woman blanch. The man was dressed in elaborate and foppish finery, a great deal of rich lace showing at the edges of his boot hose and at his cuffs.

Slowly the man turned until Marianne could see his profile. Immediately she stiffened. To her surprise and chagrin, Sir Pitney stood in the hall. Her heart began to pound as she quickly backed up the steps a short way.

How horrible! How could he be here at Falkham? He wasn't supposed to be. She didn't want him here, for he knew her face. If anyone could identify her, he could.

Don't panic, she told herself. She forced herself to relax and think logically. It was highly unlikely that Sir Pitney would recognize her unless he took the time to look at her closely. She'd seen him only once or twice before, and then she'd been only a gangly and awkward fifteen-year-old. Besides, he wouldn't expect to see her alive, for surely he'd heard of her supposed suicide.

Still, she kept well out of sight as she began to back up the stairs. Then she heard footsteps from beyond the hall and realized Garett had evidently come himself to evict his uncle. Though she told herself she shouldn't remain, her feet felt locked in place on the stairs. She couldn't tear herself away from the confrontation she knew was to come.

To Marianne's surprise, the woman spoke first. "A good morning to you, Garett," said the sad voice.

"And to you, Aunt Bess," came the earl's distant reply. Then his voice softened. "I wasn't told you had arrived, only your husband. Forgive me for not coming to greet you sooner."

As if drawn by an invisible thread, Marianne crept back down the stairs and then moved until she could just see around the door leading into the hall. Standing far back in the shadows, she watched with unabated curiosity what was happening in the other room.

Lady Bess stood staring at her nephew while he smiled at her. Then Sir Pitney moved up to clasp Lady Bess roughly about the waist. "We've come to tell you the news. My wife is with child. We were certain you'd wish to know of it."

Garett's gaze went to his aunt's face, and when her blush confirmed Sir Pitney's words, he gave her a half smile. "I'm pleased to hear of your child," Garett replied, pointedly addressing only his aunt.

"I'm so glad to see you after all these years," she said softly, and pulled away from her husband. Pitney let her go, but kept a watchful eye on her as she stepped up to Garett, holding out her hands to him.

He took her hands and lifted them both to his lips. Clearly Garett's gesture affected her, for Marianne saw her wipe her eyes when he released her hands. "You've grown so tall," she said with a forced lightness. "I can scarcely believe it's you. And you seem . . . more quiet than you were as a boy."

Garett's eyes briefly swung to Sir Pitney. "I have my years in France to thank for that."

Her husband glowered, but she paled and began, "I think you should know that—"

Sir Pitney cut her off, stepping forward to clasp her arm. "Can't you see Garett's a very busy man, my love? We mustn't take up too much of his time with talk of our private affairs."

Something in the insistent way Sir Pitney spoke made Marianne shudder. Garett clearly noted Sir Pitney's tone as well, for his brow knit in a dark frown.

"Go on, now, Bess," Pitney said with more force. "Go on back to the carriage. I'll be there shortly. Your nephew and I have a few matters to discuss."

Lady Bess nodded almost fearfully and turned away, but before she could leave, Garett stepped forward and took her hands again. "You're looking well, Aunt Bess," he said solicitously. "I hope you feel as well as you look. If you should find that's not the case and should wish my help—"

"I take care of what is my own," Sir Pitney cut in.

Lady Bess took that as her cue and, snatching her hand from Garett's, fled out the front door as Garett watched her, his eyes narrowing angrily.

As soon as she left the room, he turned on his uncle. "I'd best not hear you've been mistreating her, Tearle. She and you may have abandoned me to the wolves in Europe, but she at least is my blood, and I won't have one of my blood abused, no matter how poor her choice in husbands."

Pitney colored at that, his smooth, handsome face distorting in his rage. "You whoreson bastard! You ride into England on His Majesty's coattails, wrest from me the estates I worked hard to improve, and

then have the audacity to command me in how to care
for my wife!''

Garett laughed scornfully, his hands closing into fists
at his side. ''You improved my estates? How so? By
letting the tenants starve while you took their earnings
to pay the taxes and finance your grand schemes for
power? By abusing the townspeople in every neighboring village until the Falkham title became a hated
one?''

Garett strode up to tower over his uncle, who wasn't
a tall man. ''The only place spared your 'improvements' was this house and Lydgate. Only *you* could
have had the audacity to sell this house—my house—
to strangers, forcing me to struggle to have it returned
to me. If this is how you improve my properties, then
'tis no wonder that with counselors like you to assist
him, Cromwell despaired of it all and died! 'Twould
be enough to send anyone to his grave.''

''I poured money into these lands—''

''And took most of what you poured in back out
again,'' Garett said coldly. ''You stole more than
enough from me, so if you're here to ask for money—''

''I merely came to tell you of the coming babe!''

Garett snorted. ''Indeed!''

A slow sneer crossed Sir Pitney's face. ''And to remind you that if you should die without an heir, my
son—and it will be a son—will inherit.''

Garett's face darkened then, making Marianne shudder. She'd seen that black look before. For once, she
was glad someone else was the recipient of it.

'' 'Twould be very convenient for you if I should
die without an heir, wouldn't it, Tearle? It might even
be as convenient as certain other deaths were for you.''

Pitney instantly fixed Garett with a menacing stare.
''What other deaths? What do you mean by that?''

Garett remained silent for a moment, but she could
tell from the rigid set of his jaw that he struggled to
control himself. ''You know what I mean,'' he finally
said enigmatically. ''But it takes more than a couple
of bumbling highwaymen to bring me to earth, so per-

haps you should rethink your plans. You may not find it very easy to carry them out."

At the mention of the highwaymen, Pitney's face paled.

Garett's slow smile was mirrored on Marianne's face, for she enjoyed seeing Sir Pitney discomfited after what he'd done.

"Yes, uncle," Garett taunted with smug satisfaction. "I knew it was you who set them after me. Just as I knew you sent a man to burn my fields. But your little ploys aren't working. Your hired 'highwaymen' lie dead in the potter's field, and I dismissed the spy you'd hired from the village."

"What spy?" Pitney said, though he looked distinctly uncomfortable. "You're mad, nephew. All this talk of highwaymen and spies. You can't prove any of it!"

Garett's smile broadened, but this time the bitterness behind it transformed his expression into one filled with such hate Marianne could hardly believe him the same man who'd kissed her so tenderly the night before.

"I can't prove it yet. But I will soon. For you see, Tearle, the man whom you sent to burn my fields, perhaps even my estate, was captured alive. Your spy tried to kill him, to keep the man from talking, but was unsuccessful. So your lackey lies even now within these walls. His wounds are being well tended, I assure you. Once he's well enough to talk . . . well, who knows what things a man might reveal if given the right persuasion? He might even reveal enough to hang the one who hired him."

At those unexpected words, Marianne backed into the shadows, her stomach churning sickly. Dimly she saw Pitney's expression turn to one of rage; dimly she witnessed Garett's triumphant stare, but most of her thoughts, most of her mind was reserved for her own personal distress.

The earl was all she'd feared, and more! It was no good deed that had sent him to request her services! No, the thirst for vengeance led him to her door. She

thought back to the way Garett had behaved around
the wounded man. The earl had helped her, that was
true, but he'd never said one word of concern for the
wounded man except to express his desire the man
might live.

And for what? Merely to torture the truth from him?
Could he truly be the kind of monster who would save
a man's life only to take it again?

"You haven't won yet, nephew!" Pitney growled,
bringing her abruptly out of her thoughts. "I won't
see you lay claim to all I've striven for!"

Garett's harsh laugh was like a knife twisting in
Marianne's heart, reminding her of her aunt's words
the night before. Aunt Tamara was right, she thought
despairingly. Bitter water would always be bitter.

"Listen to me and listen well," Garett told his uncle in an ominously low voice. "In London, when I
appeared before the Parliament, I kept my anger in
check because of His Majesty's determination to keep
peace in England. But my control is tenuous. In my
own land, where none would fault me for having you
drawn and quartered, I find it difficult to endure your
presence. So I suggest you return to your powerful
friends in London, before I decide to test your fencing
abilities!"

Sir Pitney backed away from the malice on his nephew's face, clearly convinced Garett would act as he said.
Once Garett saw his uncle was truly cowed, he turned
his back and began to leave the room.

Pitney's voice stopped him. "You think you have the
final say, don't you? You're as arrogant as your damned
father. Yet even he was brought low in the end. Remember this whenever you think you're safe in your
manor—men are easily bought in these times. Even
women have their prices. Don't be too sure you've rid
yourself of all the enemies in your house."

The sneer that accompanied Pitney's words pushed
Garett beyond the limits even of rage. "I could rid
myself *now* of all my enemies," he ground out, reaching for the dagger he always kept at his side.

Marianne's heart stopped, for she felt certain she

was about to witness a murder. But Garett's gesture evidently convinced Pitney to take his leave. The man quickly backed away until he'd reached the entrance to the manor. Then he slipped out the open door, leaving Garett to stand there shaking with fury.

"I'll see you hanged yet, uncle!" Garett growled into the empty room.

And Marianne, at least, was convinced he really would.

Chapter Nine

"There's a divinity that shapes our ends,
Rough-hew them how we will."
—Shakespeare,
Hamlet

Despite the familiar surroundings, Marianne stood frozen near the stairs, feeling as if someone had just set her adrift on an unfamiliar sea of hatred and violence. Shuddering at what she'd just witnessed, she released her pent-up breath in a long, audible sigh. Then she went still in fear as the sound echoed in the stairwell and off the stone stairs.

Apparently the stairwell wasn't the only place the sound echoed. To her horror, Garett's head snapped around, and with a frown on his face, he strode from the hall toward where she stood half in the shadows at the foot of the stairs. In only seconds he'd searched her out. Instantly his scowl deepened.

"What are you doing skulking about?" he snarled.

His tone drove some of the terror from her, reminding her of the contemptible way he intended using her to exact his vengeance. "What am I doing? As if you need to ask. 'Twas you who brought me here to serve your despicable ends. And now that I'm here I'm being shown what a beast you truly are!"

His eyes bored into her like two gray coals. "How long have you been spying on me here?"

"Spying? You dare to accuse me of so unsavory an act, when you've been toying with my life and the life of that poor wounded man as if we were your puppets?

Spying! As if I'd deliberately seek to learn how thoroughly you've played me for a fool!''

A shadow passed over his face as he took in her angry expression. He didn't appear to know how to deal with her accusations. Anger still hardened every line of his face, but his eyes seemed to acknowledge the reason for her words.

''Don't speak of what you don't understand, Mina,'' he said in clipped tones. ''You shouldn't have eavesdropped on something that was none of your affair.''

That really inflamed her temper. ''I didn't intend to listen, but I'm glad I did. How you use my abilities *is* my affair. Now that I know what you intend, I shall . . . shall put an end to your contemptible plans!''

She didn't know how she'd do it, but somehow she'd move the soldier out of the earl's clutches, she told herself as she slipped past Garett and started up the stairs.

He halted her by clasping her arm with an alarming strength. ''Don't behave foolishly, Mina. What do you think you could do now? Could you, one woman, move the man out of my house without my knowledge? I think not. And I assure you none of my servants would help you. Would you murder him then to 'save' him from me? No. Whatever else you may be or might have been, you don't have the arrogance to take a man's life in order to save him pain.''

Marianne's hand clenched the banister futilely as she acknowledged the truth of his statements. Only Garett had such arrogance—the arrogance to believe he could use people in whatever fashion he wished.

She began to shake. Devil take him, but he'd exactly described her choices. Fierce words caught in her throat as she sought to gain control of her impotent fury. As much as she despised him for it, he was right. As usual, he held the reins. Nonetheless, she refused to be part of his vengeance. Possibly he'd already made her father part of it. She'd have nothing further to do with his hatred for Pitney and obsession with Falkham House.

She'd leave. That was the third choice, one he hadn't mentioned.

Silently she moved back down the two or three steps she'd climbed, refusing to look at him. He released her arm then, and she kept walking, her eyes fixed on the oak door of the manor house as if it were her only salvation.

She'd leave and not come back. Perhaps she'd even leave Lydgate. Somehow she'd find a way to determine if he'd played a part in her father's arrest. And if he had, she'd find a way to make him pay for it. Later. But not now, not while the memory of his conversation with Pitney was fresh in her mind, mocking her for being a fool.

She heard his heavy steps behind her, but she didn't stop.

"Mina, you can't leave now! The man may die without you!"

She paused, praying for the strength to ignore his words and the faint hint of alarm in the voice with which he said them.

At her silence, Garett went on. "If he dies, his last hours will be painful. You could ease his pain."

She knew he played on her soft heart, and knowing he thought she could be so easily manipulated cut her deeply. She whirled around, her face a mask of torment mixed with scorn.

"If he lives, you'll torture him. That pain would be greater than any pain he suffers in death! I can't stand by and watch it!"

For once she'd managed to astound him. He cocked his head and stared at her in blank astonishment. Then as comprehension dawned, his expression changed to angry disbelief. "What kind of heathen do you take me for? Torture him? Am I to hang him by his thumbnails until he tells the truth? My God, I've seen enough hacked and bloody limbs in war without wishing to see a man tortured at my own command!"

She watched him warily. His distinct expression of horror made her want to believe him, but she knew better than to trust him. "You told Sir Pitney there were ways to persuade a man to reveal all. 'Tis what you said! I'm not so naive I didn't know what you meant!"

"I didn't mean I'd put him on the rack, if that's what you thought. By my troth, I'm not the devil you would paint me!"

At that moment, she had difficulty believing him, for his fierce glower made him appear the very monarch of hell. He advanced a few steps, and she backed away instinctively. "I don't believe you. What else could you have meant?"

"Merely that I intend to imprison him until he tells me what I wish to know. A man whose loyalties are bought will only endure a dungeon for so long before he decides betraying his employer is the most prudent course."

Her eyes surveyed him disbelievingly. "You would merely imprison him?"

"If he lived, 'twas all I intended to do."

If he lived . . . "Even to put him in a dungeon is cruel when he's newly recovered," she pointed out lamely.

"The man strove to burn my fields," Garett growled. "Men could have been killed who would have suffered far more pain than he'd suffer in a dungeon. Be careful, Mina, that your pity isn't misplaced. The man's a villain, after all."

She half turned away, her mind whirling. Did Garett speak the truth? Would he really only imprison the man? If so, she couldn't leave yet, for the wounded man would certainly die if she abandoned him. The poor man might die even if she *did* stay at his side, but she could save him pain at the end. Yet she didn't know if she could trust Garett not to truly harm him.

As if the earl sensed her thoughts, he edged closer. "On my honor, I shall not perform any barbarous tortures on the man. If you wish, you can stay in the dungeon with him to make sure I don't. I swear you can trust to my honor in this."

Her head shot around at his seemingly sincere words. "Trust to your honor? Honor is but a paper sword when a dishonorable man wields it."

His lips thinned in renewed anger. "If you were a man, we'd duel at dawn over those words."

She paled, but didn't take back the insult.

At her silence, his eyes glittered. "I needn't prove my trustworthiness to a Gypsy. My past speaks for my honor. So does yours. You lied to me . . . you skulked about my gardens . . . you listened to my private conversations. . . . Where is *your* honor?"

"I only tried to protect myself—"

"From what? I don't even know that. I know nothing about your past, for both you and the townspeople avoid my questions."

She blanched at that. So far he hadn't pried too deeply into her past. If he ever did . . . if her refusal to accommodate him in the matter of the soldier made him seek harder for answers about her, she could be in serious trouble. Still, it galled her to be a party to his plans, even if the wounded man deserved imprisonment. She closed her eyes, trying to decide what to do.

He stepped closer, sensing her hesitation. "Why is it so hard for you to accept what I wish to do to this man? As a Gypsy, surely you've seen harsher punishments for criminals."

Her eyes flew open at his mention of her supposed life as a Gypsy. Weighing her words, she avoided his intense scrutiny. "Remember, my lord, I was raised a noblewoman. I have a noblewoman's principles even though my blood isn't pure."

"Then uphold those principles, and do what you know is best for your patient. 'Tis only your pride that's wounded now. But that man will die without you. Believe me, pride is a paltry thing next to the life of a man."

She met his piercing gaze squarely. "If pride is so paltry, why won't you abandon it and forget all your plans for vengeance? Only your pride suffered when your uncle took your lands and title. Didn't you live well in France those years you were in exile? Why not forget the past? You have everything you want now. What purpose is to be served in tormenting more people?"

When his eyes locked on hers, they were like two shards of ice, suddenly so cold and bitter. A muscle worked in his jaw. "You know nothing, nothing at all." The faraway look that crossed his face was almost fierce. Abruptly he stiffened his shoulders and said through gritted teeth, "I want you to stay and tend the man. You know what I need of you and have the ability to give it. And I know your aunt at least won't say no to the money I'll offer for your skills."

Any softness she'd ever seen in his face fled in that instant. When he continued, his voice had a hard ring of determination to it. "But be warned that no matter your choice, I won't alter my plans for him a whit. So stay or go—'tis your decision."

Having made that flat statement, he abruptly turned on his heels and strode toward the stairs, leaving her to make an impossible choice.

Garett frowned into the fire, then glanced at the man who'd lain quiet for several hours in the small, incongruously lacy bedroom that once clearly belonged to a lady of the house. The soldier wasn't dead yet, but Garett doubted he'd live much longer.

Then Garett's eyes roamed to another figure who sat curled up in a stiff-backed chair. In the end his little Gypsy had stayed. After all, Garett thought, what choice had he given her? He'd known she could be convinced. But now he felt no joy in the knowledge.

She'd seen to it he felt like a monster for what he was doing. "Damn," he muttered aloud. Who was she—a Gypsy wench without a penny to her name—to lecture him on honor and responsibility? God only knew what she'd done to survive in the last few years, she and her devious aunt.

Unbidden, his eyes strayed once again to Mina's still form. Her head drooped forward so her tangle of curls fell in soft waves over her shoulders, past where her lace-edged chemise peeked above her boned bodice, then cascaded down the front of her azure dress.

What a pretty picture she made, her legs tucked up under her as if she were an innocent child. But the delectable lips were not a child's, nor the shapely calf exposed to his view where her plain muslin skirts had hiked up. It was enough to make a monk sit up and take notice. No wonder her accusations had driven him almost frenzied with anger. He couldn't bear to have that delicious creature thinking him such a beast.

Determinedly, he jerked his gaze away, furious with himself for letting her emotions in the matter concern him. How had he come to this pass, to let a beautiful woman toy with his resolve? What she thought of him was of no consequence. No one else would fault him for imprisoning a man who tried to destroy his tenants' livelihoods.

Nor would anyone else criticize him for wanting his revenge against Tearle. His frown deepened, remembering the way she'd urged him to forget his vengeance. If she only knew. . . . But how could she? He himself had only suspicions and no proof that Tearle had betrayed his parents.

He thought back to those first painful days in France. Only after a long while had he adjusted himself to the thought that he'd never see his mother's kindly face again nor trade witticisms with his father. Most wrenching of all had been that he'd known little of what had happened. Who'd killed them? Had they suffered or had they been spared pain at the last? The emotional turmoil engendered within him by the news of their deaths had been so great he'd almost welcomed the hardships of France, which took him out of his thoughts.

And there had been hardship. Without family or funds, he'd been forced to take whatever jobs were offered him. The king's friendship hadn't altered matters, for the king himself had been destitute and eventually forced to leave France. So Garett, a boy of thirteen, had done whatever backbreaking, dirty work the French had seen fit to give him. All the while he'd had time to think about his uncle. As Tearle continued to ignore Garett's letters, Garett's suspicions had grown to a certainty that his uncle had betrayed his parents.

With that certainty had first come caution, particularly when a man had come from England seeking

Garett, intending to kill him, or so Garett had been warned by friends. At that time, Garett had stopped using his title, even his given name, convinced his uncle wanted him dead. He'd faded into the group of exiles, another nameless boy without a home, until such time as he could fight back. In the meantime, he'd nursed within his breast a hatred for his uncle bordering on madness.

Then, when Garett had been old enough to convince the Duke of York to let him serve in his mercenary army . . . Those years he wanted to forget altogether. Only his raging hatred for Tearle had seen him through the wretched, bloody battles fought not for love or country but for money, always money. He'd thought of Tearle every time he'd watched a man flogged for disobedience or a soldier friend hacked to death with a sword. Each act of violence had made Garett wonder what violence his parents had suffered because of Tearle. Then he'd forced himself to learn more, to hone his skill with the sword to a fine art, so that one day he could plunge his sword through his deceitful uncle's chest.

And now? In some of Garett's more bitter moments, he wanted to forget all caution and murder his uncle. Garett could have done it easily enough, without too much risk. But at the ripe old age of twenty-three, he'd concluded that death was too good for his uncle. He wished to see Tearle's treachery clearly revealed, not only to the nobility who'd scorn him anyway for having lost the title, but to the men Tearle considered his friends—the Roundheads who'd given him power and the merchants who'd given him the money for his ventures. Garett wanted to see Tearle so discredited, so universally vilified he'd be forced into exile as Garett had been. Exile would be a fitting punishment, much more fitting than death to a man who thrived on power.

Still, it had taken all his self-control not to thrust his dagger through Tearle's heart when the villain had appeared at Falkham House. Only Aunt Bess's presence had given him the strength to resist that urge. Yet seeing his uncle had fired Garett's desire for revenge

to greater heights. Oddly enough, so had seeing his
aunt.

Aunt Bess. He remembered her as a laughing young
woman who'd lectured him teasingly about his insolent
tongue. He'd secretly worshiped her, never dreaming
what her husband would later do to him. Now he felt
certain she didn't realize that Tearle had probably
caused her brother's death. Garett couldn't believe
she'd stay with Tearle if she realized it.

How could she stand living with his uncle anyway?
Then again, perhaps she was happy to be carrying a
child. The prospect of children seemed to make most
women happy. Yet she hadn't seemed particularly
happy.

Garett looked at Mina and wondered if she'd feel
joy at the prospect of children.

Then he cursed himself for his own perversity. Only
his Gypsy princess seemed able to take his mind from
his revenge. Only she tempted him to abandon his purpose in favor of pursuing other concerns. Well, he
mustn't allow her to do so, nor to make him forget that
his plans could very well depend upon the soldier's
confession concerning Tearle.

As if Mina sensed Garett's dark thoughts, she
stirred, her eyes slowly opening. For a moment she
seemed disoriented as she looked about the room.
Then her gaze rested on Garett, and she frowned, un-
curling her legs and sitting up in the chair.

"Is he any better?" she asked as she rubbed her
eyes.

"Not that I can tell, but I don't believe he's any
worse, either."

With a weary sigh, she stood and walked to the bed.
She bent over to rest her hand on the soldier's forehead, unknowingly presenting Garett with a very enticing picture of her derriere.

Despite his grim thoughts, he smiled at the sight,
and she turned just in time to catch that smile. "What
are you so pleased about?" she grumbled.

"Nothing you'd approve of."

She stared at him with a quizzical expression and

then with a shrug began checking the soldier's bandages. Her concern showed in her face as she raised it to Garett. "My lord, you know he may die despite my efforts. He hasn't stirred since we brought him here."

Garett nodded. "I know. We may add another death to Tearle's account. If you heard everything that was said this morning, then you know it was Tearle's spy who gutted your patient."

She glanced up at him, surprise written on her face. Clearly she'd forgotten.

"You see? Tearle's the villain in this, not I or my men."

She picked up her bag of medicines and moved away from the soldier's side to sit by the fire. "Perhaps you weren't at fault this time, but you've killed before, haven't you?"

He stared at her long and hard. "Yes. But that's what soldiers do."

She pondered that a moment. She bit her lip, then ventured another question. "So you killed men only while you were a soldier?"

Garett thought of the highwaymen and of the men he'd killed defending himself during his short term as the king's spy in Spain. "Mostly."

She paled at that. Her eyes dropped to her hands, where she toyed with the pouch of herbs that never left her side. "Why haven't you killed your uncle, if you hate him so much?"

"I have my reasons," Garett said stiffly, not at all pleased with the direction the conversation was taking. "But rest assured his time will come."

Her gaze darted to his face, and he suddenly hated that he couldn't tell her more. He couldn't bear the way she looked at him, as if he were some evil beast. "Mina, I'm a law-abiding man. I wouldn't kill a man in cold blood unless he tried to kill me."

She continued to look at him, although her expression turned from fear mingled with distaste to confusion. "You wouldn't kill for other reasons? To defend a cause, for example, or . . . or perhaps to ensure you could keep something you felt rightfully belonged to you?''

''By my troth, I don't know,'' he said irritably, wondering what had made her delve into such deep subjects all of a sudden. He thought for a moment. ''I suppose it would depend. Would I fight for my lands if some foreign army sought to take them? Of course I would.''

She leaned forward, her eyes burning into his. ''What about if someone else sought to take them? Like . . . like Sir Pitney. Would you have killed Sir Pitney to get Falkham House back . . . if he'd owned it?''

''I didn't need to kill anyone to get it, so why even ask the question? Why do you care what I did to get it back?''

She suddenly looked very nervous, which made him wary. ''I'm just trying to understand you,'' she said unconvincingly.

Garett would certainly have pursued that line of conversation further if the soldier hadn't suddenly given a loud groan. The man began to toss about in bed, mumbling deliriously.

Instantly both Garett and Mina were at his side. ''Easy, man,'' Garett muttered as the soldier tore at the bedclothes. Mina pulled the counterpane back over his body. His eyes opened slowly, but they had a feverish cast to them.

At first he didn't seem to notice either Garett or Mina. He began struggling to leave the bed, but Mina firmly forced him to lie back down. ''Hush, now,'' she murmured. ''You'll open up those wounds and make them worse.''

For a moment the man thrashed even harder. But as she continued speaking softly to him, pressing him back on the bed with gentle hands, he began to calm down. When at last she'd managed to settle him against the pillows, he turned his gaze on her. Garett noticed that the man's eyes fixed on her with a strange intentness. Then he began to shake his head and murmur, ''No, no.''

"What is it?" Mina asked in alarm.

The soldier merely dropped his head back onto the pillow, covering his face. "It can't be. You're dead," he began to wail pitifully.

At first Garett simply thought the man was delirious. He shot Mina a questioning glance, but she shrugged as if she didn't know quite what to make of it, either. She continued tucking the man's sheets back around him, ignoring his words.

"Don't talk," she soothed. " 'Tis not good for you to talk."

The soldier dropped his hands from his face and stared at her, his eyes a bright, feverish blue. "I know you're dead," he whispered.

"Nay," she replied softly as she lifted one of his hands in hers. "Can't you feel my fingers? You see, I'm quite alive."

He shook his head violently, then began coughing. "No, you're not. But 'tis all right."

"Shhh, shhh," she murmured.

"Mayhap you're an angel now," the man said, pinning her with his fever-ridden gaze. Then he nodded painfully. " 'Twould be good for me. Good to have an angel nearby if I die."

Garett thought to himself that Mina did resemble an angel, with her soft hair glowing in the lamplight. No wonder the soldier thought he was already halfway into heaven.

"You're not dying," she assured the soldier.

The soldier looked up at her with skepticism. Then his face softened, and his voice grew wistful. "You are an angel. 'Tis fitting. Always knew you were a good girl."

It was odd how the soldier seemed so certain he knew Mina. Garett wondered just who he thought she was.

The soldier struggled to rise in the bed. "Never believed the wicked things Sir Tearle said about you. Things he said you done. All lies, it was. Nasty lies about your mother, too. . . . Old lecher." He groaned, then shifted in the bed. "Always wanting her body, though she was a Gypsy."

At the beginning of the soldier's speech, Garett hadn't been so attentive, but when the soldier mentioned a mother and then the word *Gypsy* . . . Garett suddenly wasn't so certain the man was entirely delirious. He shot a glance Mina's way, his blood running cold when he saw her face blanch. She regarded Garett hastily, fear in her eyes. Instantly she dropped her gaze from his.

The soldier coughed. "Perhaps 'tis good you were sent as a vision to me. Your father—" He paused to cough again.

Mina's hands began visibly to shake. She dropped the sheets, then snatched them up again. "You don't know what you're saying," she murmured. The note of anxiety in her voice was clearly apparent. "You're thinking of someone else. Now hush, before you hurt yourself!"

But her tone didn't seem to intimidate the soldier. He fixed his pain-filled eyes on her. "Can see why Tearle wanted you and your mother. You're a good girl . . . even if you are dead," he muttered, tossing his head about on the pillow as she began to examine his dressings.

"I'm not dead at all," she said firmly, her lips thinning as she saw the blood seep through the bandages. "Now see what your foolishness has done? You've hurt yourself. Lie still, and let me give you something to help you sleep."

Wanting to hear what else the soldier had to say, Garett darted forward to stop her, but at the sight of the man's wounds, he hesitated. She was right about one thing. The man must be kept still, for he was clearly hurting himself. So Garett grimly watched as Mina forced some tepid tea between the soldier's lips, the same tea she'd given the man earlier.

As he watched her try to make the soldier more comfortable, he couldn't thrust aside the cold suspicions gripping his heart. Unbidden, Tearle's words came back to him: *Even women can be bought.* Then he remembered all her questions, all her concerns about who he would or wouldn't kill. Why had she asked so many questions?

He stared at Mina, who removed the soldier's bindings with shaky fingers. Clearly, the soldier had known her. So had Tearle. Why had Tearle known Mina's mother, the Gypsy? Tearle hadn't lived in Falkham House since long before Mina had claimed to have come to Lydgate. Yet the soldier implied that Tearle was intimately familiar with Mina's mother. He'd even hinted that Tearle and Mina . . . His mind fought that possibility even as it chilled him.

The soldier had mentioned things she'd done. Had she done them with Tearle or against Tearle? Garett wished now he'd questioned the soldier before Mina had hurried to sedate him. A bitter unreasoning rage began to surge through him. Why was it that the one thing the soldier had revealed was something he hadn't wanted ever to hear?

Unfortunately, he couldn't just dismiss it as delirious ravings. Too many bits of truth were mingled with the madness, and she'd clearly not wanted them heard. Garett had to find out more. If she was somehow connected with Tearle, she could be far more dangerous than he'd at first realized. To trap his uncle and force a confession from him, Garett couldn't have Mina telling Tearle about Garett's every move.

He clenched his fist so tightly his nails bit into his palm. His eyes sought out her face, but she wouldn't look at him. He knew she hid something, knew she feared what the soldier might reveal. What did she fear? He must know!

Whatever it cost him, whatever it took, he'd find out what she was . . . who she was. This time he'd get it out of her, he determined. For once, he'd make his deceitful little Gypsy tell him the truth.

Chapter Ten

"On a huge hill,
Cragged and steep, Truth stands, and he that will
Reach her, about must, and about must go."
                                        —John Donne,
                                            Satire 3

As Marianne washed the blood from the soldier's re-opened wounds under Garett's watchful eye, she cursed herself for being a fool. Despite having known that the soldier was believed to be Sir Pitney's spy, she'd not prepared herself for the possibility he might recognize her.

How unwise of her! If she'd thought about it, she would have realized how likely it was. When Sir Pitney had been trying to force her father into selling Falkham House, his men had been everywhere, spreading lies and rumors that her mother was a witch. Any man who'd worked for Pitney in the last few years was certain to have known about her mother, particularly after all that had come of Pitney's machinations.

Somehow Sir Pitney had learned Dantela was a Gypsy, and he'd told the people of Lydgate that little truth. Marianne vividly recalled the uproar his revelations had caused. Yet Pitney had underestimated the townspeople's loyalty to her parents and intense dislike for him. They'd remembered him during his short tenure as owner of Falkham House as being cold, hard, and cruel, unconcerned about his tenants or their needs. So when he'd come with his accusations of witchcraft and treachery, the townspeople had soundly defended the Winchilseas.

Now, Marianne thought bitterly, two years after he'd spread his lies, he apparently was finally going to succeed in ruining her life. The soldier's words were certain to have raised more questions in Garett's mind about who she was. She took only a hollow comfort in the fact that the soldier had stopped short of revealing her family name.

Suddenly a chill struck her. What might Garett think about the soldier's claim that she was dead? If he guessed why the soldier believed that . . .

She shuddered as she began to bind the soldier's wounds with fresh bandages. Oh, why had Garett heard so much of it? she thought despairingly. Why couldn't the soldier have chosen to rave while Garett was out of the room? Her heart pounding, she snatched a glimpse of Garett's face, then dropped her eyes as she saw him watching her, his expression unreadable.

Desperately hoping she could escape his questions, she lifted the soiled bandages she'd just removed and began carrying them to the door.

Garett's harsh voice stopped her. "Leave them."

"I must wash them or—"

"Later," Garett said in a clipped voice. "Now you're coming with me. We must talk."

She should refuse and insist on staying beside the soldier. No, that would only prolong her torment. If Garett wished to speak with her, he'd find a way to do so. Better to have his inquisition done and finished.

Still, as Garett ushered her from the wounded soldier's room into his own chambers, her heart began to beat a staccato rhythm that wouldn't be quelled. What could she tell Garett about her family without revealing too much? she wondered as Garett motioned for her to take a chair.

She remained standing, not wanting to give him any advantage. After all, at the moment the advantages were all his.

He seemed to know it, too. His lowering stare pinned her where she stood, giving her an uncomfortably queasy feeling in the depths of her belly.

''Had you hoped he wouldn't awaken?'' he asked, throwing her completely off guard.

Her surprise was evident in her tone of voice. ''What do you mean?''

''The soldier. If he'd died, your little secret would have died with him, wouldn't it have?''

Which little secret did he mean? she thought frantically, uncertain just what he might have gleaned from the soldier's words. Garett's imperious voice and expression unnerved her so much she started to blurt out the question she'd only thought. But she caught herself in time.

Garett's even tone was like that her father had often used to trick her into confessing some misdeed he wasn't quite certain she'd committed. She stared at the scowling earl, forcing herself not to be intimidated. She reminded herself she was no longer a child, easily cowed. So she rephrased her mental question.

''What little secret?'' she asked as evenly as an innocent.

The set of Garett's jaw revealed his displeasure. ''He knows you. And Tearle knows you. Surely you see what I must make of that?''

Again, a vague question designed to bring confessions tumbling from her lips. Well, she wasn't such a ninny.

''You can make of it what you wish, but your fabrications aren't necessarily truth, are they, my lord?''

That answer clearly tried his patience. ''Deuce take me, Mina, how does a minion of Tearle's know you, even know your parents, so well? For that matter, how does Tearle himself know you so intimately?''

She tried mightily to maintain an air of careful nonchalance. ''If I knew, I'd tell you, but since I've no idea, I can't answer.''

In frustrated anger, he ran his fingers through his hair and frowned. ''You think you're clever, don't you?'' he bit out. ''Well, you're not dealing with one of your patients. That soldier may lie down and hush when you croon to him, but I'm not as easy to placate.

I demand answers! Do you work for Tearle? Did he send you here to finish what the highwaymen began?''

He couldn't possibly be saying what she thought he was saying. It wasn't some deduction of her true identity that had him glaring at her. For heaven's sake, the wretch actually thought—

Cold indignation replaced her earlier fear. How dare he think she worked for his uncle, just because some half-delirious man linked her name with Pitney's! Never mind that she'd saved Garett's base flesh once already. Never mind that she'd even let him kiss her! He had the audacity, the overweening nerve to believe—

"Answer me!" he bellowed, and she'd had enough.

She strode boldly up to him and thrust her finger in his face, her hazel eyes turning golden in her absolute rage. "I could have killed you ten times over, my lord, if I'd so chosen. I could have slipped enough valerian in your wine to send you forever into sleep or put mustard and hedge garlic into your wounds until you screamed for me to stop the burning, but I did none of that. Nor would I ever. Think back to that night. Why, it wounded me then to cause you even a moment of pain! Surely you saw that?''

A muscle began to pulse in Garett's clenched jaw. "You saved me that night because you had to. If you'd killed me then, your own freedom would have been forfeit, for the constable would have come for you first of all.''

What he said made sense, but still she stared at him in disbelieving anger. "After the way you touched me and we . . . How can you even think I'd try to kill you, especially for some vile scoundrel like Sir Pitney?''

His eyes darkened relentlessly. "So you *do* know Tearle!''

Marianne's heart plummeted in fear, all her righteous indignation leaving her suddenly as she berated herself for having mentioned Sir Pitney at all. Now Garett's suspicions were truly roused.

She felt like Ulysses trying to steer a course between

Scylla and Charybdis. On the one hand, she couldn't deny the soldier's words. On the other, she couldn't tell the truth, nor could she let Garett continue in his errone- ous idea that she worked for his uncle. So what could she say to allay his suspicions? Would the Gypsy girl she pretended to be have known Sir Pitney? That didn't seem right somehow . . . and yet—

"I'm waiting for an answer," Garett said with a voice of softness wrapped in steel. He stepped toward her.

Suddenly certain he'd find a way to get his answers if she didn't tell him something, Marianne blurted out, "Yes. I—I know him."

That answer turned Garett's eyes a flinty, cold gray. "How do you know him? Why do you know him?"

What should she say? Marianne cast desperately about in her mind for some half-truth that might keep Garett from guessing too much about her, but nothing came to mind.

"Perhaps you were his mistress?"

Marianne's startled expression was perfectly genu- ine. "That's the most repulsive thing I've ever heard. He's as old as . . . as Sir Henry, and I've already told you I wasn't *his* mistress. Why do you always think such things about me?"

"Gypsy women often have protectors, Mina, as I've pointed out before. And an old protector is as good as a young one, if not better, for he has more money."

"For the last time, I've never had a protector! And if I were to choose one, it wouldn't be your uncle."

"Why not?" Garett persisted. "He has—or had—a great title. He still has wealth. Why wouldn't you choose him? Tell me, is he your enemy or your friend?"

"He's not my friend," she stated truthfully.

"Why not?"

Marianne stamped one dainty foot in frustration. "Faith, but you're as bad as a constable with your questions!" She whirled around, putting her back to him. He and his infernal suspicions. What could she tell him that wouldn't also reveal her identity?

"Answer me, Mina."

She hesitated, looking down at the familiar pattern of carpet as if it might provide her with something to tell him. But nothing came to mind except the truth. She sighed.

"Sir Pitney knew my father. And my mother."

"And?"

She turned back to face him. "He knew enough about Mother's heritage and her . . . her relationship to my father to ruin him."

"And did he?" Garett's face was implacable in his determination to know everything.

She tilted her chin up at him stubbornly as an idea came to her. "I'll tell you no more, or you might guess who my father was. That wouldn't do at all, for it would ruin his family name."

"By your own admission, your father's family abandoned you and never acknowledged you," he stated baldly, stepping forward until he towered over her only inches away. When she started to move back, his fingers closed around her wrists, holding her in place as if she were a mere child. "Why protect a family who never acknowledged you?"

A tear slipped from between her lids and rolled down her face. The charade was suddenly too much for her. She hated playing this role, hated not being able to shout to the world that her father was a good, honest man. But she dared not tell the truth, for her life and her aunt's life might be forfeit if she did. So she remained silent.

Her lone tear, however, seemed to touch some strain of human feeling buried deep within Garett. His eyes gazed at hers, which brimmed with other unshed tears. He muttered a low curse, then released her wrists, only to draw her to him in angry impatience.

Relieved that the inquisition seemed to be over, she let him hold her, her head dropping to his shoulder as her tears fell unbridled, soaking into his linen shirt.

"Damn you, Mina," he murmured against her hair as he wrapped his arms tightly around her waist. "You're the worst kind of Gypsy—a liar who steals into my soul to torment me when I'm least prepared for it.''

"I've never done you harm," she whispered achingly. "Why must you always suspect me of such despicable acts?''

The low groan that escaped his lips pierced her. Abruptly he released her, turning away to stride to the fireplace. He stood staring into its depths, a bleak, dark silhouette against the leaping flames. "Because you came to me cloaked in black cloth and lies. Because you have Gypsy blood." He paused, and she could see the muscles in his back tighten. "Because you know my treacherous uncle."

"Not in the way you think I do," she protested.

But he ignored her words, turning his head to fix her with an alarmingly fierce gaze. "And because you're the first woman to touch my heart since my mother was murdered ten years ago. That in itself worries me more than any of the rest."

She didn't know what to say. All breath seemed to have been sucked from her. It wasn't as if she'd chosen to touch his heart. Nor had she planned to be so terribly attracted to him, not when she couldn't even trust him.

So why did she want to go to his side and comfort him? Why did the expression now on his face, a mixture of self-reproach and desire, send a heady rush of excitement through her veins, excitement mingled with a bittersweet longing?

"What shall I do with you, sweetling?" he asked, breaking into her thoughts. He stared off beyond her to the door that led into the chambers where the soldier lay. His hand tightened into a fist as he added with fierce insistence, "If you work for Tearle, I can't let you go."

Several seconds passed before she mustered the courage to ask, "What do you mean?"

"Until you tell me the truth—who you are and why I should believe your claims of innocence—I must have you where I can keep an eye on you."

"How . . . how do you propose to : . . to 'keep an

eye on me"?" she asked, a great foreboding making her stumble over the words.

He continued to stare at the door until she thought his gaze would bore holes in it. "You'll have to be my . . . ah . . . guest here . . . until such time as you tell me the truth about your past. Until you can prove Tearle didn't send you to pry into my affairs and search for a weakness through which to strike at me."

She stared at him blankly, then shook her head in sheer disbelief. Disbelief slowly grew to anger as his gaze snapped back to hers, allowing her to read the determination written there.

"Guest? Guest?" she cried, her voice rising with her temper. "You mean prisoner, don't you? You mean to imprison me like that soldier! Are you insane? You can't do that to a . . . to . . . ." She stopped just short of saying *lady*.

"To a Gypsy?" he finished for her, his eyes narrowing. She dropped her head, furious with herself for what she'd come close to saying. He moved quickly to stand before her, his hand darting out to clasp her chin and force her head up. "All you need do, Mina, is tell me the truth. And don't give me any of your tales, for I can tell when you're speaking an unqualified lie like the one about the smallpox. Even your half-truths I'm learning to sort through very well, so you must do more than that to convince me. You must tell me it all, or I swear I'll keep you here until you do."

"You're a devil and a blackguard!" she hissed, trying and not succeeding in jerking his hand from her chin.

"You're not the first person to say so," he replied coolly. "But you're the only person who's lied to me and gotten away with it. I intend to rectify that. I want the truth. Now."

"I've given you all the truth I have to give today," she told him fervently. "If I placed all the truth in your hands, my lord, it could cost me a great deal, so I won't risk it."

For a long moment he stared at her, his obvious

outrage at her refusal feeding his already fierce anger. "You won't tell me," he growled in disbelief.

"Nothing more than I've already said. Nothing except this: I've never been, nor will ever be, a spy or mistress or anything for Sir Pitney. You can trust my word on that."

His lips thinned. "I don't think I can. You see, the last time I trusted someone, he stole my title, my lands, and—" his eyes darkened to winter sleet, as if he'd begun to say something and then thought better of it, "and everything I held dear. I'm afraid I've lost the habit of trusting people."

In desperation, Marianne tried another approach. "If you keep me here, my aunt will report you to the constable."

With a frigid smile, he dropped his hand from her chin to his side. "The constable knew me long before you even ventured close to Lydgate. He'll not countenance the foolish claims of a Gypsy wench like your aunt."

Her heart sank as she shook her head incredulously. "I can't believe you'd keep me here against my will. What kind of man does such a despicable thing?"

The farce of a smile faded from his lips. "One who's tired of being lied to. Come, now, Mina, why not tell me the truth? If you fear Tearle, surely you know I can protect you from him. You've needed a protector all along. And I'm willing to be your protector, no matter what you tell me. Even if your tale is that Tearle used his knowledge of your father to force you into his service or some equally sordid story, I can forget it all. As long as you tell me the truth."

For a long moment she gazed at him with longing. She wanted so much to unburden herself to someone. But not him! Even if her suspicions about him were unfounded, even if he had nothing to do with her father's arrest, he was still a king's man. He wouldn't harbor a woman said to be an accomplice to an attempt at regicide, no matter how much he desired her.

"I have nothing to say," she whispered.

He'd watched the emotions play over her face, his

intent concentration on her evident in his own expression, but as she gave her answer, his eyes seemed almost to empty, as if hope had fled them. Slowly he lifted his hand nearly to her cheek. Then his expression grew stony, and he dropped his hand to his side.

"Then I hope time loosens your tongue. Otherwise, you and I shall spend a long, silent winter together."

Chapter Eleven

"The brain may devise laws for the blood, but
a hot temper leaps o'er a cold
decree."

—Shakespeare,
The Merchant of Venice

Will stood outside the Gypsy wagon's wide doors,
which were shut at the moment, and glanced around
him with a frown on his face. He felt distinctly uncomfortable, although the early morning was milder than
usual for fall and not a cloud marred the blue sky.
With great reluctance he raised his hand to tap at the
doors, but they opened before he could touch them.
Tamara stood in the entrance to the wagon, her face
taut with anxiety.

"Where is she?" she demanded, putting her hands
on her hips. Without her realizing it, her action had
thrust her ample bosom forward. It was all Will could
do not to stare at her breasts. What was more, the
simple loose blouse and heavy skirt she generally wore
were tousled. No doubt the wench had just come from
her bed. Her hair, a soft cloud of sable curls, fell to
her shoulders in wild abandon. God, but the sight of
it drove every thought from his head.

Keep your mind on the business at hand, he told
himself sternly, *and off Tamara's sweet curves. 'Twill
be bad enough when she hears—*

"Well?"

"She's still at the manor."

Tamara swore under her breath. Then, her skirts
swishing about her, she marched past him down the

crude wooden steps that Will himself had built for the wagon after her nagging had driven him to action.

"Where are you going?" he cried, hurrying after her.

"To rescue my niece from your demon master."

Quickly he clasped her arm, forcing her to stop. She pinned him with a threatening glare, the kind he was getting used to seeing.

"He won't let her come back with you," he stated baldly. There. It was out. Garett's pretty little healer was staying in the manor no matter what her thoroughly appealing aunt had to say about it, and the sooner Tamara knew it, the better.

"What do you mean?" she asked, her scowl deepening.

"He— She— Oh, a pox on't! He thinks Mina one of Tearle's spies! 'Tis too complicated to explain. The truth of it is he won't let her go till he's sure of her loyalties."

For a moment shock lined Tamara's face. Then she paled and looked as if she might faint.

Will's heart sped up a pace. Damn, but she was taking it badly, just as he'd feared. He'd promised the little miss he'd tell her aunt what had happened—that much he could do without being disloyal to his master. He'd expected Tamara to be furious, to launch into one of her tirades. This deathly pale he hadn't expected.

"He hasn't harmed her," Will said in distress, stepping forward to put his arm around her. "You needn't worry about that."

She lifted her eyes to his, their deep brown suddenly so dark with anxiety that a pang shot through him. In that moment, she looked young and oddly vulnerable.

"Aye, but he will," she said solemnly. "Especially when he learns—"

"Learns what?" Will asked, his eyes narrowing.

Tamara's expression for a moment seemed shuttered. "Learns . . . learns that she's a virgin. 'Tis like uncloaking the falcon to put her so near his grasp."

Will said stiffly, "My master isn't an ogre, Tamara."

"Still, he wants to take her innocence. Haven't you seen it? The way his eyes drink her up whenever he's about? And she, innocent that she is. She can no more resist his pull than he can hers. She's like the falconer's lure to him. He means to have her, Will. Now he's found the way to keep her under his spell."

Will smiled wryly and drew her closer, delighted beyond belief when she didn't thrust him away. "Have some faith in your niece. When I left, that 'innocent' was giving him the roughest side of her tongue. She wouldn't even let him eat his breakfast in peace! She's much like you, she is. She'll not give him an easy time of it."

Tamara only shook her dark head, clearly unconvinced. "So many other things are part of this, things you don't know. . . ." She tipped her chin up stubbornly. "Understand this—your master's not for her. God knows what he might do now she's in his care. The worst of it is I shan't be able to protect her."

"Come, love, it's not so bad as all that," Will murmured, wrapping his arms fully around her and pressing her head against his chest. He decided to be even braver. "Besides, if you're right and he means to—to win her affection, what of it? Consider us. You've chipped away at my heart since the day I saw you. Perhaps 'tis the same between them."

When Tamara's body suddenly stilled, Will thought he'd touched her heart at last. But when she turned toward him and he glimpsed the scoffing expression on her face, he realized with a sinking heart he'd been too hasty.

Impatiently she disentangled his arms from about her waist. "You're as bad as he is, speaking your sweet words." Her full lips pursed as she frowned at him. "Chip away at your heart indeed! You have no heart or you'd not let him treat her so. Don't try to placate me. I shan't let the two of you ruin us both."

Normally Will was a patient man, but since he'd begun wooing the thorny Tamara, he'd discovered a capacity for impatience he'd never known he had. For the first time, he found he couldn't shake off her barbed words, not as he had before.

"What's there to ruin?" he muttered testily. "You're both Gypsies. 'Tis not as if you've lived like nuns, now, is it?"

That was certainly the wrong thing to say, he realized the instant he saw Tamara's reaction. And it wasn't one he was accustomed to. Normally she blustered and fumed, her anger obvious, but not threatening. Now she stared at him with an emotion akin to hatred in her flashing dark eyes, her silent fury stunning him.

He started forward, blurting out, "I didn't mean it, Tamara—"

But as he reached for her, she slapped his hand away and growled, "Don't you ever, ever touch me again, William Crashaw. If you do, I promise I'll cut all the sensitive parts of your body into pieces. All of them!" Then she stalked off in the direction of Falkham House.

Will had no choice then but to follow her, rueing his words. Somehow he must convince her not to engage his master in battle. Tamara might be sturdy and brave, but she was no match for the Earl of Falkham. Will couldn't bear to watch her lose all in a fight she couldn't win. If she lost, there was no telling how she'd react. She might even refuse to let him near her anymore.

Well, he certainly didn't intend to let that happen, he told himself as he went after her. If he had to annoy his master, he would, but he wouldn't let Tamara walk away from him. Not just yet.

Marianne stood in the dim stuffiness of the Falkham House library, soaking up memories of the many hours she'd spent there. It hadn't changed. Apparently Falkham had chosen to leave the entire library intact, the library her father had gained when he'd bought the estate from Tearle and which Falkham had now taken back from her father.

She ran her fingers along the tops of the books on one particular shelf until she found the book she searched for—John Gerard's *Herbal*. When Garett had entered his study, she'd slipped into the library, wishing to look at Gerard's book. If she remembered right, it had an excellent explanation of the properties of an herbal mixture she wanted to try on the wounded soldier.

But as she began to pull the book out, another volume on the shelf below caught her eye. For some reason, the volume struck a chord within her, and she abandoned Gerard's book to draw out instead the slender volume, a bit dusty now because it hadn't been looked at in some months. She held it in her hand as a wave of memory rushed over her.

Reverently she opened the volume with its intricately embroidered binding. The title page read, "A Pleasant Conceited Comedie Called Loves Labors Lost. As it was presented before her Highnes this last Christmas. Newly corrected and augmented By W. Shakespere." For a moment she paused there, savoring the familiar sight of the title. When the Winchilseas had first moved into Falkham House, she'd found the quarto and read the play often. It had once been her favorite play. The light wit had never ceased to lift her spirits when she'd felt gloomy.

But now it wasn't the play itself that concerned her. With trembling fingers she turned the page and found on the back of it the faded inscription—"To my son Garett. Continue to greet the world with a light heart even when it seems bleak, and you will never lack for strength. With love, Mother."

Marianne's heart gave a lurch. Until that moment she'd forgotten about those lines. Now the memories flooded back. As a girl, she'd found the inscription in the book and wondered about the boy named Garett. His mother's words had been so much like something her own mother might say that Marianne had adopted the inscription almost as if it had been meant for her.

It hadn't been meant for her, however, but for another child, one who'd lost his mother at a much earlier age than she had. How strange that those early days of dreaming about the unknown boy Garett, whom she'd gently been told had died in the war, had come to this.

In the imagination of her youth, he'd been a charming, happy child who loved Shakespeare's plays as much as she did. The Garett of her imagination had been mischievous, of course, but good at heart, eager to aid the sick and poor. As a girl she'd invented conversations with him about books, about Lydgate and its people . . . about life itself. Of course her image of him had made the story of his death seem more tragic to her.

In later years, she'd found other books to read, and the boy Garett had receded into the depths of memory. Until now.

Blindly she stared at the page with its inscription that now seemed so ironic. As a young girl, she'd never imagined another kind of Garett—an aloof man who couldn't trust and who didn't seem to know how to have a light heart. Last night, when she'd asked him questions about whom he'd killed and for what he'd choose to kill, she'd learned little about what he'd done to get Falkham House, but she'd learned a great deal about his pain, just from his cold and bitter manner. She couldn't imagine the Garett she now knew ever reading or enjoying the play she held. As she looked at the inscription, however, she wondered if his mother had known a different Garett altogether.

So lost was she in her ruminations she didn't hear the door of the library open and close. Too late she felt the presence of someone else and closed the book, only to have it snatched from her hand.

Whirling around, she found Garett staring at the book with torment in his eyes. Then they grew shuttered. He glanced from the book to her face and then back to the book.

She felt absurdly like a child caught with her finger in the Sunday pudding. Then his reaction roused her anger. After all, the house and library might now be his, but they'd once been hers, too, whether he knew it or not.

Wordlessly he opened the book as she'd done and

turned to the same inscription. As he read the inscription, his expression softened, making him look almost boyish. Then he snapped the book shut and lifted a probing gaze to her face.

"How—" he began, then paused. "Why did you have this book just now?"

Of course he would ask her that. And what could she tell him? The truth. "I was looking for books about herbs."

His expression showed nothing. "I see," he remarked in a tone that said he didn't really see at all. "But this book says nothing about herbs."

"I couldn't tell when I reached for it what it might concern. Then . . . then when I opened it . . . well, I found it interesting," she finished lamely.

His steady look told her he didn't believe her in the least. "Laying aside the fact that you were reading, a pursuit I didn't imagine was common to Gypsies, I must wonder why you chose that particular book to . . . ah . . . stumble across."

"It just came into my hand, that's all."

His eyes lightened for a moment as he raised one eyebrow. "Came into your hand?"

"Yes, and I'm glad it did," she plunged on, determined to move him to another train of thought. "You see, I never thought of you as having had a mother. Tell me, my lord, what was your mother like?"

His face became a mask, though she thought she glimpsed a hint of suffering in the depths of his eyes. "My mother . . . Why do you wish to know?"

Quietly she replied, "It would help me understand how the boy whose mother mentions his 'light heart' could grow into the man who'll stop at nothing for his petty vengeance."

For a long time Garett stared at her, his face devoid of expression, his eyes two quietly smoldering coals. Then he stated, "I had a light heart once, Mina, but it served me little. My mother was wrong. Lightheartedness won't make you strong. Only pain does that. And the anger that pain brings."

Something in the matter-of-fact way he stated it

made her feel as if her own heart were hollow, as if any semblance of emotion had fled. Despair sounded in its depths. She'd hoped to appeal to the part of him that once—as a boy—had found something to have a light heart about.

What a fool she'd been to think she could touch the softer parts of him in any way. He had no softer parts.

Yet even as she thought that, she couldn't push from her mind his mother's inscription. She gestured to the book he still held in his hand. "Your mother seemed to have great hopes for you. She would have thought such anger to be beneath you. I'm certain of it."

His face hardened as he tossed the book atop the shelf nearest him. "I don't want to talk about my mother, Mina. I want to talk about you. Why this sudden concern for my feelings, my future?"

When her eyes shifted away from his, he answered himself. "Ah, yes. I suppose my feelings and future are tied up with yours. Do you think you can doctor my anger like you do a disease and then I'll set you free? I'm sorry, sweetling, but the cure for my illness won't come from your hands." He went on more fiercely. "Nothing will suffice for me except that Tearle be given justice. Even your telling me the truth won't affect that. It will merely give me more weapons with which to fight him."

A lump formed in her throat at his words. "It won't give you any weapons, for I've nothing to confess that could help you destroy Sir Pitney."

Without warning, his hand went to her chin. He tipped it up with one finger until her eyes met his. "Yes, but do you have things to confess to him that might destroy me? That's my other, perhaps more important concern."

"What on earth could I tell him? You've never done anything illegal or—or really immoral in my presence."

He smiled, a hint of triumph in the curve of his lips as his hand fell from her chin. "Quite true. So why do you constantly accuse me of being some sort of monster and reprobate?"

She saw the noose closing around her, saw him dogging her on every point until she tired and took up another one. He was as slippery as glass, never really acknowledging the truth of anything she said, not when it would mean allowing her to go free. She recognized his manipulations . . . yet she couldn't stop them.

"Any man who would hold an innocent woman prisoner against her will—"

"Against her will? You have a choice, a very simple one. Tell me all I wish to know and you needn't stay one more minute."

"The choice is untenable," she said in a stiff voice.

He surprised her then by chuckling. "Why is it that whenever the choice concerns me, you find it 'untenable'? For a Gypsy, you're amazingly particular. You won't take my gold, nor my protection, nor even my trust. In fact, there seems to be only one thing you will take from me."

The words were out before she could stop them, spoken in the most tremulous of whispers. "What is that?"

At the bold, searing glance he shot her then, a slow heat began to mark a wide path through her body. She blushed. He took only one step toward her, but it put him agonizingly close.

"This," he murmured. Then once again he tipped up her chin, but this time to receive his kiss.

The moment his lips touched hers, she backed away slightly, but he caught her about her slender waist, pressing his lean, hard body intimately against her resisting one as his mouth, more inviting and warm than she'd ever felt, enveloped hers.

He didn't force so much as coax her into responding to his challenge, thrusting his tongue teasingly against her closed lips until she felt weak with dense longing.

She pulled her hands up between their bodies, trying to press him away, but he grasped one hand in his and brought it forcefully back around until he held it captive behind her back. Then he did the same with the other, until both sets of hands rested on the swell of her bottom.

She should have felt outrage at the strength that held her arms behind her. But the hands laced through hers were so warm she couldn't think past the sensations they startled within her. When his thumbs began to caress the soft skin of her hands, a trembling began in her nether regions that she could neither understand nor deny.

Then mercilessly he renewed his assault on her lips. As he tantalized her with kisses, a profound pleasure such as she'd never experienced began to seep through her, enriching her blood with a glorious tingling heat. Still, she desperately fought the pleasure, fought the temptation to surrender her mouth totally to his.

"Open to me, my Gypsy princess," he murmured as he tore his mouth from hers, his breath a warm whisper across her lips. "Let me taste more of your sweet sorcery."

The asking undid her. Like a morning glory opening its petals to the sun, she allowed him to plunge his tongue deeply inside her mouth.

After that moment, sanity left her. His hands loosened hers, but her freed arms crept of their own accord around his waist. His body pressed her back against the bookshelves, but she did nothing except strain eagerly against him.

He groaned as he felt her compliance. His hands cupped her derriere, pulling her against the full length of his firm body. His mouth made forays to other parts of her, to her closed eyelids, her delicately sculpted ear, her bared neck.

Then, while bombarding her senses with his kisses, he moved one hand up to cover her breast. She felt it even through the boned bodice she wore, and the shock of feeling his hand in such a private place dampened her ardor instantly as she realized how wantonly she'd behaved.

What had possessed her? she wondered shamefully as she tore her lips from his, her eyes wild with sudden alarm.

"Don't," she hoarsely whispered, her fingers wrapping around his wrist as she tried to pull his hand away.

His hand moved, but upward to the knot of her linen scarf. As his fingers worked the knot loose, he murmured, "Just this once, Mina, don't play the lady with me. I prefer to have the enchanting Gypsy in my arms just now."

She watched in increasing apprehension as he pushed the loose ends of the scarf aside, baring the generous swell of her breasts above the low square neckline of her bodice and chemise.

She blushed a deep pink as his eyes boldly raked over the curves revealed to him. "I can only be what I am, my lord," she said, snatching the ends of the scarf and attempting to tie them back.

He brushed her hands aside, silencing her protests so effectively with a kiss that she didn't at first notice his fingers slip behind her back to tug at the laces of her gown. Only when she felt the bodice loosen did she realize just what liberties he was taking with her. She grew frantic when his hands then reached up to slide the top of her gown and loose chemise off her shoulders and downward.

She tried to yank the edges of her clothing back into place, but he captured her hand and pressed it hard against his chest. He wore no coat or waistcoat, only a thin holland shirt. Through the material, underneath her very palm, she could feel the rapid beating of his heart.

His gaze pierced her. "What you are," he said in a low, gravelly voice, "is the first woman to make my heart race in quite some time. Like it or not, sweetling, you're too tempting for me by half. And I'm not the sort of man who resists temptation."

She opened her mouth to retort, but he refused to let her, kissing her again with a near savage eagerness that banished all thought from her mind. His tongue swept her mouth until she felt weak as a newborn kitten. Faint moans of pleasure sounded in her throat. Had those cries come from her? she wondered dimly, knowing that they had.

Then his hand slipped up to cup one sweetly rounded breast. At the shocking intimacy of it, she went still as stone. "This isn't right, my lord," she protested as she tried futilely to dislodge his hand. She would have backed away, but he already had her pressed up against the bookshelves, incapable of moving.

"You've called me debauched often enough. Surely you wish me to live up to the name," he said wickedly as he began to tease her nipple with the rough pad of his thumb.

"I—I—" she stammered, but the traitorous pleasure stealing through her seemed to stop any words of protest from leaving her mouth.

She scarcely cared that his eyes fastened intently on her face, a glint of satisfaction in them as she felt her control slipping. His hand cooled her warm breast and the sensation that shot through her as he kneaded her breast gently beneath his palm was like the first relief from summer that a fall wind offers.

When a low sigh fled her lips, his eyes lost their confident gleam as a darker emotion burned within them. "Oh, God, you could send a man into madness," he murmured gruffly. Then he lowered his lips swiftly to her mouth, brushing soft kisses first on her lips, then her neck, and then down the sensitive flesh above her breasts until he found the crest he sought. In abandon, his mouth hungrily began to caress the prized place.

As his tongue flicked over her nipple, she buried her fingers in his wavy hair, holding his head closer, so she could feel more of the exquisite sensations he engendered. All care for what he might be was temporarily forgotten. Gone were any maidenly objections, any sense of how a lady should behave. She only knew his caresses and kisses made her feel like she'd drunk an unknown liquor. She felt sweet and burning and a little wicked all at once, like the full-blooded Gypsy she was supposed to be.

The time to stop had come, she knew, but as his hand slipped up to caress her other breast and a slow, deep yearning began to creep through her, forcing her to the very brink of oblivion, she knew she could not, or rather would not stop him. That vague realization brought with it a teasing feeling of anticipation that overwhelmed any vestiges of her inborn prudery she might have been tempted to indulge.

His mouth left her breast. His eyes locked with hers as he parted her legs with one of his, then lifted and settled her astraddle his knee, placing his foot on the shelf behind her. A strange urge to wrap her legs around his thigh and hold on tight assailed her. He felt the tensing of her legs, and gave her a long, lingering kiss. Then he lowered his leg so she slid enticingly down his hard thigh until her feet rested on the floor.

"This way, sweetling," he said urgently, lacing his fingers through hers and leading her to the thick fur rug that lay by the hearth in the midst of the spacious library. Numbly she followed him.

He knelt there, pulling her down beside him, and began with great impatience to undo the ties of his shirt. She watched spellbound as inch after inch of dark, hairy chest revealed itself.

His hands had just moved to his breeches, eliciting a shocked gasp from her, when a knock at the door sounded. He suddenly stilled his movements. Instantly she blushed and he frowned. Neither of them said a word. At their continued silence, the knock sounded again.

His frown deepened. "I'll be with you presently," he barked out and reached once again for Marianne.

"My lord, it won't wait," urged a voice Marianne recognized as William's.

"If you value your life, it will," Garett growled, his fingers moving swiftly to the ties of Marianne's skirt.

But for Marianne, that knock was like a sign from God, bringing her back to the present and her sense of right and wrong.

"No," she whispered, pushing Garett's hands away.

"My lord, I really must speak with you," William urged beyond the door, though Marianne could tell he spoke with great trepidation.

With an oath, Garett stood to his feet. "Don't move," he commanded her, then strode for the door.

She ignored him, fumbling with her gown as she tried desperately to cover herself before Garett reached the door. But as he neared it she heard another voice that made her increase her efforts with something akin to panic. The voice of her aunt.

"I told you to wait downstairs—" Marianne heard William say.

"I wanted to see him now, not a century from now," Tamara retorted hotly.

Before Garett could even reach for the door handle, the door burst open and Tamara marched into the room.

"Milord, I've come to protest that—" She stopped short at the sight of Marianne kneeling in the midst of the rug, her scarf lost who knew where, her gown loose about her waist and barely covering her, and one hand held guiltily at her throat.

Shame washed hotly over Marianne. She glanced at Garett to see if he, too, felt embarrassed beyond all countenance, but his face was expressionless, though a muscle worked in his jaw.

"What's she doing here, Will?" Garett asked, his eyes coldly assessing Tamara. The calm in his voice and the nonchalant way he stood unashamed before them all told Marianne volumes. He was a nobleman for whom dalliances with maidens of lower class were not unusual. For him, their encounter had most certainly been a mere trifle, nothing to destroy his self-assurance.

But damn it, she was *not* a tavern wench that he could tumble at will! A lump of anger formed in her throat as she rose as gracefully from the rug as she could.

Tamara had remained shocked into silence until she saw her niece rise and recognized the hurt anger in Marianne's expression. Then Tamara turned on the earl, her entire body quivering with rage.

"Will told me some barbarous story about your suspicions. You claim my niece is a spy for this Tearle creature, is that it? You say that's why you must keep her here.'' She flashed a disparaging glance William's way. "A pox on that! I see your true intentions. That foolish tale was but a ruse to keep me from her while you took your pleasure!''

Tamara glared at Garett, daring him to deny her accusations.

Swiftly William stepped forward, placing his hand on her arm. "I wouldn't lie to you, Tamara. I didn't dream—''

She pushed his hand away. "I told you this would come of it. I told you he'd ruin her.''

It was Marianne's turn to be alarmed. Not for a moment did she wish her aunt to believe she'd given herself completely to Garett. "Nothing happened,'' Marianne asserted, moving a few steps toward her aunt. "He didn't . . . I mean . . .''

"What your niece is so eloquently trying to say,'' Garett bit out, "is that you interfered before I could 'ravish' her.''

"But something did happen,'' Tamara said, gesturing to the rug.

"Perhaps,'' Garett conceded. "Your niece is old enough to choose a lover if she wishes.''

Marianne cringed, then grew angry at his blunt and misleading words. How dare he imply that she, a lady of the realm whether he knew it or not, would take him for a lover! If he hadn't been so . . . so . . . seductive, she'd never have let him touch her. She opened her mouth to retort, but he went on, oblivious to her anger.

"I warn you, Tamara. What happens between your niece and me is no longer your affair. Until she—or you—tells me who she is and why my uncle knew her and her parents, I intend to keep her here. She's made her bed and now she must lie in it. And there's not a damn thing you can do about it.''

Tamara's mouth gaped open in incredulous disbelief, but her outrage was nothing compared to Marianne's. A coldness seeping through her bones,

Marianne spoke in the most distant, ladylike voice she could muster.

"I didn't choose you for a lover, my lord, so disabuse yourself of that notion. Regardless of what you believe, you've given me no choices in this matter. I certainly didn't choose to be your prisoner, nor to be accosted and mauled simply because I was here. You are the one who's made my bed, which is why I won't lie in it."

His eyes narrowed on her as she stood there, her every limb quivering with defiant anger.

"Mauled you, did he?" Tamara broke in. "Well, it won't happen again. Come, Mina." She turned to the door. "This time we are leaving Lydgate, and the sooner the better, I say."

Garett stepped quickly forward, placing himself between Tamara and Marianne even as Marianne boldly started to follow her aunt to the door.

"You may leave whenever you wish, Tamara," he said with quiet nonchalance, "but your niece stays here."

Marianne's gaze flew to her aunt. Tamara's body shook with fury. "You're a runagate, milord, despite your great title. But you shan't have your way. Not this time, by my faith. I'll go to the constable first. I'll tell him what you intend to do. I'll trumpet your crimes about the town until—"

"You won't do any such thing," Marianne said sharply. The last thing either of them needed was to draw the constable into it. If pressed, the constable wouldn't dare take their side against the earl. He might even decide it was safer to reveal Marianne's identity than to risk Tamara's forcing the issue. Much as Marianne hated being Garett's prisoner, she dared not risk his finding out who she really was.

Tamara looked at her niece in surprise. "Don't you want him to release—"

"Of course I do. But Gypsies aren't generally loved in Lydgate," she said pointedly, hoping her aunt would realize how dangerous it was to threaten Garett. Although the townspeople had given Marianne safe harbor, they might not be so eager to champion her if it meant incurring the earl's wrath. When a glint of comprehension showed in her aunt's eyes, Marianne felt a measure of relief. "The constable won't listen to a Gypsy. He might even expel you if he feels you're a troublemaker. We wouldn't want that, would we?"

"No, love, you wouldn't," William interjected, obviously alarmed by the turn the conversation was taking.

Let her go to the constable, Will," Garett remarked. "Let her see how much good it does. Then again, perhaps I should go—"

"No!" Marianne cried in alarm. At Garett's grim smile, she flashed her aunt a warning glance and continued, "No one's going to the constable, especially not you, Aunt Tamara."

Tamara's mouth snapped shut, but her expression showed she didn't like being made to listen to reason. "I can't permit him to force himself on you—" she began.

"He didn't force himself on me this morning," Marianne cut in, a slow blush suffusing her face. Much as it pained her to tell the truth, she couldn't let her aunt believe a lie, or Tamara would challenge the earl until she forced him to act. Marianne didn't even want to consider what Garett might do then.

Tamara, never one to submit graciously to circumstances, muttered, "I don't like it."

"Neither do I. But if his lordship—" She put as much sarcasm into the word as possible, as she cast a glance his way. "If his lordship can refrain from . . . from his lascivious attentions, I suppose you and I can endure this arrangement until I demonstrate I am no more a lackey of Sir Pitney's than is William."

Garett stood there with his arms folded across his half-bared chest, his eyes boring into Marianne's. Amusement was in their depths, though his cold half smile made it clear his anger hadn't entirely waned.

"I'm more than willing to do as Mina wishes," he announced as he let his eyes deliberately rest for a brief moment on her bodice, which hung shamelessly low.

Marianne turned her gaze abruptly from his face, instantly aware he was remembering the wanton way she'd returned his "lascivious attentions."

"I'd rather you did as I wish and not as my niece wishes," Tamara said, showing she, too, lacked confidence that Marianne could resist Garett's attempts at seduction.

Tamara's words proved too much for Marianne. "Your niece can take care of herself," Marianne asserted boldly. "Don't worry. His lordship may think confining me here will intimidate me into confessing imaginary crimes, but time will prove my innocence. If he insists on keeping me here, I'm willing to give him that time."

And without losing my virtue, Marianne told herself firmly. She'd prove them both wrong, particularly Garett. She'd unsettle him the next time he attempted to seduce her. After his insults today, she wouldn't be so gullible, so foolish as to let him even touch her.

"Then we've all agreed?" William said tactfully, keeping a cautious eye on both his master and the two women.

The stony silence in the room was his answer.

Chapter Twelve

Stone walls do not a prison make,
Nor iron bars a cage;
Minds innocent and quiet take
That for an hermitage.
    —Richard Lovelace,
      "To Althea from Prison"

Marianne sat shaded by an apple tree in the garden, her slippered feet tucked up beneath her and her muslin skirts spread out on the grass. The volume of *Love's Labors Lost* lay on her lap. Her finger was thrust between two of the pages to keep her place while her mind wandered.

Idly she glanced at the burly man who stood a few feet away, pretending not to guard her even though that was exactly what he was doing. Garett certainly knew how to choose the men he employed. This one had served with Garett in Spain and was completely loyal to his master. She flashed him a smile, but he ignored her, continuing to stare straight ahead.

Shrugging, she opened the book, then closed it again with a sigh. Today, reading Shakespeare's play had merely depressed her. Why hadn't she ever noticed before the somber note it struck? As one of the characters said morosely in the play's final scene, "Our wooing doth not end like an old play: Jack hath not Gill." And indeed the hint of despair in his words mirrored her own.

Two weeks had passed since Garett had announced her imprisonment—two dreadfully long, taxing weeks. First had been the death of the wounded soldier. She'd hoped he would say something more that would prove to Garett she didn't work for Sir Pitney. On the other hand, she'd feared what else the soldier might reveal. Still, she'd tried valiantly to save him. And despite everything, his death had shaken her. He'd died without ever speaking of her again. With his death, part of her hopes had also died, leaving her to wonder how she'd ever convince Garett to release her.

His death had affected Garett, too. Garett had become more distant than she'd ever seen him. Being at Falkham with him had been like being with some of her father's more serious friends. At times he ignored her completely. When he did notice her, his grim manner and intense scrutiny of her disturbed her no matter how she fought to disregard it.

She closed the book, staring forlornly off into space. Single-minded. That had been Garett during the past two weeks, obsessed with his purpose. Sometimes she thought he, too, wanted to forget that day in the library, so he could concentrate on more important matters.

When he spoke to her, which wasn't often, it was to tell her, oddly enough, about improvements to the estate or to ask her opinion in some matter of housekeeping. He kept the conversation polite and innocuous. But the ever-present Sir Pitney lay between them, the unspoken topic.

Worst of all, every day began with the one question she wouldn't answer—who was she? Every time he asked it she wanted to retort with the same question, for sometimes she truly didn't know who he was, either. Was he a calculating manipulator who'd betrayed her father and cost him his life? Was he a heartless, debauched Royalist who'd cavorted with the king in France? Or was he the winsome boy of her youthful imagination?

One thing she knew for certain. He was capable of turning her body into a raging inferno of emotion whenever he touched her. Even two weeks later, the thought of his stirring kisses made her tremble all over and an unfamiliar aching start up in her breasts where he'd caressed her. She didn't understand the feelings he summoned in her. Nothing had prepared her for them.

Her mother had once tried to describe for her the pleasures to be found with a man. But being a rather quiet person, her mother had spoken in such vague generalities that Marianne hadn't been able to relate any of the descriptions to anything in her own experience.

Marianne knew, of course, what a man and a woman did together in the privacy of their chambers. Years of studying medical books and helping her parents do their doctoring had taught her those things. She'd never given the act itself much thought, however, for it had all sounded very messy and shameful and somehow odd.

But these days she seemed to give it a great deal of thought. All the time. At odd moments, she wondered what it would be like to have Garett's body cover hers, to feel those magical hands of his touching all her private places, to have his demanding lips move lower to . . .

"Fie!" she said aloud, angry with herself for having such terrible thoughts. She'd vowed not to let him seduce her, yet here she was doing the seducing for him! Worst of all, her mind had trouble remembering who he was whenever her body started remembering how he'd touched her.

Not that she didn't have enough reminders of who he might be and the role he might have played in her father's imprisonment. Tamara reminded her often enough during the daily visits Garett allowed her.

Yet somehow everything Marianne believed to be true when she was away from Garett disappeared when she was with him. He could be a cold man, that was certain. And well she knew his hatred for his uncle. Never, however, had she seen him actually violent or deceptive. To his tenants and servants, he was an authoritative but understanding master. Even to the soldier he'd shown glimmers of compassion, bringing the man a priest when at the last the soldier had asked for one.

Still, she couldn't bring herself to trust Garett, knowing how thoroughgoing was his hatred for Sir Pitney. She couldn't be sure how far he might have gone to regain Falkham House and thus thwart his uncle.

Well, it did no good to go over and over the same questions in her mind, she told herself. She never seemed to find any answers that way. Besides, she wasn't going to sit in the sunshine on such a beautiful day and let him control her thoughts. Bad enough that at present he seemed to control her future.

Resolutely she rose to her feet, dusted off her skirts, and began to walk back toward the house, the volume of Shakespeare tucked under her arm.

Then she heard horse's hooves approaching her. She swung around, expecting to see Garett. Instead, an unfamiliar man on horseback pulled up short in front of her.

The moment she saw him she guessed he was a Cavalier, but one of a more outrageous stamp than Garett. He dressed boldly, with rich velvet on the edges of his cuffs and a flowing silk cravat tied about his neck. His waistcoat and coat were cut of a fine royal blue cloth, not too delicate for riding, but also not coarse. His hair showed his class more than anything else, for the golden curls grew past his shoulders in unabashed shining glory.

Despite his fashionable appearance, however, there was no mistaking he was a friend of Garett's, for his jaunty, arrogant stance and twinkling eyes reminded her of Garett in his better moments.

"Well, what have we here?" he asked with a sly grin. He doffed his plumed hat, exposing more of his gold mane, then dismounted from his horse and handed the reins to the groom who ran from the stables to take them.

Seeing him up close, she realized he was like Garett in yet another way—he towered over her, his broad shoulders filling out his doublet.

His eyes traveled brazenly over her. "As usual, Falkham has exquisite taste. Tell me, nymph, what forest did he find you in?"

She nearly groaned aloud. Why must all these Cavaliers be so incredibly handsome but so terribly wicked? He was worse than Garett, if that was possible.

A gleam in her eye, she met his speculative gaze with cool contempt. "Probably the same forest where he lost you," she responded tartly, annoyed with the way his eyes assessed her attributes as if she were a horse for sale. " 'Tis an odd thing about forests—they're excellent for slipping away from one's more ill-mannered friends."

Her caustic comments didn't seem to bother him in the least. He chuckled and shook his head. "Quick-witted, too, I see."

"Yes, and I have all my teeth, in case you're interested." The sarcasm in her voice was unmistakable.

"Now I've offended you," he said with a mock frown. Stepping forward, he snatched her hand up and kissed it. "I truly didn't mean to offend such a divine creature."

A low voice answered him from behind her. "Be careful, Hampden. This 'divine creature' is a Gypsy. She might just cast the evil eye on you if you persist in annoying her."

As Garett strode forward to stand beside Marianne, she glanced up in surprise, for she hadn't heard him approach. Garett was frowning, but the twinkle she glimpsed in his eyes told her she'd guessed correctly. Hampden was clearly a friend.

Hampden straightened, a look of genuine pleasure crossing his face as he saw Garett.

"I can believe she's a Gypsy," he told Garett, giving Mina a quick wink. "She's already put a spell on me." When Garett's expression turned threatening, Hampden grinned broadly. "I take it she's put a spell on you as well?"

The fading of amusement from Garett's face and his open displeasure delighted Marianne. She was so pleased to see Hampden elicit some emotion from Garett she couldn't resist teasing him herself.

"Oh, sir," she protested to Hampden, "surely you

know Lord Falkham can't be bewitched. Not the un-flustered, infallible Lord Falkham. Women have no effect on him at all, particularly women like me."

"Women like you?" Hampden asked, eyes twinkling as Garett continued to glower at them both.

"Yes. Women who don't jump at his every call." She sighed theatrically. "Alas, but I'm too strong-minded for his tastes. He prefers a woman he can intimidate, and I'm afraid I don't suit."

At that, a ghost of a mocking smile touched Garett's lips. "Mina's not being quite fair, Hampden. 'Tis not strong-mindedness I dislike but deliberate defiance."

When Marianne's eyes began to flash, Hampden suddenly clasped her around the waist and pulled her outrageously close to him. "Well, I like a little defiance, myself. Meek women are dreadfully tedious. Give me a saucy wench any day."

Marianne was beginning to regret having encouraged Hampden when Garett stepped forth and smoothly disengaged his friend's arm from around her waist.

"I'm afraid you'll have to find your own 'saucy wench,'" he growled as he rested his arm casually across her shoulders. "This one is under my protection."

"So that's the lay of the land, is it?" Hampden said with obvious delight.

Marianne bristled, tiring of their game and angry that Garett implied she was his mistress. It was bad enough to have to play the Gypsy when she was really a well-bred lady. But to play his mistress—

"No, that's *not* the lay of the land. Lord Falkham knows perfectly well I wouldn't be here if I could help it." With a frown, she pulled away from Garett and stalked to the house, ignoring them as they followed close behind her.

" 'Tis good to see you again, Falkham," she heard Hampden say. "And in such good company, too."

"I'm not certain I'm so glad to see you," Garett replied dryly. "You've only been here a few minutes and already 'my company' is ready to slit my throat. Your throat, too, I might add.''

Hampden chuckled. "I don't believe it. That face and figure alone are lethal enough to slay a man. What would she need with a knife?''

Marianne whirled around, planting her hands on her hips as she surveyed the two men, who both seemed to be laughing at her.

"If you gentlemen are quite through discussing my person, you might consider choosing another topic for conversation. One that's not quite as rude, perhaps.''

Hampden grinned wickedly. "I can't help it, pigeon. You're such a refreshing change from the women at court. Most of them simper and smirk and never let you know what they're really thinking. Only the king's mistresses exhibit your . . . er . . . strongmindedness.''

"Mr. Hampden!'' she stated in outrage, hardly believing he'd just compared her to the king's mistresses. Oh, how she'd like to give him a piece of her mind. But she couldn't, not without telling him who she was.

"I meant it as a compliment,'' he said sincerely, shocking her even more.

"Mr. Hampden, if you're going to—'' she began.

Garett cut her off. "Lord Hampden, to be precise,'' Garett corrected helpfully, unable to hold back the amusement in his expression. "I suppose I should have introduced you properly. Mina, this is my dear friend, Colin Jeffreys, the Marquis of Hampden, who served out part of his exile with me in France.''

She glanced from Garett to Hampden disbelievingly. "Another one! Just what I need—another wretched nobleman to torment me!'' She rolled her eyes heavenward, and the men laughed. Glowering at them both, she pivoted and headed off toward the garden.

"Where are you going?'' Garett called out.

"Where I don't have to put up with arrogant lords!'' she retorted.

Both men chuckled, enraging her further.

"We'll see you at dinner then?" Hampden shouted, but she didn't answer.

Garett watched her go, his eyes following the slight sway of her hips. Then he looked for the guard. Only when he spotted his man standing alert at the edge of the garden did he relax.

"My God, Falkham, where did you find her?" Hampden asked when she'd passed out of sight.

"You might say she found me," Garett answered, turning back toward the house.

Hampden followed. "Is she really a Gypsy? I can scarcely believe it. For all her sauciness, she's as graceful as any lady."

Garett smiled grimly. That was precisely the problem. Mina had this inexplicable ability to turn the most sordid task—like sewing up a man's wounds—into a polite encounter at a royal dinner. She had a true lady's approach to life. If anything unsavory came her way, she managed to turn it aside before it besmirched her.

After that day in the library, he'd been prepared for anything. Although their kiss in the library hadn't been instigated by her, she'd responded quite openly to it. Then when her aunt had discovered them . . . well, clearly Mina had attempted to use his actions to gain her release. So he'd been expecting her to try deliberate seduction, perhaps as a way of getting him to set her free. Instead she'd confounded his expectations—she'd done nothing the least bit scandalous.

That day in the library, he'd thought she was enamored of him. In fact, he'd counted on it in his attempt to gain the truth from her. He'd tried coldness, and he'd tried barbed questions. He'd been unrelenting in his inquisitions, but it had gained him nothing. Not only had she kept silent, she hadn't even seemed affected by his distant air. That irritated him most of all.

"Is she?" Hampden repeated, bringing Garett out of his thoughts.

"Is she what?"

"You know. A Gypsy."

"Yes. Partly, that is. She's a nobleman's bastard."

Hampden nodded. "That would explain it."

"Explain what?"

"Why she's here under your protection."

Garett looked at his friend and debated whether to tell the truth. He decided the truth would be the best thing. After all, Hampden might just know something that could help Garett uncover Mina's true identity. And her relationship to Sir Pitney.

"Actually she's here under my protection for another reason. I suspect she works for my uncle," he stated baldly.

Hampden stared at him in incredulous disbelief. "The hell you say! That pretty thing? She has a sharp tongue, I'll admit, but she doesn't strike me as Tearle's preference. He likes his women soft and weak." Hampden frowned. "From what I hear, he particularly enjoys seeing them cower before him. Your Mina doesn't seem to cower before anyone."

"I know," Garett admitted. "But it's possible he knows something about her and is using it to force her into doing his bidding."

Hampden snorted. "If you say so. But I can't see it."

"Well, she didn't come to you in a black cloak and mask, claiming she was scarred by smallpox and so had to hide her face. Nor did you witness her being recognized by Tearle's henchman before he died. Nor have you seen—"

"Enough. I see your point." Hampden rubbed his chin, his brow creased in thought. "Perhaps you're right, but I still can't believe it. Her eyes are those of an innocent. A devastatingly attractive innocent, I might add."

Garett gritted his teeth at the gleam in his friend's eye. "Don't even consider it, Hampden. You can't have her. Regardless of what I suspect she is, she's still under my protection."

Hampden cocked one eyebrow. "Ah, but is that all she's been under? I mean, if you haven't bedded her—"

"Don't even think it," Garett repeated emphatically, suddenly annoyed by Hampden's insinuations.

Hampden laughed. "I can't help but think it, old friend, since it bothers you so. I must admit I'm glad I came to visit. I've been here only a few minutes, and already I'm having the time of my life."

Garett gave his friend a long, steady look. "I think, Hampden, this is one time I won't be sorry to see you leave."

"You may be right," Hampden said without a trace of remorse. "You just may be right."

Marianne nervously smoothed out the simple muslin cloth of her dress, the best gown she had at present. Her other gowns had been left behind in London, not that she'd have dared to wear them anyway. What she wouldn't give to appear at dinner in one of her more elaborate gowns. She'd never cared much about them . . . until now, that is.

Now she was to dine with two men who already thought the worst of her character. She shrugged. A gown wouldn't change their minds about that.

This gown was perfectly serviceable, even attractive. Not that it was nearly appropriate for dining with an earl and a marquis. The only lace adorning it was that of her chemise, the edges of which peeked up above the low neckline. Yet the amber yellow cloth seemed to pick up the gold in her hair, which she'd carefully dressed as best she could in artful curls. Tamara had made the gown especially for her when they'd first come to Lydgate. Unlike the gowns she'd borrowed from her aunt to wear most of the time, it exactly fit her petite figure, accentuating her slender waist and delicate build.

Still, it wasn't satin, nor did it have an embroidered stomacher such as she'd always worn. Oh well. It wasn't as if she had a choice. She had to make the best of what she had. She could have refused to join them for dinner, but even that choice had been taken from her. Garett had made it quite clear he expected her at dinner. His exact words had been, "Hampden will think I'm deliberately hiding you if you don't come."

Hampden. The mere thought of having to match wits with him and Garett again all evening started butterflies in her stomach as she approached the dining room. The moment she entered, she sought the one man's face who wouldn't make her nervous. William's. Over the past two weeks, William had become something of a friend to her. He'd kept her informed about Tamara, and Tamara about her. She knew why he showed so much interest—his attentions to her aunt had been blatant—but she didn't mind. At least he didn't suspect her of being in Sir Pitney's employ.

So she looked to him for reassurance when she entered. Only after he'd smiled did she venture a glance at Garett and his friend.

She wished she hadn't. The two of them stood next to the fireplace, talking animatedly together. They didn't notice her enter at first, so she had time to observe them. To her chagrin, they both looked stunningly attractive.

Hampden she noticed first because of the burgundy coat he wore. His breeches were burgundy as well, though his stockings were a modest black. But lying over his coat was the wide lace collar of his snow-white shirt, down which his richly curled blond hair cascaded. To her surprise, however, he didn't look the fop, probably because he filled out the shoulders of his coat as she'd never seen another man at court do.

Then she turned her eyes to Garett and sucked in her breath. Why must he always look so cursedly handsome? As usual, his clothing was modest—dove-gray breeches, black silk stockings, and black coat with the cuffs of his dove-gray waistcoat emerging from beneath the coat. No lace adorned his collar. And his hair. Oh, his glorious hair with its subdued waves and roughly cut edges that made him look like some sort of highwayman. She never ceased to feel a thrill of danger when she saw that wild hair of his.

As if he felt her eyes upon him, Garett turned, his gaze locking with hers. Slowly his eyes dropped to her bodice, then lower to her tightly cinched waist. He frowned, cutting her more deeply than anything he'd said that day. No doubt he disapproved of her simple dress.

As she stood there, suddenly inexplicably embarrassed to be dressed so poorly, Hampden, too, saw her and his eyes brightened. He let out a low whistle. "Ah, Falkham. If I'd known what you hid out here in the country, I'd have come to visit sooner."

Garett's hand so tightened on the glass he held that Marianne feared it would break. "Why haven't you worn that dress before, Mina?"

Her feelings even more wounded by his words, she lifted her chin and smiled at Hampden. "I saved it for a special occasion. But I can see now I . . . I couldn't hope to dress properly for a dinner with two noblemen. So if you'll excuse me . . ."

Abruptly she left the room, a lump forming in her throat. And she'd thought she looked beautiful! How could she have forgotten how richly the nobility dressed for dinner? Had she really been playing the Gypsy so long she no longer knew what to wear to a simple dinner in the country?

She hadn't even reached the stairs before Garett came after her. As she began to mount the stairs, he strode up beside her and stayed her with one hand.

"God, Mina, I didn't mean—"

She turned to look at him. "It doesn't matter, Garett. You have your dinner with Lord Hampden and I'll—"

"No, you don't understand." For the first time since she'd met him, Garett seemed truly ill at ease. "There's nothing wrong with what you're wearing, except that it's . . . it's . . ."

"Too common?" she asked pointedly.

His eyes dropped meaningfully to her bodice. "No. Too provocative."

"What?"

"I know it's what all the ladies wear in London," he hastened to say. "By their standards it's not really even daring, but—but damn it, I couldn't stand having Hampden see you looking so ravishing.''

Relief flooded through her as she looked at his face and realized from the way he avoided her gaze that he told the truth. All this because Garett was jealous? And of Hampden, no less. She didn't know whether to be thrilled or furious.

''Come back to dinner, sweetling,'' he murmured. ''Please. I wouldn't have you miss dinner just because I . . . I made a foolish blunder.''

Two surprises in one night, she thought, blessing Hampden for having come to visit. Garett had been jealous *and* he'd admitted to a blunder. Well, the least she could do was show him she appreciated his truthfulness.

''Fine,'' she said with a regal air.

His face instantly relaxed and with a cordiality she'd seldom seen, he escorted her back into the room.

Hampden waited for them, an expression of blatant amusement on his face. After Garett seated Marianne and the two men sat down, Hampden remarked jovially, ''I'm glad my surly friend here convinced you to return, Mina. Dinner would have been dreadfully dull with only the old bear there for company.''

Marianne glanced at Garett, who struggled to keep his face expressionless.

Immediately she fell in with Hampden's teasing. ''Lord Falkham's not so awful,'' she said, lifting her glass of wine. ''But if you're hoping for interesting talk at dinner, don't ask him about his estate improvements. Not unless talk about crops interests you.''

She glanced at Garett, who lifted one eyebrow. ''I'm sure Mina would prefer to talk about her father,'' he said pointedly, any composure he'd lost earlier having been regained.

Why couldn't he ever let up? She forced back a sharp retort, deliberately sipping her wine to give her time to think. ''Actually, my lord, I'm far more interested in how you and Lord Hampden met.''

There. A safe topic. The two men could reminisce,

and she wouldn't have to worry about parrying Garett's verbal thrusts in front of a stranger.

Hampden took up the gauntlet almost gleefully. "We met in a stable," he said with a smile that broadened when Garett frowned. "You'd never know it now to look at him, pigeon, but our friend Falkham was a stableboy once."

"Really?" she asked, leaning forward with genuine curiosity.

"Yes. He and I both were. In France. We worked for a dreadful old count who enjoyed having two of the English nobility in his employ."

Garett, a stableboy in France? "Why?"

"Why did we work for the count or why were we in France?" Hampden asked.

"Why were you stableboys?"

"Oh. We couldn't do much else. When we first arrived in France, Falkham was only thirteen, and I sixteen. We weren't the only English nobility there, you must realize, and not a soul wanted us."

"But what about the king?" Marianne asked. "Surely he championed you. Surely he helped his countrymen."

Hampden smiled mirthlessly. "Ask Falkham about the king."

Marianne's gaze flew to Garett.

Garett idly toyed with his food. "The king was as destitute as we were, Mina. He could scarcely keep food on his own table, much less help us fill our bellies."

"But they told us—" she began.

"Who? Cromwell and his men?" Garett spoke, a tinge of bitterness creeping into his voice. "What else were they to tell you? The Roundheads preferred to let the English think their king was enjoying himself and living richly in France. In fact, he went from acquaintance to acquaintance, gathering what help he could, always trying to find someone to help him finance another little uprising against Cromwell. His Majesty gave us his friendship, but he could give us little more.

Then later he went to Spain. We couldn't afford to follow him.''

"Until you joined the Duke of York's army," Hampden put in.

"Yes." Garett turned somber again.

Marianne suddenly wished the conversation hadn't taken this turn. Hampden wouldn't let him sour the evening, however.

"It wasn't all bad in France," he told Mina. "Remember Warwick, Falkham?''

Garett's eyes lost their faraway look, a faint smile crossing his lips. "How could I forget? He always stank of burned wool, particularly when it rained.''

"He still does, from what I hear," Hampden responded, then turned his gaze to Marianne. "Warwick's coat caught fire one day. We managed to put it out, but the edges were quite charred. Warwick had as little money as the rest of us, so he cut off the charred parts and continued to wear the coat.''

Hampden chuckled, but Marianne couldn't join him. She found the story more sad than funny.

"Don't worry, the man didn't suffer during the winter," Garett said, correctly guessing the source of her concern. "He kept as warm as any of us. If anything, we were the ones to suffer from smelling his smoky coat. We used to say, 'Where there's smoke, there's Warwick.' ''

Hampden joined Garett's laughter and after a moment, so did Marianne.

"There was little enough to laugh about in those days," Hampden said, his eyes momentarily losing their gleam of amusement. "The count and your uncle saw to that.''

"Sir Pitney?" she asked in confusion. Sir Pitney had been in England, unaware of Garett's existence. How could he have hurt Garett?

"You didn't tell her about the letters, about the men Tearle sent to kill you?'' Hampden asked Garett.

Garett shrugged, but in that gesture was a trace of defensiveness. "I'm sure she knows.''

"I didn't know!" she protested, then turned to Hampden. "Sir Pitney knew that Garett lived?"

Hampden's face turned grim. "He may not have known at first, for apparently a servant boy accompanying Garett's parents and killed with them was mistaken for Garett and buried as the Falkham heir. But he knew well enough later. Garett sent him four or five letters with proof of his identity. Sir Pitney ignored them. Then one day a man came calling for Garett. Fortunately for Garett, he found me instead, and I was armed and more than able to defend myself." He smiled. "I'm afraid Sir Pitney's man didn't return to England."

At Garett's determinedly aloof air, Hampden quipped, "And the count complained because I'd gotten blood on his floors."

Marianne felt all at sea. Why hadn't Garett told her all this? Yet she knew why. His stubborn pride made him think he shouldn't have to explain himself to anyone.

"Tell me about this count," Marianne urged. It suddenly seemed so important to her to learn the whole truth of why Garett had returned from France an embittered man.

"Ah . . . the count," Garett remarked, taking a piece of hard bread and breaking it in half with a loud snap.

"The count was the only man to truly make me hate the French," Hampden said. "I'm sure Falkham agrees, since he tormented Falkham more than he did me. He hated Falkham. Used to call him *'le petit diable.'* "

Marianne could easily understand how Garett might have gained the nickname of "little devil." "At least he enabled the two of you to fend for yourselves. Without him, you said you might not have found work."

"I'm not sure that would have been so awful," Garett said smoothly, lifting his glass to his lips and sipping his wine. "We might have been better off begging in the streets of Paris than working for the count."

Hampden chuckled. "True. After all the beatings the old man gave us, 'twas a miracle we lived to manhood."

Marianne paled, putting down the spoonful of soup she'd been about to lift to her lips. "Beatings?"

"Actually," Hampden said, "mine weren't as bad as Falkham's."

Garett remarked dryly to Marianne, "That's because the count knew Hampden provided his best source for court news in the city. Hampden always talked the count out of beating him by offering to tell him some juicy bit about his enemies no one else knew."

Hampden smiled. "Ah, yes. I bribed him with gossip. I'd almost forgotten. Of course, it helped I was sleeping with his enemies' wives." He shrugged. "At the time, it seemed like a better way to get funds than working in the stables."

Marianne's face turned a brilliant red as she stared down at her soup.

It was Garett's turn to chuckle. "So that's how you got your tales. I used to envy you that ability to find out all of the Paris court's secrets. Now that I know how you got them—"

"You wish you'd been old enough to get a few of your own?" Hampden finished helpfully.

Garett gave him a mock threatening look. "No. I wish I'd put you onto the count's wife. Then you might have lightened the load for both of us."

"That sour-faced old—" Hampden broke off as if he suddenly realized a lady was in the room. "Well, that wouldn't have worked. She hated you as much as her husband did. It was that ridiculous pride of yours. Neither of them could stand it. They thought to teach you, a barbarian Englishman, a lesson. They loved your being a penniless nobleman. But it really infuriated them you never broke under their beatings."

Marianne's throat constricted at the thought of a thirteen-year-old Garett being beaten. She couldn't help asking the next question. "Were . . . were the beatings terrible?"

Garett shot Hampden a warning glance as he said, "No."

As Marianne looked questioningly at Garett, Hampden raised both eyebrows. "Oh? I take it you haven't shown her your back or she'd know that was a lie."

"Hampden, it's time we moved to more suitable topics of conversation," Garett stated flatly, his eyes fixed on Marianne, who turned paler by the minute.

Hampden shrugged, then launched amiably into a witty description of the latest news from the English court. But Marianne no longer listened. Images of Garett being beaten flashed before her eyes, killing her appetite.

She was beginning to understand why he hated his uncle. Sir Pitney could easily have spared Garett those hard years, but he'd knowingly let his nephew remain penniless in France while he plundered the boy's estates. What had Garett said? *Only pain makes you strong.* Now she knew what had happened to the light-hearted boy his mother had spoken of. That boy had been killed, first by his parents' death and then by his uncle's betrayal. In his place stood Garett, bitter, angry, and full of vengeance.

She glanced at Garett as he questioned Hampden idly about the court. It was a miracle he'd withstood it at all—so many heartbreaks, so many betrayals. Then there'd been his years as a soldier, years he refused even to talk about. No wonder he distrusted her, she thought in despair.

Her thoughts were interrupted when she vaguely heard Hampden mention her father's name. Careful not to show her emotions, she began listening to the conversation again.

"Winchilsea's death set the town buzzing," Hampden said as he cut a piece of meat. He put it in his mouth and began to chew while Marianne tapped her foot impatiently beneath the table. "You see," he continued after a moment, "no one really believed Winchilsea to be guilty until he was killed. The man was a high-minded noble with no reason to attempt to kill His Majesty."

"You think he was innocent?" Garett asked, his expression oddly shuttered. "From what I'd heard, the poisoned medication stayed in his possession from the moment he left his home. Clarendon seems to believe he might have been working with the Roundheads, and I'm inclined to agree. It's just the sort of thing they'd do."

Hampden shrugged. "Who really knows? But I'm not convinced. Still, I'm one of only a few who've given him the benefit of a doubt. After he died, the gossips immediately tried and convicted the old man. What else could they do? No one remained to prove him innocent. His daughter had killed herself and—"

"Daughter?" Garett asked, his eyes narrowing.

Marianne felt cold fear grip her heart at this mention of herself, and her hands began to shake. She thrust them quickly beneath the table.

"I didn't know Winchilsea had a daughter," he stated, his eyes turning to her.

Forcing a measure of calm into her expression, she met his gaze squarely. "Yes, he had a daughter. But they say she killed herself when she heard of his arrest."

"That's right," Hampden said as Garett continued to stare thoughtfully at Mina. "Threw herself into the Thames. They even seemed to think she might have been somehow involved in the poisoning."

"Did they really? Tell me, what was this daughter like?" Garett asked coolly.

Hampden sat back in his chair and wiped his mouth with his napkin. "What did I hear about her? Oh, yes. Something of a recluse. Quite plain, from what I was told. She shut herself up in her rooms all day and wouldn't come to court. I gathered she didn't like people at all."

Blatant lies, Marianne thought with a twinge of anger. Yet in this case, she should be glad the court gossip was as patently false and cruel as usual. She kept her face carefully expressionless, aware that Garett digested Hampden's bit of news with interest.

She decided she'd best keep Garett from connecting Lady Marianne with the Gypsy Mina. "Actually," she said, forcing a smile, "Lady Marianne was painfully shy."

"You knew her?" Garett asked, his gaze boring into her.

"Of course. I told you I knew her parents."

"Why didn't you mention her before?"

She made a dismissive gesture with her hand. "Why mention her? I didn't know her well. She kept to her rooms, spoke to no one, and rarely interfered with my life at all. I'm not surprised she killed herself," she continued in a nervous rush. "She was the type to faint at the slightest sign of violence. She couldn't stand blood. I can imagine how horrified she must have been to hear about her father's arrest."

Hampden snorted. " 'Twas a silly thing to do, absolutely illustrative of the fainthearted ladies at court. I could never see you, madam, throwing yourself into the Thames at such news. I wager it would never even enter your mind to do so."

"Not Mina," Garett said wryly.

She merely glanced at him, relieved beyond measure when she noted no trace of suspicion in his expression. Between Hampden's half-truths from court and her own fabrications, she'd kept him from guessing the truth. Thank God for that. Yet how long could she keep him from finding out who she really was?

Hampden began to speak of the king's newest mistress as Garett made outrageous quips about what Hampden said. Marianne listened, her anxiety growing with every word she heard. Their conversation confirmed what she'd already gathered from their talk about exile in France. Both men knew His Majesty very, very well.

Now more than ever she realized how important it was to keep her identity secret from Garett. He clearly believed her father to be guilty and could easily believe the rumors about her involvement. If he ever learned who she was, he'd be quick to turn her over to the king, that was certain. She squeezed tightly the napkin in her lap.

He mustn't learn. No matter what the cost, she must keep that secret from him.

Chapter Thirteen

"Trifles light as air
Are to the jealous confirmations strong
As proofs of holy writ."
—Shakespeare,
Othello

"Where's your beautiful prisoner?" Hampden asked
as he and Garett strode out the entrance to Falkham
House. "Didn't she wish to see me off?"

"Mina's been out all night, caring for one of my
tenants' wives who's in childbirth," Garett replied
nonchalantly as the groom walked Hampden's horse
up.

The wicked grin that instantly crossed Hampden's
face irritated Garett enormously.

Hampden glanced sideways at Garett. "Caring for
one of your tenants' wives? That's a soft heart for you.
Such a pity she couldn't be here. I was so looking
forward to snatching a parting kiss."

Only with the greatest effort did Garett keep his face
expressionless. "Then thank God she's not here. It
saves me from having to protect her from your ill manners."

Hampden's loud snort told Garett what he thought
of that. "Ill manners! 'Tis not my manners that bother
you, and well you know it. You hate she's taken a
liking to me. And I to her."

"You take a liking to every woman who crosses your
path," Garett retorted, heavy sarcasm lacing his
words.

Hampden grinned. "Perhaps. But your little pigeon intrigues me more than most."

Garett knew Hampden was baiting him. Still, it was a struggle not to lift Hampden forcibly onto his horse and send him off to London with a good kick to the seat of his breeches.

Hampden apparently interpreted Garett's somber silence correctly. "How couldn't I be intrigued by the woman who's managed to raise your ire . . . and your possessiveness? Never thought to see you act that way with a woman. Till now, you've been too busy with your plans for vengeance to take serious interest in any woman."

Garett had reached his limit with Hampden's remarks. Unable to hide his irritation any longer, he retorted, "If you're waiting for an explanation of my behavior, you might as well take yourself off to London. How serious I am about Mina is none of your damned affair."

At Hampden's broad grin, Garett realized just how truly obsessed with Mina he sounded. He gave Hampden a self-mocking half smile. "Besides, you think making me jealous will torment me, but it won't work."

"Why not?" Hampden asked, amused.

"For two reasons. First, I know you flirt with her only to annoy me and not because you truly feel for her."

Hampden suddenly grew serious. "And second?"

Garett's eyes searched his friend's face. When he found there only genuine interest, he decided to tell the truth. "As much as your overtures to her may irritate me, they're only a pinprick compared to the torment I live with every day she's here without my being able to touch her."

Hampden sighed, then shook his head. "You're a fool not to have made her yours the moment you laid eyes on her. As for your first reason—you misread me, Garett. If I thought I had a genuine chance of stealing her affections from you, you can be certain I'd attempt it."

"You've never fought me for a woman before."

Hampden shrugged. "True. And I probably never will. Unless, of course, you decide to toss away Mina's heart. Then, dear friend, I'll be more than glad to step in and comfort her."

That image disconcerted Garett tremendously. He looked away, his face growing stiff. "You assume she has a heart, and that she'd offer to me whatever heart she has."

Hampden said nothing at first, mounting his horse and taking up the reins. Then he stared down at Garett, his normally laughing green eyes for once solemn. "Oh, she has a woman's heart, that's certain. If you weren't so determined to delve into her 'deep, dark past,' you'd realize it. As for whether she'd offer it to you—that remains to be seen. I imagine that if you continue to persecute her, she won't. That would be a great loss for you, Falkham." He gave a half smile. "And a gain for me."

Without another word, Hampden turned the horse and prodded it into a trot. He didn't even glance back as he rode away.

As Garett watched Hampden leave, he felt an odd relief he'd never felt before. His claim to Hampden that making him jealous wouldn't work hadn't been entirely truthful. Hampden's overtures to Mina had cut like a knife, primarily because she'd responded with teasing, flirtatious comments of her own.

During Hampden's entire four-day stay, Mina had met every one of the marquis' wicked sallies with an impudent rebuff that delighted Hampden and annoyed Garett. Garett hadn't liked the way they teased each other. He tried to tell himself it was all harmless. For Hampden, he knew it probably was. Hampden wouldn't do more than tease. For all his words, Hampden was loyal to his friends and had instantly recognized that Garett wouldn't like his toying with Mina.

Garett wasn't so certain of Mina, however. With Hampden, she became a sparkling, delightful creature. Her cares seemed temporarily forgotten. Her ebullience had occasionally extended to Garett, but he knew he'd have missed it entirely if Hampden hadn't drawn it out of her. Garett hated that most of all. Inexplicably he wanted to be the one to make her eyes shine.

He turned back to the manor, angry with himself for letting it all matter so much to him. Of course he wanted her. That was easily understandable. Her sweet form and daring spirit would entice any normal man. But he mustn't let his desire for her become more than that. He mustn't allow her to wheedle her way into his emotions, or she'd take advantage of it. She was a Gypsy, he reminded himself, possibly one with ties to that most unsavory of characters, his uncle.

He suddenly saw her in his mind's eye, standing with her hair unbound and floating in the breeze and explaining to Hampden the difference between a toadstool and an edible mushroom. Her expression had been like that of Garett's tutors when they'd earnestly delighted in the subjects they taught. Her expression hadn't been that of a calculating spy.

Abruptly Garett wheeled away from the house and strode for the stables. He was tired of not knowing who she was, of guessing at her past. He'd played this game with her long enough and gained nothing. It was time to change his tactics. His questions and gruff manner hadn't intimidated her. The aloof demeanor he'd put on, his physical distancing, hadn't wounded her as he'd hoped it would, making her throw herself into his arms and confess all.

Instead it had thrown her into the arms of Hampden. No more, Garett determined as he saddled Cerberus. She'd responded to his kisses before. She'd do so again. Somehow he'd seduce her into telling him her true identity.

He grinned wryly at himself as he led the horse from the stable, mounted him, and rode off toward the tenant's home to which Mina had gone. Seduce her into telling her secrets. What an absurdity! If he was honest, he'd admit he couldn't touch her and keep his wits about him at the same time, much less maneuver her into telling him anything of substance. He might as well not pretend otherwise.

No, he thought as he spurred the horse on, he didn't want to seduce her for anything more than the most basic reason—that he desired her. That was certainly reason enough.

He quickened the horse's pace, suddenly very eager to see her again now that Hampden was gone, leaving them alone together again. As he neared the tenant's house where she'd gone, he heard the soft, mewling cries of a newborn.

Good, he thought, soon she'd be ready to return with him. He dismounted, his gaze going to the guard who always accompanied Mina.

"I take it the babe has come?" he asked.

"Aye." The guard, as usual, was a man of few words.

Garett joined him beneath the shade of the tree, watching the entrance to the small, neat cottage.

"How long ago?" Garett asked. Mina had left Falkham House shortly after dinner the night before.

"No more than an hour."

So she'd only just finished. She was sure to be exhausted. He fell silent, his eyes trained on the entrance to the cottage.

He hadn't waited long when Mina stepped out of the door to stand on the stone threshold. With a weary sigh, she brushed several damp tendrils of hair away from her face. Slowly she rubbed her arms and shoulders to get the blood moving in them. As she did so, her gaze went to the guard. Then she saw Garett.

He smiled at her. "Is the babe well?" he asked gently.

She nodded, her shoulders slumping. "Yes. Just like a man, he was stubborn, even during his birthing. I had to work a bit to coax him from the womb."

"Is the mother well?"

Surprise momentarily flickered across her face. "Yes. Maggie is quite well, under the circumstances."

"Good. Her husband's a fine man. He'll need her to care for the child when he tends his fields'."

"I imagine, my lord," she said dryly, "that he'll need her for other things as well. Believe it or not, some men depend on their wives for more than just raising their children."

Garett chuckled softly. "True. Inasmuch as this is their second child in less than two years, I suspect Maggie's husband won't give her long before he depends on her for . . . ah . . . more important duties."

Clearly affronted by his blatant innuendo, Mina glared at him, although her flesh pinkened considerably. Then she tilted up her chin as if to say she was far too dignified to respond to his comments.

Again he chuckled. She pretended not to notice, but didn't quite succeed in keeping a fraction of a weary smile from curving the edges of her mouth.

The tenant whose wife had just given birth stepped out of the doorway at that moment, capturing Mina's attention. So caught up was the fellow in the moment that he didn't seem to notice Garett leaning against the tree beside the guard.

"I'm coming," Mina told the man, and started to go back into the cottage.

"Nay," the tenant protested. "Time for you to go 'ome and get yer rest. You done enough already. Maggie's sister 'as come. She'll take care of me wife right and proper now that you did the 'ard part." He clasped Mina's hands enthusiastically. " 'Tis a beautiful babe, and we're mightily beholden to you for it. Yer mother'd be right proud of you, she would, if she was alive to see it."

Garett's eyes immediately swung to Mina's face. She blanched slightly, although she didn't disentangle her hands from the tenant's. She jerked her head ever so slightly in Garett's direction, but he caught her gesture. Following her movement, the tenant looked toward Garett.

He, too, blanched when he saw Garett standing there. He dropped Mina's hands and began to wipe his hands nervously on his breeches. "P'raps I'd best go back and see 'ow Maggie's comin' along," he muttered as his face turned almost purple. Quickly he walked back into the cottage, nearly tripping over the threshold in his attempt to get himself out of sight.

A long silence ensued, during which Mina refused to look at Garett. After a moment, she murmured, "I-I'd best look in on her myself," and turned back to the cottage.

"No," Garett said with authority, pushing himself away from the tree. "You're exhausted. Anyone can see that. You should return with me to the manor."

"I'm not—"

"You heard the man. They don't need you here any longer today." He strode quickly to her side.

She looked up at him as if trying to determine what he thought of the tenant's words. When Garett merely matched her stare, she turned her face away, her shoulders stiffening.

"Whatever questions you have," she said with quiet dignity, "you might as well ask now."

Garett cocked his head slightly in the direction of the guard who stood under the tree, listening to every word. Mina sighed, then let Garett lead her to his horse. He swung her up into the saddle, mounting behind her.

As they moved off, he could feel the rigidity in her body as she attempted to hold herself apart from him.

"Well?" she asked when they were a good distance from the cottage.

Though her broaching the subject was a bold thing to do, the anxious note in her voice betrayed her fear of him. Good, he thought coldly. It was about time she realized how serious he was about discovering her identity.

"It's an odd circumstance, don't you think, that everyone seems to know your blessed mother?" he asked.

She remained silent a moment. "No, not at all. We Gypsies are like mice. We creep into everyone's barns at one time or another."

He lowered his head until his mouth was beside her

ear. "*Creep* is a good choice of words, Mina. Now tell me exactly when you and your mother first 'crept' into Lydgate. From what you'd told me, I thought you'd only come here after she and your father had died."

She jerked her head forward, away from his lips. She remained silent, but he could see her hands clench the pommel.

"This refusal of yours to tell me what I wish to know has become very tiring for me," he said in a clipped tone of voice.

Her back became ramrod straight at the steely tone underlying his voice. "For me, as well."

"Until now I've kept this between you and me. And your aunt. That has gained me nothing. I think it's time to call upon the good citizens of Lydgate."

"Wh-what for?" she stammered, her shoulders not quite so erect.

"It's clear they know much more than they've led me to believe. I doubt they'll be as reluctant to spill the truth when the neighboring earl brings pressure to bear on them."

She twisted in the saddle to look back at him, gazing up into his stony face with alarm glittering darkly in her eyes. "Why must you involve them? They don't know anything of use to you. Don't you think they'd have told you if they'd known anything suspicious about me?"

He halted the horse and dropped the reins. His hands closed over her shoulders. "No, I don't. I've seen how they are with you, Mina. They're so grateful for your medicines and healing hands that they'd not deliberately cause you harm."

Wordlessly she thrust her hands up between his arms and pushed them forcefully out, off her shoulders. Then in one quick movement, she lifted her leg over the horse's head, slid to the ground, and began walking toward the manor. He rode beside her, watching as she trod the road with deliberation, her upper body shaking with some deep emotion.

"If they know nothing," he asked her as he kept

pace beside her, "why do you fear their involvement?"

"I don't fear it!" she insisted, her chin lifting stubbornly. "But I think I know you quite well by now, my lord. You'll ask them over and over questions they can't answer. When they don't tell you what you wish to hear, you'll torment them until they say something—anything—to placate the angry earl. Who can say what a people beset with fear will blather?"

The sheer logic of her argument raised his ire to even greater heights. "What do you think I wish to hear?"

She stopped short, crossing her hands over her chest and staring up at him with hurt and anger in her eyes. "I think that's quite clear, don't you? You want to hear I'm truly the despicable, devious Gypsy you believe me to be." Now she was crying, fat tears rolling down her pale cheeks. "If your . . . your damnable suspicions are confirmed, then you can truthfully say at last that no one in this world can be trusted. Then you can make your dark plans, fashion your dear tortures for your uncle, and no longer worry that perhaps—just perhaps—you were wrong!"

She wheeled away from him and the horse, ducking her head down to hide her tears. Then she began to walk away from him as quickly as her skirts would allow.

He leapt from the horse and was beside her in but a few strides. Grabbing her arm, he jerked her about to face him. Some part of him deep inside cringed at the sight of her reddened eyes and damp cheeks.

"Can you really think I want to be proven right?" he demanded, his anger still riding him hard. "I assure you I don't. I want nothing more than to lose myself in your tempting arms. But I can't. Not without knowing the truth. I don't have it in me to trust quite that much."

"I know," she murmured, tears coming afresh. "And even though I know why, I can't bear it." She lifted her face beseechingly to him. "Why not just release me, Garett? If you wish, you can send William to escort me and my aunt to the Channel. We'll leave England—'twas what my aunt wished to do in the first place. You'll never have to see us again. You can have your battles with your uncle without once fearing I'll somehow betray you to him.''

Garett lifted his hand to her cheek, brushing away a tear as he fought to get words past the lump that seemed to have formed in his throat.

"I can't do that, either, sweetling," he ground out. Slowly he trailed his fingers down the side of her face, over the smooth curves of her neck, and then to where her hair tumbled over the scarf of her bodice. Abruptly he dropped his hand.

Then he groaned and snatched her about the waist, pulling her roughly up against his rigid, fury-hardened body. "I can't let you go without knowing it all . . . without knowing you completely."

"That will never be. . . ." she whispered, turning her face to one side. He ignored her pleading protest. His large hand cupped the back of her head, forcing her face back to his. Then he swooped down, pressing his lips against hers with all the fierce fervor he'd suppressed for two weeks and more.

She tried to twist away from him. When that didn't work, she brought her hands up against his chest to push him away, but he merely clutched her closer, his lips locked hungrily to hers.

One of his hands moved down to grasp her soft bottom, lifting her up against him so he could feel her softness against his hardening loins. She gasped, and he deepened the kiss instantly, his tongue entwining with hers. Her hands stopped pressing frantically against his chest. Slowly they crept upward to clasp his neck.

Only then did he move to take his lips from hers. He rained gentle kisses over her face, tasting the salt of her tears as he did so.

She began shaking her head. "You—you can't simply kiss it all away. . . ." she whispered breathlessly.

He pulled back slightly, lifting his hand to caress her cheek and then to wind a long lock of her dark golden hair around one finger. "That's true enough. But while I kiss you, I can forget it's all there."

"I can't," she said, one tear trailing from her eye.

"My God, don't cry anymore, sweetling!" The sight of her tears made something clutch at his heart. He caught the lone tear on his thumb, then sucked it off, his eyes fixed on hers as he did so. "Your sorrow can be taken away as easily as that," he murmured. "Just tell me what I wish to know."

She shook her head violently. "That would truly begin my sorrow."

He buried his fingers in her hair, forcing her head against his chest. "Nay. You underestimate my desire for you. I have the power and wealth to give you whatever you wish—a cottage of your own, rich gowns, enough gold to make you content for a lifetime. And if it's fear that keeps you silent, I can shield you from whomever you fear . . . especially Tearle. Just trust me."

She threw back her head, her hazel eyes as wild and tormented as those of a hunted fox. "Trust you? The only one I fear is you!" The words seemed torn from her.

Then with a sob she thrust him away, lifting her skirts and running toward the manor.

He started to follow her, then stopped himself. Her parting words hammered into his brain. She feared him. He knew she disliked his being a nobleman and disapproved of his obsession with vengeance. He'd realized early she'd do almost anything to keep him from knowing her secrets. But truly fear him? That he hadn't known. Until now.

Slowly his disbelief turned to anger and then fury. He'd never hurt her once. He'd imprisoned her, true, but with silken bonds. She'd slept in a soft bed between clean sheets and eaten the best food she'd probably tasted in her life. Yet she fought his touch like he was some scarred beast. Why? Just because he was nobility? Or was there some other mystery in her past that made her dart from him?

He clenched his fist so tightly his fingernails dug

into his hands. She feared him, did she? A little Gypsy who'd probably run from soldiers and constables all her life feared him—the one man who hadn't tormented her in any way except to desire her.

Well, then. Perhaps it was time he gave her something to fear.

"A pox on you, old fool!" Pitney Tearle shouted at the moneylender who sat with stony countenance behind the oriental lacquered desk. Pitney stared in anger at the man's treasures, which were crammed into every inch of the cramped room. The sight merely increased his fury. He pounded his fist on the desk. "How dare you refuse my business? How dare you, a . . . a heretic like you!"

The moneylender's eyes were cold. He didn't flinch, but met Pitney's gaze squarely. "I no longer lend to Christians," he replied with a shrug. "One minute they claim usury is a sin, and the next they want to reap its rewards."

Pitney sneered. "It's Papists who hate usury, not good, solid Englishmen. I hate Papists and all they believe in, so you've nothing to fear from me on that score."

The old man crossed his arms over his chest. " 'Tis all the same to me. Christian dogs. I'll have no part of it anymore."

Pitney threw himself at the man, grasping him by his coat to lift him off his chair. "You've lent to me before, and you'll lend to me again. You still lend to Christians every day, old man. Don't you deny it! I know of three 'Christians' at least that you regularly lend money to."

The dark eyes that stared back at him showed no fear. "I lend to whomever I choose. I choose not to lend to you."

Pitney dropped the man in the chair with a curse and turned to pace the room impatiently. He wondered if he shouldn't try another tack. Intimidation clearly wasn't working. And unfortunately, he needed money badly. The fortune he'd gained in stealing Garett's lands was running out. Pitney had spent part of the last of it helping his friends with their fruitless attempts to regain a footing in the new government. The rest had been given over to a cause equally unsuccessful—trying to eliminate his nephew once and for all.

His handsome face twisted into an expression of murderous hatred. If only he could rid himself of Garett. Then he truly would inherit the Falkham estates. Never again would he be at the mercies of moneylenders. He scowled at the old Jew. This was the fifth moneylender or merchant he'd tried. No one wanted to lend him money—Jew or gentile alike.

"Why?" he muttered aloud.

"What?"

"Why won't you lend to me?" he asked, whirling around to pin the man in his chair with a baleful glare.

No one else would tell him and evaded his questions. But this one smiled. "You're a poor risk. 'Tis not likely I'll see my money back from you."

Pitney shook, rage filling him at the sheer audacity of the man. "I've always paid you back before. You've made a great deal of money off me, you fool."

"That was before," the man replied smugly.

Pitney planted both fists on the desk in front of him and leaned down to stare into the moneylender's face. "I'm a friend of Cromwell's son. I know half the merchants in this city, and every one of them will attest to my reliability."

"Aye? Then where are your fine friends? They don't want you now they know how you got your money. No one loves a thief—even one in fine clothes."

Cold dread gripped him. What particular stories had the man heard about him? Until now Pitney had been careful to cover his tracks well in any of his more unsavory endeavors. No one who couldn't be trusted had been left behind to tell tales. Even with his treachery toward Garett, he'd been cautious. He'd burned the letters Garett had sent. He'd made very public the funeral of the boy who'd taken Garett's place in death. When Garett had returned, Pitney had pretended to be as surprised as any.

Now he wondered if all his caution had been for naught. His temper overriding all other concerns, he rounded the moneylender's desk and thrust his fist in his face. "What do you mean, calling me a thief?"

"I know you to be one. Everyone knows. You'd be surprised how easily rumor runs its merry dance through our fair city. And who better to hear it than I, who lend to nobleman and merchant alike? Everyone knows about you, Sir Pitney." The man defied him, his eyes sparkling with malice. "Before, when you were having my fellow Jews burned for witches, no one dared cross you—especially not someone like me, with a family to feed. But now . . . now even your friends know your treachery to your own nephew. And they know he won't let it pass. So no one fears you. Including me."

Pitney cuffed the man viciously with all his might, but the old man merely winced and rubbed his jaw. Then he continued to level that accusing stare on Pitney.

"Strike me if you like," he grumbled. "But except for the paltry power in your fist, you've no other strength now. Your power is gone. Your nephew has seen to that. And I'll die under your fists before I lend you one more pence."

"Damn you and all of them!" Pitney cried, whirling on his heels and striding from the room.

He found his way down the rickety stairs with difficulty, his knees shaking with his anger. Now more than ever he must see the threat from his nephew eliminated. Until now Pitney hadn't really feared him. True, the king's championing of Garett had struck him with dread, but Pitney had felt certain he could salvage his reputation in the eyes of the court. Much as he'd hated to grovel before the king he despised, he'd done so, hoping to counteract the effects of whatever lies Garett had told His Majesty.

But the rumors that accompanied Garett hadn't been so easily squelched. The exiles had spoken of Garett's sufferings. That pompous rake Hampden had without a qualm proclaimed Pitney a scoundrel and a villain.

Then came the merchants who'd heard the stories and suddenly seemed loath to do business with Pitney.

He knew Garett couldn't prove a thing, but that was the worst of it. Garett didn't have to. Innuendo and rumor did it all. And if Garett ever suspected who had really brought about the deaths of his parents . . .

Pitney ground his teeth together in renewed determination. Garett must be rendered ineffective somehow. Or wiped from the face of the earth.

Chapter Fourteen

"Loyalty is still the same,
Whether it win or lose the game;
True as a dial to the sun,
Although it be not shined upon."
—Samuel Butler,
Hudibras

William gently led Marianne through the doorway of the finest inn in Lydgate. Although she was fully clothed, she felt wholly undressed. She hadn't appeared publicly in town without her cloak and mask since the first day she'd returned from London. It felt odd to have her face and identity so exposed, even though she knew she was among friends.

Quickly she scanned the ale room for some sign of Garett. She hadn't seen him since early that morning when he'd come to the tenant's cottage. After their encounter, he'd returned to the manor, but only to retrieve his horse, which had found its way back to the barn. Then he'd ridden off to Lydgate.

Hours later, William had come to her as she'd paced the floors in her room. All he'd said was that his master had sent a message ordering him to accompany her to Lydgate.

Now her heart beat in triple time, because she knew why she was there. After all, Garett had promised just that morning to involve the townspeople in his search for the truth. The thought of what he was planning sent a nervous shudder through her.

William's hand on her arm loosened slightly. "You mustn't let the master terrify you, miss," he whispered in her ear, leading her toward a chair near the hearth. "It's just that he don't know quite what to do with you. You and your aunt being so close-mouthed and all . . . well, that bothers him. He don't like not knowing what to expect of those around him."

Was that ever an understatement, Marianne thought to herself. "Where is he?" she whispered back as William beckoned her to sit.

William cocked his head upward. "We're to wait till they send a message down for us to go up."

Inwardly she groaned. The town council used one of the upper rooms of the inn whenever they had matters of significance to discuss. If Garett was upstairs, it could only mean he'd brought together the council. She shouldn't be surprised. He'd threatened to do as much if she didn't tell him who she was.

Still, a surge of anger hit her as she thought of what the townspeople were to suffer on her behalf. The anger wasn't all for Garett, either. She was furious with herself for ever getting embroiled with him in the first place. If she'd only acted more meekly the first time they'd met . . . if she'd just been more careful when she'd treated his wounds . . . if—

Chastising herself now served no purpose, she reminded herself. Instead she should prepare for what was to come and think about what she should do.

She could always save the townspeople from being put in the precarious position of standing for her against the powerful earl. She twisted her hands in her lap. To tell the truth—that she was Sir Henry's daughter—was one choice. If she did, she must be prepared to go to prison for it. She didn't doubt that Garett, with his loyalty to the king, would follow his duty and give her over to the soldiers.

Yes, telling the truth would endanger her, that was certain. Yet that alone didn't worry her. The truth would endanger so many others as well—her aunt, Mr. Tibbett, any townspeople who'd knowingly aided her. If she came straight out with the truth, who could know the outcome? Given the choice, the council might prefer to keep her secret, rather than risk the wrath of the king himself. At least if they said nothing, Garett could never really prove they knew all along who she was.

She gritted her teeth in frustration. No matter what she did, it would be the wrong thing. Stay silent, and she forced the townspeople to make a difficult choice. Tell the truth, and she might endanger them more than if she'd kept silent.

Of course, she might be trusting far too much to their loyalty. They might just reveal her secret to the earl the moment they saw her face. They might claim her mask had kept them from knowing the truth.

No, she thought to herself, her heart aching. They'd never betray her so easily. Nor could she betray them by telling all at the first sign of trouble. The only safe way seemed to be to keep silent and hope everything worked out.

Shifting uncomfortably in the hard chair, she glanced around the room. The guarded looks occasionally thrown her way by the other patrons of the inn were, for the most part, kind and encouraging. She took some comfort from that.

Then her eyes locked with a stranger's gaze. She knew she'd never seen the man before in Lydgate. She would have remembered him, for he had a sly coldness about him that instantly put her on her guard. He nodded his head with blatant insolence, and she suddenly had the disquieting feeling that he knew her.

She leaned over to William, who sat beside her. "Who is that man there, the one wearing a sword?"

William followed the direction of her gaze. His expression grew wary. " 'Tis Ashton. M'lord believes he's one of Tearle's men. He's the villain who stabbed that soldier attempting to burn the fields."

Unconsciously she shivered. She'd often wondered who was responsible, and now she knew. Garett hadn't lied—it was another of Tearle's men. "Why does the earl let him roam freely about Lydgate?"

"Oh, Ashton serves his uses. You can be sure he only reports to Tearle what m'lord wishes him to report, though the cursed bastard don't know it."

When Marianne looked at William questioningly, he dropped his eyes from her gaze.

A sudden suspicion twisted her insides. "That's why he's here, isn't it? To see me and tell Sir Pitney your master has caught me!"

"Nay!" William protested. Then he clasped her hand. "I'm sure m'lord has nothing to do with his being here. The bastard's a curious devil, though, and most probably heard about the council's being called. He's here to see what the whole thing's about, that's all."

Marianne couldn't quite believe him. It wouldn't surprise her if Garett's intentions were to send another of his oblique, vindictive messages to Sir Pitney. Her stomach began to churn. Regardless of whether Garett had intended this Ashton to see her or not, if the man was like the soldier and recognized her, the results would be the same. Either he would immediately tell the earl her identity or he'd pass his knowledge on to Sir Pitney. Who knew what Sir Pitney might do with that knowledge?

She cast a furtive glance Ashton's way again, but this time his head hung low over his mug of ale.

Please, God, she prayed. *Don't let him recognize me.*

After a few minutes, the man stood and left the inn. She didn't know whether to be glad or terrified. William watched the man go with a scowl on his face, which only distressed her more.

Stop it! she told herself. It did no good to worry these things over and over in her mind. She had enough trouble at the moment without inventing more. With determination, she forced herself to forget Tearle's man.

Yet she couldn't help but continue to worry, not just about Tearle's henchmen, but about Garett and his persistence. Earlier she'd suspected, even feared, that Garett had played a part in her father's arrest. But did that really make any sense? Garett was truly the king's man—she knew that now. He would only have planted the poison that implicated her father in the crime if he'd been certain he could keep His Majesty from taking it and if he couldn't be caught.

But had he planned such an elaborate plot, solely to paint her father the villain and thus regain his lands? Garett did seem obsessed with Falkham House, and he did seem to resent her father for having bought the estates. But his hatred of Sir Pitney overrode all of those. Somehow she believed Garett would more likely have plotted his uncle's ruin than her father's, for his uncle was the one truly at fault for his exile.

What's more, her heart told her Garett couldn't have done it. The same man who'd expressed concern for his tenant's well-being couldn't have also ruined her father. She couldn't believe it. Then who? Sir Pitney was a possibility, since he, too, had wanted Falkham House. He, too, had hated her father. Still, would he have done such a thing, knowing that his nephew had returned with a stronger claim to the estate than Sir Pitney had ever had?

She thrust those speculations aside. What concerned her more now was Garett's obsession with her identity. After Garett's long, hard fight to return to England, he wouldn't jeopardize it all by harboring a fugitive. If he were ever to find out . . .

She shuddered. During the long wait, she found herself growing more and more fearful, and the more fearful she grew, the more she cursed Garett for his insistence on knowing who she was.

At last the innkeeper descended the stairs and approached her and William. Avoiding her eyes, he bent over and muttered something in William's ear.

William nodded his head and stood. "We go now," he told her, offering her his hand. She took it and rose on shaky legs.

But as she passed through the room toward the stairs, she realized everyone watched her, waiting anxiously for her to give some sign that she was in control, that their futures were safe in her hands. Mustering all her courage, she forced an expression of calm assurance to her face. With as much of a regal air as she could manage, she climbed the stairs, determined that the people of Lydgate could count on her.

In far too short a time, she and William stood at the entrance to the room where the council met. William knocked stiffly, and a voice bade them enter. The first thing Marianne saw when she walked in the room was Garett standing at one end of a long table, his eyes focused not on her, but on the men who watched her enter. Then she noticed the other men's faces. Clearly Garett hadn't told them what the meeting was for, because surprise and acute distress were the dominant expressions.

Mr. Tibbett grew red, as he always did when he found himself in an uncomfortable situation. And the mayor, whose foppish mannerisms were the joke of the town, began to focus all his attention on smoothing the lace trim of his petticoat breeches as if in so doing he could make her disappear.

She felt their anxiety so acutely it was difficult to keep from bolting out of the inn and taking her chances that Garett wouldn't find her.

Slowly Garett's gaze came to rest on her face. His eyes sought to pierce her defenses, to frighten her into blurting out whatever he wished to hear. She matched his gaze with a scathing one of her own. Devil take him, she'd show him that no matter his tactics, she wouldn't be intimidated.

Finally Mr. Tibbett broke the silence by clearing his throat loudly. Then, with a glance at his still silent fellow members, he ventured to say, "My lord, perhaps it would be of use if you could tell us what this is all about?"

Garett turned his eyes from Marianne to Mr. Tibbett and went right to the point. "As you know, from the time I returned to Falkham House and reclaimed my inheritance, I've taken an interest in Lydgate. After all, my tenants come to your town for their goods, their amusements . . . their ale."

One of the men laughed nervously.

Garett went on. "As your closest neighbor, the one upon whom you depend for so much of your livelihood, I am careful to look to your needs as well. But now it is I who need *your* help.''

"How's that, my lord?" asked the mayor, leaning forward, his hands now nearly frenzied in their nervous movements.

"You all know Mina," Garett said, gesturing toward her. "You may not . . . ah . . . recognize her without her mask, but you know her all the same. From what I understand, she's taken care of many of you and your children.''

Murmurs of assent filled the room.

"Although she's a Gypsy, I realize she's been a great help to this town. It has come to my attention, gentlemen, that Mina isn't what she appears to be. She's admitted to me that she has noble blood, something you may not have realized.''

Marianne saw the look of alarm in the men's faces. Quickly she asked, "Must you proclaim my bastardy to the world, my lord? I fail to see how that suits your purpose.''

Garett frowned at her, a muscle in his jaw twitching as he attempted to keep his displeasure from showing. The men at first seemed confused by her statement, but then they quickly realized what she must have told Garett. Some of them relaxed.

"In any case, she has a past not typical for a woman who's a Gypsy," Garett continued, his eyes giving her such a quelling glance that a tremor of fear shook her. "Recently, it's also come to my attention that she has connections to my uncle." His gaze left her to sweep the men in the room. "You all know very well what my uncle sought to do, how he took my lands when I was in exile. But you may not know that since I've returned, he's also sent men to burn my fields and even to kill me.''

Angry mutters could be heard throughout the room as the men's expressions grew fierce. Marianne's pulse quickened. She knew their anger wasn't for her, but with increasing trepidation, she realized Garett knew just how to manipulate the council members to gain their sympathies.

"So you see why I must be cautious in my dealings with strangers, particularly ones who know my uncle well," Garett continued. "That's why I've come to you. I know in the past you've trusted Mina to cure your ailments, and I don't doubt your trust is warranted. But I also know she's had something to hide from the moment I met her. I must wonder what she's hiding and why she won't tell me what her connection to my uncle is."

Mr. Tibbett darted a glance at Mina, his face suddenly ashen. "My lord, I'm sure her connection to your uncle is of little consequence. As for what she is hiding . . . well, if I may be so bold, Gypsies are often reticent about their pasts. They . . . they lead rather sordid lives, after all."

Garett was silent a moment, as if considering that, though he clearly noticed Mr. Tibbett's discomfort. Then he remarked, "How then can all of you so trust one of them? Don't you question her motives in healing your ills? Haven't you wondered why she takes no coin for it?"

Marianne groaned inwardly. All her stupid mistakes were coming back to haunt her.

The mayor leaned forward. "Ah, but she does take our coin, my lord." Then he hesitated, as if uncertain whether he'd said the right thing. "I mean, 'tis worth it to give her a bit of gold for all the good she does."

Garett's eyes sought hers, cold and gleaming. " 'Tis only my coin you refuse, then?" he asked her.

She swallowed, but didn't answer.

"My lord, I do not think you should worry for us," Mr. Tibbett quickly put in, striving to turn the earl's attention away from the matter of Mina's pay. "We have dealt with Gypsies before. Some are undoubtedly scoundrels and thieves, but we will vouch for Mina's trustworthiness. She's never harmed any of us."

Garett's stormy gaze shifted to include the entire council. "Tell me this, then. Why has she lied to me, to all of us, about the reason for her mask?"

The mayor settled back in his chair and shrugged.

"Who knows? Women are funny about such matters. Perhaps she's shy."

Despite her fear, Marianne bit back a smile. Trust to Lydgate's eccentric mayor to come up with such an absurd reason.

Another man spoke up. "Mayhap she didn't want us to think she was a wh—a disreputable woman. So many Gypsies are, you know. Mayhap she feared we'd take her for one if she . . . she displayed her attractions openly. You understand." The man flashed Marianne a sheepish look, as if to say it was the best excuse he could come up with at the moment. In thanks, she gave him the barest half smile.

Garett, however, wasn't pleased. He clenched his fists at his sides. "You all seem eager to overlook Mina's odd habits. But you've still not sufficiently explained her connection to my uncle."

Mr. Tibbett drew himself up bravely. "My lord, you mustn't be concerned on that account. Sir Pitney is our enemy if he is yours. I have no doubt whatsoever that Mina stands with us in this."

"Of course I do," she staunchly declared. "I detest Sir Pitney."

"Why?" Garett asked of everyone in the room, suddenly stepping closer to the table where the men sat. He leaned down, planting his fists squarely on the table as his gaze moved around the table. "Tell me, gentlemen, why should she care? She's a Gypsy. She has no reason to side with me against my uncle as all of you do. She owns no lands nor owes me any loyalty. So why would my uncle be Mina's enemy? What has he done to her to make her hate him?"

The men looked nonplussed. The silence in the room was oppressive.

"I told you already," Marianne said hastily. "He knew enough about my father's relationship to my mother to ruin him."

"Time for you to be silent, Mina," Garett commanded without even looking at her. He didn't have to. The harsh expression he wore was enough to silence anyone.

He let his gaze rest on every man at the table, each of whom was becoming more uncomfortable by the moment.

"When did Mina first come to Lydgate?" he asked, the shift in the direction of his questioning temporarily unsettling them all.

As the men began to glance at each other, uncertainty in their faces, Mina bit back the impulse to answer for them. *Please, God,* she prayed fervently. *Let them be wise in this and not say anything that contradicts what I've told him.*

After a long silence, the mayor answered, "I—I really don't remember, my lord. One day we just—just realized she lived nearby, that's all."

Garett's expression at that moment would have frozen a hot bath. He turned to Mr. Tibbett. "Is that your answer, too, Mr. Bones?"

Mr. Tibbett's face turned several shades of red when he heard Garett stress the old, familiar nickname. It was painfully obvious he was torn between his allegiance to Garett and his loyalty to Mina. After hesitating a moment, he dropped his eyes to the table and nodded.

Garett's gaze was chilling. "Did any of you know her father?" he went on relentlessly. "How about her mother?"

An uneasy quiet reigned. That only enraged him further.

"You, my Lord Mayor," he said pointedly. The mayor shifted in his seat. "Have you nothing to tell me about Mina's true identity that will assure me she's to be trusted?"

The mayor looked as if he'd faint at any moment. "My lord," he practically squeaked, "she once threatened to thrash your uncle."

Marianne suddenly had a hysterical urge to laugh. The mayor hadn't lied about that, but she'd almost forgotten the taunt she'd thrown Sir Pitney's way the day he'd come to her father with his final offer after having sought to destroy her parents' reputations.

Garett wasn't the least amused, however. He

slammed one fist on the table. "Have you any idea whom you're dealing with, gentlemen?" he bellowed.

Their cringes gave him his answer.

"Damn it to hell, what hold has she over all of you? How can this one girl make you risk so much to protect her?"

Marianne felt her stomach wrench at his words. Oh, Lord, what had she brought upon them all? What had she done?

Mr. Tibbett rose, a solemn expression on his face. "My lord, we wouldn't have you angry with us. Do we fear you? Indeed we do. We know our town wouldn't survive without your tenants, our tradesmen couldn't thrive without your patronage, even our church would founder without your charity."

He glanced at Marianne, and his expression softened before he continued. "But we trust you to be a just man, as your father was before you. You must admit Mina has done you no harm—"

"—Yet," Garett interjected.

Mr. Tibbett swallowed. "Yet. Nor will she ever, I assure you. This I shall say—she fears all noblemen these days and thus believes she has good reason to fear you. But my lord, surely you cannot fault her for her fears, nor find in them signs of deceit."

Garett's eyes went to Marianne's pale face. "Only the guilty have anything to fear."

Marianne stared at him helplessly, waiting with baited breath for Mr. Tibbett's response to that.

"Or the unjustly accused," Mr. Tibbett said. "In any case, she has proven herself worthy of our trust from the time she came to Lydgate. Would you have us repay her kindness by betraying her secrets?"

When Garett turned the full extent of his black frown on Mr. Tibbett, Marianne could bear it no longer. "My lord, please don't torment these men anymore. I'm the only one who should bear the brunt of your anger. If you fear I'm a criminal, then charge me with a crime and hand me over to the constable. If I'm to be imprisoned, at least let it be by a true jailer."

At that, Garett's frown grew even blacker. "Damn

you, Mina, I don't want to see you imprisoned or hanged. Surely by now you realize that. But I'd welcome your trust. Clearly you're hiding from someone or something. I don't care who or what it is." His eyes passed over the entire group of men. "Even if it is my uncle," he stressed to them.

Then his gaze locked with hers again. "But I can't protect you if I don't know what I'm protecting you from. And I can't trust you if you won't trust me. So why not tell me the truth and make it easier on all of us?"

Oh, how much she wanted to. How nice it would be to trust him, to believe he really could protect her. Yet she couldn't. Regardless of his vows to shield her, he was still the king's man. He might be willing to protect her from a number of people, but would he protect her from the king? Would he also protect her aunt and the people of Lydgate?

She dropped her gaze from his, knowing she mustn't rely on him. It was far too risky to do so.

"My lord," she said in a husky voice little more than a whisper, "I've nothing more to say."

An ominous silence filled the room. At last, Garett said through gritted teeth, "Gentlemen, if I might have a word alone with Mina?"

Instantly the scraping of chair legs against the wooden floor could be heard as the men hurried to leave the room. Mr. Tibbett paused at the door as if he wanted to speak, but at the stony glare Garett shot him, he clearly thought better of it and left.

For several moments after the men left, Garett simply stood in silence at the opposite end of the table from Marianne. Her heart hammered to the beat of her fear, making her want nothing more than to flee. When at last she ventured a glance at Garett, he was staring at her as if she were some strange, exotic animal in the marketplace.

"I am impressed," he finally said, the bitter irony beneath his words cutting her. "I thought I was the only one ensorcelled by you. Now I see you've bewitched an entire town. How do you do it?"

She didn't know what to answer and could only stare at his harsh face.

His gaze flicked briefly over her. Then he rested his hip on the edge of the table, staring out the room's one window. "My mother once told me," he said with a strange calm, "that the mark of a true nobleman—or noblewoman—lay in his ability to command the loyalty and respect of those beneath him." He paused. "If I hadn't met your Gypsy aunt and seen with my own eyes the wagon you live in, after today I'd swear you were as much a purebred lady as I am a lord."

Then he turned his gaze on her, and she couldn't keep from trembling at the dark emotions it seemed both to reveal and conceal.

"They . . . they are simply grateful for my doctoring, my lord," she stammered.

He shook his head, his eyes never leaving her face. "Nay. They care deeply for you, that's plain. What's more—you care deeply for them. And trust them. Tell me, sweetling, why can you entrust your secrets to a man like Lydgate's fool of a mayor and not to me?"

Surely that wasn't hurt she heard in his voice? Did he want her trust so badly? She could hardly believe that. "He earned my trust, my lord," she said in a low voice. "They all did."

He rose from the table and came toward her. She backed away, but he caught her around the waist. Slowly his hand reached up to cup her chin. His eyes bore into hers, and this time she knew she didn't imagine the hint of pain in their depths.

"What must I do then to earn your trust, my Gypsy princess?" he asked.

His gaze, the wounded look there, deeply disturbed her. It tempted her to tell all, even when she knew she mustn't. Instead, she made one last plea. "You could set me free," she whispered earnestly.

His expression clouded with disappointment. He seemed to struggle with himself before his gaze grew shuttered. "Ask of me anything but that. I can't set you free, even to gain your trust."

The flat tone with which he made his refusal sparked

her anger. "Why not? You heard the council. I'm no friend of Sir Pitney's. You've no reason to keep me, no reason to suspect me so. I have done no wrong!"

He stared at her with a frighteningly implacable expression. "If you've done no wrong, then why won't you tell me the truth about your past?"

He had her there. Try as she might to escape his logic, she couldn't. As long as she could give him no positive proof of her true character, she couldn't escape him if he chose not to release her. She pushed herself away from him, the bitterness of her defeat rising up in her throat to choke her.

"William!" Garett shouted, his eyes following her every movement.

The door opened and William thrust his head in the room. "M'lord?"

"Take her back to Falkham House," he growled.

She stood frozen, her heart sinking as she heard the words that sealed her doom.

"Won't you be coming with us?" William asked.

"Not yet," Garett bit out, flashing Marianne a bitter glance. "I still have a few people to talk to in Lydgate."

If he'd hoped to frighten her by that veiled threat, he didn't succeed, for the one thing she'd learned from the council meeting was that no one in Lydgate would betray her. She ignored his words, moving mechanically toward the door.

Then he stepped forward and stopped her. "Mina, I warn you now. I'll learn the truth if I have to question every man and woman in Lydgate. So it does you no good to fight me like this. It just prolongs your torment."

"I'm afraid, my lord, I have no choice. I can't say more than I've said. Thus, I'll learn to endure the torment and hope that in time you come to your senses."

Quite firmly she removed his hand from her arm. Then, without a backward glance, she accompanied William from the room.

* * *

Will stole a glance at the little Gypsy. She sat her horse like a fine queen, but the sorrow in her face told him that her meeting with his master and the council hadn't gone well at all.

A shame it was that he couldn't do more to help her. But what could he do? Mina was as close-mouthed as her fetching aunt. Without knowing their secrets, he couldn't advise them of the best way to deal with his master.

The secrets didn't bother Will like they did the earl. Of course, there were reasons for that. For one thing, Will wasn't bedeviled by the past like his master. Will didn't care what life Tamara had led before. All he knew was he wanted to swing her up in his arms and kiss her every time he saw her. What was it the bloody woman did to him anyway? After all, she was older than he. A man of his youth could have a number of women. Why go to a hostile wench with a good five years on him?

But her lips were no less pleasurable for it . . . when he could get her to still her barbed tongue. Even her bold manner didn't really bother him. He'd die before telling her, but he enjoyed their squabbles. He liked finding ways to stun her into silence, so he could snatch a moment's sweetness from her.

He sighed. This time he'd have to work hard to get back in her good graces. When she saw how unhappy the earl had made her niece—

Will glanced again at Mina. Poor girl. The master had been a mite harsh on her. And all because he wouldn't be practical like Will and admit he wanted the girl in his bed above all things. The earl ought to have bedded her the moment he laid eyes on her and put to rest all his doubts. Why, anybody could see she wasn't a criminal.

As Will watched her, several tears escaped from beneath her lashes, and his urge to comfort her overwhelmed him. "Don't cry, now, miss. 'Twill be all right in time."

"He'll never let me go," she said, half in answer to him and half to herself.

About that she was probably right, Will thought soberly. The master's heart was entwined with hers, though he wouldn't admit it.

"What shall I do, Will? I can't bear this much longer without going mad."

"Don't say that. What would your aunt say if she heard you talking such foolery?"

Mina stared down at the reins. "My aunt," she said so softly he almost didn't hear her. "What will she say when she hears about today?"

Will started to retort, but something in the faraway gaze of her eyes arrested him. She appeared to ponder some idea intently. Suddenly she straightened in the saddle. Her face brightened as they rode beside the forest. She cast him a sidelong glance and asked, "Will, would you do me a great favor?"

"If I can," he replied, watching the play of emotions on her face with keen interest.

"Would you let me visit Aunt Tamara before we go on to Falkham House?"

He should have known she'd want something like that. He couldn't blame her, for she deserved some matronly comforting right now. Still, he groaned aloud. "Come, now, miss, you shouldn't ask it of me. I doubt the master would want it."

"But he needn't know," she persisted. "We could just stay a little while. Please, Will. I just need to . . . to talk to her."

The slight break in her voice made him feel awful. He shifted nervously in the saddle and looked ahead to Falkham House, a short distance from them. He shouldn't grant her the favor, but he well understood her unhappiness. It wasn't as if the earl had been refusing to let her visit Tamara. The master had allowed the visits as long as Will or the guard accompanied her. How was this any different?

He stole a glance at her, and pity welled up within him. The girl was so small and weary. Her cheeks were still streaked with tears. What would Tamara say if she found out he'd denied her beloved niece such a simple request?

Well, why deny her? he asked himself. *What could it hurt?*

"All right," he muttered, "but let's be quick about it. I don't want the master coming back to find us gone."

A mysterious half smile played across her face. "That would be wretched, wouldn't it?"

She spurred her horse down the road and then into the forest, and he followed her. In a short time they pulled up outside the Gypsy wagon.

"Come in with me," she told him brightly as she strode up the steps. "I know you want to see her, too."

He shrugged, but his steps quickened as he followed her up the steps and into the wagon. Once inside, they found Tamara sitting on her pallet, working with her needle. She looked up as they entered, and her face lit with pleasure as she saw her niece. Then she caught sight of Will, and her eyes gleamed with a different emotion.

His heart caught in his throat.

"I talked him into bringing me for a visit," Mina remarked as she sat on a nearby stool. She gestured companionably to another stool, and Will sat down as well.

Tamara's gaze shifted to Mina, and her face darkened. "Has anything happened, poppet?"

Mina sighed. "A great deal. But before I tell you, I'd like some tea." She smiled at Will. "I'm sure our guest would like some, too."

Will returned the smile. "Actually I wouldn't mind a bit of something to warm me." He flashed Tamara a wicked grin.

Tamara scowled at him, then stood and planted her hands on her hips. "The tea can come later. What happened?"

Will watched as Mina stared steadily at her aunt. "Please, Aunt Tamara," she said in an oddly strained voice. "I can't talk when I'm parched. Make us some of your chamomile tea. I do so love it. It's been a long while since I had any."

"My chamomile tea?" Tamara said, a perplexed expression on her face. Suddenly her face cleared. She flashed Will a searching look. "Ah, yes, my tea. All right, then, if you insist on having the tea first, that's what we'll do."

Her abrupt acquiescence surprised, then peeved Will. Why was it she never hopped to do what he asked? he thought as she began to rummage in a corner of the wagon. In a few moments she came back with a pot and some packets of leaves in her hands.

Dazzling Will with a brilliant smile, she prepared the pot, carefully measuring out various leaves. For a moment he wondered what all the fuss about the tea was.

Then Tamara passed him on her way out of the wagon to the fire. The sway of her hips absorbed his thoughts, and he didn't think about the chamomile tea anymore.

Chapter Fifteen

"Though those that are betrayed
Do feel the treason sharply, yet the traitor
Stands in worse case of woe."
                              —Shakespeare,
                              Cymbeline

"Is he still asleep?" Marianne asked, pulling slightly on the reins as Tamara pushed aside the curtains behind her, then climbed through the opening and up onto the seat beside her. Tamara had gone inside the wagon to check on William.

"He's coming around, I'm afraid. You gave me so little warning, I couldn't make the tea as strong as I'd have liked."

"I suppose we should have left him there," Marianne murmured.

"No, it wouldn't have been wise," Tamara retorted. "When he awakened, he would have sought out his lordship. The man would have been on our trail immediately, riding that huge horse of his. With us only in a wagon, Falkham would have found us in a few hours' time. This way we at least have Will under our control."

Marianne was skeptical about that, as skeptical as she was about Tamara's reasons for bringing Will with them. "Now we have a man to protect us," she quipped with a twinkle in her eye.

Tamara merely grunted.

Marianne trained her eyes on the road ahead of them and wondered how many miles were between them and Garett now. "A pity Will couldn't have slept longer. He won't be happy when he finds out that—"

"Tamara, you damned witch!" came a bellow from inside the wagon behind them.

Tamara grinned. "I think he's found out."

William's voice grew louder. "Untie me this minute, or I swear when you do, I'll beat that sweet bottom of yours till you wish you'd never laid eyes on me!"

Tamara tensed at that, but Marianne bit back a smile.

Tamara called back into the wagon, "Till we're safe away, you're staying put. So hush your shouting before I stuff your mouth with a handkerchief."

A tense silence reigned for a good long while after that. Marianne hoped that the quiet meant that William was resigned to his fate. She felt a slight twinge of guilt for the way she'd tricked him, but she'd had no choice. The council meeting had made it painfully clear how determined Garett was to do whatever it took to find out who she really was.

Once she'd left his side and rode out with William, she'd known she must act. She couldn't just let him lead her like a lamb to the slaughter. Thank heavens for her aunt's wonderful tea. How odd that the same tea that had begun the most terrifying chapter of her life was now to end it for her.

Aunt Tamara had been right all along, Marianne thought. Trying to find out who'd framed her father had been fruitless. She'd simply risked the lives and futures of a number of people. Well, no more. If they could just keep William tied up until they were a day or two's journey away, he'd have so far to go to return and fetch Garett that the two men would never catch up to them before they reached the Channel. Once she and Tamara were in France, they'd be free of Garett forever.

She tried not to admit how forlorn that thought made her. Yet the feeling remained. Unbidden, the memory of his lips on her neck made her quiver. Chiding herself for being so easily tempted by kisses, she blotted

out the image of him as he'd looked in the upper room
of the inn, his face clouded over with anger and determination, and his eyes the color of gray ice.

Suddenly a crash behind her startled both her and
Tamara and rocked the wagon.

"Fie on him," Tamara muttered under her breath
as Marianne tried to control the horses, who'd been
frightened by the noise.

The wagon swayed dangerously, and Tamara shifted
her position. Abruptly an arm snaked through the curtains to snatch Tamara off the seat and into the wagon's
dim confines. Marianne halted the horses, then thrust
her head back through the curtains.

William sat cross-legged on the floor of the wagon
with Tamara's rear end settled in his lap. Although he
held her tightly, most of the rest of her flailed around
the two wiry forearms wrapped about her waist, holding her in place. She kicked and struggled with all her
might, but William clearly had the upper hand. Marianne could only stare in astonishment, wondering how
he'd escaped his bonds. She saw no point in joining
the fray, for as strong as both she and her aunt were,
they couldn't subdue William long enough to tie him
up again.

"Let me go, you brute!" Tamara shouted, beating
on his arms wildly with her fists when she found her
struggles didn't free her.

William merely ignored his captive, turning an angry face up to Marianne. "Deceitful Gypsies, the both
of you! What did you do to make me sleep?"

Marianne swallowed. How could she mollify William enough to convince him not to take her back to
Lydgate?

"It was harmless, Will, really," she told him.
"Aunt Tamara put some herbs in your tea, that's all."

"You should have slept longer," Tamara bit out,
finally giving up the fight. "But fractious man that you
are, you couldn't be reasonable. How did you get
loose?"

William gave Tamara a tight smile, shifting her on
his lap as if she were a sack of meal. "I was a soldier

once, or don't you remember?'' he muttered. He thrust one leg out, and for the first time Marianne noticed the knife handle that peeked above the edge of his boot. Tamara followed Marianne's gaze. When she, too, saw the knife, she instinctively reached for it, but he jerked her back against him.

"Not so fast. I can well imagine what you'd do to me with *that* in your bloodthirsty fingers. I don't like being trussed up, wench. So I'll just hold on to it for a bit.''

Tamara began once again to struggle with him. ''Be still,'' he grumbled. ''You ain't going nowhere yet.''

''Please let her go,'' Marianne said softly. ''She can't harm you now.''

''I'll be the judge of that. So tell me—where do you suppose you're off to?''

''France,'' Tamara answered for her niece. ''Mina and I shall put as many miles between us and that demon master of yours as possible.''

''Was I going with you?'' William asked coldly.

''Aye,'' Marianne answered. ''You *are* going with us. At least as far as the Channel. Then it's your choice—return to Garett or stay with us.''

Tamara snorted. ''There's no choice for him—he's not staying with us after we reach the Channel.''

Unexpectedly, William dropped his head to plant a quick kiss on Tamara's neck. She turned a brilliant shade of red.

''You wouldn't want to lose me now, would you, love?'' he murmured against her ear, a wide grin on his face. ''I could be useful to you both. You've need of a man to take care of things.''

Tamara shook her head violently and opened her mouth to retort, but Marianne seized on his words and asked, ''Then you'll go with us?''

William's smile faded. ''Nay. I must return to my master. And you at least must return with me.''

By this time William had slackened his hold on Tamara, so she chose that moment to jab her elbow backward into his stomach. Though he grunted in pain, he still tightened his arms around her waist as she tried to rise.

"By my troth!" he complained. "Don't you ever sit docile like a woman ought to?"

"I'll not be docile if you carry my niece off," she retorted.

"Besides," Marianne put in, thinking quickly, "you can't make us go back. There's two of us to your one. You could return alone, but by the time you arrive, Garett will have decided you willingly helped us escape. He won't be likely to take you back in his employ."

William scowled. "You've thought this all out, haven't you? Trying to ruin my life after all I've done for you."

"Done for her?" Tamara fairly screeched. "You helped him keep her captive, or have you forgotten?"

William eyed them both keenly. "Well, 'tis really of no consequence what I do. Garett will find us all before we even reach the Channel. All I got to do is sit and wait."

Although Marianne hoped William was wrong, she couldn't help the tremor of fear that passed through her. "He's hours behind us. And he stayed in town to question people. He may not have even returned to Falkham House yet and found me gone."

She glanced back at the late afternoon sky and hoped that was the case. William's loud guffaw told her that he didn't seem to think it was.

"After this morning," William remarked dryly, "the master could no more stay away from you than a wolf can stay away from a tender doe. He'll be on our trail already, I warrant you. And I wouldn't want to be in your shoes when he catches up to us."

Tamara twisted in his arms to look up at him. "And how will he know what way we've gone, Sir Know-It-All? We could have taken a hundred different roads."

William shrugged. " 'Twasn't but three months past that the master tracked a man through Spain and caught up with him four days after the man fled to France. The master did that on a mission for the king. And he won't give this any less attention. He'll find us, and there's naught you can do for it.''

William's assurances about Garett's ability to find them sent dread stealing over Marianne. Then something else he said caught her attention. Three months past. Three months past, her father had just been accused of trying to kill the king. A small bit of hope clutched at her heart and wouldn't release it.

"William, when did your master return to England?" she asked.

William eyed her with suspicion. "Why do you wish to know?"

"I—I can't tell you," she stammered, then added more urgently, "But I must know. Please. What harm is there in telling me?"

He scowled, but he seemed to agree it couldn't hurt her to know. He screwed up his face in thought. "Wait a bit and let me think . . . well, when we left Spain in search of his quarry, we didn't return. We crossed the Channel from France. A rocky crossing it was, too, I'll have you—"

"When did you return?" Marianne repeated, cutting him off. Tamara was watching her closely, but Marianne didn't care. She had to know if Garett had been in England when her father had been arrested.

"I believe 'twas early August," he said at last. "Yes, two days after my birthday." He grinned broadly. "I told m'lord it was the best birthday gift I'd ever had—to see England again."

Marianne heard nothing else he said, but merely sat there in silence. If Garett had first returned to England in August, he hadn't even been in the country when the poison had been found in her father's medications. Of course, he hadn't needed to be there to have treachery done, yet it seemed highly unlikely he would have been chasing after some man in Spain at the same time he was plotting to have her father arrested.

Tamara's voice jolted her from her thoughts. "Drive on and be quick about it, poppet. We need to gain more time. Don't listen to this blatherer about the earl's

catching us. Will's hoping to frighten us into returning.''

Distractedly, Marianne closed the curtain and took
up the reins. As she clicked her tongue to start the
team moving, she mulled over her new discovery. All
this time she'd assumed that Garett had returned to
England when the king had, as had all the other exiles.
She hadn't bothered to wonder why his revenge had
taken so long for him to bring to pass, for she'd simply
assumed that planning to regain his lands from his
uncle had taken time.

But if he hadn't returned to England until after her
father had been arrested . . . A rush of relief filled
her. Garett couldn't have had anything to do with her
father's death!

That thought filled her with such pleasure she felt
almost giddy. She told herself it was because she could
never have endured thinking she'd allowed such a villain to take liberties with her. But it was more than
that. She cared enough for Garett to want him not to
be a villain.

This is insanity, she told herself as she coaxed the
horses into a brisk trot. Even if Garett wasn't guilty,
it changed nothing. She still had much to fear from
him. A man who embarked on missions for the king
wouldn't allow the daughter of a suspected traitor to
go free.

If he found out who she was, there was no predict-
ing how he might react. He said he desired her. But
he desired Mina, the intriguing Gypsy, not Marianne,
the suspect lady. At best, his suspicions about her
would take a more alarming aspect. At worst, he would
turn her and her aunt over to the king's men.

She tried to ignore the icy fear turning her heart to
stone. He mustn't find them. He mustn't!

Then she tried to reassure herself. Regardless of
what William said, Garett couldn't work miracles. He
wouldn't find them. After all, he might not even have
followed them. After their confrontation that day, he
might be glad to be rid of her.

She clung to that hope throughout the afternoon.

Hours later, after the sun had set and the horses were still clopping wearily on the road, she decided perhaps matters would turn out well after all. There'd been no sign of Garett. What's more, the moon was rising, so they could keep going for a while yet.

If she just weren't so tired, she thought, pulling her cloak more tightly about her as a cold wind slipped beneath the cloth. The day had been much too long and eventful and she wished to rest. Earlier in the evening, she'd thrust her head through the curtains to ask her aunt to take her place on the perch, only to find Tamara and William both asleep on the pallet in the wagon. William's arms had still been hugging Tamara tightly, but Tamara had worn a soft smile as her body curved into his. They'd looked so blissful in their sleep that Marianne hadn't had the heart to wake them.

Still, she envied them for having what she wanted right now more than anything. The chance to sleep. A short while earlier she'd driven the wagon through a village, and the sight of the inns with their offers of food and beds had filled her with a longing to stop. But she'd known she mustn't. Now, as unwillingly she thought of beds and how delightfully soft they were, her fingers slackened on the reins and her head began to droop.

If she could just rest a moment . . .

When next she awoke with a jerk, she realized she'd been dozing. But for how long? Her mask, which she'd worn since they'd left Lydgate, had slipped down over her nose. As she pulled it back into place, she looked around her. The horses had drawn the wagon off into a meadow and were busily munching grass. The moon was high in the sky.

She groaned aloud. Apparently she'd been asleep a few hours. Thank Providence she'd awakened while some night hours remained.

Then she realized what had awakened her—the sound of hooves plodding the road in the distance. As she sat there, listening to the faint but growing sound, she jerked the reins up in alarm. It couldn't be Garett, she told herself as she tried to coax the horses back to the road, for the sound clearly came from ahead of them. As the sound grew louder, she realized more than one horse was making the sound.

She began to panic. Who would be on the road at night? She touched her fingers instinctively to her mask as stories of highwaymen flashed through her mind. With urgency she pulled the curtains aside and called softly into the wagon, "William! Aunt Tamara! Someone approaches!" Then frantically she tried once more to force the horses from their grazing.

When they wouldn't oblige her, she leapt down from her perch and jerked on the reins in desperation. Yet they were as exhausted and hungry as she, loath to leave the pleasant meadow at the side of the road.

Then the horsemen rounded the curve and her heart sank. Nine well-armed soldiers rode wearily toward them. She went still as death, hoping they might not notice the wagon.

But the luck of a Gypsy was not on her side tonight. The moonlight clearly outlined the wagon, catching the eye of the soldier who rode at the head of the band.

"Lookee here!" he called to his fellows. " 'Tis a Gypsy's wagon. Just what we need to keep us in the captain's good graces when we tell 'im we lost that thief. He won't be as angry if we bring 'im some vagabonds."

Marianne clenched her teeth in anger although her hands shook. For once, she hoped, the soldiers wouldn't engage in their favorite pastime of persecuting Gypsies.

"Come on, now, Harry. 'Tis tired I am and not much up for anything but a good clean bed and a mug of ale," one of the soldiers responded.

For a moment she thought luck was indeed on her side. Unfortunately, Tamara chose that moment to awaken and thrust her head out the curtains.

"What is it?" she asked sleepily.

"Hush!" Marianne whispered, but it was too late. The soldier sighted Tamara's hair silhouetted against the white curtain of the wagon.

"O-ho!" the one called Harry shouted, pulling his

horse off the road. " 'Tis a Gypsy wench we have this time."

"Will!" Tamara turned back into the wagon to cry out as the soldiers followed suit and rode into the meadow.

But William was already out the back doors of the wagon, his knife in hand. The soldiers laughed when they saw his puny weapon and thin frame. Three of them leapt off their horses and rushed him at once. He fought fiercely, taking them by surprise with his wiry strength. He even managed to slice the arm of one man, who yelped and fell back, but after a scuffle the other two disarmed him. A fourth began to slam his fist into William's stomach.

"Leave him be!" Tamara cried, leaping down from the wagon and running blindly into the crowd of soldiers. One soldier caught her easily about the waist.

"Harry, you found us a good one this night," he shouted, his hands lifting to cup Tamara's ample breasts.

William strained helplessly against his captors with a strangled cry, which turned into a groan as a soldier hit him again.

Marianne's vision clouded with fury. Whipping her cloak about her, she stepped forth from the darkness. "Release her!" she cried without thinking.

The men paused to stare at her. At first her cloak and mask seemed to disconcert them.

"She's got the smallpox," Tamara told them quickly, accustomed to thinking on her feet when it came to defending herself against soldiers.

"The smallpox, eh?" the man named Harry responded. Then he said with a sneer, "Show us then the pox and we'll leave you be!"

Marianne hesitated, uncertain what to do next. That was enough to make the soldiers doubt her. Harry darted forward and grabbed her arm before she could escape. She lifted her hand to slap him, but he jerked her around and up against him so hard it knocked the breath out of her.

His fingers clawed at the mask as she fought him.

Then it was gone and the hood of her cloak pulled back, setting clouds of her hair free.

"Well, lads?" Harry asked as he dragged her struggling form before the other men and yanked loose her cloak so it fell around her feet.

Someone released a low whistle. "Faith, Harry, 'tis a bonny one ye've got there!"

Harry said, "Isn't she, though?" His arm wrapped about her waist, a brawny iron bar firmly imprisoning her petite form.

She felt him slide a knife beneath her laces and in moments her dress came apart at the back. Then he threw the knife down. As the other soldiers cheered him on, he snatched away the scarf at her breasts, pushed down her stiff bodice and squeezed one breast so hard she cried out in pain.

It was too much to bear. Marianne kicked at him wildly, grimly pleased when she felt her heel hit some part of Harry's anatomy. But it wasn't enough.

With a curse, Harry threw her on the ground and then sat atop her, jerking her arms back painfully behind her.

"Little lying witch, aren't you?" he growled. "The pox indeed! Well, then, Gypsy witch, let's see 'ow long you last the night with us. Perhaps we can teach you and your friend the right way to please a man."

Marianne groaned, certain she was to be crushed beneath Harry's weight long before he could see fit to rape her. Just as she thought she could breathe no more, one of the men began to shout, "Harry! Someone's coming!"

Marianne found only a small measure of relief in that, wondering if it was merely another assailant to add to their torment.

"So?" Harry said. "He'll go on when 'e sees who it is. No one'll question us."

Marianne lifted her head to scream, in hopes that whoever approached would take pity on her and Tamara and come to their aid, but with the breath knocked out of her, all she could manage was a squeak. Harry forced her head down into the grass, muffling even that small sound.

Then above the thundering of blood in her ears, she heard the thundering of hooves on the road. When the sound crescendoed, then abruptly stopped, she found herself hoping. . . .

"What are you men doing?" a harsh voice rang out from behind her, and she heard the sound of a horse leaving the road. As she recognized Garett's voice, relief coursed through her.

But her hope was fleeting as she realized there were nine men to his one.

"None of your business, I'm thinkin'," Harry shouted above her.

This time Garett's voice was much nearer. "Get off her! Now!" he ordered.

"Who do you think you—" Harry began, but he didn't get to finish his sentence. Marianne felt Harry's weight leave her suddenly and looked up to see Garett suspending Harry aloft with only one hand clenched around the soldier's neck.

Harry struggled to catch his breath, but it did him no good. His face turned purple as Garett held him high in livid fury. After holding him there a few moments, Garett threw him to the ground. Harry lay there choking and gasping as Garett turned his back on him. While the soldiers stared, awestruck, Garett knelt beside Marianne and turned her to her side. His eyes passed over her swiftly to see if she'd been hurt. At the sight of her partly bared breasts and slashed laces, his eyes turned cold and she read the rage in them. Standing up, he helped her to her feet. Then he snatched up her cloak and drew it gently about her.

She clutched it gladly as, with a face hard as granite, he turned to face the other soldiers, one arm clasping her to him.

"Who's your captain?" he demanded.

One of the soldiers laughed nervously. "If you think our captain cares if we have a little fun with some Gypsies—" he began.

"He'd care if he heard you'd assaulted friends of the

Earl of Falkham, would he not?'' Garett interrupted coldly.

"Earls don't traffic with no Gypsies,'' one man called out from the back of the group.

By this time William had found his voice. Struggling against the arms that held him, he cried, ''You fools. He knows what he speaks of. He *is* the earl. And I wouldn't anger m'lord unduly just now. I'm just his valet, but she—'' he nodded toward Marianne, ''she's his runaway mistress.''

For once, Marianne was silent on that subject, thankful to let them think anything they wanted if it helped her, Tamara, and Will to escape without injury.

The revelation seemed to give the men pause, but they still appeared disinclined to believe it and abandon their course. As two of the men started to edge closer, Garett thrust Marianne aside and unsheathed his sword.

"Think before you act,'' he cautioned. ''If I'm not the earl, you've lost nothing but a night's enjoyment. But if I am, you'll seal your fate by attacking me.''

The two men hesitated. Then Marianne saw Harry rise slowly from the ground behind Garett. ''Garett!'' she screamed, pointing at Harry.

Garett wheeled quickly, in time to deflect the blade that Harry thrust upward toward him. Harry thrust again, but this time Garett not only parried the thrust, but forced the sword from Harry's hand.

Then he pointed his own sword at Harry's throat. "What say you, Mina!'' he asked coldly, inclining his head over so slightly in her direction. ''Shall I slit his throat here or give him over to his captain?''

She shuddered, but was tempted to let Garett do whatever he wished.

"Please, m'lord,'' Harry croaked, ''I didn't know she was yer mistress. . . .''

For a long moment Garett stared at the soldier in disgust. Convinced he might kill the man if she didn't act, she spoke quickly, ''D-don't kill him on my account,'' she whispered.

The soft voice seemed to bring him out of a private

hell. He glanced at her, his voice unwavering as he asked, "Why not?"

How could she explain that years of mending men had made her loath to see one murdered because of her, even one so villainous? She made the only reply she could. "I don't want his blood on my head."

Then she stepped forward to place her hand gently on Garett's stiff arm. She could feel the tension in his muscles and knew exactly the moment when he chose to do as she wished, for they relaxed ever so slightly.

"Who's your captain?" Garett demanded again.

"M-Merrivale," Harry stammered, his eyes locked on the sword point at his neck.

Garett lowered the sword. "He'll hear from me, I assure you, and I'll make certain you receive a flogging for what you've done this day."

Then he turned to the other soldiers. "As for the rest of you, be glad my mistress can't bear the sight of blood. Now I suggest you leave, all of you, before I'm tempted to change my mind."

Harry scurried to his horse. The men holding William released him abruptly, and he fell to one knee. Tamara's captor thrust her aside. Then, grumbling, the soldiers followed their leader, clearly not eager to take their chances with the earl after having witnessed his skill with the sword.

Tamara rushed to William's side, cursing the soldiers as she ran her hands over William's body, searching for broken bones. Garett stood rigid as a statue, watching the men leave as his hand gripped his sword. But as soon as the soldiers were out of sight, he sheathed his sword and turned to Marianne.

"They didn't . . . they didn't . . ." He seemed incapable of voicing his fear, although she knew what he wanted to know. His expression was a mixture of concern and raw pain as he pulled aside her cloak and his eyes surveyed her again, more slowly this time.

"Nay," she whispered, suffering his gaze a moment in silence before pulling the edges of her cloak back together. "I have you to thank for that, my lord."

In the moonlight, his eyes seemed like two jewels

burning their brilliance into her flesh. "Yes." Then
his face became shuttered as he said in a clipped voice,
"We'll discuss that later."

He turned toward where Tamara sat fussing over
William, who grumbled about her ministrations.

"How is he?" Garett asked Tamara.

"No broken bones," Tamara murmured with a catch
in her voice. "He'll live."

"Good." Garett then addressed William. "There's
a village a few miles from here. Do you think you and
Tamara can make it there on your own?"

"Aye!" William answered.

"I'll go on ahead with Mina and see to the inn.
Here's gold if you think you'll need it." He tossed a
pouch to William.

Tamara caught it. "Leave Mina here, milord," she
said, handing the pouch to William. "I can tend her
as well as you."

Garett snorted. "Aye, and spirit her off. No, thank
you. You've convinced my man once to help her escape. I won't give you the chance to do it again."

Two emotions warred within Marianne's breast. In
spite of herself, she felt relief Garett was going to take
her back. But uppermost was guilt, for she didn't wish
to see poor William suffer for her actions. "Garett,"
she murmured softly, "William didn't leave with us of
his own accord."

Garett turned his fierce gaze on her. "Oh?"

"We . . . we . . ." she faltered, unable to bear the
way he awaited her answer, as if once again she was
going to prove his suspicions right.

"We drugged him," Tamara said without compunc-
tion. " 'Twas the only way to get her from you. Then
once he awakened we were so far away he saw no
point in going back."

"Damn you, wench, you know that isn't true," William protested.

In the darkness, Marianne wasn't certain, but she
thought Garett smiled.

"William felt certain you'd find us," Marianne admitted, ignoring her aunt's scowl.

"It helped that he kept throwing things out of the wagon to show me the way," Garett remarked dryly.

This time it was Tamara's turn to be angry. "William Crashaw, you wretched traitor! I ought to—"

"Now, Tamara, 'twas a good thing he caught up to us, wouldn't you say?" William said, cutting her off.

She only glared at him.

Garett shot a sympathetic glance William's way. "The two of you come along as quickly as you can. As this night has attested, the roads aren't safe for Gypsies."

"Don't worry, m'lord," William responded. "We'll leave that wretched wagon here is what we'll do and take the horses. No one will bother us then."

Tamara immediately began to protest, but Garett ignored the argument between her and William. Instead he lifted Mina in his arms and strode for his horse.

She remained silent, too exhausted from the night's events even to protest when he set her upon his saddle, then climbed up behind her. He pulled her back to rest against his hard frame as he started the horse toward the road.

"You might as well catch a little sleep now while you can," he murmured in her ear. "Because later on you and I are going to have a very long talk."

And something in his tone told her that she wasn't going to like at all what he had to say.

Chapter Sixteen

"Melting joys about her move,
　Killing pleasures, wounding blisses.
She can dress her eyes in love,
　And her lips can arm with kisses.
Angels listen when she speaks;
　She's my delight, all mankind's wonder;
But my jealous heart would break
　Should we live one day asunder."
　　　　　—John Wilmot, Earl of Rochester,
　　　　　　"A Song"

Marianne drew her cloak more closely about her as she sat in a hard chair near the newly started fire. Warily she watched Garett, who stood a short distance away with the innkeeper, discussing the terms of the room. The room Garett was presently taking for her was small and spare, but she scarcely cared.

She caught snatches of conversation about "two others to follow" and "breakfast sent up early." Only belatedly did she realize the room was meant to be for both of them.

That was what started her pulse pounding with fear . . . and the tiniest trace of anticipation. She gulped back the protest she wanted to make to the innkeeper, knowing it would do no good and would anger Garett besides.

There was no point in infuriating him any more than she already had. And she knew without a doubt that she'd infuriated him. From the time they'd left Tamara and William, Garett had refrained from speaking. Somehow she'd managed to sleep during the long ride, lulled by the slow gait of the horse and reassured by Garett's firm arms about her. But when she'd awakened at the inn, he'd led her inside without a word.

He didn't need to speak to convey his anger. She'd

known from the aura of controlled fury emanating from him as he entered the inn that he was still enraged about the encounter with the soldiers. Unfortunately, his rage would soon be directed at her.

He had good reason to be furious, she admitted to herself. As a sheltered noblewoman, she'd never come face-to-face with the kind of brutality she'd witnessed tonight. True, she and her father had sometimes treated the wounds of those who'd fallen victim to such cruelty. But her father had never allowed her to assist him with those women who'd been harmed as the soldiers had intended to harm her and Tamara. Nor had she ever seen anyone beaten before her very eyes as she'd seen the soldiers beat William.

The experience had horrified her. No wonder Aunt Tamara had always been so protective. No wonder Garett thought she needed a protector. She thought of the soldier's hands on her breasts and shuddered. Garett's offer now seemed more tempting than before. Her life lay before her, an endless stretch of battles with men like those soldiers. Wouldn't it be better just to let Garett have what he wanted in exchange for his protection?

Nay, that was the coward's way of thinking, she told herself. It also went against everything she'd been taught about the sanctity of marriage and the importance of marriage vows. After all, her father had risked all manner of disapproval to make his union with her mother a holy one. He'd married a Gypsy because he'd loved and respected her too much to have her in any other way.

Her father must be turning over in his grave to see Marianne even contemplating abandoning the teachings and morals of a lady, simply because she feared being harmed by ruthless men. For her father's sake, she must resist Garett's advances, which were not made out of love, but out of sheer desire.

She darted a glance at him. Even as weary as she knew he must be, he stood startlingly handsome before her. If she was honest, there was another more important reason for refusing to let him seduce her as he wished to do. She could never succumb to him without succumbing body and soul. But it would never be the same for him, not as long as he refused to seal it with a holy vow. If she gave in to him, eventually her pain would be far greater than if she left him behind, particularly once he discovered who she really was. Now more than ever she must find a way to flee him or lose her soul in the process.

As Garett walked out with the innkeeper, her eyes scanned the room hopelessly while she allowed herself the fleeting thought that she might escape. But she knew better. Garett still stood just outside the door. She could hear his authoritative voice echo in the tiny hall.

She waited impatiently, wanting her discussion with Garett to be over as soon as possible. In distraction she watched the shadows the firelight cast on the opposite wall. They danced, a dark reflection of the bright image they mimicked. The lightless fingers almost seemed to reach for her, to tempt her—

Abruptly she turned her head aside from the leaping shadows that hinted at the light's darker side. They mirrored far too much the emotions dancing within her at that moment—uncertainty, distress at having been caught, and . . . and much as she hated to admit it, a great deal of relief.

Then with a stab of trepidation, she saw Garett reenter the room. Alone.

He closed the door with careful movements, then shot the bolt behind him, the ominous click increasing her anxiety. Oddly enough she didn't really fear him. She knew he wouldn't hurt her. But she did fear his words, for his words seemed always to establish more restrictions for her.

An awkward silence ensued, during which his eyes surveyed her, seeming to note every grass stain and tear in her cloak from where the soldiers had roughly handled her. A muscle throbbed in his jaw, making her shiver.

"I should have killed them. I should have killed every one of the damn bastards," he said in a voice so filled with cold bitterness she marveled that he'd managed to control himself and *not* kill the villains.

She rose from the chair to face him. "There were too many of them. You'd have been killed instead if you'd attempted it."

"Would it have mattered to you?" The words seemed wrenched from him. His eyes locked on hers as he stepped closer, taking off his coat and flinging it across the other chair by the fire. "You didn't care what your leaving might do to me. Why concern yourself about whether I live or die?"

Abruptly he turned his gaze away to stare bleakly into the fire, as if he couldn't bear to watch her when she gave her answer. Her heart leapt into her throat. She could see the lines of weariness on his face, and she felt an instant desire to soften his pained scowl.

"I wouldn't have wanted to see you lose your life to those ruffians, my lord. Surely you know that. And despite what you may think, I'm terribly grateful that you—"

"Damn it, I don't want your gratitude!" he shouted, so fiercely she drew her cloak even closer about her. His gaze swung back to burn into hers. "There's only one way you can show me your thanks."

She was afraid to ask what that way was.

" 'Tis not what you think," he added as he saw her expression, "although God knows I want that, too. What I ask of you now you owe me, for the hours I've spent in torment this day, wondering what danger you might be in. And then to find you in the very danger I'd imagined . . ."

He broke off with a muttered curse. She seemed incapable of meeting his gaze, for guilt flooded her, no matter how much she told herself she had nothing to feel guilty about.

"What—what *do* you want?" she stammered.

"Your vow." He gave a short, harsh laugh. "I don't suppose it means much to a Gypsy, but you once said you had a noblewoman's principles." The earnest expression on his face was readily apparent in the firelight. "Well, then. I want the lady in you to swear you'll never take a chance like that again. Swear to me you won't leave Falkham House unless I'm with you.''

She went cold inside. His request didn't surprise her, but she certainly couldn't grant it. Escaping must be her ultimate goal, for if she stayed—

"Swear it, Mina!" he growled, advancing so close she could see the determination in every grim plane of his face.

"I can't," she whispered, her eyes dark with regret. She forced herself to meet the challenge in his gaze.

His hands clenched as if he fought the impulse to throttle her. Or do something else entirely. "You'd rather risk rape or worse from a band of dirty, wretched soldiers than live with me?"

"No. You know I wouldn't," she cried, a sob catching in her throat, for in truth under different circumstances she would have wanted to live with him. That much she had to admit.

"You do understand what would have happened tonight if I hadn't come?"

Before she could answer, he reached up to yank at the ties of her cloak. She stood stunned as the ties came loose, sending her cloak pooling about her feet. Her loosened bodice barely covered the crests of her breasts. In the firelight, the bruises on the upper swells were readily apparent. His eyes filled with a desperate anger as he saw the dark contusions.

Lightly he touched one. "This is only a sample of what they might have done to you. Yet you don't care."

"Of course I care! Don't you think I wish I could travel as I pleased, without having such men paw me and treat me cruelly simply because I'm a Gypsy? I care, my lord, a great deal more than you'd ever understand."

"Then let me protect you." He said it as if it were the only solution. "Give yourself into my safekeeping. Swear to me you won't leave. Swear it!"

"I—I can't," she repeated through the lump forming in her throat. "For all the same reasons I left Falkham House earlier today, I can't promise not to leave again."

With the firelight flickering over it, his face seemed almost diabolical as he searched for some sign in her that he could make her weaken.

She tilted her chin up, unable to stop that one little gesture of defiance. She wouldn't let him cow her simply because of what had happened that night. She dared not!

He clearly caught her gesture, for his expression altered. "Then I'll have to bind you to me another way."

For a moment she didn't understand what he meant. His gaze remained on her face as he began slowly and methodically to undo the long row of golden buttons down his waistcoat.

She saw the hardness in his eyes and irrationally thought he planned to beat her. Then a spark of something as deep and as old as violence, but far more terrifying to her, lit his face. With a jolt, she realized what he intended.

"Nay," she whispered as he slid the long embroidered waistcoat from his shoulders and threw it across the room. His fingers began to work on the ties of his full shirt, sending panic through her. "Nay, I tell you." Her voice rose a notch. "That won't work. If you force me, I'll spend every waking moment trying to escape you again."

"Force you?" he asked, one eyebrow raised mockingly as his fingers worked loose the buttons of his sleeves. "Think you I'm some grubby soldier who'd throw you down in the field and grind you into the dirt? I've no need of such barbarities."

She sidled away from him, lifting her skirts as she prepared to flee. "You're a conceited lout if you think I'd willingly—"

She broke off as he suddenly pulled his shirt over his head, baring his upper torso completely. She stood momentarily stunned. She'd seen men's bared chests before, those of her father's patients. Yet his was more magnificent than any she'd seen. Broad shoulders gave way to a well-knit, muscled chest sprinkled liberally with dark brown hair. That hair led her eyes downward, following the rough-edged line it made down his belly, then lower—

She sucked her breath in sharply as she jerked her eyes away. What was she thinking, to be standing here gawking at him? Now was the time to flee!

Yet he stood between her and the door. With a sudden agility born of fear, she threw herself across the bed, scrambling to reach the other side. He merely sat down in the chair by the fire and began to remove his boots with nonchalance.

"All of this is unnecessary, you know," he said as he dropped one boot to the floor. "Swear to me what I ask, and I'll let you continue a while longer to guard your ridiculous virtue."

Fury began to beat a steady tempo through her veins. "So you can take it later once you have me safely imprisoned in Falkham House again? I'm not a fool, and you'll never hear me swear to cut my own throat, my lord."

He paused, one boot in his hand as his eyes raked her. "You know you don't really have the desire to fight me. Only your stubbornness keeps you tilting at windmills—a foolish sport."

"You're no windmill," she hissed as she skirted the bed, inching toward the door.

Abruptly he stood. "No. But you're a Don Quixote, for your urge to fight is misplaced. What are you fighting to keep? Nothing save a distrust for noblemen that keeps you from acknowledging a few truths."

"Such as?" she asked absently, wondering if she could make it to the door and free the bolt before he could reach her.

"You want me."

That statement certainly got her attention. "Nay," she murmured, her gaze swinging to his. "Never."

"Your lips said otherwise the last time I tasted of them."

She shook her head, wishing she could deny it to herself and knowing she couldn't.

"What's more, there's no reason in hell for you not to have me."

She could think of a few reasons, among them her own self-preservation. If he so much as touched her, she'd lose half her resolve.

That thought drove her to take her chance. At her feet lay the waistcoat he'd thrown aside. She scooped it up and threw it at him, then darted for the door. She heard him swear, but she dared not look back as her hand nimbly slid the bolt open. Then she was opening the door.

But before she could open it even enough to slip through, the door slammed shut with the force of a weight that also pressed her body against the flimsy structure.

"I can't believe after what happened tonight, you'd try it again," Garett hissed in her ear.

He turned her around to face him, trapping her against the door by pressing his hands on either side of her shoulders. "By God, I'll make sure that was your last attempt."

She had no time to respond before his lips took hers in a plundering, rough kiss.

Her mind screamed a thousand warnings, and she tried to heed them all. In a panic, she bucked against him, driving her fists into his chest as she wrenched her mouth from his. He let her pummel him, even while his strong legs parted on either side of hers to clamp her limbs between his. When she wouldn't give him her mouth, he buried his face in her neck, lightly nipping the sensitive skin.

He covered her body so completely with his own that she felt like a flower encased in ever-hardening clay, destined to be imprisoned forever.

Then his lips sank lower to the swell of her breast, and he deliberately kissed one of the bruises left by the soldiers. "I'd never hurt you so, sweetling," he murmured fervently as he raised his head.

Her hands suddenly stilled at his chest, for she couldn't help being mesmerized by the glittering passion in his gaze. "You're hurting me now." She managed to choke out the blatant lie in one last desperate attempt to escape the seduction she could see he intended for her.

"Where?" he asked, not moving an inch.

She stared at him numbly.

"Here?" he continued, pressing the tips of his fingers against her throat where his lips had been moments before. She felt powerless to speak. Worse yet, she could feel her pulse beat with heightened pace under his fingers. So could he, for his eyes grew more fiery in intensity.

"Perhaps here," he murmured, sliding his palm downward until it barely rested over the breast he'd just kissed. It also rested over her heart.

Yes, she thought. That was where she hurt.

It was the last coherent thought he allowed her. Then his mouth slid over hers once again, but with less insistence and more heat. It startled into life a slowly burgeoning desire.

Her mind was taken up by flaring emotions. It was as if every part of her body demanded she acknowledge how intensely he made her feel. The scraping of his whiskery face against her cheek started one rush of sensation. Then came the tantalizing dance of his tongue inside her mouth, teasing her into responding. After that, she was dimly conscious of the way her breasts pressed up against the rigid muscles of his bare chest.

He pulled away from her only long enough to lift her in his arms. "Tonight, sweetling, you'll give me at least one of your secrets."

When she started to deny it, he bent his head to kiss her lightly on the lips.

After he set her down beside the bed and stood there unashamedly shedding his breeches and hose, her eyes grew bright with alarm. "I'll swear to you just as you wish," she whispered, trying not to look at the flesh he laid bare. "I'll swear not to leave."

A half smile played over his lips as his hands slid up to her shoulders. " 'Tis too late to swear now, my lovely temptress. That moment is past." His eyes gleamed. "But this one is filled with promise—for both of us."

She tried to deny the thrill racing through her at his words, but when he gave her one long, dizzying kiss that stole her breath from her, she could no longer deny it.

One part of her felt him slide her bodice past her shoulders. One part of her heard him curse as he fumbled with the ties of her skirt. One part of her even saw the two pieces of her dress swish downward to cover her feet like doves coming to roost.

But the other part of her heard, felt, and saw only the driving passion that rode Garett as his hands leapt to skim lightly down the length of her chemise-clad form, pausing at her firm hips. She stepped backward, but there was nowhere to go, for the bed lay directly behind her.

"Please, Garett—" she murmured, her heart hammering with both desire and fear.

His gaze caught hers and held it by sheer force of will. "In all the roles you've played, my Gypsy princess, coward has never been one of them. Don't take up that role now."

His words left her speechless, more so when his eyes traveled downward to rest at the full swells nearly completely revealed above the neckline of her chemise.

A shuddering sigh went through her when he drew the loose neckline down and began to rub his palm in ever-widening circles over the nub of one breast. She knew he watched her with those searching eyes. She knew she ought to feel ashamed, yet all she felt was a rapidly rising pleasure, a sensuous longing that danced just ahead of her like the Pied Piper charming the children into danger.

She closed her eyes against his devouring gaze, then gasped as he dropped to one knee so his lips could caress her breast. Her head fell back at the sheer wanton warmth of it. Her hands buried themselves in his dark mane, clasping him tighter and tighter to her. He seemed unable to get enough of her breast, his mouth

tugging longingly at the tip and laving the gentle swell
until her knees felt so fluid she feared she'd fall. But
he held her in place, his arms wrapped about her waist.

Had she lost all semblance of sanity? she wondered
as his body took control of hers. His hands and lips
seemed to know no boundaries where her body was
concerned. They teased, caressed, and provoked her
until every sinew of her body was limp.

Then he stood again, and she felt his fingers whisper
over her shoulders, taking with them her chemise, so
it fell to the floor to join her gown. Her eyes flew open
only to be confronted with the expression of stark desire illuminating his face.

For a brief moment she gloried in the awe that gave
a moonlight glow to his eyes as he raked her naked
body with a hungry gaze. Then shame set in. It wasn't
right for him to see her thus. Only her husband should
be allowed to gaze upon her nude body.

Yet warring with shame came the certainty that she
wanted no other man to see her thus, either. None but
Garett.

"Your body is a holy place, a cathedral," he whispered as his eyes swept back to her face.

"Is it?" she murmured, her voice catching in her
throat. She must break the spell he cast on her. She
must! She forced herself to speak harshly. "Then why
do you wish to profane it?"

A wicked half smile played over his face. "Not profane. Worship. Let me worship at the altar, sweetling,
lest I be banished to hell."

"I can't save you from damnation," she whispered,
now determined to try one last time to stop the inevitable. She used the one weapon she thought would
stop him. "If you take me now, you may forget the
past for a time, but at the slightest mention of your
uncle, you'll turn against me."

The muscles of his jaw tensed, but he didn't release
her. Instead, he jerked her hard up against him, so she
felt something pressing against her belly, something
she'd never felt before. "Nay, I can't do that, even if
you prove as treacherous as he."

She twisted away from him, but his mouth caught hers, ravaging with a wanton abandon that drove her need even more into the open. She fought the urge to lose control, fought it and lost.

Hardly aware of what she did, she clutched him to her, her hands roaming down to cup his trim, hard buttocks. With what was half moan, half growl, he pressed her backward until she fell across the bed. In a trice, he lay atop her, his body trapping hers beneath his. She felt his knee between her sprawled legs, and her eyes widened as she realized the moment was near.

A tear escaped her eye, more in anger with herself for her inability to resist him than in any pain. Garett's face darkened at the sight. His hand caressed her cheek, rubbing away the wet spot. He stared down into her passion-drugged eyes. "For once, don't lie to me, Mina. Tell me I haven't mistaken you. Tell me you desire me as I do you."

She wanted desperately to proclaim him wrong. If she did, she somehow knew he'd leave her and perhaps not touch her again. Still, she couldn't bear having him think she regarded his attentions as she did those of the soldiers. Every part of her rebelled against lying about the way he made her feel.

Yet she couldn't admit, either, that even now her body warmed and tingled wherever his skin met hers.

She dropped her eyes from his insistent gaze. "I—I don't know what I want," she murmured at last.

She expected him to be angry, but he merely chuckled softly. "Yes, you do. You're merely too proud and stubborn to admit it."

His calm assurance brought out the rebellious streak in her. "I don't want—" she began, fully intending to set him straight, but he muffled her answer with his lips.

This kiss was leisurely as he explored her soft mouth with a thoroughness that had her blushing even while she wanted more. But while his lips merely enticed, his hands enflamed, moving over her naked form like the hands of a sculptor memorizing every curve and dip and line.

When he lifted his lips from hers, shifting so he lay propped on one elbow beside her, she stared at him in confusion, incapable of speech. All she knew was she wanted to taste his lips again. Unthinkingly, she drew his head down to her, but he resisted.

"There's more of you I would taste," he murmured, then began to kiss her cheeks, her hair, her ear. When his tongue darted into that sensitive shell, a low moan erupted from her lips.

Then his hand began to inch down her belly until it rested on the soft curls hiding her most private place. She stiffened instantly. His hand remained where it was, but didn't move any farther.

"For a Gypsy, you act like a complete innocent," he said in bemusement.

"I *am* a complete innocent," she whispered urgently, attempting to turn away from him as bitter shame gripped her. She shouldn't let him touch her in such a fashion. It was sheer insanity to do so.

But he wouldn't allow her to move away. He threw his leg over both of hers and clasped her chin with one hand. "Look at me," he commanded, forcing her head around to his.

His tone of voice brooked no argument. She stared at him. For some time he gazed in her eyes, an expression of uncertainty on his face.

"I should have known you were an innocent by the way Tamara protected you. Fool that I was, I thought she only disapproved of me. But any man would have raised her defenses, wouldn't he have?"

Marianne nodded, her eyes wide as she wondered if he'd release her now that he'd accepted she was a virgin. His next words dashed that hope.

"Then I'm to be your first," he remarked, his eyes gleaming with some dark pleasure known only to himself.

She shook her head violently. "I can't do this, my lord. 'Twould not be right."

"The rightness of it has long ceased to be important to either of us," he replied in a voice so filled with husky tenderness a lump formed in her throat. "But if

it sets your mind at ease, my shy wood nymph, rest
assured this moment became inevitable the night I first
felt your gentle touch as you bound my wounds.''

He took her lips again, but she scarcely responded
to his kiss, for all her senses were taken up by the
realization that his fingers were parting her womanly
folds and—

"Oh, God, sweetling," he whispered, ''you're so
warm, so very warm. . . .''

Before she knew it, his fingers were working an in-
credible magic within her. At first she resisted the
pleasure that stole through the portals of her body. But
she couldn't resist it long, for the desire he brought to
life within her was as unfathomable as the sea and just
as timeless. Only moments passed before she found
herself arching up against the hardness of his hand,
searching for some elusive feeling that seemed to hover
just out of her reach.

"Garett . . . Garett . . ." she murmured over and
over.

His answer was to increase the tempo of his motions
until she moaned and writhed beneath his hand, still
seeking the satisfaction that barely eluded her.

She scarcely noticed when he settled himself between her legs and something else replaced his fingers
within her. He sheathed himself so quickly in her that
the sudden fullness startled her. Yet he paused at the
barrier marking her innocence.

"Hold on, dear heart," he murmured against her
ear, his hands braced on both sides of her shoulders.
"Hold on to me, for I shan't ever let you go now. After
tonight, there will be no secrets between us.''

She did as he bade because she wished she could
believe him. No secrets. How wonderful it would be
to cast aside her uncomfortable role, to bare her soul
to Garett as he'd bared her body. But in her heart, she
feared it was not to be. That thought pushed her over
the edge. If she couldn't tell him everything, at least she
could give him everything her body had to give.

So she blotted all secrets from her mind, all save
the secret of his wonderful body melded to hers. The

initial pain, which she'd known to expect, nonetheless took her aback for a moment. But he didn't allow her to hold on to the feeling. Every part of his body danced with hers until she and he were one glorious blur of dark emotion. Her arms clutched him closely as she met him thrust for thrust, savoring the feel of him within her.

She clung to him as he brought her sensual gifts she'd never dreamed existed. All was whispers and thunder together, passion and strength and sweet excess. Her head fell back as her body was rocked by tremors, then jolts, then quakes of pleasure.

Suddenly he strained with a burst of strength against her, and she felt his warmth flow into her as he cried out her name. Then the tension left his body, and he fell atop her.

Spent and satiated, she curved her body around his, loath to let him go now she'd discovered the fulfillment he could give her. After a few moments he shifted to her side, but he kept one leg and arm thrown familiarly over her body. Propping himself on one hand, he let the other trail down the glistening contours of her belly.

A sudden shyness assailed her. She ducked her head into his shoulder.

"Come, now, my Gypsy princess, don't hide that pretty face of yours," he murmured thickly. "You might lie to me at times, but I can always trust your eyes to reveal what you're really thinking. Let me see your eyes."

He tipped her face up to his. She couldn't help but meet his gaze, for she, too, hoped for some sign that their joining had meant more to him than just a moment's enjoyment.

What she saw was a raw desire so fierce it masked any other emotion his gaze might reveal. A sultry heat spread over her body again at the blatant invitation his eyes offered.

His lips curved in a soft smile. "Say it, sweetling. Tell me you found as much pleasure in our coupling as I. Tell me you wanted me. You might as well admit it, for I shan't let you have a moment's rest until you do.''

The sensual things he was already doing again to her body with his hand made it difficult to think, much less to answer him with any modicum of dignity. "It was . . . interesting," she murmured, unwilling to feed his arrogance more than that. Then she gasped when his hand darted between her legs.

"And?"

"And . . . and pleasant," she admitted breathlessly as he played on her as expertly as a musician plays a flute.

"And?"

Her head fell back and her eyelids sank shut. He was making it difficult for her to think. "Please, Garett. . . .''

He chuckled softly. "Say it, sweetling."

At that moment she would have said anything he wanted. "I want you," she whispered. "I want you . . . I want you. . . .''

With a low growl he slid over to cover her body with his once more. "Then you shall have me," he murmured before showing her yet again what having was all about.

Chapter Seventeen

"Truth is child of Time."
—John Ford,
The Broken Heart

The day was half gone when Garett awoke to find himself buried by a tangle of shapely limbs and worn bed coverings. Thick locks of honeyed hair tickled his bare chest and covered the face of the one whose body pressed down against his.

Mina. After all these weeks of unquenchable desire for her, he finally had her in his arms and in his bed. And to his surprise, he found her aunt had been right. One taste of her had merely whetted his appetite.

Lightly he stroked her hair from her face, marveling at its silky texture. How she could sleep with her body draped over his was beyond him. Yet he'd managed to sleep as well. Somehow even in her sleep she entranced him.

Unconscious of the influence her bare form was already exerting on his body, she lay with a sweet artlessness in her expression that touched some tender part within him, a part he'd thought long ago dead.

His eyes traveled to the bloodstained linen tumbled about her legs. Then he shut out the sight, letting his head fall limply back against the pillow. She'd been such an innocent. He'd never dreamed a woman with a past like hers could come to a man's bed so unsullied.

If he'd guessed the truth before, would it have made

a difference? He thought not. His hunger for her had been irrational from the beginning. He wouldn't have been able to wish it away simply by telling himself she was a virgin.

He looked again at the innately gentle curves of her face. What he wanted most to do was awaken her with soft kisses, to press her back once more against the pillows and . . . His loins tightened almost painfully at the thought.

No, he told himself with deep regret. She needed time to rest. He'd shown her little enough mercy the night before. She'd enjoyed it, even if she'd found it difficult to admit it. He'd delighted in arousing her against her will, until she couldn't help but return his desire. But she'd surprised him. It hadn't taken her long to realize the same trick worked on him, as he'd found the first time he tried to go to sleep. Never had he seen a woman find such enjoyment in lovemaking. Never had he been given such a gift.

He stared at her wistfully. Much as he wanted to, he couldn't lay abed all day watching her sleep. He needed to see how William and Tamara had fared.

As gently as possible he slid from underneath her sleeping form. Unfortunately, he wasn't gentle enough. She mumbled some unintelligible phrase, then turned toward where he lay poised and ready to leave the bed as soon as she settled. But she didn't settle back into sleep. Instead, her eyes opened slowly until she caught a glimpse of him. Then they sprang wide open.

"Garett! What are you . . ."

She trailed off as her gaze slid down his bare chest to where his desire was prominently making itself known yet again. It was all he could do to keep the grin off his face at her sudden expression of complete mortification. Her eyes widened further, her mouth formed a small *oh*, and then she turned several shades of crimson.

"Oh, heavens," she whispered. "I don't suppose I dreamed it."

He chuckled softly. "Not unless we had the same dream."

"I can't believe I . . . Aunt Tamara is going to murder me," she cried mournfully, hiding her blushing face in the covers.

"Nay. I'll wager it won't be you she'll murder."

Her head snapped up at his dry remark. She gave him a look of such earnest appeal he sobered at once. "Then we shan't tell her," she said.

A momentary twinge of uneasiness went through Garett. "Keeping it from her will be difficult, don't you think, once you're established at Falkham House as my mistress?"

She sat up suddenly in bed, dragging as much bedclothing about her naked form as she could reach. Her face paled. "Your mistress? But . . . but . . . I cannot be such."

"You already are," he replied evenly, his unease growing at her response.

She shook her head, clutching the linens to her as if they were a shield. "Last night . . . Garett, it should never have happened. It mustn't happen again."

She started to rise from the bed. He clamped his hands on her shoulders as much to have physical contact as to keep her from fleeing him once more.

"Listen, sweetling," he said in a low voice tinged with urgency, "we can't undo it even if we wished to. Why fight this tie between us? There's nothing left to keep us apart now, no reason not to find our pleasure where we may."

Her eyes flashed momentarily. "No reason except my future. I plan to marry one day. If I stay with you, no man will have me. I'm no longer pure."

He certainly didn't like the turn this conversation was taking. "Your loss of innocence wouldn't stop any man who had eyes from marrying you, madame, I assure you. But this talk of husbands is fruitless. As my mistress, you won't require a husband."

"I don't require a lover, either," she retorted. "Nor do I want one."

His grim smile masked the hurt her words gave him. "Then you deny you found enjoyment in our lovemaking last night."

She blushed again and looked down at her hands.

Her silence encouraged him. "You see? You cannot deny that you want me, nor take back the words you said last night. And God knows I want you. Can't you accept that for what it is?"

When she lifted her eyes to him, they shimmered with unshed tears. " 'Tis not enough."

"It's more than what you had before."

She shook her head. "You don't understand. You'll never understand."

He leaned forward, his fingers tightening on her shoulders. "I want you with me. That's all I care about at the moment."

"That's not true. Other matters in this concern you. Have you forgotten you don't trust me? That you think I'm in some terrible conspiracy with your uncle?"

He hadn't forgotten. He'd hoped—nay, believed—she would tell him the truth now that they'd made love. "It's you who doesn't trust me. I've already told you whatever secrets you have are safe with me. I've assured you no matter what you tell me, I'll protect you. Now that I've bound you to me as a man binds himself to his mistress, I think you can tell me about your past."

For a long time she stared at him, as if debating whether or not to trust him. Finally she wrenched her gaze from his. Staring down at the stained bed linens, she asked, "What is the worth of a man's bond to his mistress?"

When a low curse erupted from his lips, she raised her eyes to meet his glare. "Nay, I—I didn't mean that the way it sounded. But it's what I wish to know. When you speak of such a bond, what do you mean?"

He dropped his hands from her in exasperation. "You know what I mean. I'll be what any protector is."

"You'll protect my life with yours?"

He struggled to control his growing anger. "Didn't I do so last night?"

A haunted look briefly crossed her face as she seemed to remember the night's events. "Yes."

He softened his tone. "I will always do so."

She sighed. "I require more than that."

"Money. *That* I'm more than willing to give. Of course I will provide for you. You'll never want for anything."

"Until you tire of me," she whispered.

He tried to draw her into his arms, but she wouldn't allow it. A coldness crept through his veins. "I assure you, sweetling, I shan't tire of you for a very long time."

She swallowed and twisted the linens in her hands. "Men tire of women, my lord. 'Tis not that unusual."

"Men tire of common women. You are anything but common."

A ghost of a smile flitted across her face and then was gone. "In any case, it's not money that concerns me. I can get along quite well with my skills as a healer. But this bond you speak of must require other promises on your part. Would this bond force you to side with me against . . . against those I see as my enemies?"

"Of course—" he said in a clipped voice, tiring of what was beginning to sound like an odd rendition of marital vows.

"Even if they were your own friends? Would you take my part against your friends?" she went on, ignoring his irritation.

That stopped him, but only for a moment. If for some unforeseen reason he must choose between Hampden and Mina, for example, whom would he choose? The choice would be hard, but in the end he knew he wouldn't choose Hampden. "Yes. Against my own friends, though I don't see why that would be necessary."

"You'd stand for me against your blood kin? Against your country?" She paused, her eyes lit with a strange light. "Against your king?" she finished in a whisper.

Somewhere in all her questions lay the key to the riddle of who she was. A part of him suddenly recognized that. But another part was angered by what was tantamount to her conditions for being his mistress. The insult to his pride prevailed in his thoughts.

"If you wish me to swear complete loyalty to you for all eternity, Mina," he replied coldly, "you'll have to place some faith in me first. You ask a great deal of me and offer so little. I still don't know why you've hidden your identity from me when every bloody man, woman, and child in Lydgate seems to know your past. Nor do I know how you and my uncle are acquainted with each other. I'll make no promises until you tell me something. Anything."

She stared away from him into the fire that was now only ashes. He could feel her arms stiffen under his hands. "I'm afraid, Garett," she said softly.

He dropped one hand from her shoulder to clasp her hands. "Afraid of me?" he asked with hesitation, almost dreading the answer.

"Yes . . . no . . . I don't know."

He saw the confusion in her face. It twisted something within him. Unable to help himself, he drew her to him. This time she didn't resist. She laid her head against his chest as if seeking some reassurance in the beat of his heart. Then her arms stole timidly about his waist, and she clasped him to her as if he were her last refuge.

He took comfort in the way she clung to him. He brushed a kiss across the tangled waves of her hair. "You've nothing to fear from me, sweetling. Surely last night proved that. I couldn't harm you if my life depended on it."

She was silent a long time. At last she lifted her face to his. "Last night only proved you want me. But sometimes wanting isn't enough."

His eyes locked with hers. "Then let my word, my honor, be enough. I'll protect you, Mina, no matter what you tell me. I swear it on whatever god or holy book you find sacred."

For a moment she looked as if she might say something. Then she lowered her head once more to press it against his chest. "Give me some time," she whispered. "I need time to think."

He sighed. Yet he knew he must grant her wish. She was like a wild deer that must be coaxed over and over into trusting before it would finally allow a human near it.

"As you wish. I'll give you time," he murmured soothingly against her hair.

Her body relaxed in his arms. For a long time they stayed with arms entwined as he stroked her hair. Then he began to be aware of the softness of her body, the press of her breasts against his chest, the woman scent of her filling his senses. Suddenly he needed to know that her giving of herself the night before had been more than a moment's whim.

He cupped her chin and raised her head so her lips were inches from his. "I'll give you the time you need," he repeated gruffly. "But I'll be damned if I let you spend all that time just thinking."

Her eyes dropped to his lips and her mouth parted unconsciously, giving him the invitation he sought. When his mouth then closed over hers, she didn't argue.

Pitney stared morosely at the thick ledgers stacked atop his fashionable walnut desk. With a curse he toppled them over, wishing he could make them disappear. His expenditures mounted daily. Unfortunately, his income did not. His friends wanted repayment for his loans, his enemies were taking away his power, and his bankers refused to lend him any more money.

He still had some lands and his small estate. But what good was it when the tenants seemed to feel no inclination to toil in their fields? They openly defied him, and when he tried to exert his power over them, they sullenly worked for a few days, then disappeared to a local alehouse to drink their troubles away.

Pitney thought of Garett's well-tended lands and gritted his teeth. All this was the doing of Garett and his Royalist friends. For the tenth time that morning, Pitney cursed the soldiers who'd mistaken a servant boy for Garett and had killed the wrong person along with Garett's parents.

With head pounding, Pitney called for a servant. The stooped woman who answered his summons came in hesitantly with head bowed. Pitney sneered at the trembling woman. At least he was still master of his own house.

"Fetch my wife!" he ordered. "And try to move faster than the slug that you are," he added perversely, pleased when the woman's face reddened. He almost hoped the servant would respond to the insult, for Pitney badly wished to tear into someone right now.

But the servant managed to control herself, backing carefully out of the room. Pitney frowned in disappointment. He'd have to take his fury out on his wife instead.

Lately, however, that had been more difficult to do. He couldn't beat her—he didn't want to risk the life of his unborn child. All he could do was threaten. And his threats seemed to fall on deaf ears. It was as if she'd found another hope to sustain her, one that gave her an immunity to his venom.

Garett, he thought with a surge of anger. She still hoped her nephew would "rescue" her. Well, he'd make sure that never happened. It gave him just one more reason to kill Garett.

A knock at the door to his study brought a smile to his face. The servant had been quick indeed. But at his command to enter, it wasn't his wife who burst through the door. It was Ashton, his eyes bright and eager.

Ashton made a sketchy bow before announcing breathlessly, "I have important news, sir."

"Of Falkham?"

"Of Falkham. And another who interests you."

"What do you mean?"

Ashton smiled conspiratorially as he knocked the dust from his clothes. Clearly he'd rode like the devil to reach Pitney's estate. "Your nephew has a companion now—Winchilsea's daughter."

Pitney stared at his man as if he were insane. "Lady Marianne?" When the man nodded, he growled, "It can't be. You were mistaken. That chit is dead."

Ashton shook his head violently. "Nay. The soldiers who were sent to the Gypsy camp for her must have lied. She's alive. I saw her myself, and I promise you I'd never mistake that pretty face. She's in Lydgate, living at Falkham House."

Pitney sat heavily back in his chair. So the beautiful Lady Marianne was still alive, was she? He felt his member grow hard as he remembered how sweet and young she'd been, with her mother's bewitching wild look about her. Just the kind of woman he enjoyed. Except she'd been insolent, far too insolent for a girl. He'd wanted badly to press her down into submission. He'd even contemplated offering to make her his mistress once her father was safely locked away in prison.

That, too, Garett had taken away from him. Worse yet, Garett had her now. Lady Marianne and his nephew. What a potentially dangerous combination. If she'd guessed who was really behind her father's arrest and had told Garett . . .

"Did Falkham know who she was?" Pitney asked.

"I don't think so. The villagers talked of her as Mina, although you know they all knew her. When I saw her last, his man was taking her before the town council. I overheard someone say Falkham was suspicious of her and wanted to know who she was."

Pitney leaned forward, ideas forming and taking shape in his brain. "Who does my nephew think she is?"

"A Gypsy healer. Before Falkham kept her at Falkham House, she stayed in a wagon with a Gypsy woman."

Rubbing his hands gleefully together, Pitney laughed. "I suppose she won't tell him who she is for fear he'll turn her over to the king's men. Excellent! Quite a comeuppance for the aloof little bitch, don't you think? To be forced to live as her mother ought to have—a Romany slut servicing a nobleman. Her mother had no right to be rightfully wed to a pure-blood Englishman. And now Lady Marianne is paying for it. Ah . . . there is some justice in this world."

Ashton shifted uncomfortably on his feet. "But sir,

what if he finds out who she is? What if she protests her father's innocence? If she knows that you—''

"Quiet!" Pitney ordered, nodding toward the door that still stood open into the hall. No one was there, but anyone could come along. He lowered his voice. "We'll need to act before he finds out who she is. But I'll need some time to think of a way to have her discovered with Falkham. Even the king's favorite subject will have difficulty explaining why he's harbored a traitor."

Ashton's face brightened. "Aye. 'Tis brilliant. You could discredit him forever before the king."

Pitney frowned. "I doubt such an action would discredit him. After all, she's not been found guilty of anything. But if perchance I brought soldiers to capture him and if perchance he resisted the arrest . . ." He grinned broadly. "And if perchance I was there to help with the arrest and was forced to keep him from escaping . . . well, there are all sorts of possibilities, aren't there?"

Ashton nodded and patted his rapier. "Aye, sir, that there are."

With a smile, Pitney withdrew his snuffbox from his waistcoat pocket, took a pinch between his fingers, and sniffed it. "I might even find a way to dispose of Lady Marianne before she stumbles onto something that might prove that her father was wrongfully accused and murdered."

Ashton flashed him a knowing leer. "But before you do, you ought to sample what Falkham's been sampling. Lord, but she's a fine piece of work."

"And a dangerous one," Pitney retorted with annoyance. "Don't forget that."

Ashton shrugged. "What could she tell? She knows not a whit of what happened. She doesn't know I'm responsible for the poison in her medicines. And I was nowhere in sight when the medications were knocked over and the king's dogs swallowed them. What's there to—''

A slight sound from the doorway made both Pitney and Ashton turn in that direction. There stood Bess, her face white as death. Terror was written across her face. She whirled to run, but her pregnant state made it difficult for her to move very quickly.

Pitney bellowed "Come back here, Bess!" as Ashton dashed out the door and after her. In seconds Ashton had her and was leading her, struggling, back into the study.

"Shut the door!" Pitney commanded, and Ashton kicked it shut.

Bess stared at him, hatred and disgust in every line of her face. Pitney rose from his chair, wondering just how much she'd heard.

"How long have you been standing there?" he asked in as intimidating a voice as possible.

She tilted her chin upward in defiance, but her lips quivered. "Only a few moments," she said.

"Don't lie to me, Bess. You know what happens when I catch you in a lie." He opened a drawer in his desk and withdrew a riding crop. Her face turned even more ashen when he began to slap it into his palm. "How long, Bess? What did you hear?"

"N-nothing," she whispered, but her eyes remained transfixed on the crop.

He slammed it down on the table, making her jump. "Don't lie," he ground out. "Did you hear us talking about the poison?"

She dropped her eyes from his. He rounded the table and lifted the crop.

"Yes!" she cried, holding her hands up in front of her face. "Yes," she repeated more softly.

"Leave us, Ashton," Pitney muttered, and his man obeyed.

As soon as Ashton was gone, she began to speak in a rush of words. "I don't quite understand what you've done, Pitney, but I promise I won't say a word to anyone."

"Don't play the fool, Bess. You know quite well someone tried to poison the king and the poison was only discovered because some fool knocked it over and His Majesty's dogs lapped it up."

She began to shake, her shoulders slumping. "You

planted the poison,'' she murmured disbelievingly. "I know you always hated His Majesty. I know of your political ambitions. But—but to plot against the king. That's insanity. How could you do such a truly wicked thing?''

He stared into her eyes, wondering how she could be such a fool. He couldn't believe she hadn't guessed before now what his part in the attempted regicide had been.

" 'Twas not wicked, nor was it insane. When power is at stake, great men will take daring actions. Our king is rapidly undoing everything the Roundheads sought to build. I couldn't let that happen. Come, now, surely you didn't think that milksop Winchilsea was behind the poisoning?''

Suddenly her gaze seemed to shift as if she saw something within him that changed her thinking. "You truly are mad,'' she whispered, backing away from him.

For some reason, her expression infuriated him. How dare she see his brilliance as madness! Stupid woman! "Madness had little to do with it,'' he told her with a sneer. "Was it a madman that chose Winchilsea to carry the poison so that if it were discovered, he'd be the one to suffer? Was it madness to get you your precious Falkham House back?'' He smiled diabolically. "That was the main force of my intent, you know. Whether or not the king died, Sir Winchilsea was doomed once the poison was discovered. And with Sir Winchilsea gone, I could have bought Falkham House from the crown. So you see, I did it for you, my dear.''

She stiffened, her eyes blazing with outrage. "You will not blame this crime on me!''

Pitney merely strode around her till he stood at her back. "That's precisely what I'll do. If you should breathe a word of what you've heard this day, I'll make certain you're found to be as guilty as I, sweet wife.''

He lifted the crop and trailed it over her back, feeling a surge of pleasure when she trembled.

"Aye. Keep in mind what I might do to you,'' he

said with satisfaction. ''I can bribe the maid to swear you confessed your crime to her. Ashton would fabricate all manner of tales about you if I request it. You see, you had a part in my crime and didn't even know it.''

She whirled on him, her doe-brown eyes tinged with horror. ''You would betray your own wife?''

He smiled coldly. ''Only if she betrays me.'' This time he lifted the crop to the gauzy scarf draped about her shoulders and tucked in her bodice. He flicked the crop beneath the scarf, pulling it loose and baring the tops of her full breasts to his view. Then he traced a design over her white flesh with the tip of the crop.

Her face reddened, and she knocked the crop away. ''Garett won't let this crime pass. He'll find you out, and then what will you do? Already he's made your name a mockery at court and among the gentry. You can't stop him.''

Cold anger turned his blood to ice. He brought the crop heavily down on Bess's shoulder, his anger growing when she didn't so much as scream, but merely stood there, her face white and her limbs shaking.

He tossed the crop away in disgust, then jerked her up against him, squeezing her wrists tighter and tighter with his hands until she gasped. ''If you say a word to Garett, I'll kill you, do you understand? And I'll make certain you suffer in the dying. Don't think you can stop it by having me arrested. I still have men who owe me, who'll do my bidding no matter where I am.''

She struggled in his grasp, but he laughed hollowly. ''Don't think I won't do it, Bess. I have no qualms about it. So you'd best keep your pretty mouth shut.''

He pulled her hand down to feel his swollen breeches. She resisted him, but by sheer force he rubbed her hand up and down along its length. ''Be glad that even in your bloated state, I can still feel this for you. Now that you've heard my secrets, 'tis the only thing that keeps you alive—that and the babe and the few ties to the nobility you still retain. If you ever lose those three things . . .'' He twisted her wrist suddenly, making her cry out.

"I won't say anything," she whispered. "I won't."

"Good girl," he murmured, then stared into the face that bore some slight resemblance to the man he hated. Anger and a desire to punish swelled within him like an infected boil that required lancing.

He dropped her wrists and began to undo the buttons of his breeches. He couldn't take his anger out on the one who truly deserved it. But at least there was someone he could punish.

Chapter Eighteen

"A mighty pain to love it is,
And 'tis a pain that pain to miss;
But of all pains, the greatest pain
It is to love, but love in vain."
—Abraham Cowley,
"Gold"

"You haven't told him yet, have you?" Tamara asked, stooping beside her niece, who knelt in the Falkham House garden pulling up weeds.

"Nay." Marianne kept her head bent over the plants, unwilling to let her aunt see the chagrin on her face.

"It's been a week already since he rescued us. Hasn't that been long enough to wait? You should tell him."

Marianne lifted her face, shading it from the sun as she scanned her aunt's expression. "How can I?"

Her aunt plopped down in the midst of the piles of dirt strewn with already wilting ragweed and crab-grass. She gave Marianne a look of complete exasperation. "The man's besotted with you. Any fool can see that. Now that you're certain he didn't betray your father, why not tell him who you are? Perhaps he can help you discover the one who did commit the crime."

Marianne shook her head, turning back to her work although her hands trembled a bit as she tugged on another weed. "I can't believe you'd suggest it."

Her aunt sighed. "Why not? If you don't tell him soon, he'll find it out on his own. He's got persistence—I'll give him that. You've little reason to keep your secret now. What do you fear?"

"You know what I fear."

Tamara idly pulled up a weed herself. "I think I can read a man correctly, poppet. There's no way on earth that man will send you to be hanged."

Marianne twisted the long stalk of a weed, jerking it out of the ground without caring whether the root came with it. She wished she could be as certain as her aunt of how Garett would react upon learning the truth.

"He's bedded you, hasn't he?" Tamara remarked with her characteristic bluntness. "Well, then, time he knew what he got himself into. I'm thinking he ought to do right by you. And he's more likely to do it if he knows you're of his kind."

Marianne tossed down the weed in irritation, rising from the ground abruptly. Lifting her skirts, she turned and began to stride away from Tamara. Tamara jumped up and followed behind her.

"He *has* bedded you, hasn't he?" she questioned as she came astride Marianne. "I can't believe the two of you spent all that time in the inn just chattering."

Marianne stopped and glared at Tamara. For once in her life she wished her aunt weren't so forthright. She colored under the force of Tamara's searching glance.

She should have known Aunt Tamara would ask the question the first time they were alone together. Until now, either William or Garett had been with them whenever they met. Aunt Tamara had said nary a word in front of the men. Unfortunately, she had no qualms about speaking of it now that only her niece was present.

Marianne affected an air of nonchalance, but her voice shook when she answered. "I haven't asked what you and William did that night. You've no right to ask what passed between Garett and me."

"Don't start getting impudent with me, girl," Tamara retorted, her expression shuttered. "For all my faults, I'm still a guardian of sorts to you."

The rebuke stung. The thought of what her aunt had

sacrificed to come with her to Lydgate filled her mind, and Marianne felt an instant's contrition.

Tamara's expression softened. "Besides, you can't just go on this way forever."

Tamara's gentle tone broke Marianne's reserve. One hot tear slipped down her cheek, and she brushed it away, heedless of the smudge of dirt she left on her face.

Tamara licked the tip of her thumb, then lifted it to rub at the smudge. "Come, now, don't cry. 'Tis unlike you to cry."

Marianne clenched her fists at her sides in an attempt to regain control over her emotions. Aunt Tamara mustn't see her this way—so torn. After all the warnings Aunt Tamara had given her, Marianne couldn't bear to hear her say, *I told you so.*

But the urge to confide in her aunt overcame her reluctance. "I don't know what to do," she said in a low whisper.

"Yes, you do. Tell him the truth."

Marianne bit her lip. "And if I do? He knows I've lied to him in the past. What's to make him believe me this time? He might cast me aside in disgust or—" a lump formed in her throat so thick she could hardly speak through it. She finished in a whisper, "or relinquish me to the soldiers in anger. He's capable of going to great lengths to avenge himself when he feels slighted. I've seen that with his uncle."

Tamara shook her head and tapped her foot impatiently. "As if you could compare yourself to his uncle. What have you done to the earl to make him wish revenge on you? Tell him a few lies? 'Tis hardly the same as what his uncle did."

Marianne stared off at Falkham House, her heart wrenching within her as she thought of the tenderness he'd shown her the past week. He'd taken her with such sweetness. . . . Oh, how it made her ache to tell him everything. If she just weren't so afraid of how he'd react to the truth . . .

Unbidden, memories flooded back of that first morning she'd awakened in his bed. He'd made no promises. He'd been right—how could he promise anything when she told him nothing? Yet she knew it would kill her if he abandoned her now, now when she'd finally come to realize a most painful truth.

"You love him, don't you?" Tamara asked as her keen eyes followed the play of emotions in her niece's face.

Marianne's gaze swung back to Tamara. She wanted to deny it. She couldn't. "Does love make you a whimpering coward? Does it make you cautious, afraid to gamble all on the chance that your lover cares for you when he's not even whispered one word of love?"

Tamara reached out and gathered her niece to her, enfolding her in the warm embrace Marianne so needed. "Love makes you vulnerable, poppet," Tamara whispered into Marianne's hair. "If anyone knows that, 'tis I."

Something in the way her aunt's words caught in her throat made Marianne draw back to stare at her.

"Will has asked me to marry him," Tamara said quietly.

Marianne stood there in numbed shock. Pleasure for her aunt and bitterness over the contrast to her own situation warred within her. "That's wonderful," she said at last, and realized she meant it. If ever someone deserved happiness, it was Aunt Tamara.

"I told him I'd consider it. But I've half a mind to refuse him."

Marianne's half-formed smile vanished. "Why? He loves you—any fool can see that."

Tamara shook her head. "Maybe. Ah, poppet," she murmured with a careless shrug, "how could I marry him? Marriage to a Gypsy would keep him from doing what he really wants to do."

"And what's that?"

"The rogue wants to own an inn." At Marianne's quick grin, Tamara nodded ruefully. "Aye, he does, damn fool. He's even got some money set away for it. He thinks I'd be a fine innkeeper's wife. Me—a Gypsy who's more like to be tossed in the gaol than asked for a pint of ale."

"You could pretend to be Spanish as Mother did," Marianne retorted.

"I like what I am," Tamara said, a stubborn set to her chin. "I don't want to pretend to be another." Her face softened, making her look so very young. "Still, it tempts me."

Marianne stepped forward and took her aunt's arm. "Then tell him yes."

When her aunt looked at her with concern in her eyes, Marianne suddenly realized the real reason Tamara hesitated to take the chance for happiness offered her. "If you're worried for me, don't be. Just give me a few more days. I'll find the pluck to tell his lordship the truth. I promise."

Tamara relaxed. She placed her hand over Marianne's where it gripped her arm, and she squeezed gently. "I think 'tis best. You'll see."

Then she looked beyond where they stood, and her mouth twisted into a wry smile. "Speak of the devil himself . . ." she murmured, and Marianne's eyes followed her gaze to where Garett strode toward them.

" 'Tis time I return to the wagon anyway," Tamara murmured, giving her niece's arm another reassuring squeeze before she swept off across the garden, muttering and picking her way through the tangled mess.

Marianne's heart caught in her throat as she watched Garett cross the well-groomed lawn. He looked every inch the lord of the manor, for he'd just come from town and had yet to discard his plumed hat and imposing cape.

As he neared, her blood quickened. Cursing herself for being so easily aroused by his presence, she studied his face, trying to read his expression.

"Return to the house," he ordered as soon as he was near enough to be heard. "We've scarcely enough time as it is for all the preparations."

"Preparations?" she asked, acutely conscious of how grimy and mussed she must look.

A hint of amusement crossed his face as he took in her dreadful state. "My guess is it'll take you a bit

longer than I'd expected to make yourself presentable.''

She tipped her chin up, walking past him toward the
house with the dignity of an affronted princess. "What
is it I'm making myself presentable for?''

Garett strode alongside her and thrust a letter into
her hand. "See for yourself." Then without giving her
even a moment to read the letter, he began to mutter,
"Damn Hampden. Him and his parlor games. One
day I swear I'll pay him back for all his tricks.''

Between the letter and Garett's grumblings, Marianne pieced together what was happening. Hampden
had announced to Garett he was bringing a contin-
gency of six ladies and five gentlemen with him from
court that evening. He wrote that Garett had been too
long without company and needed to be reminded of
his obligations to society. Hampden further stated he
expected a good dinner and entertainment. "And,''
the letter had said, "make certain your pigeon is there
when I arrive. I wish to give her a proper greeting this
time.''

"What does he mean by 'a proper greeting'?'' Marianne asked.

Garett grimaced. "Never mind. But suffice it to say
he's most certainly already on his way. He sent me
enough notice to prepare for him, but not enough notice to send him a refusal. Wretched varlet. I ought to
abandon the house tonight and see how well he likes
arriving here to no dinner and no entertainment.''

"But you won't, will you?'' Marianne remarked
with a twinkle in her eye.

Garett snorted. "No. I'll play the host as he bids.
And you, my dear, will play the hostess.''

Marianne's gaze flew to him in alarm. "But—but I
can't!''

"Why not? I assure you none of them will care who
plays hostess for me. I'll simply tell them you're my
recently widowed second cousin who's come to visit
or some such nonsense, and everything will be perfectly respectable. You've told me many times that you

were raised as a noblewoman. I'm certain you can comport yourself as such for one evening.''

She searched his face, wondering if this was a deliberate trap of some sort. He returned her scrutiny until she lowered her eyes in consternation.

What was she to do? She couldn't be seen at dinner by a group of nobility from court. It would be madness! One of the guests might have known her or her father. It was far too risky to chance.

"I—I can't be your hostess, Garett," she told him. "I wouldn't feel comfortable." That was certainly an understatement for what she'd feel, she thought as she awaited his answer.

He clasped her hand in his and continued to walk toward the house. "I'll be beside you," he said without looking at her face. "You'll be fine."

She jerked her hand from his grip. "But I don't want to do it!"

He turned his piercing gaze on her. "Is there something you fear?"

"Aye. I fear I'll make a fool of myself."

His grim smile chilled her. He shook his head. "Nay, 'tis not what you fear. You, who stood before an entire town council and challenged me, couldn't possibly fear making a fool of yourself. So what frightens you?"

She couldn't think of what to answer. If she protested too strongly, he was certain to guess why she refused to act as hostess.

"You see? You've nothing to fear."

She bit her lip, wondering what she could say to dissuade him. The determined set of his mouth warned her nothing would change his mind. Suddenly she had a flash of inspiration.

"I don't have an appropriate gown to wear for such an occasion," she said, the weight that had begun to press down on her heart lifting a bit.

Garett's odd smile surprised her. "You will by this evening. I'd already had the dressmaker in Lydgate preparing a number of gowns for you. As soon as I received Hampden's letter, I sent a messenger to town to make certain one of them is ready for tonight.''

A quick surge of pleasure flooded her at the realization that he'd gone to such trouble for her. But pleasure was rapidly replaced by an anxiety that gnawed at her insides. She was trapped, as certainly as a bear at a bearbaiting.

As she glanced up at his enigmatic expression, she realized he knew it and was pleased. No doubt he hoped one of Hampden's friends knew her, as unlikely as that might be. Well, she'd have to hope she'd never met any of them. During her days in London, she hadn't moved in society circles very much. Still, there was always the chance. . . .

In one last desperate whisper, she asked, ''Have you any idea whom Hampden might be bringing?''

He flashed her a questing look, then shrugged. ''Who knows? Hampden has a great many friends. But most likely it's a group of exiles we both knew in France.''

She relaxed a little at his answer. She'd never known any of the exiles, although she'd been in London when they'd begun returning to England. Perhaps it wouldn't be so bad. Perhaps no one whom she knew would be there.

At any rate, she had no choice, so she'd just as well make the best of it.

''Falkham tells me your husband died recently. I'm so sorry for your loss, Lady Mina,'' said a masculine voice with a hint of mockery.

Marianne twisted around to find Hampden leaning on the back of the chair where she sat watching the glittering host before her.

''Hush,'' she whispered, though she flashed him a smile. ''He's trying not to embarrass me. Personally, I appreciate it, so be a good boy and play along with him.''

Hampden chuckled. ''Trying not to embarrass you, is he?'' His eyes darkened a fraction. ''Have you done anything to be embarrassed about?''

She couldn't stop the blush that rose to her face. Abruptly she turned her back to him and stared blindly ahead. "It's very ungentlemanly of you to ask it, Hampden," she said with a touch of iciness.

Hampden laid a hand on her shoulder. "Now, pigeon, don't be angry with me. I couldn't help but notice that the two of you are different together this time. More, shall we say, comfortable. But 'tis nothing to be ashamed of."

He patted her shoulder and moved away, leaving her tense and angry. She looked down and her eyes focused on the sparkling sea-green cloth of her new gown. Hampden was wrong. It *was* something to be ashamed of. Garett was keeping her as his mistress. Regardless of how she tried to deny it to herself and to him, that's what it was. He dressed her, he fed her, and he provided for her in every way.

She lifted her gaze to where he stood, casually bracing one hand against the wall as he spoke with a stunning young woman who wore the most outrageously low-cut gown Marianne had ever seen. Her name was Lady Swansdowne, and her widowhood was real, not that she behaved any differently for it than Marianne. Apparently Lady Swansdowne had inherited an immense fortune she enjoyed flaunting. Marianne had been told by one of the men that Lady Swansdowne was considered one of the most eligible women in London. Clearly she was also one of the most beautiful.

As Marianne watched the woman flirt expertly with Garett, tears stung her eyes, but she blinked them back. Garett was paying the woman no more attention than he did any of his other guests, but still Marianne felt desolate. She couldn't be to Garett what that woman was—a potential wife. Not as long as she remained in her guise as Gypsy.

Yet if she dropped her guise, she might lose him altogether. Her fingers closed on the arm of the chair. She couldn't go on this way. She'd go mad. No, soon she must tell him everything, and take her chances. Very soon she'd have to risk all and determine if he truly cared for her. Even life in prison had to be preferable to the torment she'd experienced lately, to the feelings of doubt assailing her.

At least she hadn't needed to worry he might discover her identity another way, by someone from court recognizing her. Hampden's friends clearly hadn't been at court the few times Marianne had been there. She hadn't recognized any of them. And though she'd stood anxiously as Hampden had introduced her to each of them, none had apparently recognized her, either.

One of the servants approached Garett and whispered in his ear. Garett nodded; then, with a few words and a bow to Lady Swansdowne, he came toward Marianne. She forced herself to smile, to ignore the pangs of jealousy that ate at her.

"You're the loveliest one here," he murmured as he picked up her hand. He turned it over and pressed his lips to her wrist. Her pulse increased to an alarming rate. He didn't fail to notice, for a wolfish grin curved the edges of his mouth. "Later, sweetling, I'll have to show you just how lovely I think you are. But now I'm afraid it's time to go in to dinner."

She allowed him to help her to her feet, but her knees felt weak. Later. And much later she'd tell him the truth. But after she did, would he still want to show her how he felt about her in the same way?

Dinner proved to be singularly painful. Garett sat at the head of the table and Marianne at the foot. Never had she felt so distanced from him. Although he often smiled at her, she could do little more than acknowledge it with a fixed smile of her own. All she could think of was when and how to tell him the truth. How on earth could she tell him who she really was and what Falkham House really meant to her?

Hampden sat beside her, but not even his witticisms could keep her mind from playing over and over that dreaded future discussion.

Then the present train of conversation began to trickle through her reverie.

"Oh, surely, Hampden, they must have learned

something by now," one of the younger men named Wycliff was saying. "Someone must have killed the man. Winchilsea didn't stab himself in his sleep. Surely someone suspects who was responsible. After all, whoever did it might be His Majesty's enemy and must be routed."

The other conversations around the table seemed to stop at that moment, while all eyes went to Hampden at Marianne's side. Even Garett seemed interested in the subject.

It was all she could do to keep her face expressionless. Mechanically she lifted a bite of venison pasty to her lips, but she didn't taste it at all as she pulled it off the fork with her teeth.

"All I know is it was a conspiracy," Hampden responded coolly.

The man named Wycliff snorted. "Everyone knows that. What's happened to your famous penchant for gossip, Hampden? Don't you have something a bit more interesting to tell us?"

Hampden sighed. "Nay. His Majesty is rather close-mouthed on the subject. He won't say a word whenever anyone asks him. I've tried to weasel information about the whole thing from Clarendon, but you know him. He's wary of everything and everybody."

"And rightly so . . ." one of the other men said, and began to tell a humorous story about Clarendon. Marianne said a silent prayer that the conversation had shifted.

Then a soft voice came from the other side of Hampden. "I know a bit of news about Winchilsea."

The bite of venison pasty seemed to stick in Marianne's throat.

"What could you possibly know?" Wycliff asked with a sneer.

The girl's voice rose a little higher. "I know something about Sir Winchilsea's wife."

"She's dead, isn't she?" Hampden asked.

"Yes. But I found out from Elizabeth Mountbatten that his wife was a Gypsy."

Marianne groaned inwardly, forcing herself not to

meet Garett's eyes. She hoped the information was too
slight to rouse his suspicions, but she dared not look
at him to find out. She just sat there praying the girl
had said her piece.

But spurred on by the chorus of excited cries of
"No, really?" she'd received from the other women
at the table, the girl who'd imparted her bit of gossip
with hesitation grew bolder.

"He actually married her. Can you believe it? A
baronet married to a Gypsy."

Lady Swansdowne leaned over the table with a
wicked glint in her eye. "That might explain why their
daughter was so unusual."

"Unusual?"

Marianne stiffened, for it had been Garett who'd
asked the question. She couldn't help it—she looked
at him. Her heart sank. His eyes were trained on her,
glimmers of suspicion already evident in them. She
didn't look away, for she couldn't find the strength to
do so. His gaze seemed to hold her there.

"Why, Lady Marianne was a perfect pedant," Lady
Swansdowne continued. "She studied constantly. 'Tis
said she even prepared her father's medicines for him.
I suppose she learned all that from her mother." Her
voice fell to a conspiratorial whisper. "She probably
prepared the poison meant for His Majesty."

Hampden remarked, "It's hard to believe any noblewoman would do such a thing, but it's possible she
was involved, or so they say. They say she gave her
father the medicines, and they never left his hand after
that. Who knows? Perhaps he was innocent and his
daughter committed the crime. If so, 'tis no wonder
she killed herself."

Lady Swansdowne added spitefully, "I wouldn't be
surprised at all if she had done it. You know how Gypsies are with their potions and poultices. I'm sure they
know all manner of poisons."

Only when Hampden clasped her hand suddenly under the table did Marianne realize how badly she'd
been shaking. Had Hampden guessed the truth, or was
he merely being kind to a Gypsy who was bound to

be offended by the woman's talk? Marianne didn't care, suddenly grateful for his gesture. She squeezed his hand, then gently pulled her hand from his grip, her eyes still on Garett.

Garett seemed oblivious to anyone and anything but her. As she stared at him, she tried to ignore the chant that stormed through her mind—*He knows, he knows, he knows.* She couldn't bear it if he'd found out like this—from a chance remark that was terribly misleading.

Someone spoke to him. He answered without taking his eyes from Marianne.

She tore her eyes away from his now piercing gaze, forcing herself to continue with her meal. She took up the fork and found herself having to order her body to do the simplest things—clasp the fork, lower it, somehow capture a piece of roast pheasant, lift the fork again.

"What did this Lady Marianne look like?" Garett asked from the other end of the table. His tone was deceptively casual. "Perhaps she was a pedant because she couldn't be anything else."

The chant in Marianne's brain grew louder.

"I'm sure she was as plain and dark as a crow," Lady Swansdowne remarked, appearing to tire of the whole conversation.

Wycliff laughed. "You never even saw the woman, Clarisse. How on earth could you know what she looked like?"

"An acquaintance of mine knew her fairly well," came a bored voice from Marianne's other side.

She darted a glance at the slightly built man who'd spoken, wishing she could just silence him with a look. But he wasn't even looking at her.

He continued, flashing a taunting smile Lady Swansdowne's way. "He was one of those . . . oh, you know, terribly earnest students who think to learn all the mysteries of life from books. Told me he was one of her father's pupils. Even claimed to have stolen a kiss from her. You'll be happy to hear, Clarisse, that he also claimed she was quite a beauty and not the tiniest bit dark at all.''

The fork dropped from Marianne's hand, clattering loudly on the pewter plate. "Excuse me," she murmured, reaching for a glass of wine. Putting it to her lips, she took a large gulp. Never had she dreamed her one innocent kiss would come back to haunt her like this.

"Sad, then, that she killed herself," Hampden said beside her. "I wouldn't have minded meeting such an intriguing creature."

Marianne tried to tell by Hampden's tone whether he'd guessed the truth, but he didn't seem to realize the irony in his words.

Had Garett? Was it possible Garett could have heard everything and not have guessed the truth? She doubted it, yet her heart clung to the hope that he hadn't pieced together the facts.

As the meal went on and the conversation drifted to other matters, she clutched that shred of hope to her in desperation. She had no choice but to do so. If he had guessed the truth, then the time had at last come for her to test the bond he claimed was between them. She didn't think she was ready for it. Not just yet.

She forced herself to look at him. She could read nothing in his expression. Determined to pretend nothing was amiss, she smiled at him. He nodded briefly, and her heart sank.

He knew. *No,* she told herself, *don't assume the worst or you'll slip and say something you shouldn't. It's possible he didn't guess at all.*

She schooled herself to act normally, to trade witty remarks with Hampden as she always had. Although she found it difficult to eat, she did so anyway, lifting the fork over and over to her lips with mechanical precision.

As she concentrated on suffering through the dinner without revealing the extent of her consternation, Wycliff suddenly stood and called for the attention of the others at the table.

"I wish to drink a health," he proclaimed, and everyone grew silent around him.

Marianne nearly groaned aloud. The drinking of healths was quite popular among both the nobility and the common folk. But she knew once it began, the dinner would drag on endlessly until every man had pledged a multitude of healths.

"Five times I drink the health," Wycliff began,

> "Of Helen, my heart's desire.
> Each of the five can only hint
> At the depths of my love's fire."

Despite her tumultuous emotions, Marianne couldn't help but find some amusement in Wycliff's crude rhyme. She suppressed a grin, watching as he solemnly drank down his full glass, then repeated the rhyme and drank four more full portions.

She'd heard once of this custom, popular on the Continent. Men drank a number of healths to the women they loved, even to their mistresses, according to the number of letters in the woman's name. Often the women were absent, as was the case with Wycliff's love. Marianne found herself wondering what Helen was like as she saw Wycliff's face grow flushed from his wine.

Then Hampden stood up, and she gazed up at him in surprise. Ruefully he winked, then began his own pledge.

> "Seven is the number of perfection,
> As perfect as my lady Tabitha,
> And though she may scorn my passion,
> I'll drink her health, as is the fashion."

When Hampden sat down after drinking his seven healths, he leaned over to Marianne and whispered, "Not much of a poet, am I?"

"Nay," she whispered back with a laugh. "But tell me, who is this Tabitha?"

"My latest love, if you must know, though she's

been playing coy with me. I thought I'd press my case. She's not here, but her brother is sitting next to Lady Swansdowne, and he'll be certain to tell her if I don't drink her health. I suppose I should thank her for her long name. Gives me an excuse to get thoroughly foxed."

Marianne laughed, but the laugh died as she saw Garett stand. The room fell silent again, but she felt certain everyone could hear the loud beating of her heart.

He gave her the briefest glance, then lifted his silver chalice.

> "Fair is the lady I speak of,
> Her walk and her speech so sublime.
> But she veils her person with false words,
> Now for us is the unveiling time."

Marianne heard the whispers that rose around her concerning Garett's odd pledge, but she scarcely noted them at all. Instead, she sat with fists clenched in her lap, silently watching Garett drink the health, then refill his glass.

Her blood seemed to race faster every time he drained the glass, then refilled it. She counted the number of healths, her heart leaping into her throat when he passed four and went to five.

The Earl of Falkham wasn't drinking to the Gypsy girl Mina. She knew that without a doubt. He was drinking to Lady Marianne.

Numbly she witnessed him give the eighth health. For the first time since he'd begun his healths, his eyes fastened on her face. For a moment he stared at her, the cold fury in his eyes making her mouth go dry.

Then he drained the glass and sat down.

Marianne was aware of several things happening at once. Hampden whispered something soothing in her ear that made her realize he hadn't guessed why Garett had drunk the eight healths. Lady Swansdowne sat back in her chair with a smug smile, apparently convinced that the eight healths were for the eight letters of her name—Clarisse.

And Marianne's shred of hope that Garett hadn't guessed the truth disintegrated in her hands.

Others were talking around her, but the clamor in the room did nothing to liven the silence in her heart. She'd taken her chance. And judging from Garett's now grim expression, she'd lost.

Not caring who noted the sudden paleness of her face or the trembling of her hands, she stood shakily to her feet.

"Forgive me," she said in a voice so soft only those nearest her could hear it. "I'm afraid I feel suddenly unwell."

Then she fled the room.

Chapter Nineteen

"Women, like flames, have a destroying power,
Ne'er to be quenched till they themselves devour."
—William Congreve,
The Double-Dealer

Garett rose from his seat as Mina fled the room. His hands gripped the table so tightly his knuckles whitened.

"Forgive me, friends," he announced with grim firmness to his whispering guests, "but I must see to my ill hostess."

As he strode from the room, he ignored the loud murmurs rising up behind him. He wanted only one thing—to corner his deceitful little mistress and determine the full extent of her lies.

He'd gone the length of the hall and was halfway up the stairs when Hampden called to him. He paused, turning to fix Hampden with a stony glare.

Hampden marched up the steps behind him, his expression filled with righteous anger. "Why don't you just leave her be and not torment the poor girl anymore? What did you expect her to do? Sit meekly by as you pledged the health of another woman?"

Garett's answering laugh mocked Hampden. "Another woman? You mean, after all that talk you didn't even guess at the truth? God, you must be nearly as besotted with her as I am."

Hampden stared at Garett as if he'd gone mad. "What are you babbling about?"

Garett didn't intend to stand there explaining everything to Hampden. He wasn't even certain such an explanation was wise. "Don't worry. Mina knew exactly to whom I drank my healths. Something else has her upset—something that is none of your concern."

Garett then turned his back on Hampden and continued up the stairs, certain that while Hampden might want to interfere, he wouldn't. Hampden knew Garett well enough to understand when to stand back.

In moments Garett was at the door to the bedchamber Mina had occupied since the day he'd forced her to remain at Falkham House. Without knocking, he threw open the door.

Mina stood beside the bed, stuffing her few meager clothes into a canvas sack. For a moment he paused to watch her, unable to reconcile the vision of loveliness before him with the criminal she was believed to be. Could that innocent face and those gentle, caring hands belong to a murderess?

No! every part of him cried out.

Still, she *had* lied to him. What was he to make of that? He steeled himself against the soft feelings that threatened to overcome his resolve.

Stepping into the room, he slammed the door behind him. She jumped at the sound. Then, her face growing ashen, she continued what she was doing without looking up.

"Going somewhere, *Lady* Marianne?" he asked in a voice heavily laced with sarcasm.

Her body stiffened, but she still refused to look at him. Wordlessly she turned away from him and went to the bureau, where she drew forth her bag of herbs and liniments. This she put in the sack along with her clothes.

The way she ignored him maddened him. He stepped forward, closing his fingers around her wrist in a grip of steel. "Stop that packing this instant! You're not going anywhere!" he commanded.

She lifted her face to his, and he felt his heart twist at the look of utter desolation in her eyes. "Am I not? I'm not a fool, Garett. Either you'll give me over to the king's guard or you'll cast me out. But either way, I'm certainly going somewhere."

He stood there thunderstruck. He'd been prepared for her to be defiant, even resentful. Now that he knew her secret, he'd also expected her to try to defend herself, to attempt to convince him she wasn't guilty. But he wasn't prepared for this silent desperation, this sad acquiescence. It tore at him like a velvet claw, making him irrationally angry with himself for tormenting her.

"What makes you think I'll do either?" he asked, unable to keep the tone of bitter reproach out of his voice.

He could see the tears start in her eyes. She brushed them away with the back of one hand. "What other choices have you? You've pledged your loyalty to the king, and I'm His Majesty's proclaimed enemy. If you allow me to slip away, you can claim I escaped and thus not lose any honor. If you give me to the soldiers, you've done your duty. But you can't harbor me. That I understand fully. Too fully."

Her sadness struck him profoundly. One part of him ached to reassure her, to tell her he'd protect her with his very life. The other part reminded him that she'd lied to him from the very beginning. She'd played on his sympathies until he was a puppet dancing to her tune. Well, no more.

"Did you commit the crime you're accused of?" he asked, more forcibly than he'd intended. The question had eaten at him since he had discovered the truth. "Did you indeed prepare the poison found in your father's medicines?"

Her entire body went rigid. Eyes ablaze, she stared at him with furious contempt. "You need to ask? Oh, but of course you do. I've forgotten what a treacherous woman I am in your eyes."

"Mina—"

"Don't call me that, my lord," she hissed. " 'Twas a nickname given to me in love by my mother. It stands for my middle name, Lumina." She gave a bitter laugh. "You'd love the irony of it. In the language of my mother's people, it means 'light.' Once you spoke it with what I thought was affection. Now I see I was misled. March me off to the hangman, then, if that's what you wish. But remember it's Lady Marianne you're sending to die. Mina died the day she foolishly gave her future into your keeping.''

''Damn you!'' he cried, clasping her by the shoulders. ''You weren't the one who was misled, who was lied to. I've risked my life for you. The least you can do is give me the truth!''

At those words, all the fight seemed to drain from her. She went limp in his hands. With a soft cry, she pulled away from him, going to stand by the window.

For several long moments she remained silent. When at last she began to speak, it was in a toneless, flat voice that Garett scarcely recognized as hers. ''The truth. I suppose you do deserve the truth. Well, then, I didn't put poison in my father's medicines. I'm certain he didn't, either, for my father was never a traitor.''

''How did it get there, then?''

''I don't know. Someone else must have planted it, knowing he would be blamed for it. I don't know who hated my father enough to do such a thing. He never had any enemies. Nonetheless, someone wanted to make certain he was forever ruined.'' A sob caught in her throat. ''Someone also succeeded in killing him.''

For a fleeting moment, Garett considered telling her that her father was alive. Then he thought better of it. First of all, Garett couldn't be certain her father still lived. Second, the king suspected that her father was part of some conspiracy. If that was the case, then she might be part of the same plot and shouldn't be trusted with the crucial bit of knowledge that her father was alive.

''You say someone else planted the poison,'' he told her. ''But by all accounts, you gave the medicines directly into your father's keeping, and they never left his sight.''

She shuddered. ''I've heard what they say. It's true that I gave them to him as soon as I'd prepared them. But what happened after that, I can't say. I wasn't with him after he left the house. Perhaps he laid the pouches down somewhere or someone switched them. I don't know.'' She turned to him, leveling on him a defiant gaze. ''But when they left my hands, they were pure. I swear it.''

Faced with her determined air, Garett was hard-pressed to believe she lied. Every part of him hoped she told the truth. If so, he would leave no stone un-turned until he proved her and her father innocent. Then he reminded himself of all the times she'd lied in the past. He didn't know if he could trust her. His parents had made a fatal error in trusting his uncle. Was he about to make the same fatal error?

And there were so many nagging questions she still hadn't answered. ''Why did you return here of all places? Why not flee England altogether?''

She gave a shaky sigh. ''I had thought—actually had hoped that if I stayed in England, I could find the man who'd painted my father a villain. That hope proved fruitless.''

She fell silent. Garett thought back to the first two times he'd encountered her. So many things he'd won-dered about before now made perfect sense: her dis-guise . . . her extreme fear of being brought to the constable . . . her ladylike demeanor. Only one thing still perplexed him.

''You feared me when you first met me. I suppose it was because you knew I was the king's man. So why didn't you flee when you had the chance? Why con-tinue to put yourself in danger?''

She hesitated before speaking. At last she stam-mered, ''I'd rather not . . . answer that . . . my lord.''

He strode up to her and gripped her shoulders with his hands. Her eyes were dry now, but they held a trace of fear—fear of him—that rekindled all his anger.

Shamelessly he used her fear against her. ''I'm afraid you *must* answer it, Lady Marianne,'' he said with cold formality. ''Right now I'm the only thing that stands between you and a dank, dark prison. I suggest you keep that in mind and tell me what I wish to know.''

For a moment her urge to revolt flared in her eyes. Then she mastered her emotions and dropped her gaze from his. "As I said before, I wanted to find the man responsible for my father's arrest. I couldn't leave until I did."

Her evasive manner made him persistent. "If you had no idea who the man was, why stay here? Why not look for him in London?"

Her gaze returned to his, steady and calm even though he could feel her trembling. "Think, my lord. Who stood to benefit from my father's demise? Who would be unable to realize all his dreams as long as my father remained at Falkham House? Who?"

A chill gripped him with such force that he felt turned to ice. "You thought that *I* had planted the poison?"

"I thought you had caused his arrest and somehow had arranged to have him be implicated in a crime. I wasn't certain who'd killed him. But you must admit you were the only one who seemed to have a reason to want him out of the way."

He released her and thrust her away from him with a curse. "You really thought me such a monster?" He shook his head in disbelief, the pain of her suspicions slicing through him. "Oh, God," he murmured, closing his eyes to shut out her steady gaze. "How long—" he began, then paused to rephrase the question. "When did you stop believing I was capable of it? Did you believe it when I made love to you? Did you actually lay in my arms believing I might have murdered your father?"

He opened his eyes in time to see her face whiten. "No," she insisted, tears welling up in her eyes. "No, by then I knew without a doubt you couldn't have been responsible."

That was something at least, he thought as he stared beyond her. It would have destroyed a part of him to believe that their nights together had been a complete sham—that she'd pretended to enjoy them when all the while she'd hated him.

"Garett," she whispered. When he didn't respond,

her whisper grew more urgent. "Garett, I wanted to tell you all of it, especially once I realized . . . I—I had planned to tell you soon. But I didn't know what you would do with the truth. I was so afraid."

His eyes swung back to her face. "When did I ever cause you to fear me? How often did I beg you to trust me? How many times did I promise I'd protect you no matter what?"

"You didn't know what you were promising. I couldn't rely on such promises."

Her answer wounded him, for he'd meant every word and had thought that certainly he'd convinced her to trust him at least a little.

In his pain, he remembered one other subject about which she'd been very evasive. "What of your relationship to my uncle?"

She seemed startled. "Your uncle?"

"Yes. How does he know you so well?"

There was no hesitation in her voice as she answered him. "He tried to buy Falkham House back from my father. He tried all manner of villainies to force my father to sell to him, including spreading rumors about my mother and me. But my father refused to sell. That's all there is to it. I couldn't tell you before because I couldn't let you know my father had owned Falkham House. That should be obvious to you."

Her answer made sense, but he couldn't accept it entirely. Other conversations now filtered into his memory, conversations with the king about the attempted assassination. "Why did my uncle stop trying to force your father to sell?" he asked.

She shook her head, clearly bewildered by all his questions. "I don't know. Perhaps he realized Father was going to stand firm."

"Or perhaps there was another reason entirely. Did you know the king suspects my uncle of having been involved with the poisoning attempt?"

She stared at him oddly. "I wondered once if he could have done it. But knowing you were returning to claim your estates, why would he have wanted to help you regain Falkham House?"

"He didn't know," Garett responded. "He didn't know I planned to return until the day I actually arrived in London."

Her face darkened. "Then it was he who—"

"Yes," Garett interrupted. "He hates the king. He truly *would* want to see him dead."

She grasped his arm in excitement. "Then—then Father was innocent! Sir Pitney did it all, then had Father murdered in his cell!"

Knowing that her father hadn't been murdered, Garett couldn't entirely accept her version. And there was the problem that Sir Henry had never let the medicines out of his sight, according to all witnesses. Besides, why would his uncle take such elaborate measures to rid himself of Sir Henry? Why not simply kill him?

"There's another explanation," he remarked coldly. "My uncle and your father could have worked out an arrangement that both found satisfying. Perhaps your father agreed to do Tearle's dirty work in exchange for my uncle's agreeing to give up any hope of repurchasing Falkham House."

Garett didn't entirely believe the theory he proposed, but once he'd spoken it aloud, he realized how plausible it was. Tearle had always been a likely suspect. And Falkham House was the clearest link between the two men.

"No!" she cried out. "You cannot think such a thing! My father would never commit such a villainous crime! Never!"

"Perhaps he feared what Pitney might do if he continued to resist selling Falkham House. He might even have feared for you and wished to save you from Pitney's dark clutches. He might have done it for you, Mina. 'Tis possible."

She threw herself at him, beating her fists against his chest. "Don't say such things! They're lies, they're all lies!"

The vehemence of her reaction made him feel like the worst runagate alive. He caught her wrists, dragging her body up against his. "Listen to me," he said as he tried to restrain her. "If your father loved you as much as you clearly love him, he might have done all manner of things to save you.''

She shook her head violently. "Not my father. He wouldn't have committed treason. He would have found another way.'' Frustration and anger knit her brow. "If you believe him guilty, you must believe me guilty as well, for I ground every powder and mixed every liniment he ever used. My mother and I, not my father, had the knowledge of medicines . . . and of poisons.''

He stared blindly past her. His mind felt bombarded with facts and pieces of information. He knew he could make sense of it all and sort out the truth . . . eventually. But in the meantime, she was here before him, twisting his insides with every trembling glance and wordless plea.

He wanted to believe her. God, how he wanted to believe her. Then he thought of his uncle, whom he now felt certain was behind the assassination attempt. Tearle was just the type of man to manipulate someone like Sir Henry. More cold suspicion washed over him. Tearle was also the type to use a woman to do his dirty work.

Garett dug his fingers into Mina's wrists, wanting to trust her and uncertain if he should.

Her body stiffened as if she could sense his distrust. "Garett," she said, her expression turning bleak. "What shall you do with me now?''

What a question, he thought, his teeth clenching. How could he decide such a thing? It meant choosing between her and his honor. His head throbbed from the choice. How he wished he could turn back time. She should have remained the Gypsy girl, the woman he could have kept as his mistress forever. Perhaps she'd been right when she'd told him not to ask who she was.

He forced himself not to think of that. It did no good to speculate about what he should have done, what she could have been. Now he must face the reality, and make some choices.

But before he could do that—

''We go to London tomorrow,'' he announced. Only
there could he find out the truth. A few possibilities
remained to be explored, and he would explore them
all before he decided anything.

''What will we do there?'' she asked in a tremulous
voice.

He surveyed her ashen face, her alarm evident in
her terrified expression. He knew what she feared and
hated witnessing her pain. But at the moment he felt
incapable of reassuring her, for he didn't himself know
what might happen once they reached London. In his
own private hell, some part of him also wondered if
her fear might bring forth the truth. Then he hated
himself for thinking it.

''Tell me what you're going to do!'' she demanded,
her voice rising a pitch in her pain and anger.

''I don't know,'' he ground out. He closed his eyes
against the image of her, wishing he could wrench
loose the hold she seemed to have on his mind. But
he seemed to see her even with his eyes closed, so he
opened them again only to find her on the brink of
tears and struggling to hold them back. He made himself ignore the instant surge of protectiveness that
raced through him. ''At the moment, Mina, I don't
know a bloody thing. But London's an excellent place
to get some answers, so we're going there as soon as
everything is ready.''

''London no longer holds any answers for me,'' she
replied. ''So all the answers must be for you. Tell me,
Garett, what exactly do you hope to find there? Do
you really think you can ferret out the truth when so
many weeks and months have passed and His Majesty
himself has apparently not determined for certain that
my father was guilty? What will you do that he
hasn't?''

Her chin came up as his gaze passed over her face.
She seemed determined to stand up to him, as if only
by doing so could she preserve her dignity. For a moment desire pounded through his blood, making him
wonder that she could still make him want her so very
much.

"Devil take it, I don't know," he answered, wanting only to get as far away from her at the moment as he could, before he made a fool of himself and forgot what she'd done. "You'd best hope I find something that vindicates you, since you're presently in bad need of my help. Though God only knows what there is to find out."

With that he released her wrists and thrust her away from him. For several seconds their gazes locked, hers defiant but hurting, his uncertain and bitter. Then, without a word, she squared her shoulders and turned away from him to resume her packing.

"We leave early, Mina," he said with finality, "and you *will* be going with me." With that he turned on his heel and strode from the room, slamming the door behind him.

"You might've told me," was the first thing Will said when Tamara opened the wagon door to his insistent knocking.

"Told you what?" she asked in confusion as she dragged her fingers through her sleep-tousled hair.

The gesture seemed to inflame Will. He grabbed her with a sudden fierce motion and kissed her hard on the mouth.

Then he pulled back from her with great reluctance. "Well, to begin with, you might've told me your niece is a damned lady an' all, and that she's in a fair amount of trouble with the king and his guard."

Tamara gave Will a more considered look. "So his lordship knows the truth now, does he?"

"How do you think I found out?" Will fairly shouted. "He's acting like a bloody madman. Lord Hampden and the guests left without getting so much as a good-bye from him. Now he's barking commands at the servants to prepare his horses for a trip and stalking the hall with a look of murder in his eye."

"Oh, my God," she whispered, her heart beating faster. Then she clutched Will's arms. "Where's Mina?"

"Don't worry. As near as I can determine it, he hasn't touched her. Poor girl's in her room. Alone."

"You mentioned a trip. . . ."

Will's face grew grim. "Aye. He plans to set off for London tomorrow with her."

"The devil you say! Is he truly that cruel? Would he see her hanged for something she'd not done?" Tamara shook her head. "She told me she feared what he'd do if he knew. But I didn't listen to her. I urged her to tell him—"

"She didn't tell him. I think that's what has him most enraged, though he won't admit it. He found out the truth by accident. Some guest of Lord Hampden said enough about Lady Marianne to let his lordship put it all together. Damn, but I wish you'd told me some of this! I might have helped you break it to him a bit more gently."

Tamara gave him a more critical appraisal, pleased when she saw he was sincere. Then she lifted her hands to his face and kissed him soundly, her eyes a bit too bright.

"You've said you love me, Will," she murmured as she stared into his eyes. "You've said it many a time. Well, then, 'tis time to prove you mean what you say. Get her away from him. I don't care how. Just get her out of that man's clutches!"

Will's eyes played over her face, and she flinched from the slight flicker of contempt she saw in them. "Would you then use my love like that? As a bargaining tool? I must earn my lady's love with noble deeds? I'm not a knight, love. I'm just a poor, scarred soldier boy who's looking for a bit of happiness. I will not buy your love, for it won't mean a whit if you don't give it to me."

She ought to be angry, but she wasn't, Tamara thought. A fierce joy washed over her to realize just what kind of a man she was dealing with. She'd played with enough men to know how easy it was to twist their wills to hers. And whenever she'd done so, she'd felt a certain loathing of them for their loss of pride. It was why she'd never remained with a one of them.

But Will had always kept himself intact, no matter what game she played. Though she might wish at the moment he weren't so strong, she reveled in his strength just the same.

"You're right," she said, dropping her hands from his face as he watched her. "I shouldn't have asked such a thing as a test of your love. Still, I need it to be done. So I ask it of you as a friend and as a lover. You have my love whether you do it or no. But Will, I still ask, do this one thing for me."

Will sighed and pulled her to him with a groan. " 'Tisn't as simple as all that, Tamara, and well you know it. I can't take her from him even if it was possible. It may not look it, but the man's half in love with her already. If she leaves him again, he'll hunt her down once more."

She shuddered as she recognized he spoke the truth. "Or worse yet, he'll have the soldiers do it."

Will held her away from him, his face a taut expression of anger. "Nay! He's not like that. I think I know my master well enough to know he wouldn't betray her. He's angry now is all. Give him some time to get used to the idea of who she is. Then all will be well. You'll see."

She gazed at him, her skepticism apparent in the way her eyes narrowed. "I'll not see her hurt, do you understand? She's all the family I have left, and I won't lose her because some man is letting his ballocks rule his brain."

Will stiffened. "She's played his mistress, and 'tis true that's clouded his judgment a bit. But he'll be fair with her, I'll see to that if I can. I'll be going to London to serve his lordship, so I'll keep an eye out for the little miss."

She flashed him a brilliant smile. "And if it looks as if he'll give her over to the soldiers?"

"He won't."

"So you say. Still . . ."

Will stared at her long and hard. Then he took her hands and kissed each one. "If I think your niece is in any danger, I swear, upon the love I have for you, that I'll protect her.''

"Even against your master."

Will looked grim. "Even against his lordship."

She gave a sudden little cry and threw her arms uncharacteristically about his neck, burying her face in his shoulder. For a moment he stood there stunned. Then his arms wrapped around her.

"Thank you," she whispered against his shirt.

"Anything for you, my love."

She drew back from him, her eyes dry but shining with love. "When you come back, William Crashaw, I'll be here waiting."

"To be my wife?"

She gave him a little half smile. "To be whatever you wish me to be."

He began to laugh. "I doubt that very much, for you always were an intractable sort. I don't expect you to change because I've granted you this favor."

She wasn't the least bit amused by his laughter. " 'Tis a good thing you don't. I'm looking forward to many long years of being your intractable wife."

He sobered. "And I'm looking forward to many long years of this," he murmured as he drew her to him and sealed her mouth with his.

So was she, Tamara thought as she surrendered her body to his. So was she.

Chapter Twenty

"How can I live without thee; how forgo
Thy sweet converse, and love so dearly joined,
To live again in these wild woods forlorn?"
                                    —John Milton,
                                        Paradise Lost

Marianne's horse stepped daintily around one gaping hole in the road only to hit another smaller rut, jolting her out of her half-drowsy state. Through the eye slits in her mask, she looked for Garett, relieved when she saw him riding slightly ahead and to the right of her.

For once she was grateful to be wearing the mask and cloak. It served two purposes—it kept the cold autumn wind from chapping her face and whipping about her body, and it shielded her from the eyes of men. All men, including Garett. It left her free to watch him without fearing he might see the emotions written on her face.

Surprisingly enough, wearing her disguise again had been his idea. She derived some small comfort from his apparent reluctance to have her identity discovered while they traveled. Didn't that say something about what he intended for her?

Yet she felt certain of nothing anymore, not even of his feelings. He'd spoken to her little since they'd risen that morning. Most of the morning he'd spent preparing for the trip and sending ahead a messenger to alert the London household of their arrival. Her observation of his extended preparations convinced her he planned to stay in London a long while. Did that bode well or ill for her?

Shortly after noon they'd left Falkham House. Despite their slow pace, Garett had ignored her with a thoroughness that wounded her deeply. It was as if her mask had cut her off from him entirely. Except for a few isolated moments when he'd glanced her way. But the expression she'd read there had made her almost glad he'd avoided speaking with her. It held a mixture of pain, anger, grim determination, and something else she couldn't quite define. Pity? No, she didn't think Garett pitied her. She wondered if he now felt any soft emotion for her at all.

William called out to Garett, interrupting her thoughts. She and Garett both twisted around to look at him where he came behind, driving the cart that carried their trunks.

"Shall we stop in Maywood, m'lord?" William asked once he had their attention. " 'Tis getting nigh on to evening. We won't be like to find a more suitable town to stop in before London."

"I'd thought we'd go on to London. It's only a few hours more," Garett bit out, turning back again to face the road ahead.

Marianne kept silent during the exchange, although her heart felt twisted into a million painful knots. Soon she would know what Garett intended to do with her. The question was, could she endure knowing?

"Begging your pardon, m'lord," William persisted, "but it's unsafe on the roads at night with all the footpads and runagates these days. And we've the miss with us."

Garett remained silent, but a muscle worked in his jaw as he frowned. Marianne wondered if he was remembering the last time she'd traveled.

William continued. "She might like a rest and some food before we get to London. The house will be in an uproar once we arrive."

Garett's gaze swung to Marianne, a gaze so wintry and aloof she shuddered from the lack of warmth. "Would you like to stop for the evening?"

She nodded, afraid even to speak for fear her voice

would reveal how much his behavior that day had upset her.

"We'll stop, then," he said in a clipped voice, then turned to repeat that decision to William, whose expression showed his relief.

At Garett's statement, Marianne stopped twisting the reins in her hands as the pressure on her heart eased somewhat. At least he cared enough to ask how she felt, even if the question was asked with the barest of civility.

When they arrived in Maywood half an hour later, they stopped at an inn William professed to know well—The Black Swan. They'd scarcely come to a halt in the inn yard before servants scurried out to help them dismount and to attend to the horses.

Marianne watched the activity—and Garett— numbly. This time was so different from the last time she'd approached an inn with Garett. Then he'd been angry, even furious, but not cold and aloof. Now he behaved as solicitously as he had then, but somehow it wasn't the same. What had happened to the fiercely protective Garett she'd known then? Had he retreated from her so completely he no longer even cared what the morrow brought?

Trying to keep herself as remote from him as he was from her, she allowed him to lead her into the inn. But when he began to discuss the arrangements with the host, she realized to her chagrin that he intended for them to share a room as husband and wife, despite the tension between them and his apparent reluctance to speak with her.

As soon as the host stepped aside to talk to his wife, she clasped Garett's arm and stood on tiptoe to whisper in his ear. "What are you doing? We can't . . . I can't . . ." How could she explain she couldn't bear to share even the same room with him in his present state?

But he seemed to read her thoughts. "Tonight, Lady Marianne, I'm afraid you must accept my company. I won't chance your attempting an escape."

She flinched, almost as much from his formal tone

as from his reason for sharing a room with her. "You have my word I won't try such a thing. Please, Garett—''

''It's out of the question.'' He stared straight ahead, but she thought his expression softened. ''You'd be in danger in a room alone without a man's protection.''

Had she just imagined it or had his tone been more than cordial? She had no time to determine one way or the other, for the host now gestured for them to follow him.

Before long, they were settled in a spacious room, the best in the house. As soon as the host left them, Garett sat down on the edge of the large four-poster bed and began to remove his mud-caked boots.

With a sigh, Marianne untied her mask and cloak. She threw the cloak across a chair, but the mask she continued to hold in her hand, staring at it sadly. ''I used to hate wearing this disguise,'' she muttered. ''And now here I am again, having to hide my face in public.''

He paused in what he was doing to fix her with an unflinching stare. ''The mask is fitting for a woman with so many secrets.''

Mesmerized by his gaze, which seemed to cut through to her very soul, she stood there, her blood thrumming in her veins as she retorted, ''I have no more secrets from you now.''

His eyes darkened as they remained locked with hers, and he looked as if he was about to reply. Then a knock at the door broke the spell.

Jerking his gaze from her, he rose with exaggerated nonchalance and answered the door. It was only a servant bringing the meal he'd requested. Both Garett and Marianne stood silent, watching the servant place several dishes and a flagon of ale on the table. When the door at last closed behind the servant and Garett sat down before the table, Marianne wandered over by the window.

''Come away from there and eat something,'' Garett commanded, his sharp tone reminding her that her face could be seen by anyone watching from the yard. She shivered and backed away a few paces.

She glanced at the table. She ought to have been eager to devour the feast he'd ordered, for her stomach most certainly protested the lack of food she'd given it. The wooden platters held boiled leg of mutton and roast pigeon, as well as a healthy portion of boiled peas. She even smelled the scent of freshly baked bread and apples roasted with cinnamon.

But her hunger was as nothing compared to the emotional turmoil she was suffering. She doubted she could eat a bite without having it come back up, so she made no move to join him at the table.

"You've eaten scarcely anything all day," he persisted, his voice oddly husky. "And little to nothing last night."

So he'd noticed. Somewhere in her deadened state, she was surprised and a little reassured that he had. "I was preoccupied."

His harsh laugh grated. "Indeed," he remarked with heavy sarcasm.

Suddenly she could bear no more. She turned to face him, twisting the mask in her hands. "Answer me one thing, Garett. If I had told you the truth when you first asked, what would you have done? Would you have turned me over to the king's guard?"

For a brief moment his composure seemed to crack, and raw anguish showed in his face. But he quickly masked it. "I'm not even certain what I'm going to do with you now. How can I know what I would have done then?"

She sighed, finding his answer not a bit satisfactory. "I wish you'd just make a decision and stop tormenting me. I no longer care what you do with me. Send me to prison, send me to hang, but tell me what you intend or I'll surely go mad."

He pushed back from the table and rose to his feet. "Have you no idea how difficult this is for me? I have a duty to my king and my country that I shouldn't ignore."

"So you'll give me over to them without a qualm."

"No, damn it!" he shouted, striding toward her. "But neither can I just pretend it never happened! If you hadn't been entangled with my uncle—"

"Entangled?" she interrupted, her eyes flaming. "Listen to me, Garett. I was not 'entangled' with your uncle, unless you call his lust for my mother entanglement."

"He's suspected of being behind the plot."

"He sought to ruin my father," she hissed. "And that's how he set out to do it!"

"How could he slip poison into your father's medications without either your or your father's help?"

"I don't know," she cried in frustration. "But any fool can see I'm telling the truth. If I were part of a conspiracy, why would I have remained in England after it was all over?"

"To avenge your father. You've already admitted that much. Perhaps you thought my uncle—"

"Your uncle. You seem far more concerned with my feelings about your uncle than with my supposed involvement in a heinous crime. Why is that? What is it about your uncle that would make you turn against me solely because I might have some tie to him? Yes, he stole your birthright. But you regained it, didn't you? Why has he so obsessed you that you would see me punished for his crimes?"

The anguish in her voice seemed to strike a part of him. He approached her, his face filled with fury tempered by concern. "I don't want to see you punished. But for him I want justice."

She clasped his doublet with both hands, her face turned up to him pleadingly. "Why? Why is it so important to you?"

He glared at her, his implacable expression making her despair. Then something flickered in his eyes, some glimmer of human feeling. As if he spoke against his will, he bit out, "He killed my parents."

She gazed up at him in numb shock. "You know this for certain? You can prove it?"

He pushed her hands from him and whirled away. "Nay. But I know it just the same. Only *he* knew they traveled in disguise. Only *he* knew the route they took and when they departed. He didn't do the deed with his own hands, but he ordered it done. More and more I'm certain of it.''

''I-I'm sorry,'' she stammered, her heart aching for him. And for her. If the root of his pain lay in this terrible thing, then it was no small wonder he didn't know what to do with her. If he believed she and his uncle had conspired together, then understandably he could have no pity for her.

But they hadn't, and she must make him realize it. Otherwise she'd be lost, for without his belief in her, she saw no reason to go on.

Hang him, she wouldn't let him do this to the union he and she had begun to form. He might not trust her, but she felt certain some part of him recognized her for what she was. The part of him that wasn't obsessed with his vengeance cared for her. She must appeal to that part if she was to save her soul. And his.

''Now you see why I can leave no stone unturned in bringing him to justice,'' he said as he turned back to face her, his eyes haunted. ''I can't let him continue to live unscathed and commit further crimes with impunity. He must be punished.''

''And he shall,'' she said fervently. ''I know you'll find a way to prove his guilt. But you can't prove it using me, for I know nothing. If I could tell you anything that would lead to his arrest, I would. Can't you at least believe that?''

He closed his eyes, his expression a twisted mask of uncertainty. ''I don't know, Mina,'' he ground out through clenched teeth. ''You've so bewitched me I don't know what to think or feel anymore.''

She trembled, recognizing the intensity of his struggle. Yet she knew she must weight the balance on her side if she was to gain his trust. And his love. More than anything she'd ever desired, she wanted his love.

The fates that had decreed he be the Earl of Falkham were not going to deprive her of that, she decided. Without hesitation, she stepped close enough to him to lay her hand on his arm.

He started at her touch, and his eyes flew open. His gaze was almost feverish as he watched her. When she had his full attention, she reached over to the table and lifted a carving knife in her hand. As his eyes followed her every movement, she hefted the carving knife, then suddenly lifted it so its point pressed against his neck.

"If I'm truly the villainess you claim, there's nothing to stop me from driving this blade into your throat. And why wouldn't I? You're taking me to be hanged anyway. What's one more death?"

He merely stared at her, no hint of fear in his eyes.

"You see, you don't believe me," she said with passion. "If you thought yourself in any danger, you'd at least attempt to wrest the knife from me. But you don't, do you, because you know I'd never harm you. Never. You trust me." Her voice broke, but she forced herself to continue. "You trust me. You just don't know you do."

Abruptly she turned the knife so it pressed against her own neck where the pulse beat, and before he could move, she pricked the skin just enough to draw blood.

He sucked in his breath. His hand shot out to grip her wrist, twisting it so the knife was held away from her. He tightened his fingers around her wrist until the pressure was too much, and she released the knife, allowing it to clatter to the floor.

Then he clutched her to him, his arms wrapping about her so tightly she had to fight for breath.

"You can't even bear to see me hurt myself," she whispered with a catch in her throat. Her voice was muffled against his doublet. "How will you bear to see strangers hang me?"

"No one will hang you," he declared. "I won't allow it."

She fought back tears. "If you give me to the king's guard, you may not have a choice."

"That's enough!" he ordered, releasing her only long enough to clasp her head between his two hands and force it up so her misty eyes stared into his. "There will be no prison. There will be no hanging.

You've proved well enough I can't bear to have them take you.''

Her heart beat triple time as she searched his face. Had she won the fight or just delayed the battle a while longer? ''What about your vows to the king, to your country?'' she couldn't help but ask, although she feared his answer.

He gazed at her steadily. ''False vows, all, if they make me act against my nature. I can't watch you suffer. I wish with every part of my being to believe you're as innocent as you say. But if you're not . . . my pride will simply have to endure a bruising, for I can't betray you, even if I'm a fool for not doing so.''

Relief flooded through her, but she still worried about what he was vowing to do. He was a man of honor—he wouldn't forsake his duties easily, and she didn't know if she had the right to ask him to do so. ''I wouldn't have you be a fool, my lord,'' she said, lifting her hands to cover his where they still framed her face. ''If you still don't believe me, I'd have you act as you feel is wisest.''

''Enough,'' he murmured. ''I tire of this talk of what I will or won't do. And wisdom? I lost all wisdom the day I set eyes on your cloaked form. I should have ordered you gone from Lydgate then. But I didn't.''

''Why didn't you?'' she asked, her throat thick with suppressed longing.

His gray eyes darkened with an emotion she'd not thought to see again. Desire. His gaze dropped to her lips. Then his thumb slid across her cheek to rub the softness of her upper lip. ''For the same reason I can't let you go now.''

Then his mouth was on hers, firm and warm. She gave herself up to his kiss, relieved he still felt desire for her, if nothing else.

And oh, what desire did he express. He clasped her to him as if he feared she'd disappear, and his mouth ravaged hers like a starving man ravages a feast. His hands roamed her body freely—she didn't stop their wandering. It was enough for her that despite all he feared, he wanted her.

She pressed her body against his, her heart filled with so much love for him she couldn't help but demonstrate it in the only way she knew how. He'd taught her how to show it, and now she took what she'd been taught, mastered it, and gave it back to him in unsurpassed lessons. Her arms twined about his waist, her lips parted for the onslaught of his demanding mouth, and her hips thrust against his.

After several intense moments, he groaned deep within his throat and tore his lips from hers. "Damn you, Mina," he murmured, his eyes bright with the force of his hunger. "I thought I'd numbed my heart years ago in France. But you'd awaken a heart beneath the breast of Death himself."

"You awakened mine," she whispered, lifting her hand to stroke his cheek. " 'Tis only fair I should stir yours."

Her words made him flinch, and he closed his eyes as if to shut her out.

"You won't thrust me from your mind as easily as that," she vowed. Then she reached behind her to clasp his hands. Lifting them from where they held her waist, she pressed them to her breast so he could feel her heart racing as once before he'd had her feel his.

His eyes flew open, and he stared at her with raw passion lending an almost holy glow to his face. "I want you past all reason," he whispered in amazement as if he'd just that moment realized it himself. "I don't know who you really are, but I want you all the same."

Her fingers tightened painfully on his hands. "You *do* know who I am. I'm Mina, the Gypsy girl who saved your life. And I'm also Lady Marianne, who wouldn't tell you the truth for fear of losing your . . . your affection. Both of us are the same woman. Both of us . . . both of us want you, too."

And to show him she meant every word, she pressed her body against his, her arms encircling his waist as she lay her cheek against his chest. His heart beat

wildly, giving her some hope at least to hold to that
he cared for her beyond just desiring her body.

"Ah, Mina, but you're tearing me in two," he murmured, burying his fingers in her silky hair. He planted
a kiss on the top of her head, then released her and
strode to the door.

Opening it, he fixed her with a impassioned gaze.
"Now's your chance," he stated. "You can leave if
you wish. I won't stop you."

Her heart plummetted as she realized what he was
saying. Did he think she'd offered herself to him in an
attempt to have him free her? She stared at him in
dumb amazement for a few seconds. Then she gave a
shaky little laugh. "Where would I go? All the soldiers in England would hunt for me if I left."

She swallowed hard at the fierce intensity of his
gaze.

"You don't understand," he told her. "I won't keep
you here against your will. Not any longer. You can
walk out of this inn and disappear. I won't stop you,
and you'll be safe forever from the soldiers, for none
of them know yet that you live."

After what he'd just said, how could he be casting
her aside? She stared at him in shocked disbelief. "Do
you really want me to leave? I—I thought you cared
for me—"

"Damn it, Mina! I don't know what might come of
this trip to London." He dropped his voice, but his
tone was no less insistent. "You could be seen and
recognized by someone. Tearle could try to rid himself
of you." His eyes turned to shards of ice. "Or I could
discover things about you that would— Never mind.
You'd be better off away from me, I tell you. At least
you'd be alive! I can give you money and whatever
else you—"

"I'm not leaving!" she shouted back at him, then
lowered her voice as she realized it echoed out into
the hallway. Striding past him, she wrenched the door
from his grip and slammed it shut.

The choice he offered wasn't for her, not anymore.
She had to stay with him to find the peace she sought

from the turmoil in her emotions. Either he found a way to trust her, or he cast her aside. But his decision had to be a conscious one based on what he wanted and not what he thought best for her.

Meeting his passionate gaze, she vowed, "I'm staying with you to the bitter end, Garett, even if it means I'm damned forever."

For a brief moment, she thought he was going to argue with her. Suddenly he lost the haunted look he'd had all evening. "Then we'll be damned together," he growled, reaching for her and pulling her roughly up against his hard body. "For I vow to you I'll never let you go now. Never."

He gave her no chance to answer. Instead he captured her mouth in a long, drugging kiss. She did nothing to resist him, for she wanted him so much she could scarcely contain her yearning.

His breath mingled with hers, as if in so doing he gave life to her. Every inch of her skin trembled with anticipation—her blood sang at his touch. A sweet tension began to build in her, endowing her with strength while it filled her with such urgency, she found herself tearing at the buttons of his doublet.

He felt the urgency, too, she knew. His caresses were less than gentle, and she reveled in the roughness. His hands cupped her bottom, pressing her hard up against the growing thickness in his groin. She gasped at the sudden intimacy, and he pulled slightly away from her, burying his face in her neck with a groan.

"You're so soft," he murmured huskily against her ear. "Sometimes I forget how soft you are. I don't mean to hurt you, sweetling."

She clasped his waist, drawing his body back against hers. "You haven't hurt me." Not physically, she thought. And she'd learn to live with the other kind of pain. But for now, she'd have him in body, at least.

She stretched up against him to kiss his neck and felt his neck muscles tighten under her soft touch. Then timidly she slid the tip of her tongue along the side of his neck up to his ear.

At that delicate caress, his control broke. With a growl, he lifted her in his arms and strode toward the bed. Then all was a flurry of leather, linen, and lace as he removed her boots and every stitch of her clothing, his gaze growing bolder and bolder as he took in the beauty he revealed bit by bit.

Although he'd seen her naked now several times, she still couldn't adjust to having her body so blatantly observed. Instinctively she snatched a sheet up to cover herself, but he murmured "Don't" and brushed the sheet away. So she knelt on the bed before him in silence. His eyes locked with hers as he began to remove his own clothing. With an almost painful longing, she watched him reveal each tantalizing bit of skin. She ought to look away, but she didn't want to miss seeing every part of him, for it might be her last time to see him like this.

In the dusky light filling the room, his body seemed dusted with gold, for the sprigs of chestnut hair that covered him caught the sun's dying rays. He reminded her of a mighty oak—solid and unyielding in its majesty.

And while she watched him with unabashed pleasure, his gaze traveled over the whole of her bared body as he knelt on the bed in front of her. Her skin shone pale as lily petals, and he reached out almost reverently with one hand to skim lightly down from the slight hollow of her neck to the ripe fullness of her breasts. There he paused to tease one nipple, which thrust itself boldly against his finger.

He smiled. Then he moved lower, down her flat belly to her hips and the smooth ivory of her thighs. His fingers stroked her skin from her hips to her knees. Then they slid slowly up inside, running along the sensitive inner skin until she thought her legs would turn to water.

A delicious shiver shook her, for everywhere he touched her she tingled. But when his hand moved higher between her legs and with no warning he buried one finger in her honeyed warmth, she could stand no more. She swayed against him and clutched at his

shoulders, wanting only to feel his body melting into
hers.

With a groan, he caught her up against him with his
free hand and kissed her deeply, even while his other
hand continued to work its magic. As he brought her
higher and higher to realms of fulfillment she'd never
reached before, she arched against him, making low
moans in her throat.

He tore his lips from hers. "That's it, my Gypsy
princess. Show me your true mettle," he murmured
hoarsely.

Then he pressed her down against the sheets and
entered her in one glorious thrust. He began to move
slowly within her, his eyes fixed on her face. "Have I
removed your disguise . . . once and for all?" he asked
her as his breathing became more labored. "Have I
. . . truly captured . . . the elusive Lady Marianne?"

"Yes," she whispered, meeting his thrusts with
abandon. "I'm yours. Yes, yes. . . ."

The words became a chant that kept time with her
rapidly beating heart and his quickening plunges. Soon
she was swept up in the pattern of the dance, in the
grafting of his body to hers so they became one limb,
one branch, one tree pulsing with life. Then they were
at the height of the dance, and he filled her with his
seed with a cry of triumph.

Afterward they lay spent and panting, their arms
and legs entwined. It took several moments for Marianne's heart to slow its frantic pace. Garett's hands
still would not cease their roaming, although now his
caresses were gentle reminders of what they'd just
shared. His tenderness made a lump form in her throat,
and she fought back her tears, knowing he wouldn't
understand them.

At last, Garett propped himself up on one elbow and
stared down at her, his face aglow. He toyed with a
lock of her hair as she gazed up at him and wondered
what was to become of them now.

"I hope you've not made a tragic mistake in staying
with me, sweetling," he murmured, his face turning
somber.

"Hush," she whispered, wanting not to lose the beauty of the moment. "Let's not speak of the morrow till it comes."

He started to retort, but she placed a hand over his mouth. "I'm hungry, Garett," she said lightly, desperate to erase the worry from his brow. "I-I'd like to eat now."

He gave her one last searching glance, then pulled her hand away from his lips with a sigh. "As you wish. We'll eat. And we'll leave the morrow until to-morrow."

A reprieve. That's what he was allowing, and she snatched it gladly.

She started to rise from the bed, but he pressed her back down. "Stay here," he told her with a sudden gleam in his eye. Then he left the bed to go to the table.

She watched as he filled two wooden platters with food, then returned to the bed with them. He seemed totally unconscious of his nakedness, but she couldn't help but stare at his broad chest, lean waist, and well-knit thighs. When he climbed back on the bed, carefully balancing the platters, he caught her staring at him and gave her a wolfish grin.

She blushed. Then she realized he fully intended for them to eat in bed, because he set the platters down between them.

"What are you doing?" she asked in surprise.

He merely lifted a piece of bread spread lavishly with butter, broke off a piece, and brought it to her mouth. She hesitated only an instant before opening her mouth to receive it, her heart giving a tiny flutter.

His fingers brushed her lips, and she shivered in delight. Such an intimate thing, to be fed by someone. She'd never done it before. Nor had she been so reckless as to eat her meal in bed. But as Garett offered her another piece of bread, his eyes burning when she took it on her tongue, she found she enjoyed this new way of eating.

In moments she was reciprocating with pleasure, feeding him bits of pigeon that she'd torn from the tiny

bones. Her fingers never left his mouth without his
licking, sucking, or kissing them, and as soon as she
discovered what a pleasure that was, she gave his the
same tribute. When taken from his hands, the food
tasted like manna—even the peas, each one placed on
the tongue with care, became fruits of the gods.

Crumbs soon littered the bed as their meal became
a game to see who could feed the other in the most
enticing manner, as they both, by silent agreement,
sought to forget what lay before them in London. He
laughed when she offered him a piece of bread held
between her teeth, which she wouldn't release until he
took it also between his. Their playful tug of war ended
when the bread softened in both of their mouths and
broke, prompting yet another kiss.

After they had eaten their fill of pigeon, mutton,
bread, and peas, he lifted a slice of baked apple, drip-
ping with juice. A wicked gleam in his eye, he offered
her a taste. She took it in her mouth. Then some of
the spiced juice dripped down onto her breast. Before
she could wipe it away, he lowered his lips to suck it
from her skin. Then his mouth traveled farther over to
fasten on the tip of her breast, teasing it until she
moaned deep in her throat.

He lifted his head to gaze at her glowing face. With
a hint of regret on his face, he stared down at the bed,
littered with crumbs and dishes. His eyes returned to
her face, and he smiled. Silently he shifted her over
so he could slide the top sheet from beneath her. Then
he climbed off the bed and lifted the sheet by its four
corners, bundling platters, bones, and all up in it.
Striding to the corner of the room, he tossed the bun-
dle down.

As he strode back to the bed, his intentions fully
apparent, she managed to tease, "But, Garett, I'm still
hungry."

He climbed into bed and drew her against the hard
length of him. "I know, love," he murmured, his eyes
alight with desire as he pressed her down against the
pillows, "but you won't be for long."

Chapter Twenty-one

"The course of true love never did run smooth."
—Shakespeare,
A Midsummer Night's Dream

The sun had reached its zenith when the travelers at last halted before Garett's London house. Marianne stared at the imposing structure, reminded of how powerful Garett had become since he'd regained his lands. Now he held her life and future in his hands. Unable to slow the frantic beating of her heart, she watched him dismount. Despite their blissful evening together, she still felt uncertain of what he intended for her.

Had their intimacy the night before been but a dream? With the morning had come a terrible foreboding to wrap its icy arms about both of them. Silently they'd dressed, silently they'd begun their somber journey again. He'd avoided looking at her most of the morning. But she took hope from the brief kiss he'd given her just before they'd left their room together at the inn.

Now a melancholy air clung to them both. Last night she'd shamelessly used his desire as a weapon to force him into recognizing she meant more to him than he'd admit. She thought she'd been successful. Yet she'd hoped more would come of their night's passion. She'd hoped to gain his trust by it. In that, she didn't know if she'd succeeded. He hadn't spoken of what they'd do in London, and his continuing silence throughout the morning told her better than any words that he didn't yet entirely trust her.

Now he helped her dismount, his gaze resting for a brief moment on her masked face. Then he accompanied her into the house. Fifteen well-dressed servants stood at attention inside the door, their smiling faces disguising any concerns they had about the hardship put upon them by their master's surprise visit. Unfortunately, fifteen pairs of eyes also followed her with curiosity as she entered the room.

When Garett introduced her as Mina, his guest, and made no explanation for the mask she wore, Marianne was surprised, but knew he was right to be circumspect. No need to make the servants a party to shielding a suspected criminal. As long as they didn't know who she was, they couldn't be held at fault for keeping silent about her presence. He made it clear she wasn't to be discussed beyond the confines of his house. The servants seemed to accept that command as if it were common for him to ask it.

Once Garett had sent the servants about their duties unloading the carts and continuing to prepare the house, he took her and William aside.

"I have some matters to attend to that may take me well into the evening," he told William. "While I'm gone, make certain no one enters this house. No one, not even tradesmen or friends of the servants."

"Yes, m'lord," William responded.

"And make whatever preparations are necessary for us to travel to France."

"France!" William and Marianne exclaimed in unison.

Garett's countenance grew stony. "Just do as I say," he told William, then dismissed him with a curt nod.

As William left, Garett turned toward the door, but Marianne laid her hand on his arm. "Why—why are we going to France?"

The muscles of his arm tensed beneath her hand, and he refused to meet her gaze. "We may not be. I don't know yet. Everything depends on what I discover this afternoon. But if matters don't go well—" He

frowned. "It would be best if you didn't remain in
England."

A knot began to grow in the pit of her stomach.
"And you? You would go with me?"

His brooding gaze shifted to her. "Of course.
Someone must protect you."

She could scarcely believe what he was saying. "You
would—you would stay there with me?"

"Until it was safe for us to return. Both of us," he
bit out.

"But Garett, what about Falkham House? What
about your lands?"

A muscle pulsed in his jaw. "What about them?"
he said with forced nonchalance as if it were a matter
of course for him to leave his estates.

But she knew better. She knew how much he loved
his land and wanted to make Falkham House a place
of glory again. "You would leave them behind for
me?" she asked thickly, emotion choking her.

His eyes glittered. At that moment he seemed almost to hate her for the hold she had on him. She felt
as if she held a falcon by one leg, and it was clawing
and fighting to be free of her, all the while realizing
it couldn't be.

"I can think of no other way to keep you from being
hanged or imprisoned," he said with a sudden aloof-
ness that chilled her blood. "If you remain in England,
someone is bound to reveal your presence eventually.
Then they'll come for you."

"I can't allow you—"

"Let it be!" he cut in.

Then he clasped her shoulders. Her questioning gaze
seemed to penetrate all his defenses.

"I couldn't endure seeing you taken, do you hear?"
he said, a raw thread of pain in his tone. "Nor could
I prevent it. So we won't take the chance."

"You could send William with me. Aunt Tamara
could be here in one day. Then we three could travel
and you could stay—"

"No!" His fingers dug into her shoulders. "I told
you last night I'd never let you go. I meant it."

"But such a sacrifice—"

He silenced her words with a quick, hard kiss, born as much of fury as of affection. Then he stared down at her with eyes clear and cold. "Speak of it no more. I will have agents to tend my estates. In time perhaps—" He broke off. "It doesn't matter. It may be the only way to keep you safe."

She wanted to tell him she loved him, to spill out her emotions for him like jewels from a tightly held bag and somehow make his sacrifice easier. But another part of her felt a terrible guilt for what he planned to do. If she told him how she felt, he would feel even more of a need to make his sacrifice. She had no right to place such constraints on him.

If he chose to take her from England, he must choose to do it because of what he felt, not what she felt. Yet he'd said they might not leave. What did he plan to do?

"Where are you going now?" she asked, a worried frown on her face.

He looked suddenly uncomfortable, and his gaze shifted from hers.

She clutched at his arm. "Garett! What are you going to do?"

He lifted her hand from his arm, squeezing her fingers in his for a brief moment before releasing them. "Just remember, don't open the door to anyone" was all he would say. Then he was gone.

For a long time after he left, she stared at the closed door with tears streaming down her face. "I love you, Garett," she whispered, hoping some day she'd have the chance to say it to his face. Then, with an aching heart, she curled up in a chair to wait.

Garett stood in the foyer of the king's sitting room, nervously watching the door. Never had he come to the king for such an important favor. Never before had he so feared being refused.

That was what came of caring for a woman. For the first time in his life, he felt true heart-pounding fear, and not for himself, either. The fear was no less real, however. The thought of Mina—Lady Marianne—being taken by the soldiers made his blood run cold. He didn't know how she'd managed to do it, but she'd crept into his soul and made a nest there. He couldn't seem to oust her from it.

He didn't even want to anymore. That was the worst of it.

"His Majesty will see Lord Falkham now," the gentleman of the chamber entered the room to announce.

Garett straightened, his pulse suddenly racing in a manner uncharacteristic of him. He forced himself to assume the air of a man of leisure. He reminded himself this was just like any other encounter in which he wanted to elicit information without revealing what he knew. Except this time, his opponent was the king. With measured steps, he followed the gentleman of the chamber into the sitting room.

Charles was at the window, watching his latest mistress play tennis with three other ladies in the gardens below. He turned as soon as Garett entered and flashed him a warm smile.

"Your Majesty," Garett said with a bow.

"So you've come out of hiding, have you?"

Garett looked at Charles blankly.

The king chuckled. "I wondered why Falkham House held such an appeal for you that you wouldn't even occasionally grant us your presence. Then Hampden informed me you'd locked yourself away at the old manor with a new mistress. That explained a great deal."

Garett couldn't halt the brief frown that crossed his features. "What else did Hampden tell you about my mistress?"

Charles seemed pleased he'd managed to disconcert his friend. "That she's exotic—a Gypsy or some such thing—and that she has a quick tongue. He says she's quite a beauty." He smiled as he added, "And that you guard her jealously."

Garett hardly heard that last phrase. So Hampden

hadn't told the king anything about Garett's earlier suspicions of Mina. That was something, at least.

"Hampden ought to keep his observations to himself once in a while," Garett said, easily falling into the part Hampden had unwittingly given him.

"Come, now, Falkham, you ought to bring her to court. Let us all have a look at her. Or is that why you're here?"

Garett met Charles's questioning gaze with a steady stare. "No, Your Majesty. This time I've come to ask a favor of you."

"A favor?"

"It concerns someone we're both interested in."

Charles strode back to the window and looked out with a frown. "Your uncle."

"Yes."

A worried expression crossed the king's face. "I don't know what more I could do about him. You've done quite well on your own. His reputation is in a shambles, he's badly in debt, and he's lost a great many of his powerful friends. No one dares champion him against you."

Garett's grim smile acknowledged the king's words. "There's still the matter of his involvement in the attempt on your life."

"Yes, there is that, isn't there?" Charles remarked, his eyes narrowing speculatively.

Garett cautioned himself to move with great care. "Have you yet to wring a confession from that physician? Has he implicated my uncle?"

Charles sighed, then shook his head. "Nay. He insists he's innocent. But they haven't used torture yet—I'm loath to allow such barbaric methods for a man of rank."

Garett hid the relief that washed through him. Mina's father still lived and was apparently unharmed. Until he'd heard it from the king himself, he couldn't be certain of it. "But you're convinced he's guilty."

The king held up his hands in clear exasperation. "I don't know. I've always had this—this instinct that he speaks the truth. Still, everyone else believes him guilty. The poison was in his medications. By his own admission, they never left his hands from the time his daughter gave them to him."

"Daughter?" Garett asked, playing dumb.

"He had a daughter who prepared his medicines."

"And what of her?"

A look of scathing contempt crossed the king's face. "A silly twit, evidently, though I would never have guessed it when I first met her. The news of his arrest so alarmed her she threw herself into the Thames and drowned."

"Silly twit, indeed," Garett murmured as he fought a second time to keep relief from showing on his face. Thank God no one yet suspected Marianne was alive. "Since she prepared the medicines, do you think she had a part in putting the poison in them?"

" 'Tis possible, I suppose. It's very odd, though. Sir Henry insists she prepared them and gave them immediately into his keeping. Then they never left his hands. He could have lied about it, or even blamed it on her now that she's dead, but he hasn't. He just seems bewildered by the whole matter. Of course, I suppose she could have planted the poison of her own accord. Then she killed herself when she realized she was to be discovered. Who knows? But I can't believe she planned alone to kill me."

"That seems doubtful indeed," Garett agreed with a calm in his voice that he didn't feel. He wondered what the king would think if he knew the truth about Marianne's death.

"But to return to your favor," Charles said, his gaze returning to Garett's. "What is it you wish me to grant you?"

Garett met the king's stare with the most innocuous one he could muster. "I wish to question the prisoner myself."

Charles gazed at him in frank surprise. "Why?"

"Remember, Your Majesty, what services I performed for you in the past. I was quite adept at gleaning information from unwilling participants."

The king's face clouded. "Yes, you were. I always wondered about your methods."

"I assure you I never did anything unsavory."

Charles studied him a moment, then remarked, "No, I don't suppose you did. You manage to intimidate a person just by turning that scowl of yours on them."

A brief smile flickered over Garett's face. "Except for Your Majesty, of course."

"Of course," Charles remarked dryly.

"If you'll permit me to question this Sir Henry, perhaps I can be more successful at dragging a confession from him."

"Or an admission that your uncle was his fellow conspirator," Charles said with a lift of his eyebrow.

"Yes."

Charles observed him closely for a moment, rubbing his chin as he thought. "I believe if anyone could do it, you could," he murmured, half to himself.

Garett schooled his features into nonchalance as he awaited the king's answer.

After a long pause, Charles shrugged. "Well, then. I suppose it cannot hurt to have you attempt it."

Garett felt the tension leave his limbs. "Thank you, Your Majesty," Garett murmured, then gave a deep bow.

He remained standing in respectful silence while the king called in his gentleman of the chambers and commanded that Garett be brought to the Tower to visit the prisoner. When the men came who were to accompany Garett, he took his leave of the king, wondering how long it would be before he saw His Majesty again.

Then he thrust that thought from his head and followed the men out of Whitehall. Throughout the long ride across London to the Tower, he focused his mind on the more difficult task at hand—of speaking with Sir Henry. When they reached the imposing, forbidding group of towers, a sudden cold fear assailed Garett—the same fear that had eaten at him from the time he'd discovered who Mina really was.

The chilly corridors of the Tower made it difficult to

focus on anything but his fear, for all he could think of was that he must save Mina from this. The snortings and roars of wild beasts filtered through the halls, because part of the Tower was still used to exhibit wild animals—bears, lions, and all manner of exotic beasts brought from England's many colonies. Hearing the noises darkened Garett's mood considerably. No matter what he discovered, no matter what she'd done, he'd never allow his Gypsy princess to be forced to lie in this place. Never!

Then they were at Sir Henry's cell. The turnkey opened the door, and Garett entered.

At least the room was spacious and well-provisioned, he thought. Then his eyes fell on the prisoner, who stood with his back to Garett, staring out the window at the sun glinting off the Thames.

Garett could tell the man had once been well-proportioned, for his clothes hung loosely on him. Now he was thin to the point of being gaunt. His hair was completely white, yet he wasn't stooped with age. He stood quite proudly in his worn doublet and breeches.

Garett motioned to the turnkey and men who'd accompanied him to step outside the cell. They obeyed, the turnkey closing the door behind Garett.

"Sir Henry?" Garett asked.

The man turned, and Garett had to force himself not to react, for although Sir Henry was a man—an older man—his hazel eyes were the eyes of his daughter.

Those eyes now filled with a hostile defensiveness Garett recognized all too well.

"So they've sent another to torment me, have they?" Sir Henry muttered. "And a good strong young soldier by the look of you. Have they decided 'tis time to use more forceful methods of persuasion with me?"

Garett was still recovering from the shock of being faced by a man so like the woman he cared for. "Nay," he said, continuing to stare at the prisoner before him.

Sir Henry grew more testy. "Well, sir, may I at least know the name of my tormentor?"

Garett hesitated only briefly before answering. "Garett Lyon."

Sir Henry frowned, seeming to search his mind for where he'd heard the name before.

"Earl of Falkham," Garett added.

Sir Henry's gaze shot up to rest on Garett's face. He scrutinized him with a keen eye. "Pitney's nephew," he murmured. "I've heard of you from the gossip among my jailers. You're the one who's put Sir Pitney to rout, so they say."

"Yes."

"Good for you. I always hated that ne'er-do-well."

Garett remained silent, pondering that statement.

"You've been given my house, haven't you?" Sir Henry asked with a certain challenging bluntness.

Garett's eyes narrowed. " 'Twas my house from the beginning. I'm the legal heir. The house should never have been sold to you."

Sir Henry shrugged. "That may be. But we thought you were dead. Dead men don't own estates. In any case, it matters little. If by some miracle my innocence is proven, you're welcome to the estate. I prefer my quiet house here in London. Falkham House was the joy of my wife and my daughter." The man's expression altered, stark pain shining in his eyes, before he went on more slowly. "It was to be my daughter's legacy. But with her dead, I see little point in fighting for it."

Garett moved closer to the older man and took his arm, leading him off as far from the door as possible. Then he fixed Sir Henry with a sincere gaze. "Suppose I were to tell you your daughter is not dead."

Sir Henry's face betrayed nothing, but his eyes lit for the merest instant. Then he frowned. "Is this a new form of torment, my lord?" he hissed. "Tantalize me with hope, then dash my hopes against the rocks? If so, it will not suffice. I know she's dead. They told me that the first day I was arrested."

"Ah, but did they tell you how she died? By drowning herself in the Thames? Now ask yourself, would Mina ever do something so foolish as to kill herself?"

Sir Henry snorted and shook his head. "I know, I know, I couldn't believe it myself. Mina would never—" He broke off as he realized exactly what Garett had said. He clasped Garett's arm, his fingers digging painfully into it. "How do you know my daughter's nickname?"

"Tamara calls her that," Garett said, staring with sudden compassion into the face of his lover's father. "It stands for Lumina, her middle name. Your wife, the Gypsy, gave it to her. It suits her well. With that golden hair and gentle smile, she *is* like a light."

Sir Henry's face turned ashen. He jerked away from Garett, moving to sit on his narrow hard bed in stunned silence. He closed his eyes, then opened them again to fix Garett with a disbelieving stare. "Is—is my daughter truly alive, then?"

"Aye. The tale of her drowning was a ruse your wife's sister used to help Mina escape London and the king's guard."

Sir Henry digested that in silence. Then he studied Garett with an intense gaze. His voice trembled as he asked, "And how did you come to know of her?"

Now came the difficult part, Garett thought. "She returned to Lydgate, and I took her prisoner." He said it coldly, deliberately failing to mention how much time passed before he discovered who she was.

Sir Henry buried his face in his hands. "Then she is a prisoner of the king now as well," he muttered despairingly.

"Nay."

Sir Henry's head shot up. "She isn't in the Tower, imprisoned as am I?"

Here was where Garett had to school himself to be hard, to refrain from showing any emotion. "Not yet. The king still believes her dead. So her life—and her freedom—are in my hands. You have the power to give them both back to her. I'll arrange for her to flee to France, and I'll make certain she's left there with sufficient money, if only you'll tell the truth about the attempt on the king's life. Tell me who your fellow conspirators are, and I'll set her free."

Sir Henry stiffened, his face reflecting his pain, and Garett felt a stab of guilt. Irrationally he wanted to assure the man he could never hurt Marianne in any manner. But at the same time, he knew this was his last chance to learn the truth. Regardless of his real intentions, Garett meant to use the one thing the poor old knight would respond to.

"Is she—is she unharmed?" the man asked in a faltering voice.

Guilt gripped Garett anew, a different guilt this time. "Yes. She's been well provided for and treated with the courtesy befitting her station." He prayed God didn't strike him dead for that last blatant lie.

Sir Henry released a long-drawn breath. "She's well," he whispered, half to himself.

Garett stepped closer to the knight. "She'll continue to be well as long as you tell me the truth. Who planned your attempt on His Majesty's life? Who prepared the poisons? Was it my uncle?"

Sir Henry stood, rather unsteadily, then met Garett's piercing stare with great dignity. "You, my lord, are a reprehensible snake. I knew your father briefly. He would have cringed to witness his son use such low methods as you use now."

That statement struck Garett to the heart, for he knew Sir Henry spoke the truth. And though he could justify his actions to himself, saying he couldn't protect Mina without knowing the whole truth, he knew he sought that knowledge for partially selfish reasons. He wished once and for all to find a reason to trust her.

Suddenly his manipulation of Mina's father seemed unsavory to him. What's more, he realized with a start it was pointless. No matter what his methods revealed, he could never believe in his heart that Mina had conspired with his uncle against the king, even if Sir Henry claimed she'd made the poisons herself. Her innocence, her kind heart—both cried out against such a deed. She truly was a light in the darkness that had so long shrouded his soul. How could he question the purity of that light when it shone before him with every sweet smile?

In that moment, Garett knew he loved her, knew he could never believe wrong of her.

Sir Henry seemed oblivious to Garett's turmoil. "My lord, you've presented me with a bargain, distasteful as it is," he told him with grim firmness. "I wish to God I could accept the terms of it, for then I could save my daughter. But I can only beg you to find some mercy in that cold heart of yours. Even to save her life, I can't tell you who made the attempt on the king's life, for I don't know. 'Twas not I."

His fervent sincerity filled Garett with even more guilt. Garett turned abruptly away, a muscle working in his jaw. How could he ever have doubted her innocence? He'd been a fool for not recognizing that the love she offered could only come from an innocent heart. If only he'd listened to his own heart more, he might have seen it sooner and saved them both countless days of pain.

"My lord?" Sir Henry asked in alarm at Garett's continued silence. "What—what will you do now?"

Garett bowed his head, then turned to face the father of the woman he loved. He lifted his gaze to meet Sir Henry's. "Whatever I can to prove your innocence, of course. And Mina's."

Sir Henry looked blank for a moment; then his mouth thinned into a line, showing his blatant distrust of Garett. "Why would you strive to prove our innocence?"

Garett said the only thing he could think of. The truth. "Because I love your daughter, sir."

There. The truth was out for all the world to hear, and Garett didn't care what the world thought of it.

Apparently Sir Henry had a great deal to think of it. Amazement soon gave way to speculation in his expression. Then he assumed a stance not much different from the one Garett's father had used when Garett as a child had committed some grievous wrong. He stood with his bony arms crossed, his jaw firm, and his narrowing eyes intended to intimidate.

"Just how long have you kept my daughter prisoner, my lord?" he demanded.

For the first time since his childhood, Garett felt true shame. He didn't regret what he'd done, but he also couldn't help but recognize how Mina's father would regard it. He swallowed, suddenly wondering what on earth he could tell an irate father. He could lie, but eventually Sir Henry would learn the truth, if Garett was successful in proving Sir Henry's innocence. Still, telling the truth presented another set of unique problems. He chose his words carefully.

"How long?" Sir Henry demanded again.

Garett looked up into unsmiling eyes. "Long enough to come to know her," was all he said.

But it was enough. Sir Henry's hands clenched into bony fists. "Has she been a prisoner in your house all these many weeks?" he persisted.

"Nay," Garett answered. "I didn't discover her identity until quite recently." That much was true, although what he implied in the way he said it was misleading.

Sir Henry's face relaxed a trifle.

"Her aunt was also with her," Garett added, hoping to mollify Sir Henry.

The older man still hesitated to accept Garett entirely. "If you've hurt her—or—or—"

"She's happy and well, I assure you, sir."

Sir Henry snorted. "I'll be the judge of that. And if I find you've compromised her, I'll wish to see the wrong righted immediately."

Garett suddenly resented being treated like a youth. Anger flared in him. He took a step toward Sir Henry. "I love your daughter, sir. By my honor, I wouldn't wish to see her suffer in any way."

Sir Henry appeared to be assessing him. After a long scrutiny, he nodded. "Well, then. Have you some plan for keeping her from going to prison for a crime she had no part in?"

Garett felt a surge of relief that he was to be spared any more probing questions about his relationship with Mina. "No," he hastened to tell him. "Not yet. We must start by trying to determine who really did commit the crime, and how they managed to involve the two of you. Mina seems to think my uncle may have done it to regain Falkham House.''

'' 'Tis possible,'' Sir Henry said with a frown, at last turning his attention to the task of clearing his name and away from Garett and Mina. "Sir Pitney sold it to me for a pittance because he needed funds. Later, when I'd improved it, he apparently decided he had the money to buy it back. But I never wanted to resell it.''

"So perhaps he thought to force you out by painting you a traitor.''

Sir Henry slowly paced the room, his hands behind his back. "It was the way he liked to work. When he was trying to compel me to sell the estates back to him, he spread filthy rumors about my wife and my daughter, seeking to discredit me among my neighbors.''

Mina had said much the same thing. With a surge of self-loathing, Garett suddenly realized what the soldier's strange words about Pitney and Mina had meant. How could he have believed Mina capable of having any relationship with his treacherous uncle? No wonder she hadn't wanted to trust Garett with her secrets.

Somehow he'd atone for the way he'd distrusted her. He'd find out who was really behind the attempt on the king's life, no matter what it took. And then he'd spend the remainder of his life making it up to Mina.

He thought for a moment, then asked, "If my uncle truly is the culprit, let's consider how he might have planned the crime. What about the medicines themselves? I know you claim they never left your hands from the time you received them from Mina. Then how could poison have been added to them?''

Sir Henry shook his head. "I cannot say. I spend every waking moment thinking about it, but to the best of my memory, that pouch never left my hands.''

"Your medications weren't in bottles?''

"No. I'm terribly clumsy. I've broken many a bottle, so I find it more useful to carry my remedies in small pouches.''

Garett pondered that a moment. "And you're certain the pouches were in your possession at all times?"

"I'd swear to it. Every time I went to court, Mina rose early in the morning to prepare my powders and fill two or three pouches with them. Then I placed them beneath my belt where they remained until I administered the treatment.''

An image suddenly flashed into Garett's mind, a brief memory of a childhood trick he'd played on his uncle, whom he'd disliked even then. He'd smeared a thin layer of soap on the inside of his uncle's mug at dinner one night. After the ale had been poured all around, his uncle had swigged his own portion heartily, then nearly choked at the foul taste of it. Later Garett had been found out and forced to apologize to Sir Pitney, who'd insisted that Garett receive a severe caning for his trick. But the trick had taught his uncle one thing—just because a mug seemed empty didn't mean it was.

Garett's mouth went dry as he leveled his gaze on Sir Henry. "The pouches you used. Were they special ones? Did you buy them somewhere, or were they made at home?"

Sir Henry flashed Garett a quizzical look. "I used the same ones over and over for the king. Mina always wanted them to be fitting for royalty, so she'd made them specially of white satin and embroidered them with furbelows and the like. Why?"

White satin. Garett began to scowl. "If someone were to have dusted the inside of your pouches with a white powder such as arsenic, 'tis likely you or Mina wouldn't have noticed when she went to fill them," he mused aloud.

Sir Henry stopped his pacing. "Yes," he muttered. Then, more loudly, "Yes! It was always early morning when Mina filled them, and she did it by candlelight in a dim room. What's more, the pouches sometimes lay for days. Anyone could have entered the house and placed the poison in them. I often had visitors and patients and students wandering in and about my house. 'Twould have been easy—''

"Easy enough even without that," Garett stated with growing excitement. "A servant could have been bribed or someone could have entered the house without your knowledge."

"Aye, aye," Sir Henry said, his expression filling with horror. "So very easy to be a villain, eh?"

Garett nodded. And so very hard to prove the villainy. But surely someone would remember seeing a stranger enter Sir Henry's or Mina's private chambers. Or perhaps if a servant had been bribed—

"What will you do now?" Sir Henry asked.

Garett laid his hand unconsciously on his sword hilt. "Somewhere there is another who can fill in the pieces. It will take time to gain more knowledge, but perhaps I can use what I know to persuade the king to refrain from questioning you more until I've done some of my own questioning."

"All that's well and good, but while you're seeking the king's enemies, what becomes of my daughter?" Sir Henry demanded.

Garett's face softened as he thought of Mina. She would be his now, forever. He would see to it. Then he remembered she believed her father to be dead. A dark frown marred his brow. When she learned how much of the truth he'd kept from her, she wouldn't be happy, that was certain.

Sir Henry's concerned voice broke into his thoughts. "What about my daughter, my lord?"

Garett wiped the frown from his face. She might not be happy, but he'd convince her to forgive him. He must. "I'll make sure she's kept safe, sir—you've my word of honor on that. And when it's all over, with your permission I'll take her to wife."

On that, he'd brook no argument.

Chapter Twenty-two

"Let secret villainy from hence be warned;
Howe'er in private mischiefs are conceived,
Torture and shame attend their open birth. . . ."
— William Congreve,
The Double-Dealer

Marianne anxiously paced the hall off the entrance to Garett's London house, every few moments casting a glance at the door. Garett had been gone but a few hours, yet she could hardly endure the waiting. Her mind kept returning to their last conversation.

He was offering to sacrifice a great deal for her. One part of her rejoiced to know it, for it proved he cared more for her than he'd admit. But another part of her wanted to refuse the sacrifice. If indeed they fled to France, what would they do there? Could Garett truly be happy knowing he'd left behind everything he'd striven for? It wasn't likely.

He'd said naught of love or marriage. Clearly he intended them to live as husband and wife, but not to speak the necessary vows. She hugged herself tightly, tears starting up in her eyes. Could she continue with him in such a manner? She didn't think so. Her heart was given to him, but could she trust him not to break it?

Yet he'd said he'd never let her go. Wasn't that a vow in itself?

Those eternal questions plagued her continuously until a pounding at the heavy oak door brought her out of her thoughts. She stood motionless, uncertain what to do. Another bout of pounding began, and she broke out in a cold sweat.

The noise brought William, who stepped into the hall and gestured to her to be silent. The noise also drew other servants. They stood there staring at the door uneasily.

Then a voice bellowed, "Open this door immediately in the name of His Majesty the king!"

Marianne paled, drawing her cloak more closely about her. Conscious of the servants' alarm, she nodded her head toward the door, indicating that William should open it. William frowned, but he motioned her into an alcove as he strode for the door. She watched from the shadows of the alcove as he opened the massive door a crack and asked what was the matter.

Before he could stop them, before Marianne could even flee, men were forcing their way inside. The ones who shouldered the door open weren't soldiers. They had frightening faces of fierce aspect, their doublets greasy and dirty. In comparison, the soldiers who then followed with reluctance behind them appeared to be almost gentlemen.

Then another man entered, one whose aging countenance did nothing to soothe Marianne's fears. Sir Pitney Tearle. What was he doing here? Had he learned of her presence or did he simply wish to harm his nephew?

She froze where she stood in the shadows, her hand lifting to brush her mask.

"Where's your master?" Pitney demanded of William.

"He's not here. And what mean you, bringing your lackeys here to soil m'lord's house?" William retorted with a sneer, gesturing to the men who were tracking mud and dirt across the stone floor.

Another man, whose uniform clearly showed him to be the soldiers' captain, pivoted to fix William with a grim stare. "Listen here, you're speaking of the king's guard, so you'd best keep a civil tongue about you. My men and I don't wish to be here. But the gentleman there has made claims we can't ignore. He says your master harbors a criminal—a woman who might have made an attempt on His Majesty's life.''

One of the more timid maids gasped, then went ashen as several pairs of eyes turned her way.

''Don't just stand there,'' Pitney told the captain, gesturing to the trembling maid and the other servants. ''Question them all before the woman has a chance to escape. If he's in London, then she's got to be with him. Why don't you start by questioning that skittish one?'' He pointed to the maid who'd gasped.

The maid began to weep as one of the other servants tried to comfort her. ''I—I don't know about no criminals, sir, truly I don't!'' she sobbed.

Pitney had just stepped forward to clasp the maid's arm when Marianne could bear it no more. She left the shadows and strode into the hallway.

''What is this all about?'' she demanded of the captain of the guard.

Her masked face and noble bearing seemed to give him pause. He gazed at her with frank suspicion. ''And who might you be?''

''I am, shall we say, a friend of his lordship,'' she replied evenly, hoping that the captain would assume she was a mistress of Garett's, perhaps even a married woman who wouldn't want her visage known. ''He isn't here at the moment, and I was just preparing to leave myself. Perhaps you could return later?''

Pitney's eyes narrowed, and he smiled smugly as if he knew exactly her game. But the captain seemed to assume what she implied, for he shifted from foot to foot in discomfort. ''I'm sorry, madam, but I—''

''You fool!'' Pitney sputtered to the captain when he realized the captain wasn't immediately going to act. ''It could be her—Winchilsea's spawn!''

The captain flushed, then gave Pitney a warning glance. Slowly he turned his gaze back to her. ''Madam, I'm afraid the gentleman here thinks you might be the one we seek. I shall have to ask you to remove your mask, milady.''

''Really, Captain, this is terribly embarrassing—''

''Don't I know it, milady. But I must ask it of you

all the same." He stood there, his manner polite, but his eyes watching her.

She realized that for all his seeming bumbling, the captain was no fool. She'd have little chance of convincing him to release her. And one look at the hatred burning in Pitney's eyes told her he'd never agree to let her pass even if the captain did.

"As you wish," she murmured to the captain. *It's over*, she thought dully as she undid the ties that held her mask. The fighting was over. At least Garett wouldn't have to sacrifice his lands for her.

When she'd removed the mask from her face and dropped it to the ground, Pitney stared at her with satisfaction.

"You see," he told the captain, whom she felt certain still didn't know who she was. " 'Tis the little Gypsy witch herself."

The captain moved forward. "I'm afraid, milady, I must ask you to come with me."

Pitney stepped into the captain's path, blocking it. "Nay, not without Lord Falkham. He's the traitor in this, for he's been protecting her."

Marianne's heart raced in sudden agonizing comprehension. Oh, God, so that was his plan—to use her to entrap Garett. His spy, that man Ashton who'd seen her in Lydgate when Garett had brought her before the council, must have told Pitney about her. Perhaps he'd even followed them to London. Pitney had taken it from there.

"Nay," she told the captain. "Lord Falkham doesn't know who I am. He—he took me for his mistress, but I never told him my true identity, for I feared he'd relinquish me to the soldiers if he knew."

Pitney laughed harshly. "You work hard to shield your lover, don't you? Such a shame you won't succeed. We'll just wait here until he returns, and see what story he gives, eh, Captain?"

The captain looked uncomfortable, but it was apparent he knew where his duties lay. Lord Falkham had been caught harboring a woman accused of trea-

son, and thus he must be questioned. "We'll wait,"
the captain said gruffly.

At his signal, his men took up a post by the door
while Pitney's men moved to the back of the house in
search of other entrances.

Pitney sidled up to Marianne, a leer on his face. He
pushed her hood off her head, then skimmed his hand
over her hair. When she slapped his hand away, he
caught her wrist, squeezing it painfully.

"A pity you went to him instead of me, Gypsy brat.
I might have protected you from the soldiers far better," he hissed softly, his face looming over hers.

His eyes fastened on her lips, and he smiled. Then
he lifted his other hand to her neck, closing his fingers
loosely about it. "Such a lovely neck," he murmured.
"A shame to see it stretched by the noose. Of course,
perhaps that needn't happen. I still have some influence, and with Garett out of the way, my power will
rise again. I could persuade His Majesty to release you
into my hands."

With utter contempt blazing in her face, she spat at
him.

His gaze hardened as he dropped his hand from her
neck to wipe the spittle from his chin. Then he lifted
his hand. "For that, you Gypsy bitch, I'll—"

"Strike her, and you forfeit your life!" a voice rang
out in the room.

Every head turned. Standing in the doorway was
Garett, his sword already drawn and his expression
one of unmitigated rage. Heedless of the soldiers who
drew their weapons, he strode into the room toward
where Pitney stood, still gripping Marianne's wrist.

"Unhand her this instant!" Garett commanded.

Pitney obeyed, but only to draw his own sword.

"My lords!" the captain bellowed, and put himself
between them. "I came to take a prisoner, not to see
the shedding of blood. Sheathe your weapons before I
have my men arrest both of you!"

Marianne held her breath as the two enemies
watched each other warily, neither moving to do as
he'd been commanded.

"My lords!" the captain repeated.

Pitney was the first to relent, for he had the most to lose by not complying. He clearly believed Garett was to be arrested in any case. Once Pitney's sword was sheathed, Garett turned to Marianne with a burning look in his eyes.

"Did he harm you?" he asked.

"No," she murmured, her eyes pleading with him not to force matters.

Only after her answer did he slide his sword back into its scabbard.

"My lord, I've something to tell you," Marianne hastened to add before Garett could reveal anything to further ruin his position. "I'm afraid these gentlemen believe me guilty of a crime. I've told them you don't know who I really am, but—"

"Silence!" Pitney shouted in outrage. "The man may speak for himself of what he did and didn't know. Let him do so."

Marianne looked at the captain in silent appeal, but he merely turned his hard gaze on Garett. "My lord, I must ask you to tell me what you know of this woman."

Marianne's eyes pleaded with him silently to save himself.

Garett gave her a long searching gaze, then turned to face the captain. "This woman is Lady Marianne, daughter of Sir Winchilsea. I have been aiding her for the last several weeks because I believe her to be guilty of no wrong. To my knowledge, no one has yet accused her of committing any crime—only her father has been accused. Thus, I don't quite understand why you've come to arrest her."

Marianne stood stunned. For her, he was risking his reputation, his lands, his very life! She wanted to stop him, but didn't know what she could say to do so.

Pitney's face grew mottled with rage. "She's a traitor to her king and her country. She only escaped being accused because she was believed to be dead!"

The captain watched both men with interest.

"I say she's blameless, as was her father," Garett retorted.

"Then who committed the crime?" Pitney asked. "No one carried his medicines but he—everyone said so. And she prepared his medicines. Nay, he was guilty, and so is she. You can't prove otherwise!"

"Ah, but I can," Garett remarked coolly.

Marianne looked astonished, as did the others in the room, particularly Pitney.

Then Pitney's eyes narrowed. "How?"

Garett turned to the captain. "I think, sir, that this discussion must be continued in the presence of those who have the power to determine a judgment. His Majesty should hear what I have to say. I won't speak further until you bring me and Lady Marianne before him."

Marianne sucked in her breath. What game was Garett playing? Had he really discovered something while he'd been gone, or was he bluffing, hoping he could prevail upon His Majesty to release them both simply by virtue of his friendship with the king? Could he really be successful? Her pulse began to race as a desperate hope was startled into being within her.

The captain seemed uncertain of what to do, and Pitney took advantage of that uncertainty.

"Don't be a fool, man," Pitney told the captain, dropping his hand to rest on the hilt of his sword. "If you bring this lunatic before His Majesty with these ridiculous ravings, the king will have your head for it. Cast them both in the Tower. Then His Majesty may question them at his leisure."

"You'd like that, wouldn't you?" Garett retorted. "Of course, before we'd spent one day in the Tower, you'd make certain we were murdered."

"You wretched—" Pitney began, then caught himself as he felt the captain's eyes on him.

The captain turned a questioning gaze to Garett. "My lord, you realize I don't have to grant your request."

Garett smiled coldly. "I know. Still, if you do, I promise to go willingly to the palace. If the king refuses to see us, then you may take us both to the Tower. But if you don't bring us to the king first, I'll fight you and your men when you try to take us prisoner. I won't win, of course, but I'll die trying. And how will you explain that to the king? He may not easily accept your tale that I fought because I was guilty. The king knows me quite well, and he's never had reason to doubt my loyalty, whereas Sir Pitney's loyalty has been doubted time and again."

"You—you damnable liar!" Pitney sputtered.

"Quiet!" the captain said irritably. "All right, then, I'll take you to Whitehall. Then we'll see if His Majesty grants you an audience."

Marianne felt some of her tension leave her. Garett knew something he wasn't telling. She was sure of it.

Then, at the captain's command, two soldiers flanked her, and two moved to flank Garett.

"One other thing," Garett said. "You must bind us both—Lady Marianne and I."

The captain looked offended. "My lord, I trust you and my lady not to—"

"Aye," Garett broke in. "I know you do. But my uncle doesn't. I wouldn't like to find my throat cut, simply because I stumbled in the street and he took it for an escape attempt."

Marianne glanced at Pitney and felt a sickening lurch when she saw his face whiten to an unearthly pale. Clearly Garett had guessed exactly what Pitney had planned. Pitney had made a potentially fatal mistake, and he knew it.

"Captain," Pitney interjected, "perhaps Lord Falkham will feel more comfortable if I don't accompany you at all. I have done my part in the king's service. I need not be there to accuse them, for their crime speaks for itself."

Garett laughed harshly. "Afraid, dear uncle, of what I might have to say before the king? Afraid it might concern you?"

The captain shot Pitney an assessing glance. "Sir, you must come with us. You must also explain how you knew of her ladyship's presence here."

For a moment Marianne thought Pitney would protest. Then he drew himself up in forced bravado. "If you insist," he murmured with a shrug, as if he'd only suggested absenting himself in an effort to be of service.

The captain motioned to one of the guards standing next to Marianne. He withdrew a pair of manacles that he clapped around her wrists. Numbly, Marianne watched as Garett stepped closer to the captain and murmured something in the captain's ear. The captain gave Garett an assessing glance, then called one of the guards over and gave him a command in a low voice that no one else could hear. The guard nodded and left the house.

Then another soldier stepped forward to manacle Garett. Garett stood only a few feet from her, his eyes never leaving her face. His expression seemed to say *Trust me*.

She wanted to do so, yet never before in her life had she been so afraid. She'd found her love in the midst of hardship, and she feared losing him so soon after knowing him. He gave her a reassuring smile, and she smiled back, forcing all the love she felt for him into her expression.

His eyes burned suddenly as his lips formed words. She thought he said *I love you*, but she couldn't be certain. It could also have been *I want you*.

Then they led him in front of her out to the street and she followed, a tiny hope growing within her heart.

The audience room of King Charles II echoed with the sounds of booted feet tramping the marble floors. The king himself sat in an oaken chair intently regarding the assembling of such a strange group of subjects. He tapped his bejeweled fingers impatiently on the arm of his chair when Pitney Tearle strode in as if he came to court every day. Then the captain of the guard brought in Lord Falkham. A frown instantly crossed the king's face as he realized Lord Falkham was manacled.

Next Marianne was led from behind Garett to stand beside him, and the king looked noticeably startled.

"Lady Marianne?" he inquired, half rising from his chair.

She managed a low curtsy despite the manacles, and he jumped to his feet.

"Take those manacles off her ladyship!" he commanded the captain. "And off Lord Falkham, too."

The captain motioned to two of the guards, who did as the king had bidden them.

"What is the meaning of this?" the king asked. "I was only told some muddled tale about Falkham harboring criminals and wishing an audience."

Pitney seemed loath to speak, now that he was in the presence of the king. Flashing Pitney a scathing glance, Garett stepped forward.

"Your Majesty," he said as he rubbed his chafed wrists, "I see you know Lady Marianne."

The king nodded. "My guard informed me months ago she was dead." His eyes flicked briefly over the captain, who colored.

"As you can see, she is not," Garett continued. "I found her at my estates some weeks ago, pretending to be a Gypsy healer."

Charles sat down, an odd expression on his face. Then his eyebrows quirked upward. "Ah, so this is the Gypsy mistress I've heard so much about from Hampden?"

It was Marianne's turn to color. Hampden and his quick tongue! If she ever came out of any of this alive, she'd make certain he suffered for his gossip.

"Yes," Garett responded, his voice a tinge harder. "Only recently did I discover who she really was. Now it seems my uncle wishes to have me condemned for protecting a traitor."

"Your Majesty," Pitney hastened to put in, "the woman clearly aided her father in the recent attempt on your life. Everyone knows she prepared his medications. Everyone knows those medications never left his hands once she gave them to him. Thus it seems obvious to me—"

"Lady Marianne," the king said, cutting Pitney off. "You never gave us the chance before to question you, but I'm sure you realize what a grave position you're in. As much as I hate to agree with Sir Pitney, he has indeed stated matters accurately. Have you anything to say in defense of yourself?"

All eyes turned to her. She swallowed, but bravely met the concerned eyes of the king. "I'm not a traitor, Your Majesty. Nor was my father. I can't explain how the poison came to be in my medicines, but upon my honor, I didn't put them there."

Charles sighed. "I see." He leveled his gaze on Garett. "Is this why you came to me this morning with a request to question my prisoner?"

Garett nodded. "Yes, Your Majesty. I think you'll be interested in hearing the results of that questioning. You may hear it from both your prisoner and myself. Before we left my house to come here, I took the liberty of asking the captain to have your prisoner brought here, so we might better unravel this tangle."

Marianne glanced up at Garett in confusion. Silently he took her hand in his and squeezed it, though he avoided her gaze.

"Bring him in, then," the king ordered.

Behind them, the double doors opened. Marianne half turned to see who was entering. A middle-aged man accompanied by two guards walked in. He was thin and worn, but Marianne recognized him instantly. Her mouth dropped open, and her knees turned to jelly.

"Father?" she whispered. Then her voice rose as he sighted her and smiled. "Father!"

Marianne gaped at him in stunned astonishment. He was dead—she'd been told he was dead! Yet clearly he stood before her, gaunt and tired, but in good spirits. In moments she was in his arms, being hugged so tightly she thought he'd break her ribs. But she didn't care. Joy surged through her as she pulled back to look at him, noting the sad disrepair of his clothing and the lack of flesh on his bones.

"Is it really you, Father?" she asked, still unable to believe her eyes.

"Yes, yes, sweet girl," he assured her, a radiant smile on his face.

His gaze took in everything about her, too. Apparently he was satisfied with what he saw, for he continued to smile broadly, making a lump catch in her throat.

Then his gaze turned to Garett. "I see you didn't lie to me, my lord," he said with gratitude in his voice.

His tone and the familiar way he looked at Garett told her a great deal. Clearly they'd spoken recently. Belatedly she remembered what the king had said about Garett's request to question his prisoner. So Garett had known. All along he'd known her father lived! She turned her face to him, her eyes accusing.

"You—you didn't tell me," she said, her voice laced with hurt. "You could have told me."

Remorse shone in every line of his face as he met her stare. He moved to her side, taking her hand and clutching it against his chest. "I couldn't be certain he still lived, sweetling, until I spoke with the king. I was returning to tell you when I found the soldiers there with you."

She shook her head in mute disbelief. She didn't know what to think. Here before her was her father whom she'd believed dead. Garett seemed to have hidden a great many things from her, and she hardly knew how to react.

Another in the room also seemed to have difficulty adjusting to the new twist in events. Pitney stood in dumb shock, then grew flushed as he apparently realized what the appearance of Sir Henry could mean.

Then he wiped his amazement from his face, replacing it with a sneer. "A touching scene. But it hardly proves anything. He's still guilty of treason, and his daughter with him."

"Is he?" Garett asked. "Another awaits outside who might have something to say about that. With His Majesty's permission—"

The king nodded his consent. From the other end

of the room entered a soldier accompanying a pale woman, whom Marianne recognized as Pitney's wife, poor Bess.

This time Pitney went completely white, as white as his hair, before he recovered himself. "Why do you bring her here?" he hissed. "She's in confinement. She shouldn't be dragged about the city with no concern for the child she bears!"

The king gazed at Garett. "Why is she here, Falkham?" he asked, his eyes narrowing.

Bess seemed wretchedly frightened, but at the sound of her nephew's name, her eyes sought him out. Upon seeing him, she ventured a timid smile.

Garett gave her a reassuring smile of his own. "She, too, may be able to help us unravel this tangle. You see, Your Majesty, I went to the Tower and questioned Sir Henry just as I requested. I even threatened to turn Lady Marianne over to the guard if Sir Henry didn't confess."

Marianne's blood ran cold. How could he do such a despicable thing? She'd meant nothing to him at all, nothing! She tried to jerk her hand from Garett's, but he wouldn't relinquish it.

"Sir Henry was understandably upset," Garett continued. "Nonetheless, he kept insisting he was innocent. I found that odd. After all, even the most reprehensible of fathers would hesitate to sacrifice his daughter for his own good, and Sir Henry is not such a man. So I could only believe he spoke the truth."

Marianne's hand went limp in Garett's. So he'd done it to test her father. Still, it was terribly wicked of him to put her father through such torment, all because he refused to take her at her word.

"This is all nonsense," Pitney muttered.

The king ignored him. "Go on."

"Yet one thing puzzled me," Garett said. "Sir Henry himself insisted that Lady Marianne had prepared the potions the morning he went to court and then had given them to him. He'd carried them on his person the rest of the day until he started to administer them and accidentally spilled them. His story corre-

sponded with the one Lady Marianne had told me as
well. So if Sir Henry hadn't committed the crime, who
had and how?''

Charles leaned forward eagerly. "Yes, who and how
indeed?'' he remarked as his gaze rested briefly on
Pitney.

Pitney stood there stone-faced.

Garett turned his gaze to his aunt. "Tell me, Aunt
Bess, do you remember a trick I played on my uncle
as a child? I coated the inside of his ale mug with
soap. Then later, when it was filled, he had a terrible
surprise. Do you remember that?''

She glanced nervously at Pitney, but seemed unable
to find any reason not to answer. Slowly she nodded.

"He was very angry after that,'' Garett said. "He
used to check every mug, every box . . . every pouch
brought to him to make certain it was truly empty
before he used it.''

Every pouch. Marianne began to shake as she realized what Garett was leading up to. She'd filled the
pouches, but she'd never checked them before doing
so. Why should she? They'd been washed days before.
There was no need to believe they might contain other
additional powders—like poison.

Her father leaned close and took her arm, squeezing
it reassuringly.

The king, too, seemed to recognize what Garett implied. He sat back in his chair, his brow furrowed in
thought. "If someone had entered Lady Marianne's
chambers and filled her pouches long beforehand—''

"The pouches were of white satin, and she filled
them early in the morning,'' Garett remarked. "She
would never have noticed arsenic dusted on the inside.
Anyone with access to her house could have—''

"This is all absurd!'' Pitney said with a shaky laugh.
"You and your talk of pouches and cups and soap. If
indeed someone else did as you say, you still have no
idea who might be guilty. It could have been anyone.''

Garett turned to fix Pitney with a piercing stare.
"Ah, but it wasn't just anyone, was it, uncle? Who
else is a known Roundhead who doesn't particularly

like His Majesty? And who else wanted Falkham House so badly he would have killed to get it? If Sir Henry were eliminated—''

"All speculation and idle flummery," Pitney protested. "You've no proof, my lord, none at all."

Garett turned from Pitney to look at Bess. "I suspect others here could provide us with proof enough if they were so inclined, eh, Aunt Bess?"

Pitney went completely stiff. "Bess, don't let him persuade you to spout lies about me, do you hear?" Pitney warned her.

Bess looked decidedly ill, and Marianne pitied her. Yet she couldn't find it in her heart to make Garett stop what he was doing. She needed too badly to prove her and her father's innocence.

"Have you anything to tell us, Aunt Bess?" Garett asked gently.

When Bess glanced in Pitney's direction, an expression of pure terror crossed her face. Garett left Marianne and her father to stand beside his aunt. "Don't let him intimidate you," he told her, taking one of her hands in his. "He can't hurt you now, I swear it. No matter what happens here and what is revealed, I won't let him harm you."

She hesitated, her free hand resting on her stomach. Then she looked at Pitney again. She swallowed, and her gaze swung back to Garett, but she wouldn't meet his eyes. "I—I don't know anything, my lord," she whispered.

The king stood to his full height. "Lady Bess," he said in somber tones. "You are in the presence of your king, remember. Lies will not be tolerated."

She seemed desperately torn. At one point she looked to Marianne, and Marianne gave her a reassuring smile.

"Aunt Bess?" Garett asked again.

Then Pitney bellowed, "I'll not have you harass my wife in this fashion, Falkham! She's with child. If she loses her child because of this absurd assertion of yours—''

"Just as I lost my father and mother because of your

greed?'' Garett retorted. Everyone in the room began to whisper in astonishment. Even the king seemed stunned.

"Think you that I don't know who killed them?'' Garett continued, his eyes boring into his uncle's. "I well remember Father's messenger saying that if he and Mother didn't arrive in Worcester at the appointed time, I was to speak with you, because you alone knew the route they intended to take.''

Bess gasped and went limp, but Garett caught her up swiftly. "Garett,'' she muttered, so low that the room fell completely silent as everyone tried to catch her words. "He—he told me he didn't know they were even leaving until after they fled.''

"He knew,'' Garett asserted. "I thought you knew as well.''

That seemed to shock her out of her faint. "No!'' she cried, twisting away from him. "No, I knew nothing at all of this until now!'' She walked clumsily to the center of the room, her finger pointing at her husband. "You killed them, didn't you?'' she cried, almost hysterically. "You always wanted Richard's lands. I heard you say so often enough even before they were murdered. You killed my own brother! What kind of monster are you?''

"He's lying, Bess. Don't listen to him,'' Pitney said in steely tones. "Remember what I told you! Think of the babe!''

"You'll never see that babe! Never! The child isn't even yours!'' she spat out. "And I'll not have the child belonging to the one I love raised by the likes of you!''

Then she turned to face the king. "Your Majesty, my nephew speaks the truth, as does this poor innocent man here and his daughter. My husband planned the poisoning so he could regain my family home. I only learned of it recently, however—''

"She lies!'' Pitney shouted. "She had as much to do with it as I! She took part in it, I swear!''

"And have you proof?'' Garett asked. "Nay, I think not. She's just another innocent you'd have take the punishment for your crimes.''

Bess continued, her eyes dark with hate. "I have proof, Your Majesty, of my husband's treachery. If you'll send your guards for a man named Ashton in my husband's house, you may persuade him to confess how it was done. He's my husband's servant, and I heard him say he planted the poison himself."

"I'll kill you for this, you ungrateful bitch!" Pitney cried.

"Seize him!" His Majesty ordered the guards, and they started toward Pitney.

Before anyone could stop him, Pitney withdrew a short sword and lunged toward Marianne where she stood beside her father. In seconds he had his arm about her waist and the sword at her neck.

"If anyone tries to seize me, she dies!" he bellowed as he began dragging her toward the door.

Marianne felt the blade too close to her neck for comfort and leaned back against Pitney, away from the threatening blade.

Garett unsheathed his own sword with a loud clang. "Harm one hair of her head, Tearle, and I'll slice you into so many bits they'll never find them all! Let her go!"

She felt the sword point quiver at her throat.

"Nay!" Pitney called out, backing away with her until he neared the door. "I'll see her dead before I let you take me, you worthless cur!"

He tried to pull her back more, but she planted her feet, fighting him. She knew if he took her from the room, all hope was gone for her. "Kill me now, then," she hissed at him.

"No, Mina!" Garett and her father shouted, but she ignored them, convinced that forcing his hand was her only chance.

"I'll not go anywhere with you," she told him more boldly when she felt him hesitate. "Kill me now. But be prepared to die afterward, for you know Garett will kill you."

Garett stood poised, his face pale as death as he kept his eyes on the sword at Marianne's neck.

"Don't be a fool," Pitney muttered, then pressed

the blade against her flesh so it bit into the skin and blood trickled down her neck.

Garett's face contorted with rage, but Marianne remained calm.

"That's just a prick!" she taunted Pitney. "Kill me. Kill me, I say, for you'll not get me out of here otherwise!"

For one terrible moment she thought he would do it. She held her breath, wondering if she had risked too much, as his arm tightened on her waist and the sword pressed even closer. Then, without warning, the blade left her neck and she was pushed hard in Garett's direction. She stumbled to the floor as Pitney lunged for the entrance. But two soldiers stepped to block his path, their swords at the ready.

Pitney whirled around and darted toward another door, but this time it was Garett who blocked his path.

" 'Tis time to give up the fight," Garett told his uncle, his sword held threateningly before him.

"Never!" Pitney cried, and like a cornered rat, he thrust at Garett.

Marianne screamed, but she needn't have worried. Garett sidestepped his uncle's thrust easily, throwing his uncle temporarily off balance. But Pitney regained his footing, holding his sword once again before him with grim purpose.

"I wish they'd murdered you instead of that servant boy," he spat. "You should have died with your parents. Haven't you ever wondered if they suffered? I could tell you—"

Garett's angry thrust cut off Pitney's taunts, but Pitney parried it with ease.

"Your mother begged at the end," Pitney continued. "I can still hear her pitiful words. . . ."

Marianne then realized that Pitney was trying to use words to make Garett slip and let down his guard if only for a second, but apparently Garett realized this, too, for his face suddenly grew expressionless as a statue's.

"Mother never begged for anything," he retorted. "But when I'm through with you, you'll beg. Like you've been begging at the doors of every merchant in town, every moneylender, every—''

Pitney lunged wildly, his face mottled with rage. But Garett sidestepped the thrust, at the same time falling to one knee and bringing his sword up through Pitney's chest.

For a moment the two seemed suspended in space, Pitney gazing at Garett with shock and horror in his face as he dropped his sword, and Garett staring at him with the same frightening expression.

Then Garett withdrew his sword, and Pitney fell to his knees.

''A wretch—'' Pitney croaked. Marianne wondered if he meant Garett or himself.

Then he collapsed lifeless on the floor.

Chapter Twenty-three

"There's nought but willing, waking love that can
Make blest the ripened maid and finished man."
—William Congreve,
Love for Love

Chaos ensued in the king's audience room. Soldiers swarmed around Garett and the body lying at his feet. Bess stood in shock as the king started from his chair and went to her side. And Sir Henry quickly moved to enfold Marianne in his arms as she went limp.

"It's all over now, Mina," he murmured, pulling her up against him.

She let him hold her for a moment, wanting to soak up the comfort he offered. But she couldn't long keep her gaze from Garett, who stood surrounded by soldiers. His face showed no sign of relief—only a deep, dark pain.

The king motioned for a soldier to lead Bess from the room, and she went willingly. Then he moved to stand with Garett and the captain of the guard. They spoke a few moments in hushed tones. Then two soldiers carried Pitney away under the captain of the guard's direction as servants scurried to clean the blood from the marble.

Tears began to fall down Marianne's cheeks. So much blood. So much sorrow, for Garett more than for her. She watched Garett as he scanned the room until his eyes locked with hers, a tender light replacing the sorrow on his face. What was to become of their love? she wondered as he made his way toward her and her father. Garett had said he'd never leave her. Still, he'd never promised to marry her, either, she thought with a lurch.

As he reached them, he looked a bit lost, as if he thought he didn't belong in the close circle formed by her and her father. Sir Henry loosened his hold on her, although he kept one arm about her waist protectively.

"Thank you for bringing my little girl back to me," he told Garett. "I nearly died when I thought she'd been killed."

Marianne felt a quick stab of remorse. "I wouldn't have let you believe such lies, Father, if I'd known you were alive. I didn't want to leave you alone in the Tower in the first place."

"Then 'tis a good thing his lordship didn't tell you about me," her father said in a voice choked in emotion. "Otherwise, we'd both be there together now."

"I doubt that," the king said behind them. "I could never have put your pretty daughter in the Tower. Once the soldiers had brought her here for my questioning, and she'd turned that innocent clear-eyed gaze on me, I'd immediately have known she spoke the truth."

Marianne pulled back from her father and gave the king a shy smile. Darting a sideways glance at Garett, she said, "Your Majesty is kind, but I don't think 'twould have been that simple. It certainly wasn't with Lord Falkham. He had trouble believing me even when I *did* confess the truth to him."

The flash of contrition that crossed Garett's face made Marianne wish to take the words back.

"Lady Marianne is right," he said, his eyes pleading with her to understand. "I'm afraid I've grown suspicious of everyone through the years, even innocent young noblewomen. But it was unkind of me not to tell her about her father. I should have trusted her with that much."

The intent gaze with which he then regarded her warmed Marianne to the bone. For a moment she forgot about anyone else in the room. " 'Tis of no consequence now, my lord," she whispered.

"You realize you've all put me in a terrible quandary,'' the king interjected with a wry frown. "Lord Falkham and Sir Henry both legally own Falkham House now that Sir Henry has been cleared of all wrongdoing. So who will retain it?''

"That should be no problem, Your Majesty,'' Sir Henry said with a wink at his daughter. "Lord Falkham and I solved the matter before he left my jail cell.''

"Oh?'' Charles asked. "And what solution do you propose?''

"I think first I should speak with—'' Garett began.

But Sir Henry was already saying, "I only intended to keep the estate as my legacy to my daughter. I prefer to remain in London if Your Majesty will allow me to continue as your physician. His lordship can retain Falkham House, which in any case is rightfully his. What's more, I need not worry about Marianne's legacy, because his lordship has agreed to marry Marianne, which should take care of the problem quite admirably.''

Marianne's mouth went completely dry. Her eyes widened as she glanced at Garett in clear surprise. Garett watched her, a guarded expression on his face.

"We've already briefly discussed the settlement,'' her father continued, "and I believe we can come to some amicable agreement without much problem.''

"Now *that* is an expert solution,'' the king remarked. "And I must say it would please me to see one of my favorite subjects married to such a beautiful, brave young woman.''

Marianne scarcely noted the compliment, for her heart was pounding. Marry Garett? That would be as close to heaven as she could reach, she thought as her blood quickened. Then the rest of her father's words sank in. Garett would have Falkham House, of course. Doubt assailed her. Surely that had no part in his agreeing to marry her, did it? Part of her refused to believe it, but the other part reminded her that Garett always got what he wanted, and he wanted Falkham House.

"Have I no say in this, Father?'' she asked bluntly.

"Am I to be married just like that without even being consulted, merely to solve the problem of an estate with two owners?"

Her father looked instantly uncomfortable. Another man might have told her she would do as he said because he was her father, but Sir Henry had always been a more lenient sort. "But I thought—" he began.

He broke off at the sound of the king's loud chortle. "This is very interesting, Falkham. Apparently the lady doesn't care about your superior title and ever-increasing wealth." He turned to Marianne. "Don't you wish to marry Lord Falkham?"

She reddened in utter mortification as Garett's face turned stony. She hadn't meant to embarrass him, but she couldn't marry him if he wanted her only for the estate.

The king's eyes darkened and his smile vanished. "He didn't force his attentions on you, did he?"

"Attentions?" her father queried with a frown.

"No, no, Your Majesty," she hastened to assure him as she avoided her father's gaze. "Of course not. But I would have wished—"

"Your Majesty," Garett interrupted. "If I could have a moment alone with Lady Marianne, I believe we could clear up any misunderstandings."

"Could you indeed?" the king remarked, immensely amused. "All right, then. That is, if the lady so wishes to remain with you here."

"Marianne?" her father asked. "May his lordship speak with you alone a moment?"

She nodded, her whole body tense. If Garett spoke of the financial advantages their union would bring, she knew it would destroy her. Yet the way Garett's gaze seemed incapable of leaving her face made her fear she'd eternally regret it if she didn't allow him to state his case.

The king accompanied her father from the room, speaking to him in low whispers interspersed with the occasional chuckle.

Then they were alone, the room completely silent. She gazed down at her hands, uncertain where to begin. "My lord, you mustn't feel it's necessary to—to marry me to keep Falkham House. I know what my father said, but I don't want it, and I'd be more than content to live here in London with him."

"Would you?" Garett asked, taking a step toward her. "You could be happy here, living for no one but your father all your life?" He hesitated. "Or perhaps you don't intend that," he said, a tinge of bitterness in his voice. "Perhaps you've an eye for some other gentleman—someone more lively, like Hampden."

She shook her head violently, tears flooding her vision so she could hardly see. "No, no one else," she whispered.

He closed the distance between them and pulled her into his arms. "Don't cry, my Gypsy princess," he murmured. "You'll break my heart. And I can't afford that, for I only have one, and it belongs to you."

She lifted her eyes to his. "Please don't say such things if you don't mean them."

"Ah, but I've never meant anything more," he said fervently, lifting one finger to brush her tears away. "I know you're angry with me for not telling you of your father. You have every right to be hurt, but I swear I'll make it up to you if you'll just marry me. I want you to be my wife, Mina. And not because I wish to keep Falkham House, either."

"Then why?" she asked, needing to hear the words, feeling as if she'd die if he couldn't speak them.

He smiled then. For the first time since she'd known him, she could truly say he looked lighthearted, like the boy Garett she'd imagined all those many years before.

"Because you're beautiful and kind. Because my tenants adore you, and my valet and your aunt would undoubtedly kill me if I left you here."

She couldn't suppress a quick smile.

Then his smile faded as his eyes darkened to the color of midnight rain. "And because I want you more than anything I've ever wanted in my life," he continued more ardently. "More than my estates or even my revenge against my uncle. But most of all because I love you. I didn't realize it until today when I talked to your father, but I know I felt it long before.''

Her heart swelled with joy. At last she'd found a way through all the barriers to his heart. After all the distrust, all the fear, he was hers.

''Well?'' he asked as she stared up at him with shining eyes. ''Can you find it in your heart to love a reprobate like me, with scars and old wounds always giving me something to grumble about?''

She raised herself on tiptoe to press her lips sweetly to his. ''Perhaps in time, my lord—'' she teased.

He growled and forced her mouth back up against his, kissing her with such passion, he left her weak in his arms. ''Say it,'' he whispered when he'd torn his lips from hers. ''Say it, Mina!''

''I love you,'' she admitted in a suddenly choked voice. ''I've loved you so long, my poor dear exile.''

''And you'll marry me,'' he added in a tone that brooked no argument.

''And I'll marry you,'' she repeated.

Then her mouth was once again covered by his.

At that moment the king and Sir Henry thrust their heads inside the room to see how matters were coming along. Sir Henry bristled immediately, ready to put an end to what he saw, but Charles pulled him back with a smile on his face.

''Don't worry,'' the king whispered to Sir Henry. ''I think they have matters quite in hand.'' Then he nodded Sir Henry from the room and followed him out, shutting the door behind him.

Epilogue

"Papa! Mama! Look what me and Aunt Tamara found!"

Garett turned to see his four-year-old daughter Beatrice come skipping across the grass toward where he stood beneath an apple tree.

Tamara followed more slowly behind Beatrice, who held something black clutched in her tiny fist and waved it like a banner over her head.

"What is it?" Marianne asked from her seat on the ground next to where Garett stood. Her face was bright with her smile.

Garett felt his breath catch in his throat as he gazed down at her tawny hair and her face aglow with the knowledge that her next child—*their* next child—would soon arrive.

Beatrice stopped before her parents, all out of breath. She looked up at Garett, the winsome smile on her face reminding him so much of Marianne that he instantly felt the same stab of protectiveness he always felt for his wife.

Gently he ruffled his daughter's hair. "What have you found there, poppet?"

Her soft blue eyes alight, she held out the crumpled piece of black silk. Garett smiled as he recognized it, then glanced at Marianne.

"My mask," Marianne murmured. "Where did you find it?"

Kneeling beside her mother, Beatrice laid it on Marianne's lap, smoothing it out reverently. " 'Twas in a box of old clothes. Aunt Tamara said I could play with them till Uncle Will came to fetch her. Then we found this!" She looked up into her mother's face. "Aunt Tamara said it was yours once."

"Aye," Garett told his daughter. "Your mother wore it the first time I saw her." An image flashed before him of Marianne in Mr. Tibbett's shop. How vividly he remembered his first glimpse of her defiant hazel eyes through the slits in the mask.

Marianne looked up at him now and smiled. She, too, remembered, he thought. He laid his hand on her shoulder, pleased when she laid her hand on his.

"Why did Mama wear a mask?" Beatrice asked him.

"She didn't want me to see her beautiful face, dearling," Garett answered with a chuckle. "She knew the minute I saw it I'd want to marry her."

Tamara's snort reminded Garett of her presence. "She knew you'd be wanting something else, I'm thinking," she remarked dryly.

The quick blush that suffused Marianne's face brought forth another chuckle from Garett. "Aye," he agreed, and squeezed her shoulder.

"You two shouldn't say such things in front of Beatrice," Marianne protested as she tried to smother a laugh.

But Beatrice had hardly noticed the exchange, let alone understood it. One of the dogs from the rebuilt kennels went racing by, and she jumped to her feet to run laughing after it, the mask suddenly forgotten.

"I'll get her," Tamara muttered as she lifted her skirts and walked briskly after Beatrice, scolding her all the way.

Garett knelt beside Marianne and plucked the mask from her lap. Marianne's eyes locked with his as he held the mask up to her face.

"You may not believe this," he told her as he surveyed her critically, "but the entire time you were treating my sword wound that fateful night, I couldn't bring myself to believe your lie about the smallpox. I felt certain your face had to be as captivating as your voice."

She looked skeptical. "My voice? But my words to you were harsh that night."

He shook his head as he dropped the mask into her lap. "Not all of them. You spoke of flowers when all that grew in my heart were weeds. That's when I first knew I had to have you. I wanted the flower you hid beneath your veils of mystery."

He settled onto the ground beside her and took her hand in his. "It took me some time to unveil you, didn't it? Thank God I managed it at last." His other hand cupped her cheek; then his thumb began rhythmically stroking her lower lip.

"And did you find the flower you sought?" she whispered, her breath quickening.

"That and so much more," he murmured. "I found a garden. The garden of my heart in yours."

Then he swallowed her smile of delight with a kiss.

Author's Note

During the first half of the seventeenth century, England began questioning the rights of the monarchy. That dispute led to the English Civil War. The Roundheads, the party clamoring for a more democratic form of government, fought for power against the Royalists, who wished to keep the monarchy. Englishmen of various ranks fought on both sides, although the nobility and Anglicans tended to support the Royalists and the middle class and Puritans to support the Roundheads. In the end, the Royalists lost, and King Charles I was beheaded in 1649.

Then Oliver Cromwell took control, declaring England a Commonwealth. Although Charles II struggled to regain his dead father's kingdom, in 1651 he lost a crucial battle against Cromwell's forces at Worcester and was forced to flee into exile in France. Many of his loyal followers fled with him. In France, a great many of those Royalists endured poverty and disillusionment, as did their king. Only after Cromwell died in 1657, leaving behind a kingdom tired of strife and a disorganized government, did the Royalists return in glory to England, where in 1660 Charles II was restored to the throne and England became once more a monarchy.

Yet life was never quite the same again for the Royalists. Those whose lands had been confiscated by Cromwell and the Roundheads had their lands returned to them. But those whose families sold their lands to pay for the high fines levied by Cromwell against the Royalists lost their lands forever. And none of them ever quite forgot what it meant to be exiled.

Don't miss the Marquis of Hampden's own tantalizing romance with an enchanting actress in *Silver Deceptions*. Coming in Spring 1994.

London, 1668

The day after New Year's, Annabelle Taylor swept into the tyring room at one o'clock, an hour and a half before she needed to be there. She found the room empty.

"Charity?" she turned to ask, but her maid was not to be seen.

Annabelle stood in thought for a moment. No doubt Charity had gone down to the seamstress's shop to determine if Annabelle's costume had been mended. Nonetheless, her absence filled Annabelle with a vague disquiet.

Already the theater was beginning to fill for the afternoon's performance, although most of the people in the auditorium were servants holding seats for their masters. Backstage, however, not a soul trod the boards, for most of the players didn't arrive until around two.

Nonetheless, Henry Harris should be here, Annabelle told herself. Charity had said he wanted to meet her at the tyring room early to rehearse their scene. If that was the case, where in the devil was he?

She shook off her uneasiness and looked for the flint box. Though it was midday, the winter skies outside were dreary, and little light filtered through the grimy window at one end of the room. She lit the candles in the sconces, then found a comfortable chair to sit in while she waited.

Clearly, Henry had been detained. There was no other explanation. She knew she hadn't misunderstood Charity, nor could Charity possibly have been wrong about the time. She was frightfully tedious about setting up appointments; she never got muddled about time and place as did Annabelle.

A soft smile crossed Annabelle's face. Charity always despaired over her mistress's lack of attention to details, but at least she understood why she was so preoccupied. Annabelle had more important things on her mind than what time rehearsal was scheduled or how her costume looked or what gallant she should appease.

At the moment, however, her mind mostly focused on how she would keep from freezing to death while she waited for the errant Henry to arrive. She swept a wayward curl from her face and wondered if she dared light a fire. Sir William D'Avenant, for all his generosity and pleasant air, tended to be a bit of a pinchpenny. Of course, with the theater only half filled some afternoons, Annabelle could easily understand his need to count every shilling with care. Nonetheless, last night the house had been full. Surely Sir William wouldn't mind if she indulged herself just this once and built a fire. In an hour's time, the servants would be coming to light the fire anyway.

With that reassurance she went to the hearth and knelt down to lay a fire. A sharp pain made her suck in her breath. A pox on her tight laces! On days like this, when the winter damp seeped into a person's bones, she had trouble with her ribs. She wondered if they would always pain her, or if there simply hadn't been enough time for them to heal. After all, it had only been eight or nine months since the squire had thrown her down, then kicked her hard enough to break three ribs.

A grim smile crossed her face. At least she no longer had to fear being tormented by her late stepfather. She fought for control over the ache and in moments had a comfortable blaze going in the fireplace.

Rising to her feet, she stood staring into the fire, thinking how different her life was here in London from what it once had been. Had it really been only last winter that she'd been forced to get up hours before dawn to stoke the dying fire in the squire's chambers, working in complete stealth lest she stir him from his sleep? And even then she hadn't minded the work, though she'd known he'd given her the task to shame her. After a night spent shivering in her own small chamber, she'd welcomed the fresh blaze.

She looked down at her simple wool gown that gave her more pleasure than all the finery the squire had made her wear when company came to call. He hadn't wanted the world to know how he treated his daughter or his wife in private. Her mother had become a master at hiding the bruises on her face with caked-on powder. And Annabelle had managed to smile her way through many a formal dinner despite her sore behind, raw from the stiff brush he liked to beat her with.

Her mother had known nothing of those private punishments, not until that horrible day when she'd come across the squire in the kitchen, his temper flaring at Annabelle's defiant words and his crop coming down on her back in a fury. Annabelle fought back tears. She'd been right to maintain the conspiracy of silence between her and her stepfather, to hide the truth from her mother all those years. She'd begun the charade early in life, when she'd realized her mother could do nothing about the squire. Annabelle only wished she could have continued it. Then her mother would be alive. . . .

She pressed her knuckles to her mouth to hold back the sobs that would otherwise escape if she let them. Her head ached just thinking about the past and her mother. She forced her thoughts away from the dangerous subject, rubbing her temples with frenzied movements. Henry would be there any moment. It wouldn't do to have him see her so upset for no apparent reason.

She pulled a chair up to the fire and stared deeply into the flames as she touched her hand to the intricately worked silver brooch she wore. The Silver Swan. Every time she heard the gallants call her that, an image flashed through her mind of the poem her mother had said was written by her real father.

The lines were engraved on her memory after all the hours she'd spent studying it, looking for some clue to her father's identity:

> The bard cannot reveal himself,
> Except in song, one last refrain,
> To beg sweet Portia tread with Beatrice
> Ever near the martyr's plain.
>
> Her heart she must keep close and mute,
> Her tongue must whisper not a cry
> Else she be forced by crown-less hands
> To sing the hangman's lullaby.

Scrawled beneath it in what had looked like a man's hand had been the words "Sincerely, the Silver Swan." Obviously the poem had been intended as a message to someone. Lately, she'd begun to form an idea of what the message might be. "The bard" could be a reference to William Shakespeare, particularly since Portia and Beatrice had been characters in Shakespeare's plays. Was the message to Portia to "tread with Beatrice" intended to be the establishment of an assignation?

Perhaps it was, she told herself, but then how would her mother have fit into all of it? And she had definitely had a part in this poem. Annabelle just hadn't yet figured out what part. All her mother had said was that many years before, during the Civil War, Annabelle's father had asked her to carry the sealed poem to a friend of his at a tavern in Norwood. The man, named Maynard, had told her mother little about the message she'd carried and only enough about the man she was to meet to enable her to recognize him. Maynard hadn't wanted to involve her any more than necessary, or so her mother had said. To ensure that her mother could verify that the message came from him, he had given her his signet ring.

Annabelle's fingers went automatically to the ring, which she kept pinned inside her gown, resting in the hollow between her breasts. She'd not yet determined to whom the crest belonged, largely because she'd not wanted to ask anyone and give away her purpose just yet. Eventually, however . . .

She thought back to what her mother had told her about her visit to the tavern. Her mother had met Maynard's friend as planned. He'd read the poem and then when some people had entered the room, he had thrust the letter back at her and told her to leave. Not certain if she should try again to leave the message with him when he was alone, she'd waited in town. But then she'd seen soldiers rushing toward the tavern she'd left. Too frightened to stay any longer, she'd returned home only to find that Maynard had fled.

At that point in the story, her mother had refused to tell her more. Annabelle had realized her mother knew more than she was saying, but hadn't been able to coax her into revealing it all. Now the desire to know the truth burned at her. Why had the soldiers come to the tavern? What had happened? Why had her father fled, leaving her mother to bear an illegitimate child alone?

Aloud she recited the lines of the poem to herself, searching yet again for the hidden meaning she knew it must hold. Her head ached, but she forced herself to concentrate on the words to the poem. She'd just repeated aloud the lines, ''To sing the hangman's lullaby,'' when a noise behind her disrupted her concentration.

''Rather a morbid poem for a beauty such as you, don't you think?'' said a man's resonant voice.

She whirled in her seat, expecting to find Henry Harris. Instead a man she'd never seen before stood in the doorway, his large frame filling it. For a second, fear coursed through her. Alone in the tyring room, she was easy prey for any stranger who chose to confront her.

Then she noted the stranger's rich clothing and rakish plumed hat. No doubt he was a nobleman with amorous intentions rather than some scruffy miscreant from the streets. She mustered her courage and reminded herself that she was the Silver Swan, the woman whose sharp tongue all the wits and rakes respected. She could handle any forward gallant.

Chin up, she stood to her feet with regal nonchalance. "You aren't supposed to be in the tyring room, sir. I suggest you return to the pit to await the play."

"Would you banish me to the pit, then, for daring to admire you?" the stranger asked. Eyes green as a forest in spring stared back at her with insolent amusement.

Something about the way his bold gaze raked her put her on her guard. The best way to deal with such impertinence was to put him in his place with banter, yet thanks to the way he surveyed her, a faint smile on his lips, she couldn't think of a quip sufficient to cow him.

When his smile broadened at her silence, however, she found her voice. "Better the pit than to be turned to stone, like those who dared to gaze on Medusa. Don't you know that an actress before her performance is as poison-tongued as a snake?"

His low chuckle contained enough charm to seduce a stone. "I hardly believe a swan could be so easily transformed into a serpent. I think Aphrodite stands before me and not Medusa."

She knew he merely played on the fact that Aphrodite's bird was the swan, but she blushed at the pretty compliment nonetheless.

Faith, but I must stop this! she told herself. *The man is a smooth-tongued devil. Any woman with half a brain could see that!* So why were her palms sweating? And why had her dreadful headache completely fled?

"Beware, lest Aphrodite pierce you with her arrows," she said a bit more sharply than she'd intended, determined to have the last word and evict this unsettling stranger.

"I'll risk it," he remarked as he stepped farther into the room. She tried not to notice his solid build, or the cleft in his very firm chin, or even the golden hair that streamed down over his shoulders from beneath his wide-brimmed hat and glinted in the firelight. She tried not to notice, and failed. She knew from mythology that one man had been spared Aphrodite's shafts—Adonis. And if ever Adonis stood before Annabelle in the flesh, it was now.

To her consternation, the stranger rested his hip against a scarred oak table that stood a scarce two feet from her.

"I'm waiting for someone," she told him coldly. "You cannot stay."

"You're waiting for me."

She thought at first he was merely being arrogant, but at the knowing expression on his face, a small suspicion gave her pause. "I'm waiting for Henry Harris," she corrected.

The smile grew a bit calculating. "But your maid, Charity, said—"

"Oh, dear heavens," she groaned as the suspicion grew to a certainty. "Devil take that woman! It's so like her to do something like this."

"I take it you were not informed of our appointment?" he remarked dryly.

"Nay." Deep in thought, she said the word with casual unconcern. But when he lifted himself to sit squarely on the table, she reacted more fiercely. "Of course not. If she'd told me, I wouldn't be here. You can be certain of that."

"Then I must thank Charity for her discretion."

She leveled a scathing gaze on him. "No, you mustn't, for her discretion will get neither of you anywhere. My maid does not decide who I will or won't see, so I'm afraid you'll have to leave."

"But we haven't even been introduced." With the

smooth, frightening grace of a tiger, he slid from the table and stood before her. Then he whisked his plumed hat from his head and bowed. "Colin Jeffreys, Marquis of Hampden, at your service."

A marquis, no less! No wonder Charity had agreed to arrange a meeting between them. But Annabelle didn't intend to let something like a title tempt her. How well she knew what farces titles were. Men with titles were just as treacherous as men without them, if not more so.

"A pleasure to meet you, my lord. Now, would you please leave?" Her voice trembled. She knew it, but hoped he hadn't heard it, especially since he stood very close to her now, close enough to touch her if he wished.

"You can't throw me out yet. We're just beginning to get acquainted." He tossed his hat onto the table, and she winced. The man clearly intended to stay awhile.

Forcing a flippant tone into her voice, she remarked, "Then we shall simply have to continue this very interesting acquaintance later, shan't we?" She flashed him a simpering smile. If she'd had a fan, she would have fluttered it coyly, as was the fashion. "Why don't you come back after the performance? Many others do so."

"Precisely, which is why I'd rather be here now than later."

From the frown on his forehead, she could tell that unlike the other gallants, he didn't like her flirtatious posturing. His suddenly sober gaze never left her face. So why could she imagine it roaming her body, searching for the chinks in her armor?

Time for another tack, she told herself. She pivoted gracefully away from him to cross the room toward the door. In the best bored monotone she could muster, she remarked, "You are becoming incredibly tiresome, Lord Hampden. If you don't leave this room now, I myself shall leave and seek out Sir William to remind you of the rules."

His low chuckle gave her pause. "Sir William

doesn't appear here until five minutes before the curtain goes up, and well you know it. Betterton is more likely to be here early. But of course, Betterton and I are good friends, so you'll find no quarter there. No, I'm afraid you're stuck with me for the moment.''

Why did his words send an anticipatory tingle through her every vein? With a jolt she realized she truly was alone with this man, and he clearly didn't want to leave.

''What do you want from me, my lord?'' Her hand on the doorknob, she twisted her head to look at him. ''What must I do to have peace?''

He crossed his arms over his chest as he leaned back once more against the table. ''Surely you could guess that yourself,'' he said as he pointedly allowed his gaze to travel the length of her.

Color suffused her face, though she fought to maintain her aloof, bantering persona. ''Ah, but that would take the enjoyment out of hearing you make the proposition.''

He pushed away from the table and approached her with slow, deliberate steps. She stared him down, all trace of amusement gone from her expression.

When he stood only a foot from her, he reached out and smoothed back one curl from her face, much as Charity might have done if she'd been there. Only his gesture wasn't soothing or helpful. His was calculated to seduce, and she knew it. His fingers brushed the skin of her cheek, the merest tickle but enough to make her heart's pace quicken.

Nicely done, she complimented him silently, and hated herself for responding to a gesture he'd undoubtedly used with many an actress in the past.

For a moment his eyes locked with hers, their glittering depths holding promises she feared he might attempt to keep. She'd scarcely realized she'd stopped breathing until he dropped his hand and she released a long, drawn-out breath.

His gaze swept downward to fasten on a point just below her shoulder. She followed his gaze and realized he stared at her brooch.

"Such a lovely piece of work," he said with only a hint that he might be talking about other things than just the brooch. "Where did you find it?"

His question put her on guard. She backed away from him while she still could. Then she lifted her hand to finger the brooch's cold metal. "Oh, I scarcely even remember. Some admirer or other gave it to me, I suppose."

"Have you so many admirers that you can easily forget who gave you such a gift?" His mocking smile returned.

"I have more admirers than you can possibly imagine," she replied acidly, hoping to discourage him.

"And not a one that you favor with your returned affection."

Her eyes widened. How did he know? Or did he? This could be a trap to find out whether her reputation was based on her real actions or not. Then again, why would he care?

She forced a saucy smile to her lips. "Of course I've favored some with my affections." She tossed her curls and fluttered her lashes. "What poor actress could resist the sweet blandishments of London's gallants?"

"What actress indeed?" he replied, his gaze probing her secrets. "Then you would not resist my blandishments, I trust."

Her smile faded. This began to feel distinctly like a trap. "At any other time, with your being a marquis . . . a very handsome marquis"—here she paused to flash a seductive smile his way—"I'd be tempted." Heavens, but it was difficult to play the part of jaded, vapid actress with this man. "But I'm afraid I have quite a *tendre* for Lord Chesterwood. I can't see how I could possibly fit in another gallant, since I spend most of my waking hours with him these days." A blatant lie, she thought, but at the moment she needed to rid herself of this importunate man as quickly as possible.

"Such a pity. The Silver Swan deserves something

better than a fop like Chesterwood. Particularly when she bears the name Maynard.''

She'd been about to give him a frosty retort on the subject of Chesterwood when his second line stopped her. ''What does my surname have to do with anything?'' she asked with studied nonchalance as she moved to put a chair between them, trying to ease the tightness in her chest that his comment had elicited.

Lord Hampden remained silent a moment, watching her with eyes that gleamed in the flickering firelight. ''As you probably know, a few Maynards reside in this town, all men of repute and title. If perchance you are related to one of them, you should at least have enough pride to uphold the family reputation and not associate with a mere second son like Chesterwood, no matter how glib his tongue and fashionable his clothing. He buys that clothing at a dear price, as I'm sure you know. He certainly can't care for a woman the way another man might.''

''Another man like you, I suppose,'' she couldn't help retorting.

He flashed that brilliant smile at her again, momentarily driving all rational thought from her mind. No man should be allowed to walk around with a smile like that, she thought. The men in town must have to conspire to keep him constantly away from their women.

''I would be the perfect choice,'' he responded without a hint of vanity in his tone.

She wanted to cut him with a biting retort, to put him in his place, but she dared not, for he hadn't yet told her what she wanted to know, and now they'd steered into other waters far more disturbing. She had to bring him back to the subject that most interested her—the Maynards of whom he'd spoken.

''You? The perfect choice? How do I know that associating with you wouldn't also put a smear on the pristine family reputation of these Maynards?'' She gave him a glittering smile of her own.

He raised one brow, then rubbed his chin with one large hand. ''You don't. That's why I'll give you time to ask about me before I continue my pursuit. I think you'll be pleased by what you find. But I assure you, if any of the Maynards I know were to have a say in what man you'd choose as a companion, they'd choose me."

Why did she get the feeling he was offering his knowledge of the Maynards as bait? Had her real father noted her presence on the stage and recruited this Lord Hampden to help him discover her game?

She surveyed Lord Hampden in silence, noting the strong square jaw, the powerful neck, the wide span of his chest. His eyes watched her with an intensity that bespoke more than just a cursory interest in her.

Yet she could hardly believe that this well-spoken gallant sought her out merely at the direction of some older lord. He seemed too independent for such manipulation. And too intent on having her for himself. The thought sent warm blood to the surface of her skin.

"So tell me, my sweet swan," he remarked, the subtle hint of intimacy in the endearment making her fight a blush all the more furiously. "Shall you allow me to call on you in your lodgings, say two days from now?"

His request threw her into a quandary. He knew about the Maynards. He might even know who her father was. What's more, if she could trick Lord Hampden as she had Lord Chesterwood into believing she'd bedded him, she'd have the ultimate weapon against her father. What nobleman could endure the thought that his daughter, a notorious actress on the stage, had been intimate with his friend, thus shaming him before the men he knew and respected most?

"Well?" he asked.

If she played it carefully, she told herself, she could use Lord Hampden to strike back at her father. And since Lord Hampden would also get what he wanted, her companionship, he'd not be hurt in the process. With determination she thrust from her mind the worry of how she would fool this forceful gallant into believing she'd allowed him to possess her body.

"You may call on me," she responded, "but in three days' time."

"Two days. That gives you ample time to determine my, ah, suitability."

His matter-of-fact treatment of the whole matter made her shudder. Was she really agreeing to take on a lover in the same way a woman chose a competent seamstress or milliner? She bit back the hysterical giggle that rose in her throat. Perhaps she should ask for written references.

Lord Hampden rounded the chair to stand right before her. "This probably seems a little cold-blooded to you," he said as if he'd read her mind.

"Not at all. If you'll just send your solicitor over with the proper papers, we can sign a contract and be done with it," she quipped, keeping her tone light. "What sort of document does one write up for formal assignations? Perhaps something simple like 'I, the undersigned, do solemnly swear to meet with actress Annabelle Maynard—' "

"Very amusing," he said, cutting her off, the corners of his mouth edging upward. "Perhaps I should impress upon you the depths of my intentions . . . so you won't have the wrong idea about what our relations to each other are to be in the future." His eyes dropped to her lips, which, to her chagrin, trembled in response.

"Truly, my lord, I don't think that will be necessary," she protested, but it was too late. His arm had already snaked around her waist and his mouth was on hers.

Her emotions immediately became a jumble of fear, intrigue, anger . . . and some other, unfamiliar emotion. Lips supple yet firm molded hers into pliancy, causing a pleasant tingling to unfurl in her belly. Struck dumb by surprise, she felt his arms press her tighter, felt his hand slide up and down her back in a caress.

Then he slid the tip of his tongue between her lips and ran it along her tightly clenched teeth. From the other kisses she'd received from men, she knew what he wanted and feared giving it to him, even though she'd given such kisses to other men without a thought. Somehow she knew such intimacy from him would affect her as those other kisses hadn't. Yet if she didn't respond in the accustomed manner, he would wonder just how experienced she really was.

So she made the mistake of opening her mouth, thus baring herself to a kiss of such fathomless intensity, it made her body ache. She scarcely noticed the faint scent of leather that clung to him; all she knew was the plunge of his tongue in her mouth, mimicking the act he meant them to share. Her pulse quickened and her eyelids slid shut as one of his hands moved to cup her neck, holding her head still closer while he stole the breath from her.

So this was seduction, she thought as an unfamiliar hunger made her want to arch into him, to pull him to her. No wonder her mother had succumbed.

When at last he drew back, after possessing her mouth so thoroughly she no longer knew where she was, she stared at him through heavy-lidded eyes, her lips slightly parted. She couldn't have spoken if she tried. His gaze locked with hers. He moved his hand from the back of her neck to cup her cheek, then stroked his index finger along her lower lip.

"Two days," he murmured, almost to himself, as his eyes darkened at the sight of her quickened breath. "How will I wait two days?"

The words sent a ripple of something through her. She feared it was desire. It most certainly was desire. She recoiled from the thought almost as soon as it came to her. Her mother had let desire ruin her life. Annabelle wouldn't make that mistake.

Yet the intimate press of Lord Hampden's lips on hers had enticed her beyond belief. Of the other fumbling gallants who'd kissed her in dark corners behind the theater flats, in the tyring room, and even in her lodgings, none had kissed her quite like this.

What was she doing, allowing this powerful lord to tempt her from her purpose? She'd never be able to control him. Only a fool would believe she could.

"This is madness," she whispered, struggling to disengage herself from his embrace.

"Nay," he said, drawing her up against him until their thighs, their hips, even their bellies met. "This seems more like ecstasy to me."

His lips lowered again. Spurred on by fear, she strained away from him, knowing she couldn't endure another searing kiss that stole her will.

Then Charity burst through the door, Annabelle's costume draped over her arm. The buxom woman quickly turned red before giving a quick curtsy. "I'm so awfully sorry. I-I didn't mean to disturb you. I'll just go—"

"No!" Annabelle practically shouted. Her breath came in quick gasps, try though she did to make it sound normal. "No," she repeated, "don't go. His lordship was just leaving."

She didn't know whose expression looked the more amused and speculative, Charity's or Hampden's. A secret conspiracy seemed to exist between the two of them, and she wanted to know exactly how much of the conspiracy rested on Charity's side.

At the moment, however, Hampden's wide grin struck her with utmost terror, and she suddenly knew she could never meet him alone without disastrous consequences. His hands clasped her waist intimately, holding her firmly next to him. She knew her lips were no doubt reddened from his kiss, knew it and hated it.

"Lord Hampden," she said, annoyed by the breathy tone in her voice. She thought of her mother, then managed to lower the intensity of her tone a notch. "I've changed my mind about . . . about your request. You need not bother me again, though I thank you for your visit today. It's been most enlightening."

He chuckled as he released her. "For me, too," he told her as he reached for his plumed hat and settled it on his wild mane of curls. Then he added, with a distinct tone of command in his voice, "Two days, Annabelle. You get two days. Use them well."